WINIFRED HOLTBY

(1898-1935) was born in Rudston, Yorkshire. In the First World War she was a member of the Women's Auxiliary Army Corps, and then went to Somerville College, Oxford where she met Vera Brittain. After graduating, these two friends shared a flat in London where both embarked upon their respective literary careers. Winifred Holtby was a prolific journalist, writing for the *Manchester Guardian*, the *News Chronicle* and *Time and Tide* of which she became a director in 1926. She also travelled all over Europe as a lecturer for the League of Nations Union.

Her first novel, *Anderby Wold*, was published in 1923, followed, in 1924, by *The Crowded Street*. She wrote five other novels: *The Land of Green Ginger* (1927), *Poor Caroline* (1931), *Mandoa, Mandoa!* (1933) and *South Riding* (1936), published posthumously after her tragic death from kidney disease at the age of thirty-seven. She was awarded the James Tait Black prize for this, her most famous novel.

She also published two volumes of short stories, *Truth is Not Sober* (1934) and *Pavements at Anderby* (1937); a satirical work, *The Astonishing Island* (1933); two volumes of poetry; *My Garden* (1911) and *The Frozen Earth* (1935); a critical work, *Virginia Woolf* (1932); a study of the position of women, *Women and a Changing Civilisation* (1934), and numerous essays.

Winifred Holtby's remarkable and courageous life is movingly recorded in Vera Brittain's biography, *Testament of Friendship*, published by Virago.

VIRAGO
MODERN
CLASSIC

NUMBER
192

WINIFRED HOLTBY

POOR CAROLINE

With a New Introduction by
GEORGE DAVIDSON

Published by VIRAGO PRESS Limited 1985
41 William IV Street, London WC2N 4DB

First published in Great Britain by Jonathan Cape Limited 1931

British Library Cataloguing in Publication Data

Holtby, Winifred
    Poor Caroline.—(Virago modern classics)
    I. Title
    823'.912[F]   PR6015.05
    ISBN 0-86068-595-0

Printed in Finland by Werner Söderström Oy,
a member of Finnprint

In Piam Memoriam
M.C.H.

Author's Note

So far as my knowledge extends, there has never been a Christian Cinema Company formed for the Purification of the British Film, there has never been an Anglo-American School of Scenario Writing, nor a Metropolitan and Provincial Correspondence College for the teaching of Journalism. But my ignorance is wide. These institutions may have an existence outside my own imagination. If so, I beg to inform their promoters and organizers that I forgive them their plagiarism in advance, and wish them the success that they deserve.

WINIFRED HOLTBY.

Contents

Introduction

Poor Caroline was hailed as 'easily the wittiest novel of the season'
upon its appearance in 1931. This represented a watershed in
Winifred Holtby's career as a novelist, since her previous three
novels had more or less dissatisfied her, and been commercially
unsuccessful. At the time of writing her fourth novel she was
well-known as a radical campaigner and journalist. But it was
with *Poor Caroline* that her fortunes as a novelist changed: it was
favourably reviewed and sold well. Sadly, this was also the year
which saw the onset of the kidney failure that was to drastically
reduce her wide-ranging literary and polemical output.

Although *Poor Caroline* was received as a tragi-comedy, its
overall tone is consciously comic. Despite a strong love element
and gradual pathos, the author's perception is satirical, in the
same mould she was to use in her next novel, *Mandoa, Mandoa!*
One contemporary criticism of *Poor Caroline* as suffering 'from
excess of cleverness' reinforces the impression of Winifred's
increased self-assurance. 'All the characters are drawn in a few
strokes with a deft touch', approved one reviewer. The author
was praised for appearing 'intelligent, unsentimental yet
benign', particularly in respect of the eponymous heroine,
Caroline Denton-Smyth. This old maid, with her vision of
perfect movies, is the improbable thread holding together her
society for the moral purification of British cinema, the
'Christian Cinema Company'. Winifred had tried to elevate
from literary obscurity another traditionally unpersonable,
depressing subject, the home-ridden young anti-heroine of *The
Crowded Street*. As *The Yorkshire Post* critic, Alice Herbert,
observed of Caroline: 'Altogether, she has pulled the comic
spinster out of her rut, which fiction has made wearisome ...

Miss Holtby's gift lies partly in taking a type that many novelists accept as ready-made, and in showing its enormously varied and complicated humanity.'

What immediately distinguishes *Poor Caroline* from Winifred Holtby's 'Yorkshire' novels is its setting in London. In so far as all the other novels are designated by location – albeit metaphorically in two instances, the very title announces a different flavour to *Poor Caroline*. Otherwise only in *Mandoa, Mandoa!*, Winifred's exotic treatment of colonialism in Africa, is the main action centred elsewhere than in the rural East Riding she knew and loved, or the small-town north of England she despised and avoided. With the exception, therefore, of the 'Opening Chorus' (a sharp stab at the complacent, provincial middle class) and two scenes, including the balancing 'Final Chorus', in Monte Carlo (where Winifred holidayed during the writing of the novel and was fascinated by the loose-living gossipy circles of artists), the events of *Poor Caroline* take place in London in the twenties. The metropolis excited Winifred right from the initial prospect of coming down from Oxford in 1921. But although she spent the greatest and most active part of her working life in the city, her only other sizeable fictional use of London is Book One of *Mandoa, Mandoa!* This apparent imbalance in favour of her childhood home is accounted for by Winifred's idyllic upbringing under a remarkable mother. The author is pinpointing a home truth in the passage describing Caroline's reflections on her own life: 'It was strange, but that child's life at Denton now seemed more vivid to her than all her subsequent adventures.'

Winifred's years in London were spent at a scarcely credible pace of production. She lectured on Pacifism and campaigned for Feminism, revelling in the atmosphere like Eleanor De La Roux, for whom 'London hummed with the activities of propaganda and reform'. Although she was generally engaged upon the writing of her next novel or short story, her lifestyle was, as we know from Vera Brittain's biography of her flatmate in *Testament of Friendship*, rarely tranquil enough to allow sustained periods of creativity. For instance, she sat on numerous committees, believing avidly in decision-making and progress by means of discussion and debate. Hence the detail and insight, in this work and in *South Riding*, with which she evokes such formal meetings. She also saw the dramatic potential of such gatherings as choice battle-grounds for the antagonistic interaction of characters.

Poor Caroline originated in a family connection. Mary Horne was an aunt of one of Winifred's early governesses, who, like so many hangers-on to the Holtby family, drew on the patient favours and hospitality of Winifred or her mother. Caroline is evidently directly based upon this Mary Horne, since Vera Brittain describes how the idea for the novel came to a regretful Winifred after the death of this tiresome, yet likeable, old eccentric, who must have impinged upon Winifred's acute conscience. Hence the dedication 'In piam memoriam M.C.H.', and the fact that one reviewer unwittingly complimented Miss Holtby upon her 'ability to create characters who are so real one suspects her of knowing them'.

Caroline's lead-part as the founding organiser of the ill-fated Christian Cinema Company is unquestioned, but her primacy among the female characters is to a degree challenged by the naturally intelligent Eleanor with her wide-eyed idealism and straightforward aspirations. Eleanor is Winifred's archetypal modern woman in the making, and as such the oracle for feminism in *Poor Caroline*. Eleanor is half South African to allow Winifred to recall her favourite foreign land, the only country outside Europe she visited, and a place to which she could remain closely attached because of her friendship with Jean McWilliam (of *Letters To a Friend*) in Pretoria. There she espoused the plight of the natives, a cause with which she became closely associated after her tour of 1926. The heroine of *The Land of Green Ginger*, who dreams constantly of far-off places, is also half South African. She came to England as an infant after the death of her non-Afrikaans father. Eleanor leaves South Africa following the same bereavement, but is an adult newcomer to England.

If Winifred's letters had been lost, or her biography not written by her closest friend, we could still glean from Eleanor a central obsession of her creator; namely, in Eleanor's words, 'this intolerable burden of immunity'. In order to overcome this inverted inferiority complex, the rich but orphaned young lady seeks out suffering and struggle, hardship and adversity: 'I have capital behind me, and education, and opportunities. All this ugliness and poverty can't really hurt me.' Winifred likewise bore the hang-ups of privilege and wealth, which her talent exacerbated. In marked contrast to Vera Brittain, she was also unscathed by the bereavements of the Great War. 'I always feel when I take my pleasures that I have snatched them in the face of fortune,' she wrote. 'But I am glad when I take them, all the same' she concluded, for she was, like Caroline, with her penchant for sweet foods, beautiful flowers and pretty clothes, no ascetic, but someone who took pleasure in rare luxuries. Winifred's nature was happy and optimistic. Believing she had no real problems, she deliberately put herself out for others in an almost self-sacrificial way to atone for being among those 'who have been gifted by fortune, we who are rich and healthy and unbound'. Overworking herself to pay back the debt she felt she owed to life, this sense of immunity was clearly cauterised by her collapse into virtually constant ill-health, which this personal complex must ironically have helped bring on.

If Eleanor voices Winifred's horror of immunity, the Anglo-Catholic curate, Roger Mortimer, represents the author's connected religious leanings. Religion, which, she once admitted, was one of the chief reasons for unhappiness in her life, was not prominent in her public utterings, but is a more obtrusive feature of her stories – Winifred had undergone a period of theological crisis, just about resolving her beliefs in an experience similar, it seems, to Roger's call to the Church one night in France. Eleanor's uncertainty about contributing to the Christian

Cinema Company is also suddenly clarified as a result of listening to Roger's sermon condemning compromise. Roger's wavering between Catholicism and Protestantism, as between the demands of his vocation and the temptation of earthly love, recalls Winifred's earlier portrayal of Wyclif in *The Runners*, her only full-length prose work never published. Roger's dilemma also foreshadows the serious mess the endearingly sensual lay preacher, Huggins, creates for himself in *South Riding*. Vulnerable vicars, whether venal or virginal, thus crop up regularly in Winifred Holtby's novels. But churchmen are not exclusively ogres or figures of fun. Roger, initially timid, develops into one of Winifred's nobler male characters, overcoming his image to Eleanor of 'a comic curate, praying among the buns'.

Love scenes, Winifred freely admitted, were difficult passages for her to write. Her own love life involved one spasmodic and unsatisfactory relationship. She wrote of 'being disappointed if I go through life without once being properly in love. As a writer, I feel it my duty to my work, but they [men] are all so helpless and such children'. Along with so many women of her generation she was affected by the dearth of adequate men after the Great War, which does to some extent account for the rarity of strong male characters in her novels and the frequency of listless survivors, either physically or psychologically crippled. Nevertheless, Roger Mortimer, despite being manipulated by Caroline and besotted with Eleanor, is healthy and shows moral strength as well as progressive views on love and marriage. Equally, Eleanor is independent and direct. Indeed, she represents a new departure in Winifred's attitude towards women's self-determination. The earlier heroines are shackled by domestic ties of one form or another. Mary Robson and Joanna Leigh, farmer's wives, are spirited individuals circumscribed by the restraints of their position in the family and in the community.

Poor Caroline is about the divergent tendencies of philanthropy and exploitation, and the humour, tinged with sadness, arising from their clash in an oddly constituted Company, bringing together incompatible people. The Jewish merchant, Isenbaum, and the dilettante, St Basil, scratch each other's backs. Johnson and Macafee are out solely for themselves. Roger and Eleanor have more palatable ulterior motives, but they too use Caroline. Eleanor is no impressionable altruist, but entertains self-professed business ambitions and involves herself in her relative's project for the sake of being associated with an apparently good cause. Even Caroline, the only true believer in her brain-child for the actual spiritual benefits she intends it to bring, is perhaps merely trying to justify herself when society has no real further need of her. Although Vera Brittain accurately described her as 'a self-deceived optimist with an unbalanced devotion to hopeless projects', Caroline is so observed as to be likeable despite her absurdity. Her world of 'uplift, good works and propaganda' was very much her creator's sphere as a fervent believer in education and the benefits of religion. Winifred, however, was no unrealistic idealist like Caroline. Her optimistic canvassing on behalf of the League of Nations or South African Trades Unions was not so earnestly self-important as to be above self-mockery – there could be an element of self-parody in her Caroline, despite Winifred assuring Lady Rhondda: 'Caroline is not a symbol of me, but an expression of herself ... I meant to leave the impression of someone silly but vital, directly futile but indirectly triumphant.'

Caroline's demise is not treated tragically, because it leads to the prospect of future benefit. Parallel with this undefeated attitude lies a positive view of progress, both moral and technical. *Poor Caroline* may not be most memorable as a discussion of the ethics of scientific progress, but the issue is not raised lightly, and admonitions concerning society's future are deliberately made. The Christian Cinema Company falls between two stools not just for lack of a unified commitment, but also, it is suggested, because the twin aims of the Company may be contradictory in practice. In *Mandoa, Mandoa!* Bill Durrant comes to a conclusion about colonial development in terms which apply to Caroline's confusion of commerce and morality: 'You can either make a profit out of people or you can lecture them for their own good. But you can't do both with any effect at the same time.' If this is a truism, *Poor Caroline*'s message would be 'to distribute uplift' rather 'than dividends among mankind. It was easier to Do Good than to Make Money.' The personal motives affecting a decision about how best to utilise a technological breakthrough show how the issue has even gained in relevance in the last half century. Johnson's every word deserves suspicious scrutiny, but amidst the regurgitated verbiage we find some valid, if gratuitous, observations, for instance when he chastises Macafee as a lover of science for science's sake: 'Ah, you scientists, who pursue the means an' despise the ends, take care.'

A fine writer's themes and obsessions continually engage important issues with a perspicacity which remains modern and pertinent over and beyond the particular fictional and historical context. Winifred Holtby was a flash of brilliant dynamism, who threw herself with a combined sense of duty and conviction into the burning issues of her day, hoping to help improve society. Her texts and speeches were persuasive in the twenties and thirties and, fortunately, she left an artistic testament which enriches posterity. For despite her dichotomy she was able to combine her dual instincts as writer and reformer without making Caroline's alleged sacrifice of one for the other: 'If I'd had more time I could have been a poet ... only between the claims of art and science I had to choose, being by nature a pioneer and fighter.' If Winifred Holtby was by nature a writer, then appropriately it is her novels which fight on as the lasting vehicle for her pioneering beliefs.

George Davidson, London, 1984

Opening Chorus

On that April evening, in 1929, the five-thirty train from King's Cross to Kingsport was half an hour late. Betty and Dorothy Smith, returning home from Caroline's funeral, had to scramble through luggage, porters and trolleys and run along the platform, nearly dropping their newly acquired parcels, in order to catch the last train out to Marshington. But their mother was waiting for them in the dining-room with sandwiches and tea; the fire leapt gaily; their father drifted in from the billiard-room professing indifference, but really agog for news, and the pleasant atmosphere of home-coming was augmented rather than decreased by the lateness of the hour and the precariousness of suburban connections.

'Tea?' Mr. Smith asked himself. 'Well, I wouldn't mind a cup as it is here. Now, girls, how's London? Have you got Caroline safely underground?'

'We have, we have,' laughed Betty, helping herself to a ham sandwich. 'We've buried her and, if you ask me, pretty nearly canonized her. What with a purple pall over the coffin, and the service so High that it nearly fell over itself backwards, and Uncle Ernest green in the face with trying to find his way among the prayers and things, it was the grandest funeral I ever saw.'

'And who is paying for all that, I should like to know?' snorted Mr. Smith. 'As Caroline's nearest relative I naturally have *some* feelings on the subject.'

'Well, you'll be relieved to hear that the actual Church service was all done free, so far as I can gather. That Father Mortimer Caroline was always writing about got his Church to do it.'

'Yes, and do you know,' interrupted Betty, 'he isn't old at all – he's quite young – young enough to be Caroline's son.'

'Grandson.'

13

'Son, anyway, and *quite* sweet. Not a bit like a curate, and a perfect lamb in his vestments, or whatever you call them.'

'A perfect scream calling him "Father." '

'I'm not surprised now that Caroline was a little dotty about him.'

'Now, Dorothy, you shouldn't say such things, really,' Mrs. Smith remonstrated, secretly enjoying every word spoken in Caroline's disfavour, but anxious to maintain her pose of broad-minded matron.

'Well, Mums, she was a bit queer, wasn't she? You ought to have heard the will.'

'The will?'

'Oh, my goodness, I wish you'd both been there. You'd have *died*. I never saw such a scream. After the funeral Eleanor insisted on us all going back to Caroline's room – that *awful* little room in Lucretia Road. There was Mrs. Hales, the landlady – *what* a dragon! – all hymn singing and vindictiveness; but we let her help herself to Caroline's old clothes, so perhaps she's satisfied. And Eleanor, as queer as ever, in the same old tweed coat, not a *stitch* of mourning, looking about seventeen and very ill, we thought, and a queer old stick called Mr. Guerdon and Uncle Ernest and us. And then Eleanor read the will.'

'And you never smelled anything like that room, cluttered with fearful old papers and all the clothes we've sent Caroline for years.'

'Mr. Guerdon looked as though he'd like to drown us all.'

'He'd come from the Christian Cinema Company – you know – the thing she was always trying to get us to put money into.'

'But, my dears, the *Will*. Do you know, she left five hundred pounds each to Betty and me, and eight thousand to her dear young friend and kinswoman, Eleanor de la Roux, and twenty thousand – yes, twenty thousand, to the Rev. Roger Mortimer, Assistant Priest at St. Augustine's, in token of all that his help and encouragement had meant to her in her lonely life. Just think of it – she must have been a little bit potty, wasn't she, Mums, dying in an infirmary at seventy-two, and making a will like that leaving thousands of pounds, that she hadn't got, to people she hardly knew?'

'Well, of course, I do think that at the end she must have been a little odd. But what I do want to know is, did she really get that three thousand pounds out of Eleanor?'

'Well, Mr. Guerdon seemed to think that Eleanor had put all her money into the Christian Cinema Company, and of course as it went bust I suppose the money was lost, but we couldn't get Eleanor to say anything.'

'Monstrous, monstrous,' said Mr. Smith. 'I always blamed de la Roux. No man ought to leave a child of twenty-two in sole charge of her capital, without trustees or anything. Eleanor came over to England simply asking to be robbed, simply asking for it.'

'Well, we did warn her against Caroline,' said Dorothy. 'We let her see the old girl's letters. We told her she would cadge, borrow or steal from anyone in the world that she could get hold of – Eleanor needn't have gone near her when she went to London.'

'Oh, catch Miss Eleanor taking advice! Dear me no. More tea, please, Mums. But she certainly seems to have got more than she bargained for from Caroline. Apparently she used to lend her money when she was alive, looked after her while she was ill, and finally arranged the funeral and saw the undertakers, and everything.'

'I always said,' observed Mr. Smith, 'and I say it again: Caroline should have gone on the Old Age Pension. She used to say it wasn't dignified, but it would have been far more dignified than borrowing from her relatives and being in debt to the tradesmen.'

'Oh, you can't alter people like Caroline. She always thought she knew better than anyone. She was always going to do something extraordinary.'

'Oh, she was extraordinary all right,' laughed Betty. 'She was an extraordinary nuisance, anyway.'

'Well,' reflected Dorothy, soothed by tea, warmth and sandwiches into toleration. 'I suppose that making a nuisance of herself was the only way she had left of making herself important. It can't have been much of a life, can it? for a woman of over seventy, living alone in lodgings, in debt to her landlady, wearing our cast-off clothes, trotting round after jobs that never materialized, writing articles that no-

15

body would publish, and eating bread and margarine for supper. There really was something rather pathetic about that awful room of hers – crowded with papers full of impossible schemes. I don't envy Eleanor the job of looking through them all. I don't suppose there can ever have been anyone whose life was much less important, or who had less influence on anybody else.'

'Well, she did get us to London, anyway. I suppose that if she hadn't died, and we hadn't gone to the funeral, we should have had to do our spring shopping in mouldy old Kingsport. Oh, Mums, I *must* show you my new blue three-piece. It's perfectly adorable, isn't it, Dot?'

'It is rather nice – and my evening frock. Do you know, skirts are getting lower and lower, Mums?'

'Well, of course, dears,' said Mrs. Smith gently. 'I don't like to seem heartless in any way, but it would have been a pity to waste the expense of going up to London, and it wasn't as though Caroline were more than your second cousin. I am very glad that you were able to do something really useful.'

'Nothing like combining business and pleasure, eh, girls?' Mr. Smith smothered a great yawn. 'Well, I'm off to bed. Don't you women sit gossiping till to-morrow.' He rose laboriously, and went to the door, but with his hand on the knob he turned. 'Good night, all. There is one thing; she'll never trouble us again *this* side the golden gates, poor Caroline.'

Mr. Smith, rope merchant of Marshington in the East Riding of Yorkshire, went upstairs to bed.

Chapter 1 : *Basil Reginald Anthony St. Denis*

§ 1

PROVIDENCE failed to do its duty by Basil Reginald Anthony St. Denis. If he had been born heir to Lord Herringdale's title and estate, instead of being merely a second cousin on his mother's side, he would have been an ornament to the peerage. The stately ritual of the House of Lords would have been decorated by his presence. The bay windows of a certain club overhanging Piccadilly would have derived distinction from his profile.

But his birth and station were unpropitious to his happiness; for he was the only son of a country rector who inhabited a Devonshire rectory seven times too large for his stipend or his needs.

His father came of Huguenot stock, and his mother was a descendant of that Countess Herringdale whose melting delicious beauty languishes from more than one of the canvases of Sir Peter Lely. If life in the Rectory at Trotover was frugal, it was dignified. Basil's infant porringer was bent and dented, but it was an heirloom of seventeenth-century silver. He cut his teeth on fine Georgian plate, and bruised his head against the angle of a Jacobean oak chest. The Rector, his father, dined easily and often with the County, and carried the ordered ritual of his Services into the conduct of his daily life.

As for Basil, he was a lovely child. His flower-like complexion and sweet fluting voice won the hearts of his papa's parishioners. Had the laburnum trees from the Rectory garden scattered golden sovereigns instead of golden blossoms on to his perambulator, no family in his father's parish would have grudged the compliment, and Basil himself would have recognized that nature did no more than her duty by him.

17

It was not that in adult life he cultivated appetites for great wealth and luxury. Political responsibility fatigued, and business adventure repelled him. He remarked upon several occasions that true civilization was incompatible with the life of action, and he disliked nothing more heartily than the untempered energy of pioneers. All that he asked of fortune was adequate opportunity to exercise fastidious taste.

It must be admitted that, considering the circumstances of his birth, Providence made erratic efforts to assist him. Lord Herringdale, charmed by the manner and appearance of his young kinsman, offered to bear the expenses of Basil's education at Eton and at Oxford. At Eton, Basil laid the foundation of a fine sense of social discrimination and achieved an understanding of the gulf which separates those who have been to the greater English public schools from those who have not. It took him several years to realize in how considerable a majority are those who have not been there.

Dependence upon charity, however, is accompanied by notable disadvantages. When Basil eventually went to Oxford, his education in the arts of civilized living involved him in certain trivial expenses. The cultivation of a palate cannot be achieved on grocer's port and Australian Harvest Burgundy. The arts of hospitality cannot be mastered without practice. The unerring discipline of the collector's taste cannot be achieved without trial and error. Naturally, such education costs money. Naturally, it was for such education that Basil assumed he had been sent to Oxford.

Lord Herringdale failed to realize his full responsibility. When the bills came in after Basil's first year, he sent for the young man and subjected him to the discomfort of an interview which, in Basil's opinion, transgressed the bonds of civilized conversation. Lord Herringdale demanded promises; he made conditions; he filled his kinsman with vicarious shame. At that age Basil blushed to see gentlemen misconduct themselves. For the first and last time he abandoned his own principle of compromise and resignation. He refused to return to Oxford on Lord Herringdale's terms.

He went home to the Rectory. He remained there for

18

several weeks contemplating the re-edition of some trifles of eighteenth-century verse which had appealed to him at Oxford. He applied unsuccessfully for the posts of assistant-curator of Chinese embroideries at the Dulwich Museum, and adviser on Adams Decorations to Messrs. Maring and Staple. But his experience only confirmed his theory that one essential condition of a civilized existence is a small independent income of – say – three thousand a year. He was beginning to consider that twelve hundred might be just tolerable.

That was in the summer of 1914. The outbreak of war came just in time to save Basil from the humiliation of his father's request to Lord Herringdale that he should overlook all earlier indiscretions and continue to pay his son's bills at Oxford. Basil was able to step into the post of private secretary to old Lord Farndale, vacated by a more commonplace and robust young man who had joined the army. There, until 1916, he remained, but the catastrophes of international war made civilized living impossible, and the inconvenience of Philistine disapproval outweighed the horror of military discipline. In 1916 Basil responded to the Call of King and Country.

He looked delightful in uniform. The crudity of army life distressed him, but he was fortunate enough to be sent as a cadet to Balliol and to find in war-time Oxford several congenial companions. When he was finally gazetted as a second lieutenant, his fastidious charm, his delicacy, and his taste were uncorrupted. Then he was sent to France.

Nobody ever knew exactly in what degree the war affected Basil. It was presumably a nightmare which on awakening he was unable to describe. In 1918 he appeared at a hospital in Carlton House Terrace with a shattered elbow. He spent the subsequent two years in tedious alternations between the operating theatre and convalescent homes. In 1920 he left the army with a stiff arm, a disillusioned though still charming manner, and the pension proper to second lieutenants suffering from partial disablement.

He returned for a time to the Rectory in Devonshire, and lay on soft but badly tended lawns or on the faded Morris chintzes of his mother's sofas. He read; he smoked cigarettes; he composed epigrams which he felt too fatigued to utter. But the boredom of country life, the inadequacy of the hot-water supply, and the monotony of his mother's catering drove him back to London.

'But what are you going to do, my dear boy?' asked the Rector.

'Well, *mon cher papa*.' Basil smiled his charming melancholy smile. 'What can a fellow do?'

There were, it appeared, a number of things that a fellow could, and did, do. Basil's acquaintances enlightened him as to the possibilities of employment in London. He could sell cars on commission, or trade in first editions, or advise newly created peeresses about the decoration of their country seats, or write occasional reviews for the *Epicurean*. But the *Epicurean* survived only six issues after its first appearance; the cars betrayed inexpert salesmanship, and the peeresses had their own preposterous notions about interior decoration.

An optimistic young gentleman called Wing Stretton, whom Basil had met in hospital, formed a syndicate at Monte Carlo for playing roulette according to a co-operative system, which he thought infallible. Once, in an expansive mood, he asked Basil to come out as secretary to the Syndicate. Basil remembered his offer when, in 1923, he had his final interview with Lord Herringdale.

'I like you. Damn it, I like you,' declared that much-tried nobleman. 'But what with the country going to the dogs and the Government taxing us out of house and home, I can do no more for you, young man. Why don't you emigrate? Emigration. That's the stuff for you younger men. Go abroad. Start afresh. This old country's overcrowded. Take my advice.'

Basil took his advice. 'Emigration,' he read in a copy of the *Spectator* which lay on his father's study table, 'gives opportunities for the display of that courage, initiative, pluck and common sense, which have made the English what they are.'

'Quite,' said Basil. He emigrated. He joined Wing Stretton at Monte Carlo.

Under the soothing influence of the Casino ritual, so elaborate, so unfaltering, and so meaningless, the memory of the brutal outrage of the war's disorder faded from Basil's mind. Listening to the monotonous whirring of the wheels, the soft melancholy cries of the croupiers performing the eternal ceremony of their unchanging Mass, he began to forget the harsh, shattering explosion of the shells. In that enchanted palace, where life is so remote from all other reality, he lost his sense of the imminent menace of death.

'It had to be Catholicism or roulette,' he observed later, 'and on the whole, I found roulette more satisfying.'

But in spite of the consolations of roulette, he had his troubles. He suffered from recurrent pain in his wounded arm. He was troubled by a dry, tedious cough. His increasing lassitude arose as much from general ill-health and weariness as from natural indolence of temperament. He was lonely. Too fastidious to love promiscuously, he was too poor to love expensively, and in Monte Carlo he had found no third alternative. His colleagues on the syndicate were business acquaintances with whom he had little in common except the desire to make a living.

In spite of his apparent detachment and urbanity, Basil knew hours when he lay on the *chaise longue* beside his bedroom window, watching the changeful blue and green of the unruffled bay and acknowledging to himself that he was ill and lonely, that his youth was passing without satisfaction, and that the malignity of providence could not be endured much longer.

§ 2

One evening about ten o'clock, after a dull and disappointing day, Basil stood on one of the small rounded balconies that lean from the windows of the Salles Privées and overhang the Casino gardens. It was the hottest week in the summer of 1923. The season was unfashionable, the room half empty. All but two tables in the room behind him wore their draping petticoats, while in the Kitchen the whirring of wheels, the jangle of voices, and the stifling atmosphere of scent and humanity, had grown intolerable. The System was doing badly. Basil's distaste for his colleagues had increased with the rising temperature of the summer.

21

He was in debt again; his head ached; neuralgic pains throbbed through his wounded elbow. He laid his arms along the stone balustrade and stared into the night.

Beyond and below him lay the warm, perfumed darkness of Monte Carlo, the lighted town seeming no more than an inverted mirror of the star-sprinkled sky. A motor-boat shot like a shooting star across the bay. A shooting star shot like a motor-boat across the sky. Far down below in the Casino garden a shaft of light from a half-shuttered window struck a pink-flowering oleander.

'I wonder,' thought Basil, 'whether there is any truth in the legend that those who shoot themselves in the Casino gardens are immediately set upon by swift attendants, who pad their pockets with notes for a thousand francs, so that the distracted relatives of the victim may not attribute his suicide to a gambler's losses. I wonder if it is true,' his weary mind continued, 'that if one throws oneself down from this balcony, death rushes up straight and sure from the ground and kills one in mid-air. Indeed, seeing that earth and sky appear so very similar, might a man not fall down to heaven, and even rise to hell?' He smiled, thinking how his father would fasten upon a similar fantasy, and elaborate it in a whimsical sermon to puzzle the yeomanry of Devon.

'I wouldn't do it if I were you,' a strange voice startled him. 'For one thing, it can't be done. They grab you before you've got one leg over the balustrade. And to go on with, it doesn't really work.'

It was a woman's voice, rich, warm, irregular. Basil turned slowly, and bowed towards the shadows, but he could see no more than the gleam of one pale arm and the denser blackness of a dark dress against the night. He sighed. Too well he knew the ritual of encounters on a shadowed balcony. He could play as prettily as any other man the game of flattery and evasion. He appreciated the ceremonial niceties of flirtation. But to-night he was tired.

'I am deeply flattered by your solicitude,' he said, 'but I assure you that it was misplaced. Had the world held no other consolation, your unseen presence . . .'

She laughed, so merry, surprising and frank a laugh that it completely disconcerted him.

22

'Come, come,' she cried. 'You hadn't the least idea that I was sitting here. And you know perfectly well that I didn't really think you were going to jump off the balcony. I spoke to you because I was bored. I've lost my shirt already to-day, so I can't play any more. I only bring down so much money with me to the rooms, and when that's gone, I just sit. But to-night it's too early to go home to bed, and none of my friends are here. So . . .'

To excuse himself from further effort, Basil invited the lady into the bar to have a cocktail. She rose with alacrity and stepped before him into the lighted room. He knew then that he had often seen her at the tables, for she was un-mistakable, a large magnificently built brunette, with warm brown colouring and mobile eye-brows. Basil, who under-stood such things, guessed that she wore her gown low, painted her face, and tinted her finger-nails merely because to do otherwise would have seemed an affectation. She fol-lowed exaggerated fashions because she was natural and sensible. As she went, she turned once and smiled at Basil over her shoulder, without coquetry, but with experienced and friendly understanding.

They drank cocktails together at the bar. They talked about Cannes, and roulette, and the heat. Basil drove her back to her hotel, a non-committal place in the Boulevard des Moulins. She told him that her name was Gloria Calmier, that she was the widow of a French officer, and that she adored bathing. They met the next day at the Casino, and the next, and the next.

§ 3

Their frequent encounters suggested to the Syndicate that Basil was attracted by Madame Calmier. Wing Stretton told everyone that St. Denis was having an affair with a rich French widow, but when he attempted to tease Basil accord-ing to the accepted convention of their circle, he was sur-prised by the ferocity of his secretary's repudiation.

'That woman?' cried Basil. 'Heavens! I can't escape her. I go to the Casino and she is there. I go to the Hotel de Paris and she is there. I go down to the beach and she is there, arising from the waves like a slightly over-ripened

23

Aphrodite. If I take the wings of the morning and fly to the uttermost parts of the earth, she will be there also, dying to tell me a perfectly *screaming* limerick about a young lady called Hilda who had an affair with a builder.'

He mimicked with such observant malice Madame Calmier's deep, laughing voice that Wing Stretton accepted his derision as *bona fide* evidence of his untroubled heart, and left him alone to avoid his own entanglements.

But Basil did not tell Wing Stretton the other confidences which Madame Calmier had entrusted to him, though they were infinitely more amusing than the limerick about the young lady called Hilda. For Madame Calmier had no inhibitions. Her candour shocked almost as much as her egotism astounded him. She took for granted his desire to know all that could be told about her past, and talked of herself with unaffected enjoyment.

During their second meeting she informed him that her name was not Gloria at all, but Gladys Irene Mabel. Gladys Irene Mabel Wilcox – 'Well, what could you do with a name like that?' said she. 'When I went on the stage I changed it to Gloria. Gloria Wilcox went quite well, and I kept the Wilcox just to spite Dad because I knew he'd throw fits if they ever found out in Peterborough that he had a daughter in the chorus.'

Her father had been a solicitor's clerk in Peterborough, but Gladys Irene Mabel had found her style unsuited to cathedral cities. When just sixteen she was expelled from the High School for an outrageous flirtation with the grocer's assistant who played the part of 'Fairfax' in an amateur performance of *The Yeoman of the Guard*. 'An awful little man he was really. Short legs, you know, and wore a bowler hat and said, "Pleased to meet you," though that wouldn't have troubled me then. For if he was common, so was I, thank heaven. There's some virtue in vulgarity that swings you over the hard places when you're young. He had a nice tenor voice, though, and I was crazy about the stage. I tried to make him run away with me to London, but he was much too pure. In fact, you know, my first attempt at seduction was a wash-out. He married an elementary school teacher and sings solos in the choir and has seven children. Oh well.'

24

But Gloria-Gladys, since she could not persuade the young man to accompany her to London, went there alone, and encountered such adventures in that city as are commonly supposed to occur to stage-struck girls of sixteen from the provinces. She found, to her dismay, that she was thought too tall for the chorus. She walked on in pantomime as one of Dick Whittington's young men friends in green tights and a leather jerkin, and she eventually crossed to America with a vaudeville producer in a capacity never clearly defined by contract. She sold cigarettes in the foyer of a New York hotel. She acted as hostess in a dance saloon. She displayed models as an outsize mannequin in a Chicago dress store, and in Rio de Janeiro she bore a child, which died, to an Italian real-estate agent whom she had met in Illinois. During the war she returned to Europe with an extremely respectable semi-amateur concert party under the auspices of the American Y.M.C.A.

The concert party went to Paris and there she met Gaston Calmier, a childless widower, no longer very young, the son of a Lyons silk merchant. He was a gentle, ineffective little man, but Gloria liked him, and when, in a panic of loneliness before he was finally called up to join his reserve regiment, he asked her to marry him, she accepted even before she knew that he had a small but pleasant fortune, carefully invested. 'A nice little man. He wouldn't have hurt a chicken. And he was killed six weeks after he'd reached the front. It was murder to send little creatures like him to fight. Well – life being what it is, perhaps it was better so. For him, and me.'

Basil, perforce, listened to this autobiography. While in Monte Carlo, he could not escape from Madame Calmier, and could not leave Monte Carlo while his sole means of livelihood lay there. But after three weeks of unsuccessful attempts at evasion, he suddenly succumbed to a sharp attack of gastric influenza. He thought then that Providence had sent his illness as an order of release, but on the third evening he awoke from an uneasy sleep to find Madame Calmier sitting on his *chaise longue*, placidly polishing her rose-tipped finger-nails with his ivory-backed polisher.

'Nobody seemed to know how you were or what was

25

wrong, so I came to see for myself. Your landlady tells me it's *la grippe*. You certainly do look pretty mouldy.'

Basil was unshaven. His bed was rumpled, his fair hair tousled as threshed straw, his room squalid, his head aching; and he knew that he was going to be sick. For the first time in his life, he swore at a lady.

'God damn you, go away!' he cried in agony. Then that which he feared must happen, happened.

Madame Calmier was neither embarrassed nor insulted.

'My *poor* lamb!' she cried. 'You *are* in a bad way.'

Then she rose, and with sensible promptitude set about making him more comfortable.

She made his bed and washed his face and found him clean pyjamas and gave him milk and soda and bullied the landlady, secured a room for herself in the same house, and sat down to nurse him. She was lonely, and she had found a friend. She was bored, and she had found an occupation. Too indolent for professional efficiency, too feckless for prolonged caution, she made a good enough nurse to justify her presence in his room.

As for Basil, his first horror melted into acquiescence. He derived a measure of comfort from her affirmation that there was nothing about a bedroom to embarrass her. The nature of his illness stripped him of all dignity. To his surprise, she never seemed to see his nakedness. Or perhaps, he reflected, she never saw men or women as anything but naked. Her cheerful glance ignored the masks and the ritual behind which men like Basil seek to hide themselves. She set no value on the decorum which he had cultivated with such care. At first he was too ill to do anything but surrender to her unperturbed initiative. Later he was amazed by the restfulness of complete collapse. As he grew stronger he found himself even enjoying her shameless intimacy, her Rabelaisian anecdotes, her absurd yet amicable limericks. He had found somebody before whom he could relax completely the rigid discipline of his pose, and he was grateful.

A month after his recovery, he married her. 'And quite time too,' said she. 'Anyone could see with half an eye that you were a neglected only child from a country rectory. If I hadn't rescued you, you'd have been a finicky old maid in no time.' And that was the extent to which his grand poses had impressed her.

§ 4

For nearly five years Basil and Gloria drifted about the continent, losing a little money here, speculating profitably there. Gloria once did a good trade in Viennese embroideries, and once she lost money in a stupid venture in Hungarian gas works.

'If the worst comes to the worst,' said Gloria, 'I'll sell out my French bonds and buy a little hotel somewhere between Nice and Cannes. We ought to do quite well there. You understand all about food and wines, and I know how to deal with people.'

'That will indeed be the worst,' said Basil.

'Well, my friend, life being what it is, it's as well to have a way of retreat mapped out. Still, we won't despair yet. What about London for a change?'

They went to London. Gloria found a post as saleswoman of outsize models in a Hanover Square dress-maker's establishment. She and Basil took a small flat in Maida Vale, and Basil went home for a week-end to the Rectory. He showed his parents a photograph of his handsome wife, and they were too thankful to learn that she was a wife to ask disturbing questions.

By this time Basil had succumbed almost completely to Gloria's dominion. In her presence he relaxed his heroic tension of deportment. He had learned to drink port out of a claret glass, to scribble a note on unstamped paper, and to sit down to supper in a lounge suit. On the other hand he could now sleep for more than two hours consecutively. He ate better; his cough left him: he was less cadaverously thin, and more handsome than ever. His wife was well pleased with her handiwork.

One August Sunday morning in 1928, just before noon, Basil lay on his bed in the Maida Vale watching Gloria, who, in a brief apricot-coloured chemise, wandered about the room performing a leisurely Sabbath toilet. She painted her eyebrows; she examined a ladder in a silk stocking; she criticized London in August; she complained of the price of

27

invisible mending; and she turned up the ends of her thick curling hair with a pair of heated tongs. She was trying out the tongs on a sheet of the *Churchman's Weekly*, left in the flat by an Anglo-Catholic charlady, and the smell of scorching paper mingled pleasantly with the scent of *Quelques Fleurs* and cigarette smoke.

'You know, Basil,' she said with her habitual irrelevance, 'you ought to get a job.'

'My *dear* Gloria! What next? And why that now?'

'This loafing's bad for you. You'll lose your figure. You'll develop into the Perfect Clubman – all smile and stomach. Incidentally, Mitchell's won't let you have any more credit, and I'm not exactly rolling in money at the moment. You ought to do some of the world's work.'

'I have a wife who works. Surely one member of the family suffices to satisfy this Anglo-American god of commercial Go-getting? Besides, I have the very strenuous job of being your husband.'

'Well, you're going to have something else very soon if you're not careful. I've been thinking. It doesn't matter so much what you do, so long as you do something.'

'Jobs, my charming Gloria, do not seem exactly to fall into my lap.'

'I know. That's why you've got to make your own job. You know, where we go wrong is that we always try looking for money in the same place. That's no good. I remember a man in America telling me, "You can't go on hammering the same nail for ever. One day it'll get right down into the wood." I remember him telling me that if I wanted to make money I must keep off cabarets and clubs and go in for uplift. He said that there was an enormous lot of kick to be got out of uplift, and that what people liked best in the world was to feel that they were getting fifteen per cent. interest and the pleasant sensation of doing good at the same time.'

'But, my dear Gloria, do you suggest that I should attempt to uplift anyone?'

'Rather. Why not? I want you to listen to this.' She cleared a place on the dressing-table by sweeping aside bottles of pomade, talcum powder and cosmetics. She spread there the scorched and goffered sheet of the *Churchman's*

Weekly on which she had been testing her tongs, scattering brown flakes of charred paper like faded rose petals on to the bedroom carpet. 'This paper's called the *Churchman's Weekly*, and it's got the largest circulation among the real uplift Press – or so it claims. Now it's been running a series of articles by bishops and schoolmasters and M.P.'s and all that sort of thing on "Our Scandalous Cinema" – all about the harm done by immoral pictures to the young, and calling up the churches to make a great effort, before the talkies come right in, to get 'em pure.'

'I believe you.'

'Well. This week there's a woman called Caroline Denton-Smyth writing a letter to the editor saying that some months ago she had an idea of a Christian Cinema Company which should combine profit with pioneering and produce only absolutely one hundred per cent. guaranteed pure films – talkies and all – made in Britain. You know. The sort the curate could take his mother to.'

'Loathsome idea. Well?'

'Well?'

'Well? What has this to do with me, my dear?'

'Rector's son. Second cousin of Lord Herringdale, a great Evangelical peer – or his father was, anyway. Eton. Oxford. Ex-service. *Noblesse oblige.* Secretary or – no – chairman of the Christian Cinema Company – modern but moral. Happily married. Artistic. Wants to help the youngsters. Make a happy England, and beat the Yanks at their own game. *Can't* you see it?'

Basil lay speechless. Gloria gathered a tumbled but vivid silk kimono about her and proceeded to sketch her scheme.

'Enormous appeal to fathers of families, Conservatives, patriots, Nonconformists, chapels, school teachers, town councillors – can't you see it? Get the Press to take it up. "See British films. The Christian Cinema Company earns dividends (at least, it may one day) while doing its duty." This Caroline Denton-Smyth. There must be thousands like her. Spinsters and widows in stuffy boarding-houses in Bayswater and Bournemouth. Longing to do good to somebody before they die. Aching for a little flutter with their

29

money. I bet you Caroline's got thousands and thousands
put away in Brazilian railway stock or something, and keeps
a depressing companion, and quarrels with the Rector about
candles on the altar. But she's hit on a great idea. There's
nothing on earth people like better than to feel that they're
doing good and making money. What's more, when it's a
question of charity and causes and all that, they never ask
for the same security as in a purely commercial speculation.
I remember all those collections for clubs and missions and
all that at Peterborough. Dad had shares in some sort of a
holiday home. Never paid a *sou* in dividends, but he always
hoped it would, and he felt that he was doing good. We
don't want to offer a steady three-and-a-half per cent. We
want to offer a chance of twenty per cent. and a sure sense
of virtue.'

'We?'

'We – the Christian Cinema Company Limited. Properly
registered and all that. Semi-charity. You know old Guerdon, that Quaker stick we met at Aix-les-Bains. He knows
all about Company law and so on. We'll have him on the
Board as a director. Nothing like the Quakers, my dad
always used to say, for money and uplift. Righteous Recrea-
tion for the People – issue £1 shares – up to £500,000 say –
to produce *wholesome* British entertainment. We'll get them
on the "British" – catch all this anti-American feeling that's
floating round. Even if it never comes to anything much
there should be directors' fees and a few commissions, and
so on. There's that fellow Johnson – the Canadian who
knows all about films and runs that correspondence school
business.'

She was absurd, of course. But so was life absurd. Basil
lit a cigarette and lay blowing exquisite smoke-rings toward
the ceiling, and listened. The sight of Gloria in her crêpe-
de-Chine chemise and scarlet kimono, so engagingly incongruous to her subject, tickled his sense of humour. He enjoyed the thought of Caroline Denton-Smyth and all her
type of moralizing churchwomen finding a protagonist in
his wife. He appreciated the comedy of vengeance which
he could exact upon all the hours of boredom spent during
his boyhood while sitting in the Rectory drawing-room,

30

hearing his mother's conversation with the ladies of the Mothers' Union. He sat up and laughed at Gloria.

'Almost thou persuadest me to be a Christian.'

'And then, just think how excited poor old Caroline what's-her-name would be to see an idea of hers come true. I don't suppose she's ever had many of her ideas catch on, do you? Oh, Basil, we must do it. Think of her, fluttering about her Bayswater Boarding House, collecting subscribers, or shareholders or whatever we decide to call them. The more we can make it sound commercial, the more of a novelty it'll be to them. Oh, we'll give her a run for her money before we've done with her, poor Caroline!'

Chapter 2 : *Joseph Isenbaum*

NUMBER 987 Sackville Street, London, W.1, though registered in the Street Directory as the Gentleman's Tailoring Establishment of one Augustus Mitchell, was less of a shop than a club, and less of a club than a sartorial chapel. Mr. Augustus Mitchell's clients did not enter his heavy swing-doors idly, carelessly or wantonly. They came reverently, soberly and discreetly to consult the High Priest of their temple upon matters of religious solemnity, the cut of a trouser, the width of a stripe, or a change in the shape of a collar so subtle that it would have been invisible to the untutored eye. None knew better than Mr. Mitchell the profound and mystic significance of that distance between two buttons on a waistcoat which makes all the difference between the well-groomed gentleman and the outsider.

Mr. Joseph Isenbaum was aware of that significance, and he respected Mr. Mitchell's mastery of it. There were several things about Mr. Mitchell which he did not respect, but this knowledge of detail was impressive. Mr. Isenbaum was a ritualist by racial tradition. He knew what it meant to tithe anise and cummin, and to broaden or narrow the phylacteries. A Jew by birth, name and temperament, an exporter of agricultural implements by profession, a free-thinker by religion, a family man by accident, and a connoisseur by inclination, he regarded his visits to Mr. Mitchell's shop as unpleasant but sacred obligations.

For Mr. Isenbaum cherished a wistful and often misplaced devotion to the Best. He maintained that a man's possessions should be Few but Good, that his habits should be Restrained but Splendid, and that his associations should be Eclectic but Intimate. Unhappily his worship was hampered by his limitations of taste and judgment. In pursuit of the Rare and Beautiful, he had filled his house at Richmond with a catholic collection of monstrosities, picked up at auction sales all over London and the Home Counties. Though he went to Mitchell's for his clothes, the eccentricity of his figure prevented even that master from fulfilling his highest possibilities. Though he belonged to two tolerable clubs, the dissonance of his name, and a certain hesitation and obsequiousness of manner, prevented him from forming those few but choice friendships which he desired. His desire for a son involved him in a disastrous sequence of five daughters, at the end of which had come at long last his beloved, his Benjamin.

Benjamin Isenbaum. Benjamin Isenbaum. As Mr. Isenbaum sat on one September afternoon in Augustus Mitchell's shop, he repeated the name over and over to himself as though it were a painful yet exciting charm. Whenever Joseph had nothing else of special moment to think about, his thoughts turned to his son. Yet always the contemplation hurt as well as comforted. For Joseph had inflicted upon this splendid son, this lamb without spot or blemish, this glorious boy, an intolerable burden. Benjamin Isenbaum. Benjamin Isenbaum. What could a man do in the world with a name like that?

Joseph had originally intended, if ever he had a son, to change his own name to Bauminster and to call the boy William or Richard. He had discussed the matter with his wife, who was content to acquiesce in all his decisions. As a free-thinker and modernist, he was bound by no tie of piety or interest to Judaism.

But when it came to the point of taking out letters patent, the delicacy of spirit which was with him a motive stronger even than his paternal love, frustrated him. Three weeks before the birth of the boy, he heard an ex-Jew, Ferguson, whose father had been called Abrams, talking to a group of men about his recently acquired membership of a coveted club. 'Thank God,' cried Abrams-Ferguson. 'You can eat without meeting any Jews there!'

Joseph saw the polite acquiescence of the Gentile listeners. His pride and his hunger for perfection combined in revolt

33

against both the meanness which inspired Ferguson and the scorn which greeted him. He made a vow to the God in whom he professed enlightened disbelief that if he had a son he would call him Benjamin, and that he would remain an Isenbaum till death.

The decision was made. The son was born. The name was given. But Joseph lived to repent daily and hourly his magnanimous gesture. The boy was everything that a boy could be. Nothing could be too good for him. Eton or Harrow, Oxford or Cambridge, the best clubs, the best companionship, the best profession. The Bar and then Parliament? Harley Street? A Professorial Chair? The presidency of the Royal Academy? All these pinnacles of achievement appeared accessible to Dicky Bauminster. But to Ben Isenbaum?

Torn between obstinacy and compunction, his father laboured to undo the harm of his rash oath.

He endeavoured to enter Benjamin for one of the big public schools. But he learned by bitter experience that the son of Joseph Isenbaum, exporter of agricultural implements, might knock in vain at the gates of Eton or Harrow unless he could go sponsored by some more welcome visitant. House-masters wrote politely to say that they had no vacancies. Non-committal replies left Joseph sick with apprehension. Fear lest he should have ruined his son's chances lay like a weight of indigestion across his chest.

But if he could secure a letter of introduction from an Etonian, a Bishop or a Peer, or even a plain gentleman of good standing, then the situation would be changed.

Among his acquaintances were men who had been to public schools, but not one of them, Joseph felt, was the right man for his purpose.

He was thinking of his need when he sat in Augustus Mitchell's show-room, handling patterns of gent's autumn suitings.

Here in this sombre, spacious room he was surrounded by the Best that English tailoring could offer. The bales of cloth dripped to the floor their smooth dark drapery. The assistants trod silently up and down the rich fawn carpet, moving like acolytes at their priestly task. Here was taste not to be bought with money, and dignity which was incorruptible. Yet even here were barbs to prick Joseph's sensitive conscience. There was one characteristic of Mitchell's shop which he found almost intolerable.

Mr. Mitchell was an autocrat. He was an undiminished Paternal Despot surviving from the Victorian era. He refused to employ a member of a trade union; he refused to employ a professing agnostic; and he refused to call his assistants by their names. His ideal, he confided sometimes in more favoured clients, was Anonymous Service. While at his work no man of Mitchell's save Mitchell himself, was permitted to exercise Personality. His clients were attended not by Smith, Jones, or Robinson, but by assistants number 49, 17, or 63.

To Joseph Isenbaum this custom was odious. He knew too well the importance of a name. Every time he saw Mitchell, he intended to revolt against the barbarous humiliation of his adult skilled, competent and dignified assistants. But he never did.

To-day, however, as he sat brooding and dreaming, he became aware that farther down the room Mr. Mitchell himself was talking to a client. Too unhappy to choose autumn suitings, Joseph looked up idly, and began to watch the comedy displayed before him. For very soon he realized that something unusual was happening just beyond the palm in the brown china stand, and the oval table supporting copies of the *Spectator*, *Debrett*, *Who's Who* and the *Tailor and Cutter*.

Mr. Mitchell's client was a tall, very fair, very slender and handsome gentleman, with a foppish, drawling, languid, elegant manner. He was exquisitely attired, a credit, thought Joseph, even to Mr. Mitchell's tailoring, and a consolation for the discomforts and encountering assistants number 17 and 63. He lounged against the long table which served in Mitchell's for a counter, and with the point of his stick drew patterns in the nap of Mitchell's turf-like carpet. Of all odd things in the world, he was discussing cinemas.

Joseph bent over his cloths again; but he was listening. The elegant gentleman was talking about films, Russian

35

films, German films, Hollywood and English films, their actual vulgarity, their potential excellence. He talked well, with a knowledge which seemed topical rather than profound. Could Mitchell find suitable entertainment in the cinema for his three daughters? He could not.

'Of course, æsthetically, they are contemptible. Educationally,' the client shrugged slender shoulders. 'Well, of course, personally, I find it a little difficult to gauge the taste of the average schoolboy. When I was at Eton . . .'

Eton. Eton. Eton, echoed Joseph's conscience. This exquisite creature was a product of Eton. Benjamin . . . He missed several sentences.

'. . . from the ethical standpoint,' concluded the client.

'Oh, there you have it. There you have it, Mr. St. Denis,' said the tailor. 'From the ethical standpoint I agree with you. I endorse your sentiments. I uphold you. We do not want Hollywood morals in our English Homes. As for the Empire. Look at the effect that this sort of thing must have upon the natives. As an imperial responsibility, Mr. St. Denis, the Government ought to take the matter in hand. British prestige is being lowered, reduced, degraded by the obscenities – pardon the word – the indecencies of American actresses.'

'The Government? Hum. Now, as a Conservative, Mitchell, I put it to you. Do you really approve of Government interference with industry?'

'Industry, sir? Industry's a different matter. This is a question of morals.'

'Ultimately, Mitchell. Ultimately. I grant you that the final judgment upon the cinema may be ethical. But the immediate motive is – I put it to you – commercial.'

'What we need is a censor, Mr. St. Denis.'

'We have one. We have one, Mitchell. An entire Board of Censors. And what do they achieve? – What is the use of banning a few bad films? The demand is there. It will be supplied somehow. What we want, I suggest, Mitchell, is enterprise – competition. We want to place upon the market a film which will be worth showing.'

'Very pretty, Mr. St. Denis. Very pretty. But where is it to come from, sir? America? Can we make silk purses out of sows' ears? England? British enterprise is dead to-day. Dead. Killed by the Dole and Government interference.'

'Not dead, Mitchell. Not dead. Sleeping. The Sleeping Beauty waiting for Prince Charming.'

'I dare say. I dare say. And where is he, Mr. St. Denis? Where is he, I say?'

St. Denis laughed.

'I am a modest man,' he said. 'Far be it from me . . .'

'You, Mr. St. Denis?'

'Well, Mitchell. And why not? Don't you think it about time that I did something to justify my existence?'

And then it seemed to Joseph as though he were watching a very intricate and expert duel, which proceeded according to the ritual of all good sword-play. The elegant client called St. Denis was clearly determined to interest Mr. Mitchell in some scheme for the formation of a company to reform the British cinema. Nor did the interest appear to be purely impersonal. Joseph had himself an hereditary understanding of finesse. He understood why Mr. St. Denis pressed so lightly, so ironically, the claims of his cinema company. He understood the heavier retreats and defences of the tailor.

The tailor, of course, was in the superior position. He only had to listen and deny. St. Denis had to do more than that. It became evident to Joseph, watching, that St. Denis, like many other exquisite young men, was in financial difficulties. In short, he could not pay his tailor's bill. He sought instead to prolong his credit by dazzling Mr. Mitchell with the prospects of a new cinema company of which he was, it seemed, to be the chairman of the directing board.

'So suitable, don't you think, Mitchell, being a rector's son?' murmured Mr. St. Denis.

A rector's son who had been to Eton, noted the father of Ben Isenbaum.

But the rector's son who had been to Eton was not by any means winning his match. For all his light fencing, his delicate thrusts and agile ripostes, he was being beaten back by the slow pomposity of the Christian tailor.

Joseph's imagination warmed towards the conquered. His love of elegance endeared St. Denis to him. His romantic heart softened to this rector's son who wore his clothes so admirably. His alert sense of business observed that here was an Etonian in a difficulty. Of all things in the world that Joseph needed at that moment was an opportunity for placing an Etonian under an obligation to him.

Still, the opportunity had not yet arisen. St. Denis broke off, raised his eyebrows, and turned to go. He was defeated, but he was unbroken. He strolled three paces down the room, then turned.

'Oh, by the way, Mitchell. I told Hollway that I wanted that suit by Friday.'

'Hollway, sir?'

'Hollway. That fellow you call 17. My dear Mitchell, you surely don't expect me to adopt your degrading practice of calling your assistants by numbers as though they were Dartmoor convicts, do you?'

'Degrading, sir? Ah, hardly that, I think, surely. Our ideal is one of impersonal service – impersonal anonymity, sir. Look at the Gothic cathedrals. We do not know who built them. Look at *The Times* newspaper.'

'Yes. Look at it. Damn dull, my dear Mitchell. Damn dull. In any case, these numbers confuse me. They are worse than the streets in New York. In future, please, when I am here, kindly call your assistants by their proper names.'

'Splendid, splendid, splendid!' applauded Joseph's heart. His tongue was silent, but he rose to his feet in an impulsive tribute of gratitude and admiration.

Then St. Denis saw him.

'I'm afraid that I've kept you too long from your other customers,' said he. 'This gentleman.'

'Not at all. Not at all,' cried Joseph, perspiring but composed. 'I was only looking through some patterns.'

He swallowed hard. What St. Denis, insolvent but indomitable, had done, that Isenbaum, solvent as he was, could do. 'I gave my selections to your assistant, Griffin.'

'Griffin?' Mr. Mitchell flushed. St. Denis was an old customer. He was a relative of Lord Herringdale. He was privileged. But Isenbaum, the fat, stinking little Jew, Isenbaum had defied the Rubric, and blasphemed the Holy of

38

Holies. Mr. Mitchell grew calm with fury. 'You mean my assistant, 17?'

'I mean your man here, Griffin,' repeated Joseph, flushed but resolute. 'I agree with this gentleman, Mr. Mitchell. I prefer to call your assistants by their proper names.'

'Admirable,' smiled St. Denis. 'You see, Mitchell, I have a fellow protestant.'

If fury could destroy long-set tradition, if rage could master business advantage, if a life-time of discipline had not overlain Mr. Mitchell's passions, he would then have ordered both his customers from his shop. Had Isenbaum been alone, he would have done it. But St. Denis was St. Denis. He did not pay his bills, but he was well connected. One never knew how far the repercussions of insulting Lord Herringdale's kinsman might resound through the small world of quality. Mr. Mitchell tightened his lips and bowed in silence.

But as he bowed, he conceived another and more subtle means of vengeance. Mitchell's was a club, over which he had hitherto presided with inimitable discretion. Never had he affected an introduction which cast the least shadow of embarrassment on either of the parties. Now he remembered that the Herringdales hated Jews; and he suspected that St. Denis borrowed money from all men of substance. The pair were well matched to inconvenience each other.

'Ah,' said he. 'I believe that you do not know Mr. Isenbaum, Mr. St. Denis? Mr. St. Denis, Mr. Isenbaum.'

Mitchell had made one miscalculation. Of all his clients there was none who appreciated better than Basil St. Denis the fine shades of etiquette at Mitchell's. He knew that Augustus Mitchell did not introduce his Jews. He knew that Mitchell sought to make himself unpleasant. He quietly spiked the tailor's guns.

'Ah, Isenbaum, we are two revolutionaries. Mitchell will have none of us. I am desolate. We must console each other. Were you going anywhere?'

'Only eventually back to the city. But not in any hurry,' smiled Joseph nervously.

'Then come and have a drink first,' said Basil, as though

39

Joseph Isenbaum were the one man in all London whom he had hoped to meet.

They left the shop together, leaving the tailor more harassed, angry, outraged and discomforted than he had ever been since Mitchell's stood in Sackville Street. But Joseph was elated. He knew that he had done a good day's work. If a few hundred pounds invested in a wild-cat enterprise to purify the cinema could buy him the friendship of an old Etonian, the investment was as good as made.

§ 2

A week later, Joseph Isenbaum asked St. Denis to bring Miss Denton-Smyth to lunch with him at Boulestin's. He had devoted some thought to the details of that party. 'It's not enough for the man to be indebted to me,' he had told himself. 'He's got to like me.' He felt that the liking depended to a great extent upon the choice of a restaurant. The Savoy was too hackneyed, Claridge's no place for business, Simpson's too beef-steaky and he-mannish. He chose Boulestin's.

Sitting in the ante-room, uneasily turning over smooth new copies of the *Sketch* and *Tatler*, he waited for St. Denis and the lady who had inspired his interest in the cinema. He was anxious to meet this Miss Denton-Smyth, for though still uncertain of St. Denis's honesty and intentions, Joseph felt perfect confidence in his taste. Any lady whom St. Denis brought to lunch would be worth entertaining.

Joseph tried to imagine what she would be like. He pictured her walking down the shallow rose-carpeted stairs, and pausing to look at the glass case imprisoning bags and scarves and fantastic glass beads displayed by an amusingly expensive store. Would she be young, shy, ardent, the least little trifle absurd in her fanaticism, like the charming young thing who had once tried to interest him in a dancing school? Or would she be a business woman, keen and competent as a greyhound, and unruffled as a fashion-sketch from *Vogue*?

She was late of course. They were both late. He imagined that St. Denis would always be a little late. Unpunctuality was the privilege of charming people. Joseph himself always

40

arrived everywhere a little too early, and then suffered anguish from the embarrassment of waiting.

He was perturbed to-day by other considerations. Should he offer cocktails? Or was St. Denis one of those gourmets who accuse cocktails of blasphemy against the well-trained palate? And if a cocktail, which?

He studied the little list. 'Moonshine,' 'Kingston,' 'Alexandre'? This lunch was going to cost him a pretty penny. It would be worth it, of course, if only Benjamin could go to Eton. But though aware of the advantages of extravagance, he could not refrain from reckoning his losses. His generosity and his economies were spasmodic. After a lunch at Boulestin's, he would ride for weeks in buses, and snap at his wife for buying her stockings in half-dozen pairs.

He thought he would smoke. Smoking gave a fellow self-confidence. The sight of his cigarette-case reassured him. He had exercised commendable self-control in choosing plain tortoise-shell with a gold monogram, when he might so easily have carried platinum set with diamonds. His cigarette-case, he considered, was All Right, and it was immensely important to be All Right when one was the father of a prospective Etonian.

His attention was diverted from his contemplation of Ben's future by the sight of a woman entering the restaurant. She was so remarkable a woman that Joseph stared at her with indignation. For when one has gone to all the trouble and expense of choosing to entertain acquaintances at Boulestin's, one does at least expect to be spared nuisances of that kind. Joseph wanted her to be removed immediately, not rudely of course, and not in any way that would cause discomfort to a spectator, but gently and firmly lured upstairs again, and out into the more appropriate neighbourhood of Covent Garden. Seated among the fruit boxes and orange cases of the market, she would seem almost commonplace.

But she did not appear to be abashed by her intrusion. She halted in the doorway, and fumbling among the chains and beads about her neck, found a pair of lorgnettes, clicked them open, and stood peering through them into the anteroom, turning her finger a little as she peered, so that all her chains and beads clashed softly together, like the trappings of an oriental dancer at a cheap music hall. The lorgnettes imparted to her short, plump, eccentric figure an air of comic but indomitable dignity. Her preposterous red hat, with its huge ribbon bows and sweeping pheasant's feather, bobbed triumphantly above her fizzled hair. Her green coat shone with age, but it was elaborately decorated with lumps and bands of sealskin, the fur worn to that soft ruddy opalescence which it acquires with extreme decrepitude. Her shoes – Joseph had taught himself always to look at a woman's shoes – were worse than inadequate, they were shameful.

It was quite hideous that she should be there, destroying the muted perfection of that subterranean refuge from distressing things. Her poverty, her oddity, her jaunty air of unintimidated resolution were abominable.

Joseph was a soft-hearted man. He did not wish to be reminded of the poverty and loneliness of odd old ladies when about to enjoy himself at a good restaurant. Supposing St. Denis came in and saw her there? Joseph shuddered, and tried to turn his mind to the anticipation of *crêpes de Volailles*.

But through the open door he saw now, coming down the staircase, a pair of elegant feet with immaculate spats, followed by beautifully pressed trousers, followed by a lounge suit of Mitchell's most perfect cut, followed by the thin, pale, handsome, supercilious face of Basil St. Denis. Horrors! St. Denis would see the old hag in the doorway. There was no remedy for this nightmare situation.

He did see her. St. Denis paused and looked at the woman. The woman turned and looked at St. Denis. Then she let her lorgnettes fall and held out her hand with a little cry of pleasure.

'Oh, I didn't see you and I knew I was late, and though I know it's silly, I always say to myself now has he been run over by a bus, or have I come to the wrong restaurant?'

'You've come to the right restaurant, and I was not run over by a bus, and here is our host waiting for us. Mr. Isenbaum, may I introduce the honorary secretary of the Christian Cinema Company, Miss Caroline Denton-Smyth?'

Joseph gasped; Joseph stared. With a terrific effort he tried to pull himself together and to assume the careless

42

courtesy of an Etonian's father. He heard his treacherous voice stammering:

'Pleased to meet you, Miss Denton-Smyth.'

After that there was nothing for it but a cocktail.

If Miss Denton-Smyth looked strange in the restaurant, she made it quite clear by her manner that she felt quite at home there. She settled herself at the little painted table, and talked to the waiter with smiling familiarity. She would certainly have a cocktail. If Alexandres really had whipped cream in them, she would have an Alexandre. She adored whipped cream. She adored those very curious paintings on the wall. A little *Bohemian* perhaps; but then it was nice, once in a way, to be Bohemian. And now that she was connected with the cinema trade it was important to get to know all sorts and conditions of men – and women. She caught sight of a lovely blonde, trim as a magpie in black and white, dazzling an enamoured stock-broker at a corner table – '*Men* and women,' repeated Miss Denton-Smyth, sipping her Alexandre with satisfaction.

Joseph watched her, fascinated. He noticed that St. Denis took her entirely for granted, treated her as though her oddity were an asset, or, even more subtly, as though she were not odd at all. And following St. Denis, attempting to imitate St. Denis's delicacy of feeling, Joseph found himself regarding Miss Denton-Smyth with acquiescence. For though she was shabby, pretentious and a little absurd, she was not insignificant. Seen more closely, her shabbiness wore an air of picturesque and debonair eccentricity.

She was a little woman, short, plump and animated as a kitten. Beneath her hat bubbled and curled the dyed and frizzled fringe that almost hid her lively arched brown eyebrows. Her eyes were large, handsome, brown and romantic as a spaniel's. She might have been any age between forty-five and seventy. There was youth in her eyes, in her vitality, in her soft, eager hurrying voice and merry laugh; there was youth in her girlish skirt and sturdy legs; but her skin was old. Her round brown face was wrinkled as a walnut; her neck was old, and her busy restless hands were knotted with rheumatism.

St. Denis let her talk. It amused Joseph to watch how he

43

prompted her with casual questions, as though her flow of discursive, excited, emphatic conversation gave him exquisite entertainment. Joseph could not keep up with her at all.

He heard her say, 'And so, you see, if we can really buy the rights for six months of the Tona Perfecta, we shall soon raise the capital for manufacture.'

He gathered that the Tona Perfecta was some newly invented talking film.

'Yes, Mr. Johnson met him, and of course although he is perhaps a rather *rough* diamond, I always say he has a heart of gold, and then these Canadians are somehow so *winning*, and Mr. St. Denis went with Johnson to the laboratory, didn't you, Mr. St. Denis? It's out at Annerley, you know, in a really extraordinary place, although he is undoubtedly a genius.'

Joseph's mind leapt panting after her eager affirmations, but he was handicapped by the necessity of instructing the waiter, of choosing wines, and of paying attention to his other guest. He could not follow her.

'And so I've written of course to my Yorkshire relatives and told them that as an investment which will really bring them both financial and moral satisfaction, of course, the Christian Cinema Company is unequalled. Only, of course, we must have offices, and I have seen exactly what we want in Victoria Street, because though Mr. Johnson has very *kindly* lent us his just until we get somewhere of our own, I always say that one little *corner* of your own is better than a palace of someone else's.'

Whatever else might fail, thought Joseph, the *crêpes de Volailles* at least fulfilled their purpose. They were perfect; they were marvellous; they were so unequivocally The Best of their kind that they set at rest all his natural impulses of uneasiness.

Miss Denton-Smyth also found them admirable. 'Of course, I always say that the Good Lord wouldn't have given us stomachs if he had not meant us to enjoy our food. Of course, I *belong* to temperance organizations because I think that one ought to encourage all good work, but I'm very glad that we haven't had prohibition yet in England. I

44

always think that the miracle of Cana, if you know what I mean, is somehow so *stimulating*.'

Clearly she had been stimulated by something; but whether by the wine, by the food, by the suave leisureliness of the restaurant, or by her own vitality, Joseph did not know. St. Denis talked little, and ate almost as little as he talked. But his manner assumed that Joseph was as much interested in Miss Denton-Smyth as he was, and that the Christian Cinema Company was a rather complicated personal joke which they would share between them. Before they left the restaurant, Joseph knew that he was committed to a preliminary investment of five hundred pounds to enable the Christian Cinema Company to establish its offices in Victoria Street, to negotiate for the rights of producing Tona Perfecta Films, and to open its propaganda campaign for the purification of the British cinema.

§ 3

Towards the end of November, 1928, Joseph Isenbaum sat at the Board table of the Christian Cinema Company Limited in Victoria Street reckoning his gains and losses. The gains were substantial, for St. Denis had at last promised him an introduction to the house-master of his old house at Eton, and had manifested adequate interest in little Benjamin. Moreover, St. Denis himself was an agreeable fellow. He would make no fuss if, after Benjamin was safely entered for Eton, Joseph quietly withdrew from his directorship.

For Joseph had no intention of letting this business cost him very much more. Already, one way and another, he had spent upon it six hundred and thirty-seven pounds, twelve shillings and eightpence, and while he was prepared to spend far more for Benjamin's sake, he had no wish to throw away his money. Five hundred pounds he had subscribed to the company, one hundred and six pounds he had spent at Mitchell's, unobtrusively clearing St. Denis's account and restoring his diminished credit. The rest had gone on luncheons, drinks and taxis. It was enough.

The company, of course, was in itself a farce. The honorary secretary saw herself as an alluring combination of Sir Oswald Stoll and Josephine Butler, a great financial power

45

whose influence purified British entertainments. She wanted to be rich as much as anyone; but from practical experience she knew that it was far easier to distribute uplift than dividends among mankind. It was easier to Do Good than to Make Money. Joseph's five hundred pounds and the small investments of the other directors had evaporated upon office equipment, printing and advertisement, and although public opinion might have derived education from the result, the company had certainly derived no substantial pecuniary benefit.

Still, there it was, and there was the Board assembled at five o'clock in the afternoon, waiting to begin a meeting. St. Denis sat at the head of the table, acting his part as chairman with ironic exaggeration. One of the amusements of a business career lay in the opportunity for dressing-up. St. Denis as the Complete Business Man, in a morning coat and striped trousers, his sleek fair hair brushed back, and a gardenia in his buttonhole, was a glorious sight.

On his left sat Hugh Macafee, inventor of the Tona Perfecta Talking Film, a gauche, raw-boned, sullen young Scot, his gaunt face thrust down on to his roughened fists, his badly fitting Norfolk jacket hunched up round his ears. Macafee had a grievance, and Joseph Isenbaum was not at all sure that in Macafee's place he would not have had a grievance too. For the other directors might find the company one incident among many in their lives, but the Tona Perfecta Film meant everything to Macafee. He had worked for it and starved for it and dreamed of it, and had, Joseph considered, a right to sell it in the best market. If he were wise, he would break away from Johnson's clutches and get clear of the company. Once or twice Joseph had been tempted to tell him so. But after all, was it his business? He was a director of the company. The Tona Perfecta was its sole substantial asset. What right had he to play a double game with Macafee? Far better leave well alone. After all, even Macafee was not a child.

He turned from Macafee to John Fry Fox Guerdon, the Quaker director, an unhappy, timid, middle-aged bachelor, with a long egg-shaped head, very bald and highly polished. A semicircle of white hair fringed his oval skull; small surprised tufts of white hair jutted from his eyes and eyebrows. He twitched his long nose and blinked disconsolately through his gold-rimmed eyeglasses, alarmed at every manifestation of activity on the part of his fellow-directors, ill at ease in the proximity of Johnson, and obviously only remaining upon the Board because his family tradition impelled him to good works, and St. Denis had persuaded him that this was a noble cause.

Poor Guerdon, thought Joseph, forced by his principles to associate with a brigand like Johnson. For if ever villainy was writ large upon a man's countenance, that man was Clifton Roderick Johnson, 'of Toronto and Hollywood' according to his own account, of Birmingham and Chicago still more probably, thought Joseph, a huge, hulking, clumsy, disreputable, oratorical creature, who had just missed being superbly handsome and obviously gave himself the benefit of the doubt. Johnson affected a picturesque and conspicuous style of dress and manner. His decorative blue shirts with open necks, his broad-brimmed black hats, huge flapping cloaks and free dramatic gestures, made his appearance remarkable in any company. Tall and finely proportioned, his otherwise impressive figure was spoiled by the ugly forward thrust of his head and neck. His black brows almost met above dark flashing eyes, which were unfortunately disfigured by a slight cast. His really handsome profile was marred when he smiled and showed his big, yellow neglected teeth. He was as dirty as St. Denis was fastidious, forgot to shave after a night's drinking, and would appear at a lunch at the Café Royal with his shoe-laces undone. In moments of excitement he had been known to roll down a woollen sock and expose on a hairy ankle the scars left by a bear's claws during a rough encounter in the Rockies. He gave acquaintances to understand that on less accessible parts of his person were even better scars. He was a clever, bragging, untidy, talkative, malicious, romantic fellow, with the face of an artistic scavenger and the amatory impulses of a tom-cat. The thought of his concern for the purity of the cinema was sufficient to afford St. Denis adequate entertainment for a year.

On the other side of Johnson was Joseph's seat, and between Joseph and the chairman sat the honorary secretary of the company, Miss Denton-Smyth. It was she who had arranged the austere but imposing furniture of the office, she who had laid before each director a sheet of pink virgin blotting-paper, a writing-block, and sharpened pencil. It was she who had written in the large leather-bound book the minutes of the previous Board meetings; she who sent out the circulars, drafted the prospectuses, soothed Macafee's impatience and curbed Johnson's eloquence. For all the ironic insinuations of St. Denis, Joseph knew that Miss Denton-Smyth was the Christian Cinema Company. It had come into being at her word. It existed upon her labour. It aspired toward her ideals.

'What a woman,' thought Joseph Isenbaum. 'What a woman!'

As Joseph watched her open her correspondence file, smooth the papers neatly in front of her, and beam round the table at her Board until her eyes came to rest with adoring solicitude upon her chairman, Joseph thought, 'Almighty God, the woman's fallen in love with St. Denis.' But later, when she went through her correspondence, spoke of the growing public interest in the enterprise, displayed the company seal that had just arrived at the office, and described the interview which she had had with the Rector of Mayfair, Joseph thought instead, 'The woman's fallen in love with the Company!'

The meeting began.

St. Denis nodded his head, and drawled in his charming, musical voice, 'Well, Miss Denton-Smyth and gentlemen, we may as well begin. I call upon the secretary to read the minutes of the last meeting.'

Miss Denton-Smyth cleared her throat and ran her tongue over her lips. She began to read.

'A Board meeting of the Christian Cinema Company, Ltd., was held on November 1st, 1928, at 396 Victoria Street. Present, Mr. St. Denis in the chair, Mr. Johnson, Mr. Guerdon, Mr. Isenbaum, Mr. Macafee and Miss Denton-Smyth, honorary secretary. The minutes of the last meeting were read and confirmed. The hon. secretary reported that she had received seventeen letters of inquiry in response to the advertisement in the *Churchman's Weekly*, four through the *Protestant Gazette*, two from *The School Teacher*, and seven from *The Homes of England*.'

The eager, gentle voice went on. There was no doubt, reflected Joseph, that to Miss Denton-Smyth these letters were as wonderful as love-letters. Each circular was to her a royal mandate. Geography radiated from one central point, this office in Victoria Street. History dated from her first interview with Basil St. Denis. Mathematics was a system for calculating how many shareholders buying ten £1 shares would be necessary to start the manufacture of Tona Perfecta Films. Art was the inspiration and direction of purified and educational films. The universe centred round the success or failure of the Christian Cinema Company Limited.

'It's not as though she, or any of them, cared two straws for the purity of the British film,' thought Joseph. 'She wants her two hundred per cent., as much as any of them. If the business were selling saucepans or rubber or instituting laundries or building a college, it would be all the same. She's in love with the work, with enterprise, with getting something done, with running an office, and flirting with St. Denis. But she can't take it easily. She's a fanatic. It's a religion with her. Well, I suppose it's about as satisfactory as any other religion and may last at least as long.'

The Christian Cinema Company had at the moment a bank balance of £87. Its assets were the company seal, the furniture of the room in which the directors sat, and the rights, not yet formally acquired, to reproduce Macafee's Tona Perfecta Films. The appeal for shareholders was now being made, but it was perfectly clear that the British public was slow to realize its possibilities. Up to date the investments amounted to exactly £528 11s. 6d., apart from the directors' contributions.

Miss Denton-Smyth explained all this without uneasiness, 'These of course are only preliminary inquiries, Mr. Chairman. Now that our circulars are printed, I expect to see a great difference. I have up to date managed to get two thousand envelopes addressed, but of course I work single-handed, and I do not like to wait too long. I wondered if I might get a little clerical help. That was one of the things I wanted to ask the Board. There are another five thousand I could send out, and I hate to think that we may have lost a really valuable shareholder, just because I was unable to address the proper envelope. And yet I find that I cannot do any more than I do now.'

It was amazing. If she did all the work that she claimed to do, she must have slaved from morning until night.

'These women, Almighty God, these women,' thought Joseph. 'If I had her in my office . . .' But all the same he was glad, on the whole, that he did not have her in his office. She set a pace which only fanaticism, not business method, could maintain.

'Well, Miss Denton-Smyth,' St. Denis was saying. 'I think we must trust to your discretion. You know the state of the company's finances better than anyone. You know the need for economy. I am sure that the Board will agree with me that in this matter of clerical help we can safely leave all decisions with Miss Denton-Smyth.'

'Agreed, agreed,' growled the directors, all but Hugh Macafee, whose Scottish voice broke harshly in upon the meeting.

'I suppose we have some guarantee that the company's funds will not be squandered in unnecessary clerical extravagance,' he said angrily, looking round the Board with fierce challenging eyes. 'We're out to make Tona Perfecta Films, I take it. Not to provide employment for a lot of girl typists.'

'Quite. Quite. But you will see, I am sure, Mr. Macafee, that before we make the films, we must raise the capital.'

'If we go on at this rate we shall be waiting till Doomsday. I always said that these £1 shares were like trying to empty the Atlantic with a thimble. If the thing's a decent business proposition . . .'

'It is, Macafee. It is. But you remember that we agreed that in an enterprise like this, run not only for commercial but for artistic and moral profit, the wider we throw our nets, the better. We want to make it possible for all those interested in the future of the cinema to contribute.'

50

'That is so; that is so,' interpolated Johnson in his hybrid, pseudo-American accent. 'We're idealists, Macafee, idealists. We want to allow all practical idealists to co-operate with us to put Beauty on th' map of England.'

'I take it then,' St. Denis said, 'that we authorize Miss Denton-Smyth to employ occasional clerical help, remembering of course the need for strict economy. Thank you. Now – let us see. The next item on the agenda – ah! the circulars. Would you be good enough to let the Board see the various suggestions in proof, Miss Denton-Smyth?'

The circulars had been compiled by the chairman and the honorary secretary. Their composition had given Basil exquisite pleasure. He had designed appeals to captivate country clergy, Anglo-Catholic missionaries, Nonconformist town councillors, pious maiden ladies in seaside boarding houses, Puritan manufacturers with strong prejudices, and artistic young ladies and gentlemen from Chelsea, Macclesfield, or Liverpool, who longed to strike a blow for Liberty in Art, against the Philistine horrors of the commercial cinema.

St. Denis was proud of his circulars. He had baited his hooks cleverly. He had been charmed by his occupation, and the earnest co-operation of Miss Denton-Smyth added the final flavour of delicious unreality to the business. Miss Denton-Smyth was his criterion. Her eager affirmations or criticisms provided the tuning-fork which gave the pitch of commonplace credulity. She prevented him from becoming a victim of his sense of humour. What she passed as possible that he too accepted.

He was eager to watch the reactions of his fellow directors to his work. He feared that they might refuse to take seriously these lyrical appeals marked 'Seaside Spinsters,' these common-sense proposals 'To business men.' But he had reckoned without the entrancing fascination of a new technique. He had not experienced, as Joseph had experienced, the spell wrought upon a bored and lethargic meeting by the necessity of passing judgment upon green- or orange-tinted paper, type, and capitals, borders and spacing.

'Look here, St. Denis. We ought to alter the lay-out of this cover. These wavy lines are too indefinite.'

51

'. . . Good straight block capitals. *Black* – easy to read.'

'Well, I always say, Mr. Chairman, that a little verse breaks up the lines and gives a sense of – of . . . *intimacy*.'

'I like these with the Old English lettering for the parsons. An ecclesiastical air to them. What about a violet-coloured border?'

'Now, what we want, gentlemen,' roared Johnson, in his backwoods, lumber-camp voice, 'is psychol'gy. Psych'logical appeal's the thing.'

They forgot that the Christian Cinema Company was a crazy adventure, without adequate capital, without prospects, without even strict business honesty. They forgot that each of them except Miss Denton-Smyth had entered it for entirely irrelevant reasons. They had become completely absorbed in the excitement of the thing-in-itself. They wanted those circulars to conform to their own individual notion of what circulars should be. They were swept by a wave of excitement. They scrambled over the proofs; they argued; they shouted. They drew diagrams on the nice, clean rose-coloured blotting-paper. They wasted recklessly sheet after sheet of the smooth cream writing-pads. Even Joseph, who had come to watch his fellow directors expose their capacity for self-deception and dishonesty, found himself carried away from his detachment. He disagreed about the appeal to business men. He had suggestions for the circular marked 'High-brow Artistic. Chelsea. Bloomsbury, etc.' He began to scribble designs, suggest, correct, or argue, like any of them. He grew hot and excited. He became eloquent. He even forgot for a moment that he was enduring all this nonsense so that St. Denis might make it possible for Ben to go to Eton.

In the middle of his excitement he glanced up from a violent dispute with Johnson, and saw Macafee sitting aloof, sullen, indifferent, scribbling private calculations on his writing-block; and he saw St. Denis, whose enthusiasm for the circulars had had time to cool since the completion of their design, watching him with amusement, entertained to see that even the little Jew could not resist the excitement of quarrelling about lay-out and type-setting.

Joseph was about to leave the office after the meeting when Miss Denton-Smyth approached him. 'Could you spare a few moments when the others have gone? I want to speak to you. It's rather urgent.'

'Well, let me see. I have a dinner engagement.'

'I really shan't keep you a moment.'

The other men were collecting hats and sticks, continuing arguments, and shaking hands with the secretary. Joseph waited. The thought that he would arrive home too late to see the boy before he went to bed made him irritable with impatience. Ben was splendid in his bath – great at gymnastics on the nursery floor. He looked forward to half an hour with his father. Damn the woman. Damn the woman. Why did she want him now?

Guerdon and Johnson followed St. Denis. Joseph was left with Macafee and Miss Denton-Smyth. The young Scotsman stood by the table, unhappily turning over slips of paper.

'Well?' inquired Joseph.

'It's all right, Mr. Isenbaum. Mr. Macafee can stay for our little talk. It concerns him.'

Macafee did not look up. His young sullen face was heavy with trouble.

'What's the matter? What can I do for you?'

The nurse would be taking Ben up from the drawing-room now. Probably he would resist, kicking and shouting for Daddy. A boy ought to be full of spirit.

'It's Mr. Macafee,' said Miss Denton-Smyth. 'I told him to go to you himself because I always say that there's nothing like the *direct* appeal. But he asks me to explain. You see, Mr. Isenbaum, I've been *trying* to make him understand that *pioneer* work is not like ordinary business. We must expect rebuffs, mustn't we? We must take the *long* view and the *broad* vision. When crushing the commercial octopus and fighting against principalities and powers and spiritual wickedness in high places. But I keep telling him that the ultimate reward is certain if we have *only* faith, though I do know the temptation to catch at glittering prizes.'

53

'What is it, Macafee? How does this concern me?'

The Scotsman raised his head.

'I wanted to tell them all at the Board meeting, but Miss Denton-Smyth asked me to wait and speak to you. I want to know when the company's going to start making Tona Perfecta Films, Isenbaum. You're a business man. Guerdon's an old sheep and Johnson's an adventurer and you never know what St. Denis thinks. But you're a business man. I want to ask you a straight question. Is the company going to be able to manufacture my films? If not, I'll go elsewhere.'

'Why, Mr. Isenbaum, tell him he mustn't be so impatient. We couldn't do without the Tona Perfecta, could we? It's just because the thing's so big that it takes time. It takes time, of course, to tell the public all about it. Why, the circulars haven't gone out yet.'

'I asked you a straight question, Isenbaum.'

'Look here, Macafee. I haven't much time now. Lunch with me one day next week.'

'I've got an interview to-morrow with the managing director of British-American Movietone Company. I want to know if I'm to put the Tona Perfecta into his hands.'

'That's a dud concern, anyway. I happen to know. But why didn't you bring this up at the Board?'

'It's my fault, Mr. Isenbaum,' cried Miss Denton-Smyth. 'I didn't want him to raise such a very, very serious subject just when everything was going so nicely. You *know* how easily frightened Mr. Guerdon is, and Mr. Johnson makes things just a *little* difficult to deal with, and besides there was your other proposal, Mr. Macafee. And I thought that really, perhaps, seeing that Mr. Isenbaum could really settle everything quite easily, it wasn't worth while making it all a matter for the Board at this stage.'

'What do you want me to do?'

'I've made a very reasonable offer, Isenbaum. I've said that if the company can show £3,000 capital raised before the New Year, I'll stick to it for a bit longer. If not, I go.'

'And I thought,' panted Miss Denton-Smyth, 'that seeing you are *sure* to be putting some more capital in sooner or later, it would be just as easy for you to put in three

54

thousand now just to show that you *do* believe in the company, and to convince Mr. Macafee that all his fears are simply the result of inexperience and over-anxiety.'

'This ought to have come before the Board. It's a very serious proposition.' Damn them, damn them. He'd paid enough already. They'd bleed him before they were through. God Almighty, there were other Etonians beside St. Denis. There were other schools beside Eton. Three thousand would almost pay for the boy's entire education.

'I can't deal with a matter like this now,' he said brusquely. 'I'm very sorry you kept Mr. Macafee from raising it at the Board meeting. Naturally you know my interest in the company. But you can't deal with a matter of this importance now all in a hurry. When's the next Board meeting?'

'Not in the ordinary course of things till after the New Year, you know. Oh, Mr. Isenbaum.'

'Can't you wait, Macafee?'

'No, I can't. And I won't. I'm seeing these British-American Movietone people. I want to know what to say to them.'

'You'll have to call another Board meeting,' said Joseph. 'Of course this must come before the Board. I don't think you need have any fears, Macafee. Naturally I see your point of view. Let me know when a meeting has been arranged. Good night. Good night.'

He took his hat. He ran down the stairs, his small feet in their patent-leather shoes twinkling below his rounded waistcoat. He had got away very cleverly. He had done the adroit, the sensible thing. Postpone. Postpone. And then slip quietly out of further responsibility. After all, he was the only man who stood to lose. Five hundred was five hundred.

He rang for the lift, climbed inside and shut the door. His eyes were just on a level with the corridor when Macafee's worn brown shoes slouched into his vision. He did not reverse the lift, but shot down to the ground floor, let himself out of the lift, and out of the building. In order to make doubly sure his own escape, he left the lift door ajar. Macafee would have to walk downstairs.

Only when he jumped upon a bus, he remembered that

unless Macafee closed the door – an unlikely courtesy for that gauche young man – Miss Denton-Smyth would have to walk down also. Well, after all, the Christian Cinema Company was her hobby, not his. She must take the rough with the smooth, he thought. Poor Caroline.

Chapter 3 : *Eleanor De La Roux*

IN the autumn of 1928, Eleanor de la Roux came to stay with the Smiths of Marshington. She was the daughter of Mr. Smith's young sister, Agatha, who in 1903 had been sent for the sake of her health to South Africa with a school friend from the West Riding, whose father had business on the Rand. And there a terrible thing happened to her. She had fallen in love with a Boer veterinary surgeon, and married him. A Boer. One of those fellows who lay in ambush to shoot on the white flag and the red cross and all that. And a veterinary surgeon. A common vet. It was incredible.

Naturally the Smiths had been very much upset. There were family consultations at Marshington, cables to Pretoria, collapses at Kingsport, and visits to solicitors. The West Riding family were warned never to communicate with a Smith again. Three Smith ladies approached the brink of a nervous breakdown, and had to recuperate together at Torquay, where in the hotel lounge they discussed and rediscussed the astonishing folly of poor Agatha.

Agatha herself, after her first long, rambling, joyful letter to tell of her engagement, only wrote home three times. The first letter described her marriage. The second defended her husband, Hugo de la Roux, in terms more creditable to her heart than her discretion. The third announced the birth of her son. The next letter from South Africa came a year later and was from Hugo de la Roux himself. It told of the death of his wife in giving birth to a second child, a girl called Eleanor. After that, the Smiths heard of the de la Roux's no more, until years later a business friend of Mr. Smith's described a pleasant visit to the de la Roux's home outside Pretoria. 'De la Roux's a very decent fellow – very well thought of. In the Government service. Of course, the

57

veterinary service in South Africa's quite IT. Different to a vet in England. Yes, the boy's A.1., going to study mining engineering in the U.S.A. he tells us. The girl? Oh! a fine little girl – quite a kid. High-diving champion of the Transvaal Girls' schools, they tell me, and plays a top-hole game of tennis. Clever too. Going to college next year. Says she's going to be a vet like her father. Not much sort of a job for a woman, *I* say, but you never know what girls will do in these days. A game little lass. Quite the hostess and all that. Thought a lot of out there, I should say, the de la Roux's.'

That was in 1926. Two years later the Smiths heard that Hugo de la Roux had been killed in a motor accident, that the boy was in America, and the girl quite alone. They decided to let bygones be bygones. Mr. Smith asked his wife to invite Agatha's child to Marshington. Somewhat to their surprise, she came, and within forty-eight hours of her arrival, the Smiths decided that they had been right in their original estimation of the catastrophe of a mixed marriage and its products. They did not like Eleanor de la Roux. They did not like her small, thin figure, her lean brown hands, nor her boyish tweed coats and tailored shirts. They did not like her disconcerting silence, nor her equally disconcerting questions. They did not like her low husky voice, with its faint suggestion of a colonial accent, and her frequent use of Afrikaans ejaculations. She was not what Mrs. Smith called an easy guest. The girls confirmed this condemnation.

'Well, anyway, she won't be here for long. She says she's going to London to a secretarial college.'

'Why on earth? When she *has* done two years at science in South Africa, why doesn't she go on with it?'

'She says she does not want to be a vet, now.'

'I expect she's the sort of girl who never knows what she does want.'

'I don't like this idea of a girl at her age on her own in London,' said Mrs. Smith.

'Well. We don't want her here, do we?' asked the practical Betty.

'And she's of age, isn't she? And her money's all her own. She can do what she likes.'

58

Eleanor was of age. She had nearly four thousand pounds of her own. She could do what she liked. She was going to London to a secretarial training school to learn shorthand, typing and business method. She did not consult the Smiths about her future. She went forward very quietly, using introductions from her university in the Transvaal, writing her letters, making her plans. She told the Smiths just as much as she thought it necessary for them to know about her business, and she sat for hours, her small hands folded in her lap, her grey eyes staring straight before her, saying nothing, doing nothing.

'If you ask me,' concluded Betty, 'I should say she was a bit queer in the head.'

It did not occur to the Smiths to attribute any of their cousin's eccentricity to the shock of her father's death, to her loneliness, her grief, and the disruption of all that had been her former life. They did not know of the agony which kept her wakeful night after night, feeling in her nerves the jolt of her father's car as its wheel caught in the rut, and the axle snapped, turning the whole world upside down in a crashing nightmare. They could know nothing of her torturing wonder whether her father had been stunned immediately, or whether he had lain conscious, helpless, and in pain, pinned beneath the car through the long night and through half the dusty day. The road had been lonely, and a wandering native found him late the following afternoon; and neither the Smiths nor anyone else knew that.

Eleanor had refused to go with him on that six days' tour in the northern Transvaal. She had wanted to finish her term in the laboratories; she had wanted to play in a tennis match at Potchefstroom. Being a convivial creature, her father disliked driving alone. He enjoyed Eleanor's company. And she had not gone. And because she had not gone, he had probably drunk rather too much whisky at his last stopping-place and he had driven carelessly, and he was dead. Eleanor felt that it was all her fault. There was, it seemed to her in the weeks which followed, no remedy for remorse. Grief might soften; disappointments could be conquered; fears might be proved false. But the pain that gnawed at her mind was constant and untempered.

She could not endure the Transvaal, because he had died there. She did not want to take her degree and train as a veterinary surgeon, because it seemed ignoble to step into the career thus taken from him. She had come to England because she was sure that she would hate it, to the Smiths because she was sure that they would hate her. Only by inflicting upon herself the discipline of discomfort could she endure her father's death.

The Smiths had justified, indeed they had exceeded her expectations; they were as vulgar, complacent and stupid as her imagination had depicted them. But irritation can provide an antidote to sorrow, and the Smiths served their purpose.

Two days before Eleanor left Marshington, she came down rather late to breakfast to hear her relatives sitting in judgment on a letter. The letter was, she gathered, from someone called Caroline. She heard 'Poor Caroline' this and 'Poor Caroline' that, until, for the sake of conversation rather than from any active curiosity, she asked, 'Who is this Caroline, Aunt Enid?'

'Well, my dear, her father was your Uncle Robert's second cousin. He was a farmer at a place called Denton in the North Riding, and married beneath him, a chemist's daughter. There were two children. The elder girl, Daisy, married, I believe, a jeweller in Newcastle. We never see anything of her now. But Caroline . . .'

'Caroline's the skeleton in our family cupboard,' cried Betty. 'She's our prize cadger, prize idiot, prize bore, and prize affliction. She lives in some place in London, *on* her relatives, writing stuff that nobody ever wants to read, and trying to dodge her creditors.'

'She's an author?' inquired Eleanor, impressed.

'Well, dear. I should hardly call her that. Authors are people who get their works published. Caroline of course *did* contrive to get one book into print. It was called *The Path of Valour*, a devotional volume. But her family had to meet the cost of publication.'

'Fifty pounds, Mother, wasn't it, eh? eh? Fifty pounds. Eh? Couldn't read a word of it myself,' said Mr. Smith.

'She's not a very near relation then,' observed Eleanor in

the dry, precise voice which the Smiths found so unattractive. 'Did you know her very well?'

'Well, I remember that after her father's death we all spent a holiday together at Hardrascliffe. Your uncle and I were first cousins, you know, Eleanor. Caroline and her sister were just grown up, but we were children. I remember so well that Caroline had a grey serge dress that we thought rather smart – with rows of black velvet round the bottom, and black buttons down the bodice. She was always rather dressy – but too short, and inclined to be plump even then.'

'Rather go-ahead in those days, wasn't she, Mother? Frizzy fringe and rather fine eyes, and used to carry on with the officers. I remember someone teasing her about lifting her skirt to show her petticoat as she came down the steps along the sea wall. There was a young Carter, wasn't there, a bit sweet on her?'

'Yes, but *he* married one of the Miss Peaks of Huntingthorpe, and Caroline had to go and be governess to some people near Selby. It was there that she first became artistic, and set up as the local poetess in the parish magazine. And then she took a situation in a private school near Malvern where she had one of those silly friendships with the head-mistress. A clever woman, that Miss – Miss – what was her name, Betty? I've told you, I know – Thurlby. Adelaide Thurlby. Newnham or Girton or something. But I never liked her from the first. She used to trail round in olive green and old gold tea frocks – Pre-Raphaelite, Caroline called them. Prehistoric, *we* said. And when the school failed, as of course it would, and Miss Thurlby lost all her money in it, Caroline brought her home to Doncaster where her mother was living, to have a nervous breakdown there very comfortably, though it killed Caroline's mother, we always said. At any rate, she had a stroke just then, and Miss Thurlby got engaged to the local doctor, though Caroline had rather fancied him for herself, I imagine, and then they had a quarrel or something, and Caroline had to borrow money from us to pay for her mother's funeral. She's been borrowing ever since.'

'More coffee, please, Mother.' Mr. Smith pushed forward his cup. 'Eh, yes. Let it be a lesson to you, Eleanor. Don't

61

fall in love with scheming school marms, and stick to one job if you want to get on, eh?'

'Well, certainly, Caroline must have tried almost everything. She has been a school matron, and an agent for some sort of educational books, and secretary to a Rescue Home, and travelling companion to Lady Bassett-Graham's imbecile daughter, hasn't she, Mums?'

'Yes, and it was when she came back from Italy because Lady Bassett-Graham took a dislike to her, that she changed her name to Denton-Smyth – with a *y*. Smith wasn't good enough for her.'

'Well, the *y* does not seem to have done her much good,' said Betty. 'Has anyone waded through that letter yet?'

'I have, nearly,' said Dorothy.

'What's it all about?'

'Oh, she wants my brown coat when I've finished with it, of course. She always wants something. And there's a lot of rot that doesn't seem very important about a cinema company or something.'

'That's a new craze. Cinemas. She moves with the times. It'll be flying next.'

'Here, Eleanor, you'd better read this. And learn what you've got to avoid in London.'

Betty handed to Eleanor the letter headed '40 Lucretia Road, West Kensington, S.W.10.'

'My dear, dear Enid and Robert,' Eleanor read. 'I feel that I cannot wait any longer to tell you of the great good fortune which has befallen me. The Christian Cinema Company is not only formed, but marching triumphantly along the Road to Victory.' There were eight pages of letter, and Eleanor read them all.

§ 2

Eleanor dug her fingers on to a cracked button, and the syren of her car uttered a long melancholy screech. To Eleanor its note was sweetest music. She pressed again. An errand boy fifty yards ahead nearly fell off his bicycle with surprise. Eleanor steered cautiously round the back of a bus, between two coal carts, a motor ambulance and a taxi, and found herself facing the stormy splendour of the November

62

afternoon. She was looking due west down the Richmond Road. Above the roofs, where the road swooped down upon itself, hung the wild drama of the setting sun. It gleamed on the polished surface of the road. It gilded the metal caps of the coal hatches on the pavement, until they danced like sovereigns dropped by the passers-by. It caught the windows of the taxi, the bottles on the milkboy's bicycle, and the brass on the bonnet of Eleanor's own car. It transfused with jubilant gold the exciting frosty freshness of the November air. The whole of London rose in a golden flame round Eleanor, as she drove for the first time her new car in triumph along the Richmond Road.

In her new car Eleanor forgot that her heart was broken.

She had seen the car five days ago in a second-hand shop in the Edgware Road. It stood in the window, a 1925 Clyno, bearing a ticket on its bonnet – '£35. Splendid order.' She had driven a Clyno in South Africa. She knew the engine, and she could do running repairs. She walked into the shop and asked if she might have a trial run. It was good to feel a wheel under her hands again. Because it was in a motor-car that her father had met his death, motoring brought no additional pain to her. She was running the same risks that he had run. She might be killed in a motor accident herself. The possibility of death took away her desire for it. She spent a rapturous week-end overhauling the Clyno, and could hardly wait on Monday until her classes at the secretarial school were finished before she rushed round to the garage. She meant to explore South-West London before supper-time.

She was glad that her engine was uncertain, her brakes worn, her mudguards battered. There was all the more prospect of fun ahead for her. She enjoyed tinkering with machinery. Her head was clear, her fingers firm and steady. She could apply her attention to mechanical problems with diligence. The more perplexing the problems, the better protection they brought her against sorrow. She beat back remorse by gears, sparking-plugs and carburettors.

She drove along the Richmond Road, enjoying herself.

To make quite sure of her lights, she tested them, turning the switch up and down. Twice it responded. The third

63

time it clicked impotently. 'Damn!' muttered Eleanor. 'I knew the battery was a dud.'

She looked round hopefully for a garage, slowly making her way along the darkening road.

'Fool. You ought to have made sure about those lights.' It was only a ten-minutes' run back to her own garage, but she had no mind to turn again. She saw a slightly dilapidated establishment on her right, which was, however, far smarter than the garages of the Transvaal. She hooted and screeched her way across the road. The grease-stained mechanic speculated that he would take about half an hour to put her lights in working order.

'But it's only a five-minutes' job,' protested Eleanor.

'We must take orders in rotation. No "Ladies First" now that you've got the vote. It's all Equality now,' he leered.

Eleanor drew herself up to the whole height of her five feet three inches.

'Certainly pursue your usual routine,' she said, her small nose in the air. 'I was not asking for favours. I shall come back in half an hour.'

She left the garage and strolled along the road. Even if she had not the car, this still was London, an unknown city, to be investigated, criticized or admired. Richmond Road was clearly no fashionable thoroughfare. Eleanor looked into shop windows displaying glass dishes on which drowsy winter bluebottles crawled, befouling pink sugared hazel nuts and Liquorice All Sorts. She inspected the garments for sale in a Court Dress Agency, wondering who wanted to buy tarnished tinsel slippers and stained georgette frocks, dripping their beads and sequins from dismal threads. A household store offered for sale jars of cheap mayonnaise sauce, soup and tintacks, piled between cracked enamel dishes and feather brooms.

While in her car, Eleanor had felt majestic and detached from London and its people. She rode along, a stranger, regarding splendour and squalor with indifferent curiosity. Now on the pavement she felt herself part of the loitering or hurrying crowd. She read the ill-written notices pasted along a board outside a stationer's shop. 'Comfortable bed sitting-room for quiet gent. Use gas-ring. 18/-.' 'Respectable married woman wants morning work.' 'Family Bible for Sale. Best offer.' She began to worry about the people who passed by her, wondering whether the man selling shoe-laces was really starving, and whether the two young girls with brightly painted faces and wiry bunches of curls protruding from scarlet tam-o'-shanters were really prostitutes 'below the age of consent.' This London was full of problems. Even without a Native question it offered work enough for Sociologists. In South Africa, Eleanor had followed her father, supporting the Labour-Nationalist Pact. She believed in Women's Franchise, and had read *My Own Story*, by Mrs. Pankhurst, and the *Life of Josephine Butler* and the first volume of *Fabian Essays*. But her interest in politics had been purely academic. Here, in the Richmond Road, she was no longer protected by happiness and her father's companionship from her consciousness of human misery. She could not help wondering whether she was right to plan for herself a prosperous business career, in which she was determined to 'make good,' to 'do decently,' to show her brother in America that a girl could get on as well as a boy at money-making. How far was one justified in making use of one's immunity? 'I have capital behind me, and education, and opportunities. All this ugliness and poverty can't really hurt me. I'm immune,' she told herself. 'Had one any right to be immune? Ought one not to hand over one's three thousand pounds to the I.L.P. Winter Campaigning Fund?'

Eleanor's uneasy questioning brought her to the corner of a street. She found herself standing by the tables on which a second-hand bookseller exposed his desolate wares. Inside the shop were broken chairs, cracked dishes, fans, embroideries, toilet utensils and stained engravings. At her elbow were theological works, school books, and old faded novels, jumbled together in an open box. The books seemed to have taken on the characteristics of the neighbourhood. Once they had been full of vitality, the glory of their writers. Now, nobody wanted them. Compassion and melancholy descended upon Eleanor. She looked around her with distress, and in the fading light her eye caught the name of the street which turned beside her away from Richmond Road.

'Lucretia Road,' she read. Lucretia Road, now where had she come upon that name before? 40 Lucretia Road, West Kensington. She remembered that breakfast with the Smiths at Marshington six weeks ago, their contemptuous dismissal of Poor Caroline as the skeleton in their family cupboard. Eleanor's instinct was always to open doors and look at skeletons.

She glanced at her wrist-watch. A quarter of an hour still remained before she could return to the garage. She might as well stroll along Lucretia Road to number 40. In her mood of melancholy curiosity she liked to think that she had a relative living in this street. She was not utterly a stranger.

Lucretia Road itself depressed her. It had evidently once known better days. The houses were large, with deep cavernous basements, and heavy porches supported on peeling plaster columns above the doors. On many porches stood flimsy erections of coloured glass, that once had been conservatories; but now discoloured clothes flapped idly there, growing damper and dirtier through misguided efforts to make them dry. Children with sore faces and dirty coats scrambled up and down the area steps or squabbled drearily in the gutter. Shabby women with slack, dispirited figures trundled prams heavily laden with bulging parcels and cross, unappetizing babies. 'Poor whites,' thought Eleanor. 'This is far worse than Johannesburg. Oh, Lord,' she groaned in spirit, 'what a country.'

Number 40 was distinctly more respectable than its neighbours. No children clambered up its yellow-stoned steps. If the columns of the porch were peeled like the bark of the plane tree on the opposite pavement, the brass knob of the door was newly polished. The hideous conservatory of coloured glass above the balcony was in a state of tolerable repair.

'So this is where Caroline lives,' thought Eleanor. 'How very angry Aunt Enid would be if she thought that I had called upon Poor Caroline.' Yet why shouldn't she? She was not sociable, but she was adventurous. Curiosity allured her. The South African habit of never passing a friend's house influenced her. The temptation to do something of which her Aunt Enid would disapprove decided her. With

66

her lips compressed, her eyes dancing, and her heart beating quickly under her trim tailored coat, she tripped up the steps and rang the bell.

§ 3

'And so I knew that something nice would happen to-day,' said Caroline.

They sat together in the leaping firelight, 'two bachelor girls just on our own,' giggled Caroline comfortably. They drank tea out of chipped cups of rather fine old china, and ate bread and margarine and very stale seed cake.

'If I'd known you were coming, I'd have got a walnut cake,' said Caroline, then added hastily, lest her guest should take this as a hint that her unexpected visit was not welcome, 'but of course a surprise visit is far, far nicer. Only it's you who suffer, because I've been so busy these last few weeks that my housekeeping has gone just all anyhow.'

The firelight was kind to the crowded room. It revealed only for fleeting moments the large brass bedstead attempting with awkward bashfulness to hide behind a torn pink curtain and the desk in the window almost drowned in papers. Papers overflowed on to the floor, the chairs, the bed. Another curtain hung bulging over an alcove by the fireplace. A row of bookshelves beside the window, a screen round an untidy washstand, a table and two chairs beside the fire filled all the available space.

When Eleanor had arrived, she was shown up three flights of steep stairs by a gaunt, very neat and thin-lipped woman, who knocked peremptorily on a door, and announced, 'Visitor, Miss Smith,' and left her standing there on the dark landing, wishing she had not come, longing to turn and fly.

But from within the room had come the sound of doors banging, papers rustling, curtain rings squealing along a metal pole, and the door had opened, revealing a short, plump, animated woman, little taller than Eleanor herself, who peered with short-sighted eyes into the gloom, and cried, 'Who's that? Who's that, Mrs. Hales?'

'I – I – is that Miss Denton-Smyth?' Eleanor had stammered. 'I'm Eleanor de la Roux. I think we're sort of cousins. My car broke down in the road just outside, and I had to wait a few minutes to get it mended. So I came to call – just – just . . .'

The little woman fumbled among the many chains and beads and ribbons which hung against her crimson bodice. She found one at last from which were suspended a pair of tarnished but decorative lorgnettes. Up they went with a click, opening against her round, peering, battered, vivacious face.

'Who's that? What did you say?' And then as though the lorgnettes had indeed enlightened her, though, in that dark landing she could not possibly have seen anything clearly, she cried with rapture. 'Why, Eleanor – Eleanor de la Roux? Of course. My little cousin from South Africa!' and dropping the lorgnettes that chimed and jangled against all her festooning beads and seals and pencils, she stretched out short arms in tight crimson velvet sleeves, and drew Eleanor into a warm embrace.

'Well, isn't this nice? Well, isn't this nice? Come in and let me have a look at you,' she chirruped, taking the girl by both hands and pulling her into the firelit room. 'My little cousin from South Africa. Dear Agatha's daughter. Why, of course I remember Agatha. A lovely girl. One of the sweetest girls I knew. And you're like her, my dear. You've got her eyes, I believe. Real hazel. I always say there's nothing like hazel. And long lashes. But she was taller. You're like me, my dear. Little – little but good, they say. Small body, large heart. Well, well. And to think you should come and call upon me. That *was* nice of you. I *am* pleased. And you are stopping in London? When did you arrive? You haven't had tea, have you? I've just got the kettle on. And your car broke down? Do you drive yourself? Oh, you modern girls, how I envy you. I should certainly have had a car. *And* flown. Do you fly? I always say now that I shall have to wait until I'm an angel. Still, you never know. Perhaps I shall do it yet, now that I'm making my fortune at last.' She bent over the fire, poking it vigorously. The flames leapt up. The kettle sang. The firelight illuminated her face with grotesque lines and shadows. She crouched above her kettle like a witch brewing enchantments.

68

'She *is* like a witch,' thought Eleanor. 'You're cosy here,' she said aloud.

Caroline caught at the compliment. 'Yes, I am!' she cried. 'There's nothing like a bed-sitting-room, I always say. Then you have your books and papers all around you and can work to any hour of the night or day.'

'Do you often work at night?'

'Oh, *quite* often. Especially now since I went into business. The director of a company has great responsibilities, I can tell you. Dear Enid would tell you of my work, didn't she? I expect she's been very busy preparing for Christmas and that's why she hasn't had time to write to me herself. I know that those grand old-fashioned Yorkshire Christmasses take a *great* deal of preparation, and I'm so glad, dear, that you went straight to Marshington when you came to England. It would never have done to miss seeing our real *Yorkshire* hospitality.' She was laying the cloth, fetching cups from the fireplace, and bringing teaspoons and knives from a battered tin biscuit-box. 'Of course, here in London I can't offer my friends the hospitality I should like. You know the pioneer is bound to go through some rather dark and lonely times. Wasn't it Robert Owen who said, "Pioneering doesn't pay?" But that was in a moment of bitterness, and of course we all have our moments of bitterness.' She made tea in a chipped brown tea-pot. She bade Eleanor draw up her chair. 'But now, *of course*, I am reaping the reward of my labours. I suppose you never heard how much dear Enid and Robert intend to invest with us, did you? Perhaps they would not talk about it in front of you. Of course, I am hoping to be able to reserve quite a number of shares for them. But if you *are* writing you might just mention that it would be as well to let me know *soon*. You might just say casually that I thought about three thousand, just as a kind of beginning. It's a *really* good thing. We're going to sweep the country soon.'

As though she had never had a listener in her life before, Caroline poured forth the details of the Christian Cinema Company. She told Eleanor of its vicissitudes, its hopes, its possibilities. She told her of the wonders of the Tona Perfecta Film, the obstinacy of Mr. Macafee, and his final ultimatum. She told her of the last Board meeting. 'An Extraordinary Meeting, my dear, and you're a relation or I would not tell you company secrets, for of course in a way it's all confidential, but you're a Smith and I want you to understand exactly my position so that when you see dear Enid and Robert you can put it to them.' She told her how Mr. Macafee had repeated his offer, and how Mr. Isenbaum had not been present. ' "Unavoidably detained," he wired, and of course I was terribly upset because of course I had felt sure that he was the man who was going to save us; but of *course* I always say God moves in a mysterious way His wonders to perform. And if it's not Mr. Isenbaum, it will be someone else. These delays are sent to *try* us – to purify us as by fire. And in any case I persuaded Mr. Macafee to give us another month – till the end of January. I must say that I take a little credit for that. I had him out to lunch, you know, and talked to him like a *mother*. I felt afterwards that I had been wrestling against the powers of darkness. But he gave way.'

She was a witch. Her brown eyes glowed; her bosom heaved. She built up for Eleanor a glowing, romantic picture of High Finance and Big Business inspired by Idealism, of Art and Ethics reconciled at last.

She did not deny her poverty, her loneliness, her frequent failures. But she spoke of them all in the past tense.

'I've sometimes thought,' she said, 'that when the dreamer's dream comes true, he takes a little while to realize that he isn't still asleep. To be *really* affluent at last – to be able to repay all the kindness that people have shown one in the past, because I always say that it's just the art of being *kind* that's all this sad world needs. You know, my dear, as we grow older we do like to do a little of the *giving* as well as the *taking* in the material things of life. I have always tried to be a spiritual giver. But circumstances have often compelled me to be a material borrower. I've tried to take generously, because I always say that it takes two to make a gracious gift, the generous giver and the generous taker. But there comes a time when one would like to be the *giver* for a change. And so you see how doubly glad I was when I realized that it might be in my power

70

not only to repay, but to enrich those who have helped me.'

'Yes, of course,' murmured Eleanor inadequately.

'That's why I made my *Will* as I did.' She turned and rummaged among the papers in her desk, opening drawer after drawer, each of which spilled new contributions to the general confusion on the floor. But at last she found a long blue envelope. 'Ah. Here it is. I want you to read this, my dear. Just in case.'

In just what case, Eleanor did not know; but she took the envelope and drew from it a long blue document, written in Caroline's delicate sloping hand.

'The last Will and Testament of Caroline Audrey Denton-Smyth, Journalist and Secretary, of 40 Lucretia Road, West Kensington, in the County of London.

'I, Caroline Audrey Denton-Smyth, being in my right mind and in active bodily health do hereby cancel and revoke all other wills, testaments, and legacies whatsoever that I may at any former time have made. And I will and bequeath hereby to my dear friend and cousin Enid Smith of Marshington in the County of Yorkshire, and to her husband, Robert Harold Smith, 10,000 Ordinary £1 Shares in the Christian Cinema Company, to be held jointly if both are alive when this Will comes into force, or severally by the survivor. And I will and bequeath to my dear cousin John Robert Smith, son of the above, the sum of £500, and to my dear cousins Dorothy and Elizabeth Smith, sisters of the above John Robert, and to his brother Harold, the sum of £250 each. To my cousin the Reverend Ernest Albert Smith, Rector of Flynders in the County of Lincolnshire I will and bequeath 1,000 £1 shares in the Christian Cinema Company, in the hope that he will continue to use his influence as a clergyman to bring the Church of England to a full sense of its Responsibility in the matter of the Purification of the Amusements of the People. To my nephews, Claude and William, sons of my late dear sister Daisy Shotwell (*née* Smyth) of Newcastle-on-Tyne, I leave the sum of £50 each in token of my true forgiveness of all their past neglect. To my friend and landlady, Eliza Hales of 40 Lucretia Road, I leave the sum of £200 in gratitude for

71

all her kindness and consideration to me, and in testimony to our sisterhood in Christ through the Fellowship of St. Augustine's Church. The rest of my fortune I leave to the Church Fund of Saint Augustine's, Fulham, in the County of London, in memory of all the inspiration and help that it has been to me in my lonely work of pioneering, and in the hope that my friends there may see fit to commemorate any small service that I may have been able to render to my fellows by a memorial tablet to be placed near the pew in the Southern transept where I used to worship.'

Eleanor read to the end and sat silent, the document in her hands, her face bent over it.

'Well? Well?' asked Caroline. 'What do you think of it? It's fair, isn't it? It gives an impression of Christian justice and magnanimity, doesn't it? Or do you think I ought not to say that about forgiving my nephews? But you know, my dear, I always say that bitterness is the first infirmity of *ig*-noble minds, but really they might have written or come to see me when they were in London.'

'I think it's a wonderful will,' said Eleanor truthfully. 'And how splendid to be able to leave all that money, after . . .' She meant to say 'after you have been so poor.' But the evidence of present poverty was all around her. The details that Caroline had told her of the Christian Cinema Company's fortune perplexed her. 'I didn't realize that you had invested all *that* amount of capital in the company.'

'Oh, of course, dear, you must understand. I haven't *yet*. That is what *will* happen when we come into our own. Of course, we've got to find *three* thousand to begin with before the end of January, or else Mr. Macafee will withdraw his patent and then I don't quite know what will happen. But what's the good of Faith if you can't gamble on it a little?'

'You mean you've left this money without having it yet?' asked Eleanor slowly.

'Why – but I've as good as got it, my dear. Quite as good. Because if I don't, if I don't get it – why, what's the good of waiting and starving? Yes, starving through all these years of pioneer work, if I never see the promised land? Oh, I shall get it. Life won't let me down. God won't let me down. I always say that wills are like epitaphs – you know the poem.

"Write your own epitaph in high-flown phrases,
    Paint every virtue in its brightest hue,
Fill all your lines with glowing, golden praises –
    Then live a life that shall prove it true."

Well? Isn't that wonderful? Isn't that beautiful. "That's Faith, my dear. I live on Faith. My will is a great act of Faith, and will be justified. You'll see, my dear. You'll see.'

§ 4

Eleanor left Lucretia Road disturbed, amazed and curious. She had never met anyone like Cousin Caroline before. Her bizarre, animated, decorative little figure, in the crimson velvet dress which, Eleanor reflected, had probably once belonged to Dorothy or Betty, her crowded room, her fantastic will, her large, glowing, beautiful brown eyes, all these epitomized the unexpected quality that Eleanor found in London. The Christian Cinema Company was to her the personification of all that she found strange in England.

She had little leisure during the following few days in which to think of Caroline, for the novelty of London life absorbed her. She had come to the club in Earl's Court bristling with prejudices, prepared to dislike everybody and to wear the discomfort of English society as a hair-shirt under her sensitive shyness. She found to her astonishment that she was popular, and that her fellow residents in the club, though frequently second-rate and silly, were almost invariably kind.

Being a modest person, and, until her father's death, not given to introspection, she found it odd that something of a fashion should arise for her society. She was surprised to find herself regarded as a person of unusual courage and initiative. Her car, her mechanical efficiency, her Afrikaans expressions, her enterprise and independence all won respect and interest. The girls were refreshed by her appearance of unself-conscious interest in feminine society. They had their own standards of social value, and according to these, within a week of the acquisition of the Clyno, an evening drive with Eleanor de la Roux ranked almost equal to a date with a

73

young man. Eleanor could not understand their eagerness for male society. She herself was so well accustomed to the companionship of her father, her brother and their friends, that she found a certain attractive novelty in association with girls, and, anxious to return any kindness shown her by the English, she invited one member of the club after another to accompany her upon her voyages of discovery through London.

But Eleanor's expeditions were by no means all idle pleasure-trips. During her first week at the club she had been taken to an I.L.P. meeting by a fierce, untidy, ink-stained amusing young fanatic called Rita Hardcastle. There she listened to a thin man with black heavy hair, a disarming smile, and a mind of virginal unsophistication piling one indictment after another upon the British Empire. He reminded her of the speakers at the Nationalist Convention at Bloemfontein. Translating in her own mind his most telling phrases into Afrikaans, she felt that at last she had found her spiritual home in London. She joined the Independent Labour Party, and later on placed her car and her services in the evening at the disposal of its London speakers.

Then began a period of superb adventure. Throughout the rest of the winter she spent bright orderly days at the secretarial college, where she worked with punctual neatness and efficiency; but her days were threaded together by nights of daring splendour. Backwards and forwards through the lighted streets of London Eleanor drove, conveying chairmen to conferences, lecturers to week-end schools, and humbler speakers to little meetings at Croydon and Ilford. She learned the elements of English politics through heated discussions in small schoolrooms and Labour clubs. She learned the geography of the Home Counties by poring over maps in the light of an electric torch, and she saw the landscape of England as a flurry of moving darkness, through which she rode behind the silver spear of light thrown by her lamps on the sleek ribbons of asphalt or the winding caprice of country lanes. She drove in a cool fury of concentration, tilting at the huge December darkness with her spear of light, and as she drove she felt that she was indeed tilting against slums and poverty and economic oppression and the hidden menace of vested interests. She surrendered herself to the strong sweeping urgency of speed and propaganda. Though temperamentally cool-headed and suspicious of enthusiasm, she found that the physical excitement of driving an uncertain engine down strange roads in darkness, and the mental excitement of political indictment of half-realized evils, relaxed the painful tension of her nerves. She was so tired when she went to bed that she no longer lay tormenting herself about her father's death, but fell into the dreamless sleep of exhausted youth.

In this new life, Eleanor's first visit to Caroline lost its dream-like fantasy. Caroline soon appeared no stranger an enthusiast than the many other Eleanor encountered. Caroline starved, prayed, toiled and exalted over the Christian Cinema Company with a faith no more foolish than that of Rita Hardcastle, who hunted a crock of gold at the Rainbow's End of family allowances, of Ben Sanders, who cheerfully courted imprisonment while demonstrating on behalf of the Class War Prisoners' Aid Association, or of Brenda Clay who shuddered at Marble Arch on frosty evenings, preaching passionately the gospel of Total Abstinence from Alcoholic Liquors.

London hummed with the activities of Propaganda and Reform. Wherever Eleanor turned she found societies for the ultimate perfection of Society. She was invited to Youth Rallies for Peace, Feminist Teas, and protest meetings about China. She was asked to address envelopes, buy calendars, act as steward at meetings, sell papers at the street corner, and drive enthusiasts from one revival to another. And whatever society she encountered, she found always that it was short of money, living on the margin of subsistence, bluffing with magnificent effrontery about the size of its membership, the influence of its resolutions, and the condition of its bank balance. The relationship between cause and effect was more remote than her scientific education had led her to believe. Institutions which she had thought concrete and stable enough, such as newspapers, political conferences, and business companies, rested upon a large measure of unsubstantial fantasy. 'Far be it from me to judge Reality,' thought Eleanor, 'when the world is so very much

75

more odd than I had thought it, and when, according to Professor Ipswain's lectures on the Operation of Credit, the most powerful source of wealth and the dominating economic influence is nothing more concrete than a supposition.'

But if Eleanor was prepared to recognize an element of mysticism in the hidden dynamic which controls society, she was prepared to tolerate nothing but the most brisk and orderly realism in an office. She took to her lessons on business method like a duck to water. Files and book-keeping, card indexes and records were the instruments of a regular and beautiful orchestration. It jarred on her methodical mind to hear a single instrument out of tune. She had no experience of the crises and confusions of an active office, staggering blindly but gallantly from one emergency to another. She had yet to learn how little the life of reform and moral welfare lends itself to the niceties of precise routine. The office of the Christian Cinema Company in Victoria Street shocked her profoundly.

Too shy and too kind to tell poor Caroline how terrible she thought her unchecked lists and unsorted letters, she contrived to suggest during her second visit that she might come along one evening, after the classes were over, and bring two or three girls who would help to put the office straight. 'It will be such good practice for us. Do let us do it.'

Caroline's eyes glowed with gratitude and anticipation. She envisaged Youth and Efficiency taking charge of her office and reducing its chaos to order. She saw young girls, fresh as daisies, filing her letters and laughing at her difficulties, and picnicking round her gas fire when the work was done, drinking tea out of the bright orange cups from Woolworth's and sprinkling crumbs of walnut cake joyfully on the floor. Her eager imagination leapt to this vision of gaiety and hope.

'My dear, my dear. You are too kind to me. Life is *too* wonderful. You know, I knew from the very moment I first saw you that you were bringing luck to me. I've felt quite differently about life ever since.'

'Any word about the three thousand?' asked practical

Eleanor. It was almost the end of January. Mr. Macafee's ultimatum was due to expire within a week.

A shadow crossed Caroline's face.

'No. No. Not yet. But we've got six days more, and I've had sixteen inquiries about the company circulars, and an application from a lady in Brighton for two shares this afternoon, and that brings us up to £542 10s. 0d. up to date. *Any* day now we may find our millionaire.'

'But if not?'

'If not? If not? My dear child, when you've lived as long as I have, fighting and striving for what *seems* impossible, you'll know that there are some questions best left unasked. It *will* be. It *must* be. Faith. I will have faith although the heavens fall. Don't you see, dear, that for people like us, who step off the beaten track and dare to scale the heights, there is no retreat, no turning back? There is no *If not*. It must be.'

'Yes. But – surely one has to face the worst, Cousin Caroline.'

The little lady turned fiercely upon Eleanor, all her beads and pendants clashing together like a soldier's armour. 'The worst, child? What do you know about the worst? Wait until the iron has entered into your soul. Wait until you have gone down to the depths in utter loneliness and risked everything, *everything*, even your own self-respect, in the Cause of Right. Who are you to tell me about the worst, when you have always led a sheltered life, with capital behind you, and a university education? When have you accepted the conditions that lead to utter nakedness of spirit, when people say, "There can't be much in it or she wouldn't look so shabby?" Yes, and when people say, "She still keeps on at it, poor thing, she must be a bit cracked." When have your relations wondered if it wouldn't be safer and more economical to get you certified and put away quietly in a nice mental home? When have they told *you* to give up the struggle and live on an old-age pension in a club for decayed gentlewomen? When has there been nothing, nothing left except success? If you could strip yourself naked of all privilege, my dear child, you still couldn't understand the nakedness, the loneliness, the – the unshelteredness of my genera-

77

tion. Even then you'd have youth and health and a good education, and people's approval of you to help you on. But I and women like me, we started from nothing – *nothing*, I tell you. You've been sheltered all your life. You can't escape from the immunity of your generation. And then you come and talk to me about "facing the worst!" '

She confronted Eleanor, her breast heaving, her eyes blazing, her face white with emotion. Then suddenly she collapsed, crumpling up into the office chair, her head on her desk, sobbing with an abandon both childish and terrible, with the stormy anger of a child and the difficult, painful weeping of the old.

Stricken by remorse and embarrassment, Eleanor stood behind her, repeating stupidly, 'I'm sorry. I'm so sorry. I didn't understand.'

For a minute or two, Caroline sobbed uncontrollably. Then she sat up as quickly as she had sunk down, pushing her fringe back from her red-rimmed eyes, endeavouring to compose her distorted face. The strength of prophecy had gone from her and the sudden dignity of revolt. She was as incoherent and garrulous as ever. 'No, no,' she cried. 'It's all right. You couldn't possibly understand. I had no right to expect it. I expect it's because I'm tired – not quite my-self to-day – a little difficulty with Mrs. Hales, of course I *should* have paid the rent. I quite see her position, but going to the same church I thought would make a difference, and always such a nice woman, more like a friend than a land-lady even though a woman of that class, and of course rather painful for me in my position to be in debt to the lower classes. I can't help thinking about it at night and then if you don't get your proper sleep they say that it is much harder to bear the responsibilities of big business. I've al-ways understood—' she was pulling herself together, dabbing her eyes, and stifling from time to time a half-suppressed sob—'I've always understood that Mr. Lloyd George was able to bear the great burden of winning the War for us so splendidly, because he always got his sleep at nights.'

'Oh, Cousin Caroline. I didn't know. Is Mrs. Hales be-ing beastly to you? Can't I – I mean – I'm not offering money or anything – I'm not presuming – but as a loan –

78

just until your director's salary comes in?' Eleanor stammered and blushed, torn by pity and discomfort. Caroline's tears were too painful to be borne. She must take action immediately, and escape.

'Well, just as loan – I wouldn't ask you. I wouldn't have dreamed of asking you if you hadn't offered. But it makes such a difference to me, when I come in at night tired out, to be able to go down to the basement, always so clean and nicely kept to have a word with her and perhaps a cup of tea in front of the fire. Not so lonely as going up to that room alone, night after night. It's only seven pounds, eight and sixpence. But I *can't* speak to her when I'm in debt like this.'

'Seven pounds, eight and sixpence – let me write you a cheque. I have my cheque-book here in my bag.'

Caroline was tidying her dishevelled hair in the little office mirror, but her face remained stained and crumpled as though someone had taken a cardboard mask and crushed it into a ball and thrown it away, and then tried to straighten it out again for use. She was, however, her own mistress again.

'You might make it out for the eight pounds,' she said. 'It won't make much difference to you and it'll mean I can give the dairyman something on account.'

'Why of course – I mean – of course. Why didn't you ask me before? It's dreadful of me. I should have asked.'

'Not at all. It's very natural. You've not seen much of life really yet, I mean to say, I always think that one half of the world doesn't know how the other half lives. It's a *loan*, of course, and I shall pay you back with interest.'

Eleanor handed her a cheque for twenty pounds.

'Well, thank you, dear. I'll make a note of it. Now take no notice of what I said to-night. It's lovely to see youth, I always feel, and you're going to come with me on Sunday night to hear dear Father Lasseter preach, and then coming with me round to the vestry afterwards, aren't you? Because you know at the last Board meeting we decided that we must have a representative of the churches with us. A bishop if possible, and I want to get Father Lasseter to speak to the Bishop of Kensington-Gore about it. You will come, won't you?'

Eleanor had meant to evade the invitation. She had promised to attend a Young Socialists' Social at the 1918 Club. But she could not refuse now.

'Why yes,' she said. 'Of course I'll come. And you must come round to supper afterwards at the club.'

She could not escape. As she walked behind Caroline down the two flights of stairs to the lift, she felt that her fortunes were bound up inextricably with those of the Christian Cinema Company. She could not let her cousin starve. She could not let her be snubbed by the unmerciful rectitude of Mrs. Hales. Life would not be tolerable if the three thousand pounds did not materialize before the end of January.

Yet she did not want to be bound to Cousin Caroline. She did not want to spend much time at Victoria Street when she might be driving propagandists to I.L.P. meetings, or attending lectures on Company law and scientific management. She had not come to London to act as office girl to the Christian Cinema Company. Or had she? What had she come to London for? What did one do anything for? Why was she alive? What did life mean? Why had her father died and she been left alive? Was there any discernible intention behind it all? Immune? Of course she was immune – from poverty, from ignorance, from death itself at present. This was what had been troubling her all the time, ever since she saw Jan du Plessis walk up the path to the stoep, with that queer white face, and heard his strained voice, 'I say, Eleanor. I've got bad news for you.' One could not shake off this intolerable burden of immunity.

All the way home to the club, Eleanor felt the old familiar pain at her heart. She went up to her room and lay on her bed in the darkness, seeing again the stoep, overgrown with feathery plumbago and deep magenta bougainvilia. She saw her father's big wicker armchair, its one arm broken and bound up with string. She saw the table with its pile of crumpled papers, and the fly whisk, and the empty soda syphon, and the pipe rack and tobacco tin. She could hear again the heavy shuffling tread and laboured breathing of the men who carried the stretcher across the stoep and into her father's room. Every detail of the interval between Jan du Plessis's message and the arrival of the body reacted itself in her awakened memory. 'Immune. Immune.' She beat her small clenched fist against her forehead, hoping to find relief in physical pain. Her father's big signet ring, which she wore on her second finger, cut her eyebrow. She did not care. She welcomed pain. Oh Father, Father!

There was a knock on her door.

'Hullo. de la Roux! Are you in?'

A pause.

'I say. Hullo!'

She made no answer. She held her breath, praying that they would go away. She heard Rita's voice saying to someone else, 'She can't have come in yet. Well, she'll miss the meeting.' She heard footsteps vanishing down the stone corridor.

Hour after hour she lay in the darkness, thinking about her father, and immunity, and poor Caroline.

§ 5

The first thing that struck Eleanor about Saint Augustine's Church was that it might have been a building in the Cape. It was about fifty years old, large, ugly, dark, and built in an awkward combination of Gothic and Classical styles.

Eleanor had been brought up as a member of the Dutch Reformed Church, but both she and her father had been agnostics without much interest in religion. She had attended Anglican services only twice before.

She noticed the pictures round the walls – 'The Stations of the Cross,' Caroline whispered. Eleanor thought them crude and rather repulsive. She disliked the smell of incense, and the attitudes of the shabby men and women who dropped almost to their knees facing the chancel before they turned in to the pitch-pine pews.

She did not know why people wanted to meet together at fixed intervals in the formal discomfort of a church, to kneel down and stand up and sing preposterous words about their bones melting and their enemies flying, and the king's daughter wearing clothing of wrought gold. Those fragmentary readings from the Old and New Testament, those prayers repeated so often that the words flowed smoothly past the consciousness of the congregation, those ridiculous hymns; why did anyone want them? Why did they imagine that such performances could possibly be agreeable to Almighty God – if there was a God? Why didn't they see what a waste of time it all was, when there was so much to be done, infant welfare centres to be established, and indexes to be prepared, street directories to be marked for canvassers, slum landlords to be confronted, facts about India and China and the wickedness of international oil trusts to be made known? All the best people were over-working themselves into nervous breakdowns, and these smug Christians bobbed up and down before a grotesque and ugly altar. There was so much to be done. In four days' time, on Thursday night indeed, Macafee's ultimatum expired. The Christian Cinema Company would be saved or lost. It seemed to Eleanor only too probable that it would be lost. Mr. Isenbaum remained completely inaccessible. Mr. St. Denis had gone to Paris for Christmas, and there had inconsiderately fallen a victim to the influenza epidemic. He was better, and returning at the end of the week, and had wired asking Macafee to postpone his action. But Macafee was obstinate.

'I see his point. I see his point,' Caroline had said. 'It's his invention. He says he needs the money. He has postponed it once. But then pioneer work is like that. Friends will come with you part of the way. Then they get frightened. They begin to ask for their reward to be given on earth as it is in heaven.'

'We must pray,' Caroline told Eleanor as they walked to church. 'Pray for the miracle. I believe that this is being sent to try our faith and that at the eleventh hour we shall be saved. They talk about the excitement of gambling. We could tell them something about that, couldn't we?' Her protest of the previous week was quite forgotten. She drew Eleanor into the circle of her experience by that inclusive 'we.' 'I always say that the ordinary racer or gambler doesn't know what risk is. Why, we've staked everything – everything – on a hundred-to-one chance, we pioneers. And we're going to win, aren't we?'

It was perfectly true, thought Eleanor. Caroline with her

82

gallantry and enthusiasm and recklessness took enormous risks. Moreover, that one moment of weakness over, she faced the odds with magnificent gusto. She seemed even to enjoy the situation. Whatever fears of anguish of spirit assailed her during the long nights when she found herself unable successfully to emulate Mr. Lloyd George's gift of sleep, she showed no signs of faltering by day. On her way to church she had seemed radiant, even exalted, as though 'facing the worst' for her meant looking into a vision of forthcoming glory.

But in church, after the organ had played, and the short procession of choirboys in rumpled lace-trimmed surplices and scarlet cassocks had stumbled along the aisle, Caroline turned to Eleanor with a look of dismay.

'He's not here,' she whispered. 'Father Lasseter's not here. It's a stranger.'

'Oh well,' thought Eleanor. 'Even if he had been here, I don't suppose he would have done anything. I wonder how seriously other people do take Caroline? I wish I'd seen this Mr. St. Denis. Well, in any case, it will be all over by Thursday. Nothing really can save them now.'

For she was very sure that Mr. Isenbaum meant to evade all further responsibility and that the dilettante Mr. St. Denis did not really care. The Christian Cinema Company could collapse unmourned by anyone but Caroline.

She was not interested in the service. She wanted to get away, from the church, and from Caroline. She told herself that the Christian Cinema Company was nothing to her. If no more fantastic than a dozen other semi-philanthropic enterprises, it was impractical enough. It annoyed Eleanor that Caroline should hitch her wagon to so remote a star.

'The psalms for the 27th evening of the month,' announced the priest who was not Father Lasseter. 'The 126th psalm.'

Caroline nudged Eleanor. Her eyes were shining.

'I had forgotten it was to-night,' she whispered. 'Surely this is a sign. I always count so much on the psalms.'

The choir sang,

'When the Lord turned the captivity of Sion: then were we like unto them that dream.

83

'Then was our mouth filled with laughter: and our tongue with joy.

'Then said they among the heathen: The Lord hath done great things for them.

'Yea, the Lord hath done great things for us already: whereof we rejoice.'

The tears were rolling down Caroline's cheeks, but she held her head high, and joined in the singing with her husky, tremulous voice.

'Turn our captivity O Lord: as the rivers in the south.

'They that sow in tears: shall reap in joy.

'He that now goeth on his way weeping, and beareth forth good seed: shall doubtless come again with joy, and bring his sheaves with him.'

After that even the *De Profundis* seemed an anti-climax. Eleanor could feel Caroline beside her sailing through the service on the crest of a wave of excitement. Even she herself was moved, though she distrusted her emotion. It was nothing more than a coincidence that this was the 27th evening of January, and that the 126th psalm happened to fall upon that day. Almost any other psalm in the prayer book could have been as significant. This pretence of seeking signs in the accidental choice of a psalm savoured of necromancy. Caroline belonged to the foolish if not adulterous generation which sought after a sign. Eleanor could not forget that vision of her as a witch, bending over the kettle beside her sitting-room fire, the flames flickering upon her crimson velvet dress, and painting curious shadows on her face. Caroline was a witch. She believed in magic. She sought for signs in the psalms.

Eleanor began to long for the society of plain practical people who earned a respectable living, and kept their feet on the firm ground of common sense, and talked about cattle diseases and the condition of the market.

Yet her heart burned with pity for Caroline. Life was so short, the future so unstable. Some people walked so richly endowed with friends and wealth and fortune and success. Others had nothing. Caroline had nothing. The benevolence of fortune was too wholly dissociated from merit.

84

If Caroline had forgotten her cry of protest against the cruelty of Eleanor's privileged youth, Eleanor had not. She thought that she would never again forget. The contrast between her own comparatively enviable future and Caroline's loneliness and poverty haunted her throughout the service. She watched Caroline's head bent devoutly over her worn woollen gloves. She watched her raise it proudly as she stood up for the responses. She watched the grand-ladyish air with which she snapped her lorgnettes open to follow the lesson in her Bible.

'If I were God,' thought Eleanor, 'I would make Caroline's miracle happen, just because it's time that something nice did happen to her. What's the use of being a snorting, magical, bull-roaring, miracle-working, storm-quelling, Jehovah-deity, if you can't have a little fun sometimes?'

'He hath put down the mighty from their seat,' Caroline sang with robust conviction, 'and hath exalted the humble and meek.'

That was a pious hope, thought Eleanor, not a statement of fact. The mighty generally remained firmly established in their seats, and if they fell, they crushed the meek and humble in their fall.

By the time they reached the anthem, she was in a condition of prickly irritation, disliking God more than ever, for His failure to make good use of all His opportunities. But Caroline at her side seemed to be drawing spiritual sustenance from every sentence of the service, even from the prayer for the Royal family.

The young priest who was not Father Lasseter climbed the pulpit steps.

'A good-looking young man,' whispered Caroline with interest. 'I always say that looks are half the battle in the pulpit.'

Eleanor acknowledged that he was good looking, though his inquiring nose was too long and his mouth too wide. Still, he was tall and straight and pleasing; his attractive brown hair swept in an unruly wave across his intelligent forehead; his hands that clutched the little desk as though their owner were none too happy in his elevated position were long and delicately shaped.

85

A pleasing young man in many ways, Eleanor decided, but that made his ordination all the more regrettable.

She could never look upon young and personable clergymen without distrustful interest, for she found it incredible that a man who was normally strong and intelligent should seek to shut himself off into that company of persons claiming to be able to instruct their neighbours in morality. It seemed as though, once a young man had put on the uniform of the church, he consecrated himself to unreality, and was no longer entitled to normal human consideration.

This particular young man was neither pimpled, nor gauche, nor sickly, nor did he exhibit any other external disadvantage which Eleanor associated with Anglican curates. He bore himself with shy, abrupt dignity. He announced his text in a quiet, unclerical voice. 'Jesus said unto him, If thou wilt be perfect, go and sell that thou hast and give to the poor.' He did not speak very well. His manner was too stiff, his voice too diffident, his diction a little forced. But as he developed his theme, he twice forgot himself and his congregation, and became for the moment almost eloquent. To Eleanor's amusement, on both of these occasions, he dropped his deliberate simplicity and became the young college don lecturing on Ethics to a class of undergraduates. Then he pulled himself up abruptly, blushed a little, and with an effort resumed his shy colloquialisms.

Eleanor, who had expected to be bored, found herself delightfully entertained, for it seemed to her that here was a clever young man of the donnish type, who had been commanded by his superiors to be simple. His inclination was to dispute with an All Souls Fellow, his duty to convert a tired charwoman. He had brought notes to the pulpit, but he screwed up his blue, short-sighted eyes at them as though he could not see, and ultimately abandoned them altogether.

'Poor young man,' mocked Eleanor. 'He's not at all comfortable. Well, if he'd resisted this temptation to spiritual pride and remained quietly at a university, he'd probably have been a great success. He's got intelligence and personality, and he'll soon develop a pompous prig.'

Her interest in the young man's dilemma made her give some attention to his words, and from criticizing the manner she passed to consider the matter of his discourse. And indeed, this seemed to her to be aptly chosen. For his theme arose quite naturally from his text. Following Lord Morley, with whose essay he was obviously acquainted, he spoke of Compromise, its leaden weight upon idealism, its fascination for the mediocre. His commendation of enthusiasm came quaintly from lips so plainly diffident; his indictment of the half-hearted, his praise of audacity, his conception of an aristocracy of gamblers, those who dare to risk all their fortune for an ideal, conveyed to Eleanor an impression of romanticism which discomfited her, at first because she disagreed with it, but later because she applied it to herself. For as he spoke, she found herself fitting the cap of those who play for safety on to the Smiths of Marshington, on to the respectable bourgeoisie, the protected, the sensible, the timid followers of convention. The true aristocrats, who sought perfection, were those who like St. Francis of Assisi, and St. Francis Xavier, and Joan of Arc – yes, and like Caroline, even poor Caroline – counted no cost, but made the splendid and reckless gesture of independence. And she herself?

Suddenly Eleanor saw herself as one of the compromisers, who could make the Great Refusal, because of their possessions. Caroline had said that she could never strip herself as naked as the women of the older generation. That was true. She was protected for ever by her education, her freedom, and her father's sympathy for her ambitions. All that Caroline had cried out to her that night in the office became here part of the young clergyman's argument. It was she who compromised, she who was immune. She had chided God for His failure to perform a miracle. The miracle was within her power as well as God's. She had three thousand pounds. She could save the Christian Cinema Company if she would, and thus with one act teach God Himself a lesson and strip herself of part, at least, of her intolerable immunity.

Directly the thought entered her mind, it seemed so patently clear that she wondered why she had not done it

87

before. She had the money. She did not really need it. At the end of her six months' course she would be equipped to earn her living, and she had funds enough to last her, with economy, through her training. It was idle to deny that she was the best student in her class. She had had a good scientific education, and her Commercial Dutch was an additional asset. Even now she could, if she liked, accept a part-time job of translating Dutch correspondence for a firm of merchants. What need had she for three thousand pounds? She would use it for the salvation of the company.

What a triumph for Caroline, what a snub for the indifferent Board, what a reproof for the Marshington Smiths, who always thought that Caroline would achieve nothing. Why had she never thought of that before? The nice young man! A Daniel come to judgment. Indeed, thought Eleanor, it is appropriate that my association with the Christian Cinema Company should be inspired by a sermon, sermons being so little my customary mental diet.

Directly she had made her decision, the depression of the last few days vanished. She was happy, happier even than when she bought her car. She felt as though she had already effected something. She was about to take an action which would change the course of history, even though it was an obscure and local history.

She did not hear the conclusion of the sermon. So far as she was concerned, its message had been delivered. She joined in the final hymn with gusto equal to Caroline's, though she had no voice and little ear for music. She followed Caroline from the church, her nerves tingling, her pulses dancing, her lips twitching into a triumphant little smile.

She could hardly bear to wait until they had boarded the bus, before she observed casually, 'You know, I've been thinking, Cousin Caroline, what about that three thousand pounds that Father left me? I think that 5 per cent. War Loan is deadly dull, don't you? What do you really think about putting it into the Christian Cinema Company?'

Afterwards she always told herself that whatever her rash
88

impulse might have cost her, it was worth while, if only for the amusement of watching Caroline's face tremble into ecstatic eagerness. 'At least,' thought Eleanor, 'I've taught God his duty by answering one prayer prayed by a faithful Christian. Poor Caroline!'

Chapter 4 : *Hugh Angus Macafee*

HUGH ANGUS MACAFEE, so far as he was made at all, was a self-made man. The great disadvantage of making oneself lies in the difficulty of getting both sides to match. Hugh's development was distressingly one-sided. At twenty-six he was a brilliant technician. He could calculate to a nicety the acoustical properties of any given buildings; he could compose accurate but unilluminating treatises on colour photography, electrical reproduction of sound, the uses of cellulose or the synchronization of light and music: he could write examination papers which would win him First Class Honours in Physics, Chemistry or Engineering in any European university; he could live on fifteen shillings a week without experiencing conscious hardship; and he had invented a film to synchronize with sound-production which was almost as effective as the Glasgow Galloway Patent then in use at Hollywood. But he could not order a dinner, interview a patron, market a patent, recognize a song-tune, make a woman fall in love with herself, or work for more than half an hour with any man without antagonizing him.

To do him justice, he was not dissatisfied with his own production. Disapproval was his favourite hobby, but he rarely applied it to himself. He disapproved of the Oxford accent, of modern novels, of Bittniger's electrical process, of classical education, of a supernatural deity, of all women – except mothers – of Anglo-Catholicism, central heating, *hors d'œuvres*, studied courtesy, Gomschalk's atomic theory, and the English nation. He approved of Robert Burns, Highland scenery, honest poverty, oatmeal porridge, scientific education, and himself.

He was a peasant's son from Perthshire, who when fifteen

years old had looked around upon his home and prospects and found them not at all what he desired. He was an imperious lad, and he found his father enslaved to winds and seasons. He was impatient, and he saw his mother bound to the slow wasteful routine of natural reproduction, having reared five children and buried seven. He was intelligent, controversial, alert and curious, and he found himself doomed to agricultural passivity.

His teacher commended his aptitude for mathematics, and thrashed him for obstinacy and insubordination. Hugh asked his father's leave to try for a bursary to continue his education, and met with curt refusal. But his mother understood something of the boy's ambition. When Hugh ran away to become odd-lad to a third-rate photographer in Perth, he told her of his destination. She sent him surreptitiously little parcels of soda scones and oatcake throughout the lean, long years of his apprenticeship.

Photography fascinated him. At nights he read in the public library, attended evening classes and looked into a new enchanting world of order. He read chemistry and physics and works on technical photographic processes. Beyond the casual chaotic appearance of things lay perfect symmetry. Too small for the clumsy eye of man to see, moved systems exquisitely attuned to clear precision. The coarse deal chair in his lodgings became a thing of wonder. The law which bound to an appearance of solidity its spinning electrons, the law which changed the texture of its wood, the law which governed the expansion or contraction of its measurement, became to Hugh an absorbing interest. The joy which some men find in music, others in form, and others in contemplating the spiritual majesty of God, Hugh found in natural science. Chemistry and physics introduced him to an ecstasy of wonder that changed his whole relation to the universe.

This was his inner life. His outer life was passed in making himself indispensable to his firm, living upon an incredibly small income, saving with heroic concentration the tips and windfalls which came his way, and informing everybody who had patience to listen to him that he would one day go to college. And to college he went. When he was nineteen he borrowed two hundred pounds from his richest relative, a pig-dealer in Dundee, and took himself to Edinburgh University. In Edinburgh he worked all day and half the night. He denied himself friendships, recreations, luxuries and hobbies, and lived in an isolated world where matter became transparent, where it seemed to him that with his naked eyes he could watch the solid world dissolving into the rushing activity of unsubstantial protons. But he took his engineering and his chemistry examinations and fulfilled his promise to succeed in both. At the end of his course he had won a unique reputation for dogged ability, resourcefulness, and the power to make himself objectionable. His professors were prepared to recommend him for academic posts in any university but Edinburgh. The further he removed himself, the better pleased they would be. When he won a travelling fellowship and went to Germany to study colour reproduction, they congratulated themselves with warm sincerity.

Hugh went to Germany. He remained there for two years, doing admirable work, strengthening his disapproval of the English, and acquiring a rough mastery of the German language and scientific methods. He returned to join National Cinema Products Limited as experimental chemist at a salary rising from £600 a year. He endured the really liberal conditions of commercial employment for just eighteen months, during which time he treated the company's laboratory as though it were his private experimental department, quarrelled with all his colleagues and insulted the managing director. But the few ideas which he presented to the company were so valuable that it treated him as a chartered libertine, until he declared his intention of working only three days a week at the firm's own business and devoting the rest of his time to the Tona Perfecta Synchronizing Sound Film. Then that laden camel, the managing director, faltered. He threatened to resign if he had to soothe any more tempers ruffled by the eccentricities of Macafee. He had nothing to say against the Scotsman's efficiency, which was brilliant, nor against his honesty which was clear to the point of insult. But he could not work with him. He could not induce other members of the staff to work with him. Less originality and more co-operation might bring greater profit to the firm.

The Board sent for Macafee. The directors approached him as friends and brethren. They suggested tact to him; they counselled co-operation; they urged meekness and moderation. Hugh heard them out for twenty minutes, and then he turned and rent them. He told them his true opinion of business methods, advertising ethics, publicity, compromise, and the English character, and he said that if they came grovelling to him on their hands and knees, beseeching him to work for them, if they offered him £10,000 a year and a free run of their laboratories, he would not cross the road to enter their buildings.

Then he put on his battered Homburg hat, and marched incontinently from the room.

While drawing his salary of £600 a year, Hugh had been living at the rate of 35s. a week. He now regretted his extravagance, but he had at least a pleasant sense of solvency. He tramped round London and found one day the half-ruined buildings of some derelict Chemical Works at Annerley. The main block had been bombed during the war, and never rebuilt, but the laboratories were in tolerable condition, having been used for some years by the manufacturers of a patent medicine. The lease of the two acres of ground on which the works were built was due to fall in at the end of three years, but until that time the owners were only too charmed to find in Hugh a tenant for such undesirable property. It was just what he needed. It was adequate, it was isolated; it was cheap. He spent almost the entire sum of his savings on its equipment, then settled down to complete the Tona Perfecta Film.

When this was done he went to the Patents Office, secured the registration of his invention, and returned to National Cinema Products Limited with his offer. They might have his film, completed without their help, at his own price. Had the directors been moved only by those motives of enlightened self-interest discerned in economic man by textbook writers, they would have accepted his proposal and his terms. But they were human and they had been insulted. They never wanted to hear of or from Hugh Macafee again.

They wrote, politely but triumphantly, advising him to go elsewhere. A week after their bold refusal they learned of the Glasgow Galloway Film, and almost wept with joy. For the Glasgow Galloway process was in several details better than the Tona Perfecta. But they did not inform Hugh Macafee of his rival.

Hugh received their refusal with proud and angry triumph. 'Poor worms,' he thought, 'how little they know their own best interests.' He shut himself up in his grim laboratory, while late in the night his light streamed out on to the broken bottles and rusting tins, the oily pools and tufts of dock and nettles that decorated the waste land surrounding it. He was, however, in a difficult situation. His concentration upon technical details had entirely blinded him to the importance of legal and commercial knowledge. He did not realize that designing an invention is merely an amusing prelude to the serious business of selling it. In his innocence he thought that men had only to do good work in order to be paid for it. But the truth was that he simply did not know what to do next about his film.

Had he made friends, he could have sought advice from them about it. But he prided himself that he neither sought nor took advice. He declared that he valued no man's opinion, but he was terrified of the least suggestion of criticism. Ridicule flayed him. Patronage caused him anguish. In the world of business competition he was about as capable of looking after his own interests as an unshelled tortoise below a herd of charging elephants.

He had taken a small unfurnished back bedroom above a monumental mason's shop in Penge. He paid six shillings a week for it, and thought the rent extortionate. Between his rooms, his laboratory, and the Public Library, he walked with dour regularity, sometimes for days speaking to no one but Campbell, a discredited and unemployed chemist whom he employed as his assistant. He regarded with contempt the people whom he saw in the London streets. He hated the fat women who fell into trances in front of Stupendous Sale Reductions. He loathed the fatigued but insatiable mothers who pushed laden perambulators like battering-rams through the spell-bound crowd, pausing in front of

Genuine Winter Bargains – Lady's fur-trimmed Coats, only 49s. 6d. – Celanese Silk Underwear – and 'Beauty Cases – everything for the Toilet.' He loathed them because they were ugly and stupid and futile, because they blocked his way when he was hurrying on serious business; he loathed them because they were leisured and happy and convivial, while he was lean, hungry, and distracted, consumed by unattainable desires, mastered by dreams, lonely and fierce and arrogant. He loathed them because there was not one individual in those gaping crowds who would tell him how to sell his Tona Perfecta design, nor who would care the farthing's change from a 1s. 11¾d. bargain, whether it ever was marketed or not. At such times he longed for a machine-gun to mow down those loitering figures, those gaping vacant faces. He wanted a bayonet to thrust his way through the crowd. He wanted an earthquake to rend the earth beneath their dragging feet, almost content that he should perish like Samson in the general ruin. On one such occasion a small child lolling half-drowsily on its mother's arm looked up and saw his white staring face and furious eyes and burst into a roar of terror, dropping the dummy from its mouth. Hugh, wedged in the crowd, saw its mother stop, retrieve the dummy, dust it on her black coat, suck it herself to remove further impurities, and thrust it once more into the child's wide mouth. Sick, furious, wretched, Hugh turned away and nearly ended his life under a motor-bus as he strode angrily down the street.

§ 2

One evening in the early autumn of 1928 Hugh was kept waiting at the Public Library. He wanted Fowell's *Experiments with Light*, and he wanted it badly. He was irritated almost to the verge of insanity, fatigued, despondent and hungry, and he wanted his book so that he could return at once to the soothing solitude of his back bedroom. He was at work on a new preparation of cellulose which he believed would increase by 100 per cent. the subtlety of colour reproduction, but at the moment the composition baffled him. All this exasperation with his own failures kindled his wrath against society, and at last he turned on the assistant

95

librarian and told her what he thought of public library methods.

She was a foolish-looking young person with large romantic hazel eyes and a soft drooping mouth. Her high Cockney voice was pitched to refinement, and a tiresome affectation of squirming her shoulders beneath her blue crocheted jumper set Hugh's teeth on edge. The more he railed at her, the more she squirmed.

'But Mr. Macafee,' she protested, directly she made her voice heard above his flow of ferocious Scots, 'I have mentioned the matter to the chief librarian. I have really.'

'I put it down in the suggestion-book six weeks ago.'

'I know. And I did go to Mr. Bruce about it. I said you'd told me it was very important.'

'I hope you did.'

'And he said that it was not the kind of book that there would be much demand for. He said that these technical books aren't really what we're supposed to supply.'

'Oh, he did, did he?'

'Well, we must consult the needs of our rate-payers.'

'I see. And I'm not a rate-payer, I suppose?'

'Mr. Bruce said that if you wanted the book in all *that* hurry, you'd better go to the British Museum Reading Room for it.'

'And do you think, woman, that I'm going to waste good shoe leather tramping to the British Museum because some gauntless, pop-eyed, yammering half-wit doesn't know the value of a great book when he hears of it?'

'Oh, come, come, not a great book now. Even in its own line, not a great book.'

At the rough jovial voice, Hugh spun round, and found himself confronted by a very singular person. He was a large, heavily built, picturesque, slovenly and almost handsome man, of whose low-collared, ill-laundered blue shirt, broad-brimmed hat carried in stubby blackened fingers, and thick grizzled hair Hugh immediately disapproved. Everything about him seemed over-decorative and under-washed, while the slight cast in his handsome bold dark eyes confirmed the air of Bloomsbury-Wild-Western villainy suggested by his swaggering manner and Spanish whiskers.

'You did say that Fowell's *Experiments with Light* was a great book, I believe, sir?' asked this individual.

'Ow, Mr. Johnson!' giggled the assistant librarian appreciatively. 'What a start you gave me: I never thought you'd be coming here to-night!'

'No? And again, Yes! My dear Miss Brackenbury, the spirit like the wind bloweth where it listeth. And I am indeed most interested to hear Mr. – Mr. –'

'Macafee,' suggested the girl.

'Mr. Macafee called my friend Fowell's little treatise a great book.'

'What the Hell do you know about Fowell's Book?'

'Ah, what indeed, my friend? Well, in the first place Fowell and I ran up against each other in Los Angeles way back in '23; an' in the second place he shot his book across to me when he'd written it; and in the third place, I've read it, and I can tell you, sir, that it's just ten years out of date. It was outa date, 's' matter a fact, before it was written. 'Smy belief that the Russians an' Germans have been putting across that kind o' thing since '25, but poor old Fowell never would look beyond his own nose. Never would have a look-see at what was going on on the other side the duck pond. And what happens? What happens? I tell you, sir, there's no man on earth so wall-eyed as an expert with a kink.'

'And may I ask why Fowell gave you his book? Have you anything to do with kinematography or theatre engineering?'

The new-comer thrust a dirty hand into his waistcoat, then into his trouser, then into his coat pockets, and at last produced a rather soiled and crumpled card, on which Hugh read:

'Clifton Roderick Johnson of Toronto and Hollywood. Director of the Anglo-American School of Scenario Writing, 18 Essex Street, Strand, London, (Eng.), and 247 East Twelfth Street, New York.'

'Indeed,' said Hugh. 'And what is a school of scenario writing, if I may ask?'

'My dear sir, my dear sir. You are interested enough in the cinema to wanna wade through Fowell's wretched outa date punk on lighting. Can't you see the need for a movement to raise the standard of the scenario? Why, 'smy belief that the scenario supplies the fundamental brain work behind the cinema. Getta good scenario, and with luck you gotta good film. There's Art in the scenario; there's intellect. There's Psychol'gy. My job is to put across Art an' Psychol'gy to the multitude. Catch 'em young and give 'em high ideals. That's our motto.'

'Indeed,' said Hugh, frigid with dislike.

'Now, take your own case. You're a young man who thinks you're int'rested in lighting. You go to a film you think you like an' say, "Jehosaphat, that's great stuff! Yet sure-ly a fine girl like that would never let a third-rate crumpet-muncher like that simp get away with her mother's secret like that?" *Don't* you? An' *that's* the beginning of criticism. An' criticism's the first step toward construction. You go to a film. An' you starta getta hunch you could go one better. An' before you know where you are, you *have* gone one better. Every man, woman or child has at least one first-rate scenario in him. But until you've learned the technique, your ideas are bottled up inside you – not a word saleable – not a syllable. Now, I'll put it to you another way. When you go to a cinema . . .'

'I never go to a cinema,' said Hugh.

'You never go to a cinema? You? I beg your pardon. You mean that literally? You *never* go?'

'I am an expert chemist and electrical technician. I invented the Tona Perfecta film, and the Macafee projector, and directed the National Cinema Products experimental department until three months ago. I am interested in problems of lighting and acoustics. I have no use for the osculatory performances of half-clothed young females.'

Mr. Johnson was not daunted. He stared at Hugh, his big head held sideways. 'Now that is verra interesting. Verra interesting. As a problem in psychol'gy. I call that verra interesting. You concentrate on the means. You spend long days an' spend laborious nights – at least so I imagine – on constructing the means. Science at the service of Democracy. The technician *in excelsis*. An' *yet* you despise the ends. You despise the ends. You don't care what comes of your work. 'Svery interesting.'

98

'I'm glad I interest you. But I'm a busy man. Good evening.'

'Oh, not so fast! Not so fast!' shouted Johnson. 'D'you *still* persist in wanting to read Fowell's book?'

'I am not in the habit of changing my mind at the discouragement of a casual stranger.'

'Then better come round to my lil' place an' borrow it. You'll see for yourself then it's old stuff. 'Smy belief Fowell's goin' gaga, poor chap. But if you won't believe me, see for yourself. The only true means of education is independent investigation.'

'Where is your place?' Hugh was prepared to calculate possible wear and tear of shoe leather, his distaste for the personality of Mr. Johnson adding quite four miles to any distance from his home. He wanted to read that book.

'Battersea. Facing the Park. Not as artistic as Chelsea, but quite as pleasant. And I've got the automobile here, and I've got the books I wanted and if you're through, we can get off right away.'

'Very well,' said Hugh ungraciously, and followed Johnson out of the Public Library.

It was a mild October evening. The brown and sherry-gold of the London afternoon had faded into clear violets and blues lit by the primrose lamps, that made a spring fantasy of the autumn night.

'Glorious evening. Marvellous colouring. Colour. My God, Colour. I could eat it. *Eat* it,' cried Johnson, folding his vast bulk into the driver's seat of his small car. 'Why don't you chemists getta work on a really good colour medium? These so-called colour films are crude stuff – crude. 'Smy belief that what this age is suffering from is a lack of colour. Black an' white. Straight lines. Half tones. Damn this bus! She's always a bad starter. I'll have to crank her. Hell!' Hugh saw no reason for putting his mechanical skill at Johnson's service. He sat in his seat while Johnson lumbered in and out of the car. The engine snorted and trembled. 'This mechanical age robs us of warmth an' beauty. We gotta get back to Nature. Passion.' The car leapt forward, almost bouncing Hugh from his seat. 'Steady, girl, steady! 'S I was saying,' shouted Johnson, gripping the

99

wheel as though it were the rein of a refractory bronco. 'Hell, these cars are! When I was out West I could ride anything with four legs an' a spine. But these *Machines*.' . . . He threw into the word 'Machine' the concentrated hatred of a lifetime. The car narrowly avoided a bus, mounted with one wheel the left-hand pavement, then bounded forward on its erratic way. "S I was saying, look at all these straight lines. Houses. Sky-scrapers. Machines. So on. Watch 'em. Look at their design. Straight lines. Stripes. Carrying the eye forward to a logical conclusion. Rational. Logic. No compromise. Where's it leading to? *Must* lead somewhere. Revolution. Revolt of men against machines, perhaps. Or of machines against men. What happened during the French Revolution? Stripes fashionable again. Straight lines. Logic. No compromise. Revolution. Mobs. Terror. Guillotine. Then look at our Victorian era. Sprigs. Sprays, patterns. Break up the lines. Break up thought. Albert. Tennyson. The Great Exhibition. The great middle-classes. The great humbug. Who wants to think thought on to the end when its design is smothered in wax flowers?'

'Really?' gasped Hugh, whose whole attention was fixed upon the progress of the car. He felt as though he were being winnowed, flesh from bone, but he clung nimbly to the bouncing vehicle.

'Psychol'gy. That's what we gotta study. 'Smy belief the cinema's the greatest force in breaking up revolution in the world. Cuts across the straight line. Gives 'em beauty, passion, Art. Why – Beauty – Hell, you son of a bitch! Where the devil d'you think you're going to?' By a miracle he avoided the slaughter of an errand boy, and returned to his flowing monologue. 'We've gotta democritize colour. Give Art an' music to the Masses. Counteract the Machine *by* the machine. Satan to cast out Satan. Yes – sir!'

Frail as a cockleshell among great whales, the little car burrowed its way between buses, dived under drays, and span around huge lorries. Hugh's heart had turned into a heavy lump lying below his waistcoat, but he scorned to show fear to the man beside him.

'Ah, you scientists,' chanted Johnson above the tumult of the traffic. 'Ah, you scientists who pursue the means an' despise the ends, take care. Take care. The day will come when you may be thankful to go to school with babes and sucklings to learn the elements of psychol'gy. *Here* we are. Nip out, an' I'll just park her round at the back.'

Hugh climbed out with surprised relief, finding real pleasure in release from fear. Five minutes later he was seated in a warm and unusually comfortable room, half buried in the brown plush cushions of a large leather chair, his feet turned to the blaze of a bright fire. Johnson at a small table was mixing whiskys and sodas.

'Great little place. Rented it furnished for three months. I'm a rolling stone. Mayfair one minute, Alberta backwoods the next. Gotta have action. Well, here's how!'

Hugh bowed stiffly over his whisky.

He had not altered his opinion of his host, but he told himself that with scoundrels, at least, you knew where you were. Johnson was obviously an adventurer. Dirty, garrulous, probably dishonest, sensual and ignorant. But his fire was warm, and his whisky was like soft flame, and it was clear that the man knew something, however inaccurately, about the cinema. He had Fowell's book and he might possibly understand the marketing of patents. It was the kind of commercial, second-rate knowledge which one might expect such a man to have. Hugh determined to keep to the forefront of his mind his two immediate necessities. He wanted to read Fowell on Lighting, and he wanted to sell his Tona Perfecta Film. If Johnson could help him to do either, he would endure the peculiarities of villains.

He found himself listening drowsily to Johnson's scheme for raising the moral and æsthetic standards of the British film.

'Friend o' mine – Basil St. Denis – nephew or something of Lord Herringdale – I'm a democrat. I sold papers in the streets of Toronto when I was knee-high to a grass-hopper. But I know what I'm talking about when I say that in a matter of taste Eton or Oxford put it across the *Hoi Polloi* nine times outa ten. Mark my words, Macafee, in matters of taste give me heredity and devil take environment. We're forming a Company – I don't cotton much to the title, but Caroline – she's Miss Denton-Smyth, our secretary – says that we've gotta get the churches in. Christian Cinema Company. Don't you forget it. Rake in the parsons, and the pence'll look after themselves. Of course we gotta get the Jews – Isenbaum's the right stuff though. Money without millions. None o' this Jew Süss run-a-cabinet nonsense about him.' In Hugh's mind, drowsed by warmth and whisky, the staccato sentences danced upon the flames. They pirouetted round him while he lay in a pleasant stupor, only half conscious that his host from time to time refilled both glasses and carolled jubilantly, 'Here's how.' Enormous, through blue smoke clouds, rolled Johnson's figure; enormous, boomed his voice; enormous, rose and fell the rhythm of his monologue.

'Service,' he cried. 'Science and Art walk hand in hand in Service. I'm British. C'nadian. Lived in the States, but my heart's with the Lil' old Home Country. What I wanna see is the British sound film circling the world from Huddersfield to Honolulu. While we had the silent movies, Hollywood got 'em. Climate gets away with it every time. But now we've got the Talkies, Culture counts more than Climate. I wanna see Science counteracting Climate an' puttin' the British culture on the map. I'm writin' a book now – like to see part of it? dictate two hours every morning to my sec'try before I go down to the Schools. I'm gonna prove the English film 'll put Old England back as the hub of the universe. . . . The speech of Shakespeare against the California sun.' On and on it flowed. Hugh's mind detached single phrases. 'Midwife to ideas.' 'Science the handmaid of beauty.' Art. Science. Psychol'gy. Absolute Form. Design. The Christian Cinema Company. Hugh was unaware that he had contributed any sentence to this rhapsody, yet it seemed to him as though the Christian Cinema Company and its vast ideas swept round him in a fiery flood.

'Of course. The Tona Perfecta's jussa thing we need. . . . Synthesis of sound an' form. Abstract patterns of sound an' movement. Have another whisky? Gotta meet St. Denis. Whassatelephonenurra? Give youring.'

Like warm swirling waters, Johnson's eloquence closed over Hugh's head. He was not actually drunk. When at last he rose from the leather chair, he found that he could stand and walk quite steadily. But he was not master of his speech. The whisky acting upon his empty stomach had robbed him of his habitual secretiveness. As he walked homeward through the emptying streets he realized that he had committed himself to go and see a paragon called St. Denis about the sale of the Tona Perfecta design to the Christian Cinema Company.

§ 3

Hugh lay awake in bed that night, calling himself every kind of fool. He had wasted an entire evening. He had acquired a headache. Instead of eating a sensible dinner, he had drunk too much whisky. The pangs of hunger gnawing at his vitals rivalled the hammers of headache tapping behind his eyes. If he chose to drag himself out of bed and grope his way to the inverted packing-case which was his larder, he could quell his hunger with part of his breakfast loaf. But he could not recall his lost evening, his sense of dignified isolation, nor his opportunity of acquiring without expenditure of time or money Fowell's *Experiments in Lighting*. He had forgotten the one thing he set out to obtain. The book which he had taken such trouble to borrow still lay in Johnson's flat at Battersea.

'I've got nothing out of the fellow but a headache!' raged Hugh.

He was mistaken. Two days later, while working at his laboratory, he was interrupted by knocking and voices. He shouted to his decrepit assistant.

'Go and tell whoever it is to get to Hell out of here!' He was unaware that he had learned this phrase from Johnson.

Campbell opened the door, but before his message could be given Johnson pushed his way past him and rolled forward into the room, followed by a tall, slim, dignified, blond gentleman to whom Macafee took an immediate dislike.

'You thought you gonna getta way from me?' shouted Johnson effusively. 'But here we are. Aw! The Hellova time we had to find you. Mr. Hugh Macafee, inventor of the Tona Perfecta Cinema Film, meet Mr. Basil St. Denis, Chairman of the Christian Cinema Company. Now, I hope we're going to do business. I hope this is going to be a real historic occasion.' He looked round him with dramatic expressions of wonder and admiration. 'Now, then, where's this wonderful sound film of yours? Can't you fix us up a little private demonstration?'

'I'd hate to disturb you,' said the tall fair gentleman. 'But Mr. Johnson, before whom I am as a babe when it comes to technical matters, assures me that you have done something marvellous.'

Hugh looked at Campbell. The experimental film prepared for National Cinema Products Limited was there. The apparatus for trying it out was there; but the acoustical properties of the laboratory were imperfect. He began to explain this with angry emphasis. Johnson interrupted him.

'Aw, cut that. Cut that. We know all about laboratory trials. We're willing to take fifty per cent. for granted. What we want is something new and something safe. You say your films are non-inflammable?'

'Compared with the ordinary film on the market, yes. I wouldn't guarantee it fireproof if you threw it on a furnace.'

'That's good enough for us. If we can advertise films safe for the kiddies – morally *and* physically we've got the matinee market!'

Hugh saw no harm in exhibiting his treasure. He needed money. His new ideas on colour photography had just reached that stage when the first delicious movement of creation stirs the faculties. Afterwards would come labour and disappointment, but at the moment no details clouded the fluid and radiant vision of achievement. And just because of this, he needed money. He would require more apparatus, more materials, more assistance, more leisure, before he could bring to birth his new conception. If the Christian Cinema Company would pay him cash for use of the Tona Perfecta, he was prepared to tolerate even the acquaintance of the too-effusive Johnson and the dandified St. Denis.

It appeared that the two directors of the Christian Cinema Company were satisfied with what they saw. Three days later Hugh received an invitation from the company, signed by St. Denis, asking him to join the Board. If that was the first step, Hugh was prepared to take it. He could endure the attendance of a monthly meeting. He could look after himself in a nest of villains. But he wished that he knew more of company law and the ways of the world.

For when he first visited the offices in Victoria Street, his co-directors puzzled him. Miss Denton-Smyth might be cracked, but she seemed too poor to be a crook. Having been brought up on the morality of the 'Cotter's Saturday Night' Hugh cherished a naïve illusion that honesty and poverty were interdependent qualities. Isenbaum was a Jew, and should therefore be rich and shrewd. Guerdon was a Quaker and should therefore be cautious and honourable. St. Denis was a dude, but possibly he could not help that, and Johnson was clearly a scoundrel, but he had the one merit of professing his boisterous belief in the qualities of the Tona Perfecta Film. Hugh was prepared to forgive more than he guessed to men who praised the Tona Perfecta and called him a great man.

He listened to discussions about raising capital. It all seemed wonderfully easy.

'We've only got to find a millionaire!' cried Miss Denton-Smyth.

They talked in thousands and millions of pounds. It was only after Hugh had been a member of the Board for two months that he realized its hazardous pecuniary state. Its circulars provoked little interest and less money. Isenbaum's original investment was almost exhausted. The minimum sum required in order to induce the Ferens Milmer people to manufacture the film was thirty thousand pounds. 'A mere trifle!' roared Johnson. 'A bagatelle!' said St. Denis. 'Get it, then!' said Hugh. In the panic of anxiety for his invention, he devised an offer which filled him with admiration for his own business acumen. The Christian Cinema Company must show solid signs of its forthcoming prosperity. It must produce before the end of the year three thousand pounds, five hundred as retaining fee for Hugh, and two thousand five hundred as a guarantee of future payments. Miss Denton-Smyth invited him to lunch, thanked him for his generosity, but explained the difficulty of collecting cheques at Christmas. Hugh shrugged his shoulders and gave her grace until the last day of January. Then he re-turned to his own work and shut himself up in his laboratory.

But his peace was broken. The affairs of the company could not be wholly excluded from his daily life. While he tramped back and forth between his bedroom and the works at Annerley, he would chuckle to himself, thinking of Basil St. Denis and the fat Jew, Isenbaum. He had 'em on a string. They'd to raise that money, or he'd make them all sit up. He'd break their pretty bubble. Company? They were a pack of children playing at the serious and important business of adults. Business? He'd show these business men what he thought about them. He brooded bitterly on the National Cinema Products Limited and their treatment of him. He reflected upon the inevitable loneliness of all great men. He sat shivering in his wretched room, gloating over his power to break so futile and dishonest an illusion as the Christian Cinema Company.

When the end of January arrived, and he found himself walking along Victoria Street towards the office for his last directors' meeting, he told himself that he had been in-famously treated. He had been led on false pretences to believe that the company would pay him for his invention. He had given them liberal terms which they had not ful-filled. He had lost other possibilities of marketing his inven-tion through their refusal to face reality, and reality meant for them the acknowledgment that their whole enterprise was an expensive farce. He worked himself up to a mood of righteous indignation as the lift carried him up past one floor and another.

He opened the door and found the other members of the Board already assembled. Isenbaum was back, sleek and ingratiating and self-conscious. Hugh did not know that the Jew had now gained his object in joining the company, and that this was the last Board meeting which he would attend. Guerdon polished his pince-nez very timidly. St. Denis, a white carnation in his buttonhole, was softly chaffing John-son, who greeted the new-comer with boisterous geniality.

Hugh came forward and took his place at the table, Miss Denton-Smyth pushed the leather-bound attendance book towards him. He signed his name in his precise, legible writing, carrying back the tail of the final 'e' under the other letters with malicious triumph.

The chairman, in his habitually gentle voice, called the meeting to order. The minutes were read. The usual correspondence was discussed. Hugh waited impatiently. All this kind of thing was waste of time. Why couldn't they come to the point and tell him straight out that they could not raise the money?

Miss Denton-Smyth put down her file.

Her chains and beads rattled together. Her lorgnette tinkled. She snapped it open again with trembling fingers. She coughed. And then she spoke in her quick trembling voice:

'Well, I ought perhaps to deal next with a communication which might otherwise have had a place in the agenda to itself, but I really had no time after it was officially made to alter the agenda, and I think the Board will give the clemency already suggested by the chairman that I should read it now.'

She looked round the table. The papers rustled beneath her shaking fingers. But even a man so little expert in Psychol'gy as Hugh Macafee could not mistake her excitement for distress. There was no doubt about it. Miss Denton-Smyth was delighted about something.

'I have received an application, that is to say, the company has received an application, from Miss Eleanor de la Roux, late of Pretoria, now of the Earl's Court Club, London, S.W.5, for three thousand pounds' worth of ordinary shares. I have already Miss de la Roux's cheque before me, and have made proper inquiries that the bank will honour it. And that at once disposes of another little item which is down on the agenda, the purchase of the Tona Perfecta design.' She beamed joyfully across at Hugh. 'What I mean to say is that the Board now is able to fulfil Mr. Macafee's conditions, and I suppose that we may congratulate ourselves on having prevented the breach of a relationship which we all value.'

Hugh listened in amazement. He was so much overcome by surprise that he lost his head completely. Had he retained full possession of his faculties, he would undoubtedly

107

have chosen this opportunity to escape completely from the company. But instead he heard his own voice saying: 'Well, gentlemen, I have no objection. I suppose this means that I sell you exclusive rights of reproduction for ten years for £500 cash down as a retaining fee, £2,000 when you begin to manufacture, and a royalty of ten per cent. on each 1,000 feet of film sold.'

There was more talk. There were technical details and business details. The company was to launch forth into a great campaign of advertisement and propaganda. It was to make every effort within the next three months to raise the thirty thousand pounds. The company's fortune was as good as made already. The clergy and educationalists who had hung off a little, while the affair was still uncertain, would come rushing forward to buy shares now that its business prospects were secure. A bishop was to join the Board at once.

'Well, I haven't exactly got his lordship's *promise*,' said Miss Denton-Smyth. 'But the Reverend Father Mortimer, a very *distinguished* young priest and scholar, you know, who has been doing temporary duty at Saint Augustine's, *he* has said that he will speak to the Bishop of Kensington-Gore about it, and knowing Father Mortimer I may say that I am quite *certain* of success, indeed, I hope soon to add an archbishop to our list of directors.'

'An archbishop?'

'An archbishop, Mr. Johnson. Do you not remember that at our last meeting we decided to invite a number of distinguished ladies and gentlemen, representing the Stage, the Church, the Schools, the Universities, Art, Music and public service, to become directors so that when we send out our appeals we may make it *quite* clear that we have the highest possible authority behind us? My idea was, if possible, a *Cabinet* Minister, even the Premier might, being so greatly interested in English culture. I confess that I should like to see Mr. Baldwin's name upon our Board and possibly the Archbishop of Canterbury. I always say *aim* high and you may keep on the level.'

Hugh listened in a dream. He learned that there were to be new directors, that there were to be new circulars, that there was to be a big public meeting. He heard Miss Denton-Smyth outlining her proposals for this final function.

It was, if possible, to be held at the Albert Hall, that is to say, if Miss Smyth could induce the Prime Minister or Mr. Lloyd George, or the Archbishop of Canterbury, or Mr. Bernard Shaw to speak for them. 'A great public expression of protest against the present condition of the cinema,' said Miss Denton-Smyth. 'Possibly with extracts from some of the worst films to be shown, because I always think that a *graphic* example goes a long way, but of course avoid all that *sex* or stuff which can be more delicately handled verbally by the dear Archbishop.'

'Aren't we being a little ambitious?' asked Guerdon sadly, repolishing his polished glasses.

'Of course we are!' cried Miss Denton-Smyth, bringing down her open hand on the table with such emphasis that all her chains rattled again. 'Of course we are ambitious. And why else have we met together? I always say that great oaks from small acorns grow. What does it matter if there are very few of us who have the faith yet? We are few in number, but *great*, very great, in unity and in inspiration, and then look how our contagion spreads! When dear Eleanor – when Miss de la Roux approached me about the shares I *knew* our faith was justified. We shall go forward. Was there ever a great cause launched without a few apparently obscure people coming together in an upper chamber to deliberate about impossibilities? I always say that nothing is worth doing unless you do it when it seems impossible. We are going to raise *England* to get a clean cinema!'

§ 4

The world into which the Christian Cinema Company now led Hugh differed not only from the worlds which he had previously known, but from those also which he had any desire to know.

He understood the farmer's life in Perthshire, its intimate relationship with heat and cold, and wind and weather, its simple animal necessities of hunger, fatigue, toil and mating, and its occasional excursions into the fear or fortitude of Calvinism. He understood the life of a modern university, with its intellectual emulation, its job-hunting and sublimated gossip. He knew the austere and excellent world of scientific order, which he entered each time he closed behind him the doors of his laboratory, and he knew now the semirespectable poverty of his lodgings in Penge and the Free Library.

But Miss Denton-Smyth's world was the world of uplift, good works and propaganda, and it was a world in itself. It had its own inhabitants, busy middle-aged women in drab clothes, elderly, rather querulous Quakers and Socialists, blossoming round-bellied Liberal Philanthropists, earnest young women with spectacles and pimples, clergymen with saccharine manners, social workers carrying bags heavy with reports and pamphlets. It had its own activities, committees, annual general meetings, public demonstrations, At Homes, bazaars and lectures. It spoke its own language. All round him, Hugh heard phrases such as 'educating public opinion,' 'creating the right atmosphere,' 'getting a good press,' 'non-party,' 'non-sectarian,' 'pioneer work,' and 'approaching the younger generation.' Especially he heard of appeals to the younger generation. What is it, thought he, about this younger generation which makes it so important? Why should the conversion of a young man of twenty-two to temperance or disarmament or public hygiene be more important than the conversion of an older man of fifty-five? Hugh looked round about him and observed that in spite of all this touching enthusiasm, one generation appeared very much like another. He considered that the young were sadly over-rated.

Indeed, thought Hugh, the young possibly find this world as strange as I do. He could understand the pursuit of wealth, or the pursuit of truth. He could accept, though he despised, the pursuit of pleasure. But Miss Denton-Smyth and her associates apparently cared for none of these things.

They despised wealth. They spent laborious days and nights on work which was either unpaid or was rewarded by infinitesimal sums called 'nominal salaries.' Protesting against sweated labour, they permitted themselves to be exploited shamelessly. They travelled uncomfortably in trams and buses, they lunched off milk and baked-beans-on-toast, they darned their cotton gloves, and knotted their brows over budgets which rarely balanced in back bed-sitting rooms and basement flats.

They despised pleasure. Their wildest dissipations rarely exceeded a Social Evening, enlivened by sandwiches and coffee in a bleak suite of cellars resembling a public lavatory, below a building owned by the Christian Mothers' Guild.

They had little use for truth, even though they paid lip-service to it. Those facts which failed to support their own particular vision of the perfect world, they tacitly ignored. They spoke of scientific research, meaning the exploration of phenomena advantageous to their cause. They inquired if men or women were 'sound,' with the intention of dis-covering not their habitual rectitude or sanity, but the degree of their devotion to a particular point of view. They had no use for laboratory investigation, unless its results could be predetermined in their favour. They had no love for the world as it was, no mercy upon its contradictions, no appreciation of its variety. They sought to mould society according to some self-designed pattern of good, to impose their wills upon the shifting wills of men, their ideals upon the mobile framework of the universe. And they called upon Hugh to help them secure Anglo-American Alliances, a national home for Armenians, the suppression of informa-tion about birth control, the propagation of information about birth control, the abolition of African Native mar-riage customs as social atrocities, the preservation of African marriage customs as anthropological curiosities, the ad-vancement of the British Navy, the abolition of all navies, the suppression of vivisection, the defence of medical re-search from anti-vivisectionists, the prohibition of alcoholic liquors, the defence of the human right to choose one's own liquors, and the complete and absolute emancipation of women.

Hugh gazed in wonder on this vast machinery. He had hitherto believed that social phenomena developed spon-taneously. He had imagined that economic, sexual and traditional motives pulled men and women hither and thither into the strange postures of society. He had not seen these arbiters of human destiny directing knowledge and

111

desire, appetite and ambition, making articulate the needs of democracy, and effecting those other miracles which might have been so revolutionary had they not apparently cancelled out each other. What, thought Hugh, would happen if all the societies quietly disbanded? Would this not have the same effect as pairing in a parliamentary division? Why take all this trouble, why endure all this labour, in order to make people do things which they would probably do in any case?

But he was too much interested in his own problems to trouble greatly about the vagaries of human nature. He had never thought much of his fellow creatures. The Christian Cinema Company did no more than confirm his dark suspicion. When Miss Denton-Smyth wrote imploring him to attend the At Home to be given by the company to clergy and social workers, his first instinct was to ignore the letter. Then he remembered that he had to see a man on business in Victoria that evening, concerning his new apparatus, and that the refreshments mentioned on the invitation would save his supper. He said that he would go. It was with the intention of finding a free meal that he strode down two flights of stone steps to an underground room sprinkled with wooden chairs. At one end a row of trestle tables formed a buffet, behind which hatless women stood pouring thin straw-coloured tea and pallid coffee from large metal urns, and handing plates of very small sandwiches and very large buns to the jostling company.

Hugh saw the Quaker, Guerdon, unhappy and alone as usual, balancing a large bun on a small saucer, and twitching his long helpless nose. He saw Miss Denton-Smyth trotting from chair to chair, scattering sandwiches, smiles and benedictions. Her appearance was as wonderful as ever. Her dress of vivid blue brocade was adorned with feather trimming. Her frizzled brown hair supported an erection of fancy combs and nodding tassels. Her beads, chains and lorgnettes tapped and swung and jingled, so that she walked to a musical accompaniment. Around her moved a sparse company of clergymen, secretaries of welfare and educational societies and dreary women. Here and there a younger girl, earnest and spectacled, shook her bobbed head above the queen cakes. Fragments of conversation drifted round him. 'So I said, Well, if she moves that amendment *and* carries it, I resign.' 'My dear, an absolutely atrocious thing to do. Absolutely *atrocious*. And at the deputation to the Home Secretary, she took ten minutes, not a second less, and we were only supposed to have four and a half . . .' 'brought her to the Home, four months gone, and won't be fifteen till next March – Her own uncle.' 'I'd give them the lash. That's the only thing that'll ever teach them.'

'I can't stand this,' thought Hugh, gobbling ham sandwiches from a plate conveniently marooned on one of the chairs. 'I can't stand this.'

Then he became conscious of Johnson's huge bulk careering towards him across a barrier of benches.

'You here? Good man. Good God! Hold on. I'll come round.'

Wading through seated ladies, Johnson reeled slowly round to Hugh, and stood against the wall with him, looking across the company.

'Oh, Mr. Johnson, won't you have some tea?'

'Tea? Never touch it. Never touch it.'

The amateur waitress retired sadly. Mr. Johnson was a rather intriguing novelty to her. His height, his self-assurance, the rich male smell of tobacco and whisky round his clothes, and his Wild-Western air, were all refreshing. He watched her go, then turned to Hugh.

'D'you know what they all need?'

Hugh shook his head. 'Who?'

'These women. 'Smy belief it would be the salvation of half of 'em to be raped by the butcher's boy.'

Hugh was shocked.

'My dear fellow,' muttered Johnson, squeezing his arm with the familiarity which Hugh detested. 'Don't you see what's wrong with 'em all? Sex-starved. Sex-starved. Must use their energy somehow. Good works. Purity and social welfare. Nosing round to find nice juicy stories about child assault an' prostitutes. Rescue work. Excuse for bishops to talk sanctimonious smut to a lot of sex-starved spinsters. Anti-Slavery. Feminism. Peace. Pshaw! Relax their complexes a bit. Get on a box an' spout at Marble Arch.

Exhibitionism. "Oh, my friends, give ears unto my cry. Harken to the woes of my poor down-trodden sisters in Melanesia!" Purity? Fugh! "My Lord Bishop, do you know the terrible things that go on in Hyde Park? Terrible, terrible. Kissing? *Far* worse than kissing. *I* should never think of rolling about on the turf with a grocer's assistant." No grocer's assistant would think of asking you, Madam. Peace crusades? Women's Peace movement? *Don't* they enjoy them? Did you ever see women enjoy themselves as they do when raising Hell in Trafalgar Square over a peace crusade?'

Hugh grunted. He thought it possible that Johnson was right. He was prepared to believe any evil or stupidity of women. But he wished that Johnson would stop talking.

'Why do they come here?' Johnson continued. 'They might be eating to the sound of jazz in a Lyons' Pop; they might be hearing music; they might be tending to their own or someone else's children; they might be reading, roller-skating or going to the movies. They might . . .' He suggested, with painful audibility, other occupations which they might pursue, but which are not commonly mentioned by name in public places. 'But they don't. They come here. Why? Do they care a tinker's cuss for the cinema? Not they. Do they care for more civilized education? Pshaw! What they care about is interference. They're doomed to die, poor things. They're ugly, poorish, unattractive, unsuccessful. The burden of their mortality is upon them. They gotta hitch their waggon to some durable star. I tell you, there's a sorta spurious second-hand immortality in uplift. We die, but the Cause goes on. We are poor, ill, weak, despised, obscure. But the Cause is great. The Cause prospers. Here they *are* somebody. They feel they've got their fingers on the world's pulse. Why, look at old Miss Foxton there. Two hundred a year, invalid father to nurse, housekeeper who bullies her, can't raise an eyelid at home. Now she's on the committee of the End all Wars movement or something, and feels that the Chancellories of Europe stagger when she sneezes. I tell you – it's *the* game, this uplift . . .'

'If you think like this,' asked Hugh in his slow, Scotch,

rasping voice, 'why do you come here? Why do you take such an interest in the Christian Cinema Company?'

'Because you never know. Hell! Macafee. Why d'you want everything always so cut an' dried? 'Smy belief that most of life is punk, anyway, and this Uplift stunt is as much part of life as any other. Besides, we gotta do something. You care for this science. Can you get what you want without Caroline's uplift? No. Can I get my cinema without Caroline's committees? Who's going to finance it? Artists? How much capital d'you think art controls in England? A few Jews buy up Old Masters once they've been approved of for about five hundred years. Then they're safe. No risk of making a fool of yourself over a Rembrandt or Titian, by God. But the new ideas, vitality, art, new flexible media – before it's got set an' stereotyped by custom. Who cares? No one I tell you. 'Smy belief the British public's scared of Art. Scared stiff. Look here, Macafee. The truth is we've gotta take the world as we find it. St. Denis is right. By God, St. Denis is right. It sometimes takes a blood 'un to be right. Not that he's got brains, mark you. Not brains particularly, nor guts. But he's gotta flair. He says Uplift Pays. And, by God, he's going to make it.'

'Do you believe that the Christian Cinema Company is going to succeed?' Hugh was becoming more expert at keeping his feet on the solid ground of his own interests while Johnson's conversation rolled around him.

'I do. I do. Mind you, last week I mighta told you differently. *C'est le premier pas qui coûte* an' all that. If this de la Roux girl – by the way, have you met her?'

'Who? The woman who put up the three thousand? Our principal share-holder? No –'

'Woman? Why, she's a kid! A cute, dandy little kid. I went round to the office two nights ago and met her there helping Caroline write to the parsons. An orphan – *and* an heiress from South Africa; cousin of Caroline's or something. Hands out three thousand as if it were threepence in the plate on Sunday. Now, Macafee, there's your chance. She likes scientists. Told me so. Went to college in South Africa and read zoology or something. Not pretty, you know. One of those little quiet ones. A dark horse. She's coming to this bun fight. That's partly why I'm here. *And* to see Gloria. By the by, have you met the great Gloria?'

'No. I don't know who you mean, but I have never met her.'

'Gloria St. Denis. By Gosh, there's a woman. 'Smy belief between you an' me an' the gate-post, she's not his wife at all. Not the marrying kind – either of 'em, I should say. But a fine woman, not one of these female anchovies, all leg and lipstick. There'd be a bit of something to get hold of with Gloria. And there she is!'

And there she was, straight from her establishment in Hanover Square, Gloria in her full loveliness, artistically subdued for the occasion. Her black gown was the one in which she entertained customers. Her pearls were admirable. Her soft turban hat, her fur coat drooping from one arm, her air of quiet dignified effrontery, were startling in that assembly. She walked like a goddess; vitality radiated from her; she was strong and splendid and serene, as alien in the hall as Johnson himself. She moved to a table and sat down.

'Gotta to go and speak to her. Come an' be introduced?' said Johnson.

'No thanks!' Hugh returned to his sandwiches and watched Johnson lumber between the chairs and hurrying waitresses until he greeted the lady with a laughing compliment.

Hugh had eaten his sandwiches, and was about to set down his empty plate and flee, when Miss Denton-Smyth's voice at his elbow made him start and turn.

'Mr. Macafee. I'm so glad to find you disengaged. I want to introduce you to Miss de la Roux, my cousin, whose name I think you know already. Now, Eleanor, see that Mr. Macafee gets some coffee, will you? I always think that men are so helpless at this sort of function, and I've just seen *dear* Father Mortimer *with* Father Lasseter, so very good of them to come when they are both such busy men, so I must *fly*!'

Miss Denton-Smyth flew, trailing conversation like her scarves and beads and lorgnette cords behind her. Hugh was left facing the grave scrutiny of a very small brown-haired girl.

'Good evening, Mr. Macafee!' she said. 'I think it was you who invented the Tona Perfecta Film, wasn't it?'

'I did,' he replied, still looking for a resting-place for his empty plate.

'Give me that. Thanks! Do you want any coffee?'

Hugh did want coffee, and said so.

'I'll get you some. Will you wait there? Bag those two seats. I'll get a tray. If you come too, we'll lose the seats.'

She was gone, picking her way neatly between the shifting throng, and returning almost immediately with a tray, which she placed on the radiator.

'Now we can eat in peace,' she said. 'Thanks for keeping the chairs. I wanted to feed, because I shan't have any supper to-night. I'm driving a speaker out to Goswell Garden City, and they never give refreshments there.'

'I'm missing supper too,' said Hugh.

'Good! Then we can both feed properly. Do you like ham sandwiches? I loathe them. I've learned they're the staple food of propagandists.'

'Are you a propagandist?'

She lifted her serious face to his and considered for a moment. Then her eyes twinkled. 'Well, I don't know. I work for the I.L.P. It's all very interesting. But I think sometimes that I should have stuck to science. You know where you are in a laboratory.'

'Science?'

'I was reading for my B.Sc. in South Africa. You did chemistry, I suppose.'

'And engineering.'

'Edinburgh?'

'And then Germany.'

She nodded. 'I want to go to Germany. There seems so much to learn.'

'It's a country where they take serious things seriously,' said Hugh.

She twinkled again. 'What are serious things?' Then, seeing his frown because he hated rhetorical questions and irony and all conversational evasions, she added gravely: 'But I think I know what you mean. Try one of these buns. They're not bad really, and they fill up the corners. Of course, you really know everything there is to be known about films, don't you?'

'Most things that are known at present,' he said calmly, meaning what he said. He was inclined to like this girl who reminded him in many ways of the only other young woman he had really respected, a student of chemistry in Berlin, with whom he could talk for a whole afternoon without being made aware that she was not a man. This Miss de la Roux, with her short boyish hair, and her boyish tweed coat, and her queer husky voice with the South African accent, might have been a small dandified young man.

'I wish you'd tell me about the Tona Perfecta. Why is it different from other films? How do you secure perfect synchronization? Isn't that partly a matter for the producers? Caroline has tried to tell me, but she doesn't make technical subjects awfully clear, you know.'

Hugh was happy. He turned his back upon the disturbing hall, consumed large currant buns and two plates full of sandwiches, and gave this restful, intelligent listener a full account of the innovations distinguishing the Tona Perfecta.

'Do you know,' she said at last. 'This makes me feel quite differently about the company? I wanted to do something about it before because of Caroline, but now I think I *really* want it to succeed for its own sake.'

He was pleased. He, who had scorned all pleasure but that which comes from work well done, felt a warm glow of satisfaction. He remembered that this little creature was an heiress. She could put down three thousand pounds as easy as three pence, Johnson said. And she was keen about the Tona Perfecta. She might be interested in his new and yet unrevealed invention. She might put down more thousands.

He blushed. He actually blushed.

'Well, then,' he said, and was about to invite her to come and see it for herself in his laboratory at Annerley, when Miss Denton-Smyth was again upon them.

'Oh, Mr. Macafee, I want you to meet Father Mortimer. Father Mortimer is, I hope, going to be of the very *greatest* help to us. He is using his influence with the Bishop of Kensington-Gore. This is the man who made our *wonderful* Tona Perfecta, Father. One of the cleverest inventors now living, I believe. And this is my young cousin from South Africa, Eleanor de la Roux.'

Hugh looked with disgust at the interrupter of his conversation. He saw that Miss Denton-Smyth thus addressed as 'Father' a man young enough to be her son, if not her grandson, a tall, slim, debonair young man, whose black clerical cassock accentuated his height, his slenderness, and his youth, a handsome enough young fellow, damn him. Hugh hated all parsons categorically, and parsons who interrupted him particularly.

'Do you remember coming with me to hear Father Mortimer preach, Eleanor?' chirruped Miss Denton-Smyth.

'I'm not likely to forget,' said Eleanor. 'And I don't know yet,' she twinkled, 'whether I'm likely to forgive!'

'Forgive?' asked the priest.

'It's a long and possibly absurd story, and in any case you couldn't help it, so I suppose I must forgive you.' She smiled at him, but he remained looking at her with a queer disturbed attention.

'I was telling Miss de la Roux about the Tona Perfecta,' Hugh broke in abruptly. 'I was saying I want her to come to my laboratory one day and see it. Will you, Miss de la Roux?'

'Thank you. I should like it very much.'

'You've seen it, Cousin Caroline, of course?' the girl asked.

'No, I haven't, dear. Well, not exactly. Only the plans and so on. It was Mr. Johnson and Mr. St. Denis who really *saw* it.'

'Can't we come down together, Mr. Macafee? I've got a car.'

'*And* Father Mortimer,' cried Miss Denton-Smyth. 'He's going to help us. He ought to see the justification of our faith!'

'Well – perhaps. Is this a secret process, Macafee?' smiled the priest.

Hugh was lost. Before he knew where he was he had committed himself to show a car-load of the Christian Cinema Company round his workshops and laboratory on the following Friday evening.

He meant to qualify his offer; he meant to encircle it with such conditions that he would secure either Miss de la Roux alone, or nobody. But at that moment, the buzzing conversation round him faded; Miss Denton-Smyth with a clink and a jingle sprang away and made off up the room, while a small procession filed on to the platform. There was Mrs. St. Denis, now holding a large bouquet of red carnations, and a plump parson, and Johnson, and a tall emaciated actress with scrupulously unreddened lips and emphatically unparisian clothes, the sort of actress, though Hugh was unaware of it, who compensates for lack of professional ability by assiduous devotion to good works. Miss Denton-Smyth brought up the rear, tripping up to her seat, bowing and smiling from it, and beaming upon the company as though she had achieved her heart's desire.

'Speeches,' murmured Eleanor de la Roux. 'And I'm stewarding. Good-bye!'

She stole silently to her stand beside a pamphlet-laden stall and left Hugh with Father Mortimer to watch Johnson rise from his chair, spread his vast fingers on the green baize table-cloth, and begin:

'My friends, ladies and gentlemen.'

The chairs screeched as their occupants turned to face the speaker. A scattered fusillade of clapping drowned the screeches. Hugh looked to see whether escape were possible, but the way to the door was now completely blocked. He stood with his arms folded, his eyes closed, leaning back against the wall and hearing Johnson explain to the assembled company that among all ways of saving this wicked world, the quickest, cheapest, most spiritual and most artistic was the creation of a Christian Cinema Company. When he turned to scrutinize Father Mortimer at his side, that young man was again looking across the room to where Miss de la Roux stood, a thin, childish, quiet sentinel upright behind her laden stall.

§ 5

Very early in the morning after the Christian Cinema Company's At Home, Hugh Macafee woke up to the sound of a cat's serenade on a neighbouring wall. He had tried to train himself to constructive action, even when suddenly aroused from sleep, so that no waking hour of the night or day might be lost to him. That morning his Puritanism was rewarded by two excellent ideas flashing almost unsought into his mind. The first concerned a new arrangement of chemical sensitizers to facilitate the colour reproduction for which he was striving; the second concerned his own domestic arrangements. Why, he wondered, should he pay two rents, when he could perfectly well make himself some sort of a bed at the laboratory? There he would be close beside his work. He could economize in time and money. It was absurd that he had never thought of this before.

Directly he had breakfasted he gave notice to his landlady and hurried off to the chemical works. Now everything went splendidly. He had been working along all the wrong lines in his colour film. What he wanted was a medium which would reproduce not only tone but opacity and depth. He began to study the crude elementary colour photography of Joly, Ives and Lumière, seeking for the right foundation for his own projected work. He became completely happy and absorbed, moving about the laboratory among his newly acquired apparatus, delighted with his new financial liberty. His only grievance lay against Campbell. Campbell did not care for colour photography. The definite and practical purpose of the Tona Perfecta he could understand, but he could not see the importance of this colour business. Hugh's desire to photograph more perfectly the subtle variations of light and tone, to catch the sense of solidity or transparency in colour, appeared to Campbell as highfalutin' nonsense. He became surly and obstructive until Hugh, in a frenzy of impatience, paid him a week's wage in lieu of notice, and told him to clear off.

He was working alone on Friday night when he was interrupted by a sharp rap on the door. Startled, he put down his pen and sat listening. His first thought was that this must be Johnson, but then he remembered that Johnson was out of town. Who could it be? A policeman new to the beat, unused to seeing his light in that strange place? A tramp?

Again came the knock, persistent, not peremptory.

121

Hugh rose and shambled slowly towards the door. For a moment he hesitated, then quickly turned his Yale lock and pushed the door, which opened outwards into the main building. The light from the laboratory fell on to the figure of Eleanor de la Roux, who stood with Miss Denton-Smyth and the young priest whom Hugh had met at the At Home.

'Gaw!' gasped Hugh.

He had completely forgotten his reluctant invitation.

'Good evening!' smiled Miss de la Roux. 'You did mean us to come, didn't you?'

Hugh stared and stared.

'Didn't you get my post card? I said we should come unless you told us not to, you know.'

'Where did you send it?'

'To an address in Penge that Cousin Caroline gave me.'

'I've moved,' said Hugh, and suddenly remembered that he had made no arrangement for the forwarding of letters.

'I'm so sorry. Then we are interrupting you? And had we better go away?'

He remembered now that this de la Roux girl was an heiress. She put down three thousand as easily as some people put three pence into the collection-plate on Sunday. She was interested in the Tona Perfecta. She might be interested in his other work. She was intelligent – for a woman. She might even be useful to him in other ways.

He continued to stare awkwardly, until Miss Denton-Smyth took up her tale.

'Oh, Mr. Macafee, it's *so* exciting! I declare it's quite like a scene out of a spy story or something – we made for the broken door just as Mr. Johnson said, and Eleanor left the car outside, and then we looked in and saw your light shining from the ruin and knew it *must* be you because it's such a *very* strange thing to see a light shining out of a *ruin*, and I always say that castles and abbeys never look really themselves until their roofs have fallen in, but a *factory* when *it's* gone to pieces looks *really* ruinous!'

'Well, as you are here, you'd better come in,' said Hugh ungraciously. 'Though I don't think there's much here that can interest you.'

They entered the lighted laboratory. Hugh's provisions

122

for his own comfort might be inadequate, but he knew exactly what he wanted in the way of equipment. The laboratory was a large room, already provided with gas-pipes, bunsen-burners, electric lights and sinks. There were lamps and stoves and cameras. There were delicate instruments for testing acoustical properties. There was a draughtsman's desk and revolving lamps. When Hugh switched on more lights all these were illuminated in a white dazzling blaze. The room was an oasis of complex and civilized activity in the middle of dark ruin.

Hugh looked on his work with justifiable pride.

'You can look round. But you must not touch.'

Miss de la Roux at least might appreciate something of all that he had done. She knew nothing about the possibilities of sound and colour reproduction, but she had received an elementary grounding in scientific values. She was not quite a fool. Hugh liked her appearance as she trod with her quick light step along the room, pausing here and there to question him about an instrument, bending forward, her ungloved hands clasped behind her, holding her leather gauntlets. She looked as though she were at home here, as though she would move nimbly and effectively in this place. Her quick quiet questions were intelligent. Devil take the girl! What was she doing with that snivelling young parson and that half-witted old woman?

Hugh had no use for parsons. Miss Denton-Smyth, on the other hand, could hardly hide her enthusiasm for Father Mortimer. When the girl and the priest had moved across the room, Caroline turned to Hugh, bubbling over with confidences.

'Oh, Mr. Macafee, I can't tell you what it means to me to be here to-day, and to be able to bring Father Mortimer with us. You know I always felt that we needed the blessing of the *Church* on this enterprise, and though at Saint Augustine's dear Father Lasseter has always been such a *great* help and comfort, it's not the same as securing the interest of a really *distinguished* young priest and scholar – Oxford, you know – New College and *very* brilliant. Greats – I think they call it, or is it *Smalls*? I always think it's so confusing, the difference between *smalls* and *shorts*, not having had the advantage of a university education myself, though I've often regretted it, but in my day opportunities were so much more limited, and I'm always telling Eleanor that I really wonder whether she was *quite* wise to stop short in the middle of her college course, but the poor child was so terribly upset losing her father like that, they being *all in all* to one another, that she could not bear to remain in South Africa, and though I always say that we must not let our affections be our *sole* guide, I do think that a *father* is different, and then having no *mother* too. . . .'

'Umph,' grunted Hugh, but he was thinking rapidly.

There across the room stood the South African heiress talking to the parson. She had neither father nor mother to advise her. Sorrow had driven her to England, and sorrow or loneliness had forced her into the arms of Caroline Denton-Smyth. She had given up her university work, but she was obviously fitted by nature to be an inventor's assistant. Had she herself not said that she preferred the honest work of a laboratory? It was all wrong that she should waste her youth and intelligence among the confusions and falsities of propaganda and uplift. She was too good for it. It must be stopped. Was not this the solution to the problem caused by his dismissal of Campbell?

Missionary zeal consumed Hugh. He had to save Miss de la Roux's soul, and to enrol her as a worker in his own service. He left Miss Denton-Smyth without an explanation and strode across the room. Eleanor bent over the diagram on which he had been working when she interrupted him. Now he interrupted her. 'I want to talk to you!'

'Well?'

'Why don't you come back to laboratory work!'

'I beg your pardon?'

'You're still messing about with this Christian Cinema Company?'

'Not as much as you are, I understand.'

'What d'you mean?'

'You're a director, aren't you?'

'They say so.'

'Well, I'm not. I'm only a shareholder – pretty well the only shareholder, I believe.'

'Well, being a shareholder can't take all your time.'

'No, it doesn't.'

'What do you do with the rest of it?'

'Work. Drive a car. Explore London. Listen to Labour speeches. Learn how to be a business woman.'

'Business. Why business?'

'I want to make money.'

'Is that why you gave up your university work before you got your degree?'

She paused. 'I suppose you could say that.'

'You're throwing yourself away!'

'Thanks! I think I'm the best judge of that.'

But she smiled as she said that. She was not rude or snubbing.

'Give it up!'

'For what?'

'Come and give me a hand here. I need an assistant. I don't suppose you know much, but I daresay you can obey orders, and you look as quick as most.'

'Are you asking me to be your assistant?'

'Oh, I know it's taking a lot for granted. You may be as much of a nuisance in a laboratory as most girls. But I could start with you for a week on trial.'

'Well.' She stared at him, amused, surprised and quizzical. 'You are an amazing person! Is this a serious offer?'

'I don't waste time making offers I don't mean.'

'How much could you pay me?'

'Do you mean a salary?'

'Naturally.'

'You wouldn't be worth a salary for a long time. I should have everything to teach you. It would be a great opportunity for you. You really ought to pay me a premium.'

'Do you talk like this to the men who work here with you?'

'What do you mean?'

'Aren't you a little precipitate?'

'Well, if you want time to think it over, you can take it. But I warn you that you're running the risk of ruin while you hang about with Miss Denton-Smyth and her friends. How can anyone preserve their capacity for honest thought

in that atmosphere? They all lie and compromise and pre-
varicate. They sell the truth if a lie can be of any use to
their meetings and wretched causes. It's all – it's all dishonest – rotten. There's nothing in it.'

Hugh had not the eloquence of Johnson. He was unac-
customed to the missionary's task. He stumbled and fought
for words, dominated by an unfamiliar emotion. He saw
Eleanor de la Roux swept down into the whirlpool of Miss
Denton-Smyth's activities. He saw her honest brain defiled
and muddled by sentiment, her clear vision darkened by
confused emotions. It was not good enough. She would be
destroyed. She would become just like all other women,
feeble and sentimental, incapable of rational thought. She
watched him with grave wonder, opening wide her hazel
eyes, surprised, but neither embarrassed nor wholly dis-
pleased. When at the end of his tirade she said quietly,
'Don't you think I'm the best judge of my own interests?' he
stammered: 'No. No. Of course you're not. No woman is.'

'What do you know about women?' she asked. 'And what
do you know about me?'

'I know you're – you're . . .' He had reached the end of
his resources. He knew, indeed, nothing about her, except
that she was intelligent and self-possessed, and that he
wanted to have her working in his laboratory, concentrating
her grave attention upon him, and not lounging about with
that long slug of a priest.

But he could not say that. He could only glower at her
and snap: 'I hate any waste of time and of ability. Look
here, Eleanor – what's the good of mucking round with
those old women – of both sexes? Miss Denton-Smyth talks
about purifying the cinema – making an honest film, and
all that. She doesn't know the first thing about an honest
film. I can show you honesty. The only sort of honesty you
can get in a show of this kind is honest workmanship. Cut
all that propaganda. I'll teach you how to do good work.'

She smiled suddenly, a smile of quick friendliness and
liking.

'Well, well,' she said. 'You're very persuasive, though I
don't like the way you talk about my friends. I'll see.' And
she was off, leaving him in a fine flutter of uneasiness.

Miss Denton-Smyth immediately approached him. 'Oh, Mr. Macafee – I hate to bother you,' she began, 'but there's just one thing I wanted to ask you.' She hesitated, then went on boldly. 'I suppose you couldn't let me have a little loan of ten shillings or a pound? I'm just a little short this week. Of course, I'll pay you back. My embarrassment's only temporary. We're all going to make our fortunes. I'm just a little short now.'

'But, Miss Denton-Smyth.' Hugh stared at her in amazement. 'Johnson told me you had an independent income and a lot of rich relations.'

'Well, naturally,' she said with a little toss of her head, 'I'm not going to confide all my domestic affairs in Mr. Johnson. Between you and me, I am having rather a struggle just now, though dear Eleanor has been very good during the past few months, but of course I don't like to take too much from her because I know that since she invested her capital in the company she's only got just enough to last till she finishes her training, and of course until the dividends come in, which they must do soon, I've got five and four-pence halfpenny at the moment, but I'll go to dear Father Mortimer to-morrow. That's what's so wonderful. I always say it doesn't matter about *money* if only you've got good *friends*!' She smiled a little fluttering smile.

'You mean you're living on that parson and Miss de la Roux?'

The smile died, and she gazed at him.

'Why, it's only a loan – until we *all* make our fortunes. And it's wonderful how little you need when you're my age. It's only natural they should want to help me when I'm doing important work, because you know I don't think that my dear relations in Yorkshire quite understand just *what* the work is. Of course, that's why we've *got* to make the Christian Cinema Company succeed. Having staked *everything* on it, I mean.'

'I see.'

So she was really penniless, and the company was not a rich old woman's whim, but a desperate gamble against fortune. Hugh felt sick at heart. He did not yet know what complications might result from this exposure of poverty, but he knew that all poverty was dangerous. He knew that it interrupted work, disturbed the mind, and came between a man and his ideas.

Sullen and disappointed he stumbled across the laboratory to a small safe where he kept his plans and papers. Unlocking the door he turned his papers over until he found a leather case. Counting out four pounds deliberately, he returned four others to the case and locked the door again.

'You'd better take these. And now if you don't mind, I should be glad if you would all go away. I want to do some more work to-night.'

'Well, thank you very much. It's only a loan, mind you. I'll send you an I.O.U. I'm very much glad to have this, not only for what it is but because it shows that we're all working together and that you really believe we're going to succeed.' She called her party together, and they said good-bye and went away.

It was no use, Hugh decided, trying to do anything with a woman like that. She was incorrigible. Of course, it was madness to lend her money. He had a strong impulse to run after her into the street and take his four pounds back again. Still, in justice to her he must admit that she had created the Christian Cinema Company. He was indebted to her for the sum of £500 and possibly more to come. He might, through her, secure the de la Roux girl as an unpaid assistant. He knew now that the prospect of this arrangement was very pleasant to him. Well, he ought not to grudge her a loan of four pounds, he supposed, poor Caroline.

Chapter 5 : *Roger Aintree Mortimer*

WHEN Caroline reported at the Board meeting on January 30th that Father Mortimer had promised to speak to the Bishop of Kensington-Gore about the company, she was not strictly accurate. What Mortimer had promised to do was to inquire further about the business for Father Lasseter.

The Reverend Father Mortimer was at that time assistant priest at Saint Augustine's, Fulham, in the diocese of Kensington-Gore, a position which he mistakenly believed to lay upon him the obligation of working for sixteen hours a day on seven days in the week.

All day he rushed on his bicycle about the streets, taking services, visiting the sick, arguing on committees, and wrestling with the pert, irrepressible, undisciplined and tedious members of the boys' clubs and young men's guilds. The streets down which he strode, his long black cassock swinging to his swift stride, were drab and ugly. The houses he visited were poor, squalid and overcrowded. He knelt in prayer beside tumbled and dirty beds. He strove in bare, dilapidated clubrooms to ignite sparks of enthusiasm in the breasts of unemployed cynical adolescents. It was hard work, but its rigour was his consolation. The ugliness of the Clergy House where he lodged had a certain charm for him. He found it necessary to drug his nerves with work and to stupefy his intellect with fatigue.

His trouble was not the common one. He found no burden in asceticism. The desires of the flesh rarely vexed his lean young body, hardened by constant exercise, plain food and the perpetual discipline of action. But his wanton mind distressed him. The child of a cultured, debonair and ironic Oxford family, he had returned for his school holidays during the first two years of the war, to find himself exasperated by its aloof superiority and academic indifference. Responding recklessly to the challenge of 'He who is not with me is against me,' he flung himself when he was just eighteen at once into the bosom of the Anglican Church, and the ranks of an infantry regiment. A mood of chill but exquisite exaltation carried him through the ordeals of medical examination and adult baptism, confirmation and army latrines. He took his first communion three days before his draft left the training-camp for France.

He was not, on the whole, unhappy while in training. The lack of privacy, the rigour of physical effort, the harsh discomfort and rough community life resembled his vision of an unsanctified but adequate monasticism. His spiritual detachment left him outwardly cheerful, docile and a little shy. Charmed by Franciscan ideals of brotherhood and poverty, he refused to let his squeamish nerves shrink from the ugliness of physical contact with men less fastidious than himself. He listened with courteous interest to jokes about square pushing, to smutty gossip, and to the brutal violence of a sergeant who, in giving bayonet instruction, yelled at him to hate the Germans, to eat 'em, bite 'em, and tear their bowels out. These were the men whom he had undertaken to love, and since love was the order of the day, the harder the task, the more meritorious its fulfilment.

Even when he at last arrived in France and reached the trenches, his exaltation acted as a general anæsthesia, dulling the perception of horror which might otherwise have driven him mad. He marched, dug, sweated, ate, slept and endured the absence of sleep, and crawled on his belly along reeking mud, and it seemed as though a curtain hung between the objective world in which all these things happened, and the subjective world in which he really lived. When he went sick with pneumonia in the winter of 1917, he lay in hospital choking and coughing, but mentally in bliss. The outward appearance of things became refined to extraordinary fragility. It hung like a transparent curtain between him and the real world of the spirit. Under the influence of fever the curtain sometimes blew aside a little and he saw straight into the dazzling light of absolute realities.

He passed his twenty-first birthday in a camp near Abbeville in the spring of 1919, waiting for demobilization. Behind the camp stretched woods with long green rides leading past glades yellow with daffodils. In the mild spring evening he walked by himself, pushing his way through tangled thickets of hazel and hawthorn, stopping to watch a squirrel chattering with anger on the low bough of a beech tree, and listening to the liquid whispering of evening birds. He was radiantly happy, not only with spiritual ecstasy, but with normal human and egotistic pleasure. The war was over; he was alive and well; life lay before him, Oxford, liberty, learning, the mellow leisure of academic life, the loveliness of the English country, Tubeny woods, the Cherwell, Magdalen tower, the admirable sherry at Wadham, good talk round well-furnished luncheon tables, women – a vague yet rapturous adventure, for he was still a virgin – philosophy, travel.

Down into a hollow glade he strode, knee-deep in daffodils, then struck his boot against something dull yet soft, hidden below the flowers. The instinct of more than two years made him start back in horror, expecting and almost smelling the stench of putrifying flesh.

It was not a corpse under the daffodils; only an old log so rotten that it crumbled at a touch. But horror had pierced his triumph and brought him face to face with a reality which was not spiritual. Retching and shivering, he stared at the log, seeing instead of the damp wood the body of his friend Arnot, who had slipped when half-drunk with fatigue from the duckboard into deep mud and been trampled to death by the feet of his own company. He saw Linden, coughing his life away after a gas attack, and Meer, suddenly mutilated by an exploding shell. The revulsion of strained nerves and tortured senses came upon him, and he cried out in anguish against the fate which had doomed him to bear the burden of life while they were dead. He saw with horror his complacency in settling down to enjoy the pleasure of which they had been robbed, and in a sudden passion strode round the glade, tearing up the daffodils, and trampling into the earth their broken trumpets.

He was absent that night from roll-call, and next morning

was found, crouched on a fallen tree, his head in his hands, incapable of speech or effort.

The war was over; discipline was not what it had been; the army doctor liked young Mortimer, who had struck him as intelligent, alert and keen. Brain-storms were not unknown among young soldiers, and it certainly caused less inconvenience to have them after the Armistice instead of before it. Mortimer was sent to hospital in Abbeville for a fortnight to be treated for influenza, a convenient disease which indeed opportunely attacked him. He apparently recovered from both of his disorders simultaneously and was able to report for demobilization on the appointed day.

But the result of his revulsion was his determination to take Holy Orders. Because he had no right to live, he would renounce the world. He played for some time with the thought of becoming a missionary to the lepers; but he discarded that idea as a piece of sentiment which he must not permit himself. His work lay in England.

He went up to New College with his government grant for the shortened course in Greats; then passed on to Lichfield Theological College.

Since he left Lichfield, he had lived in slum parishes, fasted and prayed and spurred himself forward to new efforts of endurance and toleration. The endurance was mental as well as physical. He compelled his complex and subtle mind to produce Simple Talks for Working Mothers and Manly Addresses for Young Lads. He schooled his lively and inconvenient sense of humour to docility in the face of care committees and church workers. His speculative habits were smothered beneath an avalanche of drudgery. Thus he was able to flog himself into a state of chilly happiness, sensitively alive to small pleasures. An unexpected leisure hour in the London Library, an exhilarating spurt on his bicycle between two rushing streams of traffic down the Edgware Road, or a rare holiday, swimming and walking in Cornwall, sufficed to make him in love with this world as well as with the next.

But his trouble lay in his intellectual uncertainty. The Catholic ideal of unity, of discipline and organization appealed to him, but his temperament was fundamentally Protestant. He found himself compelled to refer questions of faith to his individual conviction instead of to authority. The spectacle of his friends who collapsed into Catholicism on attaining middle age revolted him. The Anglo-Catholic position failed to satisfy him. It was engaged in a battle which he thought unimportant. Though he loved and admired Father Lasseter, he was fatigued by the older man's pre-occupation with sectarian controversy.

But he despised himself for vacillations. When on Septuagesima Sunday he preached at Saint Augustine's instead of Father Lasseter who had laryngitis, he condemned compromise in order to elucidate his own position. He thought that by preaching to suit himself, he might meet the needs of at least one member of the congregation. Quite unaware of Eleanor's presence or of the Christian Cinema Company's distress, he pronounced sentence upon his own half-heartedness. Two days later a funny little woman called Miss Denton-Smyth lay in wait for him outside the vestry door, and asked him to find a bishop for her. He murmured something about Father Lasseter, and left her, promptly forgetting all about the incident.

But if he forgot the Christian Cinema Company once, he was not allowed to forget it again. Almost every time he took a service in Saint Augustine's, he was haunted by the small bright figure of Miss Denton-Smyth. It was impossible to ignore her, for she was vivid as a parrakeet in her unsuitable green and crimson dresses. On the coldest mornings she appeared at Early Mass among the faithful. She lay in wait for Roger at the door; she hunted him down on his way to Parish Meetings with inexorable, gentle, unhurrying pursuit.

Roger spoke about her to Father Lasseter.

'Poor old thing. She's desperately poor and inclined to be a nuisance. I'm really glad she's found a hobby at last. Be thankful it isn't parish visiting or Church work. You'd better humour her.'

Roger humoured her. He listened to her story, walked back to her room in Lucretia Road with her, accepted bundles of circulars, which he promptly threw into an overfilled

133

waste-paper basket in the Clergy House, and promised to attend the At Home to Clergy and Social Workers which the Christian Cinema Company had arranged.

He went in a mood of detached and melancholy amusement. He had been reading the *Summa Theologia* and the terrific power and knowledge behind the dry sentences goaded him. He felt that Aquinas would have had nothing but contempt for his fluctuating impulse. He knew that he was working himself up for another nervous and spiritual crisis. References to Catholicism stung him. He found the Communion Service a fierce ordeal, every word and movement challenging him to justify his Protestantism in the face of that huge claim upon Christian unity. If he was to face his problems calmly he must, he felt, divert his attention from these larger problems and amuse himself by trivial encounters.

He knew one or two people at the party, but his habitual shyness isolated him, and though he busied himself handling cups of tea and rearranging chairs, he had opportunity to observe the people round about him, and especially one girl sitting eating sandwiches beside a radiator across the hall.

The things he noticed about her were odd things. She wore very trim country shoes, with low heels and boyish worsted stockings. She had removed her hat, and her brown fringe overhung her straight sullen brows. She was talking with grave attention to a lean gawky youth whom Roger knew to be Macafee, the inventor. She listened to him as though what he was saying were interesting and important, but there was no coquetry in her clear, critical glance and abrupt questions. Roger knew far too well the earnest and unintelligent response of womanly women who hung upon a man's words, inhaling through open mouths with indiscriminating favour his most commonplace remarks. This girl was listening as an equal listens, nodding her head from time to time, so that her brown, heavy, silken, lustreless straight hair swung back and forth. Then her face broke suddenly into a charming smile, and he noticed the band of freckles across her nose, and the clear line of her well-moulded chin. Of all the people in the room, he felt that he would like to know her, and laughed at himself for acting so well the curate, threading his way through impenetrable forests of chairs, carrying tea, and sustained by the prospects of conversation with an unknown girl.

'I don't suppose I shall ever see her again,' he thought. 'This meeting's rather a frost. I imagine that this Cinema Company will go the way of many other companies. And I?' He did not know where he would go.

'Father Mortimer,' – Miss Denton-Smyth was at his elbow – ' I want you so *much* to meet my cousin, Eleanor de la Roux; you know we owe *her* the continuance of the company and everything.'

She led him across the room to the girl whom he had noticed talking to the young men and introduced them. 'Do you remember coming with me to hear Father Mortimer preach, Eleanor?'

To Roger's surprise the girl greeted him with a remarkable phrase. 'I'm not likely to forget,' she said, 'and I don't know yet whether I'm likely to forgive.'

Forgive? Forgive? He could not even remember what he had preached about that night at St. Augustine's. But the incident excited his imagination. He had noticed the girl. He had wanted to make her acquaintance. And already he had unconsciously affected her life. It was amusing; it symbolized the curious diversity of experience which went to make the pattern of life. 'We are so oddly interrelated,' he thought. 'We are members of one another. An inescapable communion. We cannot avoid incurring responsibility for our brethren.' With half-comical dismay he contemplated the glib complacency with which good Churchmen referred to this intricacy of mutual relationship as though it were not one of the most alarming qualities of the universe. He committed himself to go down to Annerley on the following Friday to visit Macafee's laboratory.

He wanted to see Eleanor de la Roux again. He wanted to find out exactly how his sermon had affected her. He felt as though he might use this brief diversion to dam the rising tide of his own intellectual disturbance. Was he withheld from Rome by loyalty or indolence? Throughout half that night he knelt in his cold cell-like room, wrestling with the angel of his honour, and calling in vain upon his sense of humour to save him from the madness of apostasy.

§ 2

His first visit to Macafee's laboratory remained in Roger's memory as the occasion when he first became aware of the reality behind St. Paul's laconic injunction that it is better to marry than to burn. When he saw Eleanor de la Roux at the Christian Cinema Company's At Home he had been amused and intrigued by a situation in which an unknown young woman had acknowledged his influence upon her life; but when he joined Miss Denton-Smyth and her young cousin to motor down to Annerley, he immediately knew that Eleanor de la Roux meant more to him than a casual acquaintance.

Standing in the laboratory, listening to Miss Denton-Smyth's hurrying monologue, he followed the girl's pilgrimage from desk to table, watching with novel excitement her assured and unself-conscious movements. Driving back in the car he suddenly knew that he could not bear the expedition to end like this. She would just drop out of his life like the hundreds of other men and women whom he met by chance and parted from without regret.

When they had set down Miss Denton-Smyth at Lucretia Road he turned to Eleanor. 'Must you go straight home?' he asked, 'or will you come and have coffee or something with me?'

'I don't really mind,' she said indifferently. 'Isn't it pretty late?'

'There's a place in the Earl's Court Road quite near your club,' he insisted. 'It won't take you out of your way.'

'Oh, very well.'

They drove almost in silence back to the Earl's Court Road. It was a clear cold evening, and the polished roads gleamed as though they were transparent and lit from within. The lighted city seemed like an alabaster globe in which electric lights are veiled, a lovely and fragile bubble that one blow could shatter. Roger felt that his new mood of happiness was as brittle. He sat very still, hardly daring to move or speak lest he should break its magic. He was content to

136

watch the houses fall away from him, and Eleanor's firm gauntleted hand upon the wheel.

In the Earl's Court Road is a small foreign restaurant, open till midnight. There Roger took Eleanor, and they sat together at a table beside the window, lit by a pink-shaded lamp. He ordered coffee and sandwiches, and while they waited for their order to be carried out, Eleanor smoked.

'I want to know something,' Roger said at last. 'You needn't tell me unless you like, but my curiosity is piqued.'

'What is it?'

'Why did you say, when I first met you, that you could not forget me, and you might not forgive?'

She smiled at him quizzically over her cigarette. 'You remember that? Oh – Well.' Then to his surprise a sudden rosy blush poured over her cheeks and neck, and she pressed out the stump of her cigarette with firm brown fingers. 'Well –' she began again.

'Don't tell me if it's only absurd – or embarrassing. I assure you that it's the idlest curiosity tempting me to ask. Also I should hate to feel unforgiven by you, if it were possible to rectify the evil.'

'Well, the position's this,' she said at length. 'You've cost me three thousand pounds.'

'I've what? I beg your pardon –'

'Well – it was like this. Caroline took me to church. I don't often go. I'm really a member of the Dutch Reformed Church, and anyway, I'm an agnostic.' She looked up with a sort of challenge, but he only nodded gravely.

'Yes?'

'Well. I'd been rather unhappy and very dissatisfied with a good many things, myself most of all. But you preached about the dishonesty of compromise, and the young man who went away sorrowful because he had great possessions. It wasn't – excuse my saying so – an awfully good sermon. But I'm a Socialist. And I was tired of doing things by halves. So I took your advice.'

'I – see.'

He did not pour out the coffee, but sat looking at her.

'And now that I've done it, it all seems rather stupid, because I've got to work much harder than I used to do,

137

simply to get my own living, whereas, when I was a capitalist, I could do quite a lot for other people. I believe I was more useful before.'

'Do you mean to say that you gave away *all* your money?'

'Not quite all. I reserved enough to finish my training and keep me till I could keep myself. I shall have to sell the car, though.'

'You gave it all to the Christian Cinema Company?'

'Caroline calls it an investment. But I don't suppose I shall ever see any of it again. What do you think?'

'I don't know. I really don't know much about the company. But –'

'But?'

'Aren't you interested in the company?'

'No. I think it's rather a frost really, don't you?'

'Then why on earth –?'

'Oh, I don't know. It's difficult to explain. I suppose that I wanted to play providence a little. That's what most charity is – a way of making oneself an amateur God. I don't think it's the right way, though. It's too easy. And it doesn't bring any real satisfaction. You'd better register that for future sermons. One can't buy peace of mind like a block of shares in government securities. It doesn't work.'

'Will you sell your shares then?'

'Would you?'

'That's hardly to the point. I seem to have done enough damage without inflicting any more of my opinions upon you.'

'Damage?'

'Well –'

'How typical of the Church! You preach the most uncompromising doctrine that was ever invented and as soon as anyone takes you literally, you're shocked beyond expression. I suppose you're not accustomed to converts. Am I your first?'

'If you were a convert, I suppose you would be. But I'm not going to put you down to my credit yet.'

'Yet?'

'Well – Hope as well as Faith and Charity were commended to us.'

She sighed, as though she were tired, and dropped her chin on to her hands.

'You don't seem very jubilant about it. I don't know that I expected anyone would be, except Caroline. And of course, you're right. If all the members of your Church obeyed its precepts literally there'd be the most frightful economic revolution to-morrow. We'd all be taking off our coats and giving them away with our cloak also. Every working man paid to walk one mile would walk two, and so upset the foreign markets by undercutting all our commercial rivals. The banks would crash, because everyone would be selling all their securities and giving to the poor, and the only hope left to us would be an immediate Second Coming to get us all out of the mess we'd fallen into.'

'Ah, but that is where the Catholic Church has learned wisdom. She safeguards us so cautiously from the consequences of our impetuosity.'

'Humph. You think then that my running amok and flinging away my capital is the result of being an unbalanced agnostic individualist, and that if I'd belonged to your Holy Mother the Church I should have known that you didn't really mean what you said about refusing to compromise, because every saying has its symbol, and only the barbarians have not learned how to avoid their literal interpretation. Is that it?'

'Something like that, perhaps. But I really didn't want to score points at the moment. I'm wondering what can be done. I feel a certain responsibility about your investments. Of course, if the Christian Cinema Company were to turn out a financial success you'd be all right.'

'And God's mysterious ways would be justified, I suppose? Well, Caroline of course says I'm going to make my fortune. I doubt it, and still I think that Macafee is a clever fellow and there really may be something in his inventions. What do you think?'

Roger did not want to talk about Macafee. He wanted to discuss Eleanor and her predicament. He was distressed and at the same time excited to discover that he should have exerted, however unconsciously, a decisive influence upon her actions. He was perturbed about her possible difficulties.

He pressed her for further information about herself, about her home in South Africa, and her brother in the States.

'But of course, he's practically a stranger to me now,' she said. 'And I never had much in common with him. What a farce it is, all this talk about family feeling and blood being thicker than water. I am quite prepared to accept the physiological fact that blood is thicker than water. But what does that prove? That I can make my brother understand how I feel about things? Nonsense!'

The sleepy waiter was hovering by their table. It was long after eleven, but Eleanor made no move to go, and Roger was well content that he should sit and watch the pink light from the lamp flushing her grave and rather stubborn face. He thought her casual, grave, reckless, and a little scornful. Her contempt for the Church, her indifference to her own interests, and her half-mocking admiration for her cousin Caroline attracted him. When at last she rose, pulling on her big gauntlets, and yawning, he was conscious of acute regret.

'Must we go?' he said.

'It's nearly midnight, and I've got to garage my car – and work to-morrow.'

'So have I – to work to-morrow, I mean. Can't I garage your car for you?'

'Can you drive?'

'My people had an Austin – and I had a tumbledown Singer for some years.'

'I forgot that clergymen did those sort of ordinary things that real men do.'

'And I am not a real man?'

'Well, clergymen somehow aren't quite proper men, are they?'

'Aren't they? The devil they aren't,' he laughed, but he was stung. He could have borne deliberate insult, but this indifferent assumption infuriated him. Not quite a proper man? He'd like to show her.

Inwardly raging, outwardly polite, he walked back with her to the car, escorted her from the garage to the club and said good night. Then he set off to walk home through the empty lamplit and moonlit streets.

140

Somehow or other, he told himself, he was responsible for Eleanor de la Roux's rash investment. It was therefore his duty to inquire into the prospects of the Christian Cinema Company and make quite sure what damage he had done. Eleanor must not be allowed to lose all her money. It was absurd – a girl like her, throwing away her capital like that. He became quite excited about it, and determined to call upon Miss Denton-Smyth as soon as possible, extract the whole truth from her and prevent her robbery of orphans.

Then he called himself a fool, for the girl was perfectly capable of looking after her own interests. She was hard and keen and efficient. She did not want interference in her affairs, especially by someone who was not quite a proper man. The comic curate, he said to himself. That is how she sees me – the comic curate, living on milk and buns.

He strode home to bed, his long legs devouring the distance between Eleanor's club and his Clergy House. He went to his bleak, cell-like room and spent a very long time in rather violent prayer. When he fell asleep he dreamed that he attended again the Women's Social Evening of an East End Club in which he once had worked.

In the gaunt whitewashed hall a band played jazz music. On the floor three couples of young girls were dancing together, their charming faces intent, their young slim bodies moving with grave precision. Their hair was waved, their lips scarlet, their dresses of cheap satin or mercerized cotton symbolized their youth, their pride, their vitality and self-respect. They danced with sensuous yet sober pleasure, proud, sweet, slim, lovely, unbroken things. Against the wall sat a row of older women. Their wedding rings had sunk into the flesh of their crippled fingers. Their grey sagging faces drooped into slackened necks which slid into huge, shapeless bosoms and distended stomachs. Their swollen legs bulged out of broken shoes. Life, work, child-bearing and poverty had torn their bodies, making hideous what had been lovely, draining their vitality and robbing them of self-respect. They laughed with toothless pleasure over bawdy jokes; they tapped their feet in response to the music; they clapped their gnarled, grime-stained hands. They watched the young girls dancing, making from time to time unseemly jests in husky undertones.

And it seemed to Roger that as he watched one gross and toothless and misshapen hag, she changed slowly before his eyes into the straight, clean, definite personality of Eleanor de la Roux, and began to dance, gravely and quietly, among the girls. He rushed out to greet her, calling to her, 'Eleanor, Eleanor. Dance with me. Dance with me!' But she turned her indifferent contemptuous face towards him, and said, 'A comic curate. Not even a proper man.' In fury he leapt at her, catching her by the shoulders and shaking her, until she changed again, while in his arms, to the toothless, shapeless, quavering old woman.

He woke up suddenly, sweating with terror, to find himself alone with a sword of moonlight falling across his bed.

§ 3

Three or four days passed before he found time to call upon Miss Denton-Smyth. He found himself at about six o'clock one evening passing close to Lucretia Road, and decided to find out if she were in. He would insist upon knowing just what was the position of the Christian Cinema Company. After all, she had frequently asked him to help her. He could not be expected to give his support to a movement that he did not understand.

He hardly noticed the external appearance of 40 Lucretia Road. He was accustomed to dark staircases and grimy corridors. He knocked at her door, but heard no answer. He knocked again.

This time there was a faint movement inside the room.

'Is Miss Denton-Smyth in?' he asked. 'It's Mortimer – Roger Mortimer here.'

'Oh, wait a minute. I've only just got in. I'll put the light on.'

'Is it an awkward time to come? Shall I go away?'

'Oh, no, no, no.'

She opened the door now, and he moved forward into an unlighted room.

'I can't – I can't find the matches,' half-whispered a muffled voice.

142

'It's all right. I've got some.'

He felt for his matches.

'Shall I light the gas?'

'Oh, please.'

He lit the gas. He saw the comfortless disorder of her room. He saw her coat and hat flung on to the bed where she too had obviously been lying until he came. He saw her face working and quivering with emotion.

'I – hadn't time –' she gasped. 'Just in from the office. Rather tired.'

And she crumpled up into a chair and began to cry.

'Ah – look here – you're tired – can't I light your fire for you?'

He had encountered similar situations before and invented a technique with which to face them. He lit the fire, plumped out the cushions and drew the faded curtains. She could not speak, though her tears were drying, and she could lie back against the armchair into which he had pressed her, and wait there for more miracles to happen.

Gradually she recovered her self-possession, laughed a little, and asked him to fill the kettle, explaining that she had come in from the office too tired to make the tea, or shop, or do anything.

'Well, you'll have to let me be your errand-boy. What do you get for tea?'

'Anything. Everything. I don't think there's anything in the house at all. But there's about sevenpence halfpenny in my purse.'

'Very good. I'll see what one can do on sevenpence half-penny.'

He ran down the stairs again, thinking rapidly. Caroline's condition had entirely destroyed his earlier intention. She looked really ill as she lay back in her chair, unable to control her tears of exhaustion. This was not the moment for stern reproaches and the high hand of pastoral indignation.

He went from shop to shop, buying recklessly milk, eggs, cheese, butter, bread, tea, a bottle of brandy and a large Madeira cake, a box of crystallized fruits and a pound of sugar. Returning, laden with parcels, he passed a boy wheeling a barrow bright with mauve, pink and scarlet tulips. His purse was almost empty, but on an impulse he stopped, bought a tight scarlet bunch of tulips, and ran back to Caroline's room, dropping butter and the Madeira cake on the stairs.

She heard him coming and opened the door. She had recovered a little by this, tidied her hair and spread the tablecloth. The fire blazed; the kettle puffed. With a child's pleasure she watched him unpack his parcels; but when she saw the tulips she almost wept again.

'Oh, flowers –' she cried. 'Oh, flowers.' And buried her face in them.

Embarrassed now by his exuberance, uncertain if it had been in the best of taste, he murmured, 'Oh well, when one is tired flowers are rather pleasant. And I am always looking for an excuse to buy them.'

He cut the bread and butter, boiled the eggs and insisted that she should drink one tablespoonful of brandy in strong tea before she filled her cup up properly.

'My mother swore by it as a pick-me-up.'

'Won't you have some?'

'I'm not tired.'

'Your hair's wet. Is it raining?'

'No. I've been bathing – in the Victoria Baths – rather absurd it sounds, doesn't it? But it's about the quickest means of getting exercise, and I take a batch of young urchins on Thursday afternoons straight after school and make 'em dive. All my scouts are going in for their swimmers' badges.'

'Do you dive?'

'Mildly.'

He was a brilliant diver. Too short-sighted for proficiency at games, he had specialized in running, swimming and hurdling. Since he came to London he had found that his athletic accomplishments gave him a greater hold over the boys' clubs and young men's classes than either his learning or his asceticism.

'I'll tell you something, Miss Denton-Smyth,' he confessed, chasing an egg round the pan with a small teaspoon. 'I use my diving purely for effect. It's the only spectacular accomplishment I have. The Boy Scouts and Young Men's

144

Guilds and so forth think me rather a poor worm, for I'm no good at all at Bright Brief Brotherly talks. But I learnt to swim in the Cher when I was about four, I should think, and diving and so on are almost second nature to me. Salt? Salt? Where do you keep it? In this cupboard? Are the eggs hard enough? It's a disquieting reflection upon the influence of the Church, that one can't really do anything with these young creatures by precept or practice, but if one says "Come and see me do swallow-dives on Thursday" they sink into the most complete docility.'

'I should like to see you do it.'

'Oh, it's a remarkable performance, I assure you. The trouble is that I had the arrogance to think that my work was to lead souls to God, whereas what I can really do is to lead bodies to the bathing-pool, –

"And all that teacheth man to dread
The bath as little as the bed." '

He was talking nonsense to gain time while she recovered her strength and spirit under the influence of tulips, tea, and miracles. She squared her shoulders again and a bright spot of colour burned in each cheek. She began to make jokes, to talk jubilantly and criticize his latest sermon. In the face of such recovery, he felt able to get to business.

'You know, Miss Denton-Smyth, you asked me a little while ago to use such small influence as I have on behalf of the Christian Cinema Company.'

'Yes, yes indeed, and I can't tell you how pleased I am, because once we can have the interest of the Church I know that is just what we are needing. You see, the omens have been very propitious lately. Did I tell you about the *very* nice notice we had in the *Christian Herald*? And another in the *Methodist Free Press* about the little lecture I gave at Willesden last week? I tell you, it spreads; it spreads.'

'What I really wanted to know,' Roger began; but she interrupted him.

'You see, I've written to Lady Huntingdon, and her secretary says she's coming back in March. I know she's very well off, because I read in the papers about her husband's will, and she is sole legatee, and that means *quite* twelve thousand a year, if not more, and really with all that money she *should* be able to spare us just a little, say five thousand, and I *know* she's interested in the cinema.'

'But Miss Denton-Smyth –'

'Oh, I *know* you'll agree with me. And then you know there's Mr. Macafee. Of course he's difficult. You know, I always say that genius is the converse side of abnormality and of course you can't expect a *brilliant* man like that to have the common sense and practical knowledge of the world which people say, for instance, that I have, though I'm sure I don't know. And speaking of the company – I suppose you couldn't *lend* me five shillings just as a loan over the week-end? I did send a post card to Eleanor asking her to call round to-day, but then she has to be down at that firm she works for in the city this evening, and of course she mayn't have time to come in. Young people *will* be young people.'

So she not only swindled Eleanor as a director, thought Roger. She borrowed from her as a relative. She was a dangerous and tiresome old woman. He braced himself for condemnation; but his sympathies ran counter to his reason. For when he looked at her, he observed her debonair vitality rising above her fatigue and loneliness. Her large romantic eyes gazed at him with adoring trust. It was so obvious that she saw herself as a brave if battered adventurer steering through storms and perils towards a splendid harbour. She was talking now of the great things which the Christian Cinema Company would one day accomplish, of the need in England for an organization to purify public taste. The glory of her theme caught her up like a wind and swept her to the heights of her idealism. Her gallant spirit triumphed above her weary flesh, until Roger saw, acted before his eyes, the drama of the mystic whose strength transcends the limitations of mortality. He could not force himself to break in upon her ecstasy. Also he had a committee meeting for the Church Bazaar at 6.30 and it would take him quite a quarter of an hour to reach it.

Across the emotional world was woven the net of practical routine. If he was late for the committee, Mrs. Rawlins would bully the wretched secretary, Beattie Laver, into gibbering incompetence, Mrs. Masters would push the Romney girls out of the Sweet Stall, and time would be wasted, nerves shattered and dignity lost over absurd confusions. He must deal with Miss Denton-Smyth another time. Meanwhile he fumbled in a shabby leather case where a pound note lay in wait for such emergencies. If Eleanor came that night she must not be troubled by the old lady's importunity.

So he handed Miss Denton-Smyth his pound note with matter-of-fact indifference as though it were the most natural thing in the world that he should lend her money, and decided to return within a day or two to complete his rescue of Eleanor. Meanwhile he made his excuses to his hostess.

'Well, if you must go, of course you must, but I can't *tell* you what your coming has meant to me. A light in a dark hour – a *wonderful* privilege to pray for help and *find* it. It's this kind of sympathy that makes us *know* that God is good. I shall never, never forget it. Never. And I won't keep you because I know that you must go. But before you go, won't you say just one prayer? It would be such a *help* to me. I should always have it, as a sort of memory – blessing this room.'

Mrs. Rawlins, Beattie Laver and the Romney girls must wait. Roger had prayed in too many similar rooms to feel any self-consciousness now as he cleared a little space among the discarded tea-things and knelt beside the table. Caroline got stiffly to her knees, her head pillowed among the broken springs of the armchair. Father Mortimer's quiet voice was music in her ears. It was enchantment. It was wonder. She did not hear the soft tap on the door, nor the faint sound of its opening.

But Roger saw.

'Lighten our darkness,' he prayed, and raising his eyes saw the figure of Eleanor in the doorway. She stood against the darkness of the passage, buttoned up in her trim leather coat, her eyes shining, her cheeks glowing from the cold wind. For one instant she paused there, seeing Roger on his knees, his hands clasped among the egg-cups, and the

147

broken leather of Caroline's upturned shoes. A flicker crossed her face – a faint ripple of amusement, embarrassment and something that might have been contempt. Then the door closed.

'. . . and by thy great mercy defend us from all perils and dangers of this night,' Roger repeated. Then he pronounced the blessing and remained for a moment quiet.

When he rose, Caroline lumbered up after him, her joints creaking.

'It's been too wonderful – too lovely,' she cried, her voice trembling, 'the tea, the flowers – your coming, everything. Do you know who you remind me of? Barnabas, the Son of Consolation.'

He bade her good-bye, escaped from her clinging knotted hands, and ran down the stairs. At the front door he paused. He had come just in time to see Eleanor's motor-car disappear round the street corner. He heard the arrogant scream of her syren as she turned into the Richmond Road. Then she was gone.

He stood, his hand unconsciously crumbling the damp plaster of the pillar, his face livid with pain. For he had thought that he had cured himself of his folly and now he knew that the cure was an illusion. He had lashed himself with the whips of his ridicule, but Eleanor's smile lashed him with scorpions. He saw himself as she saw him, a comic curate, praying among the buns. 'Not quite a real man.' Just so; just so. And she had not even troubled to wait to see her cousin. But he had seen, in that swift vision, all that she meant to him. He knew that her scorn could wither the universe. What did he care for his soul's safety or the honour of the Church (which Church in any case?) if she could look like that at him? He needed her respect. Yes, and by God, much more than her respect. He wanted her, loved her, lusted for her. 'Think straight, then, think straight,' he gibed at himself. 'Call things by their proper names. Face up to this, you fool. You are a priest, and to an intelligent modern young agnostic like Eleanor de la Roux a priest is slightly comic, and entirely despicable. If your prayers amuse her, the knowledge of your love would afford her delicious entertainment. This is not the place for heroics.

148

In ten minutes you are due at a meeting of the Church Bazaar Committee, to adjudicate between the rights of Fancywork and Home Produce to hold the place of honour just before the platform. This is the life you have chosen. Down these steps, hurry along the road, catch your bus, stand to allow the fat woman with the parcels to sit down. Pass right along the car, please. One penny fare, please. Now shall I back the Romney girls or Mrs. Masters? Ah, God, God, God. How can a man live in this agony of frustration? That's right. Call upon God. You chose Him as your consoler – the illusion conjured up by generations of chained and frustrated men – the protest of the human soul against the limitations of experience. This is reality, this blinding pain, this shame, this agony – Eleanor de la Roux is reality. And you have chosen – Church bazaars. God. I can't stand this bus – these hideous drivelling stupid people – no – there's no time to walk. Five more minutes now before the committee meeting. That's what? I beg your pardon. My ticket? Oh, Hell – a comic curate never is able to produce his ticket for inspection – ah – here it is. But this isn't tolerable. This is not to be borne.'

He swung himself down from the bus, crossed the pavement, entered a building and took his place at the committee table just as a timid secretary polished her pince-nez and began to read the minutes of the last meeting.

§ 4

Committee meetings do not drown sorrow, but they can sometimes prevent sorrow from drowning its victims. Roger's pain was not mitigated by the state of his engagement book, but the necessity for constant action strengthened his endurance. He could not think continually of Eleanor when he was rushing from the church to care-committees, from boys' classes to funerals, from baptisms to swimming classes and bazaars. For nearly a month he drove himself forward on a self-imposed routine of work which aroused Father Lasseter to faint protests.

'You need not think you have to bear the whole burden of the shortage of clergymen on your own shoulders, my dear boy.'

'I don't,' laughed Roger. But when he heard of the demand for an assistant at Saint Saviour's, Bermondsey, he told Father Lasseter of his desire to make the transfer.

'Graves is a noted slave-driver.'

'I know. I think that just at the moment I want to be slave-driven.'

'Well – go if you must. These phases pass. I suppose you don't feel like telling me what's wrong.'

'There's nothing wrong that time and a little diversion of interest won't put right.'

'You'll get diversion of interest in Bermondsey. But there's no need to kill yourself.'

'I shan't. I'm extremely fit. Don't I look it?'

'You look as if you were heading for a nervous breakdown.'

'Nonsense, sir. I'm going to make my team win the London Junior Diving Cup. You can't associate that ambition with nervous breakdowns.'

They had both laughed, and Roger left the older man somewhat comforted.

He did not, however, forget the business which had taken him to Lucretia Road. He had gone twice to the offices of the Christian Cinema Company, and after another interview with Caroline and one with Johnson had decided that there was only one chance of salvaging Eleanor's money. If the Tona Perfecta Film was all that Johnson and Macafee claimed, it was just possible that somebody interested in the film business might think it worth financing. Then at least Eleanor would perhaps get her capital back.

It was then that Roger rang up D'Aynecourt. D'Aynecourt had been at college with him and an erratic friendship survived between the two men on the basis of an amiable incompatibility of interests. D'Aynecourt lived in Paris and Chelsea, wrote intellectual film criticism and pursued as a hobby the wholly disinterested amusement of deciphering the more scandalous riddles of film finance. He always knew whose money supported which film and why, and recounted the reasons with sardonic amusement.

To D'Aynecourt's rooms in Cheyne Row Roger went with his tale of the Christian Cinema Company, and in a spirit of malicious benevolence, D'Aynecourt at once produced his Big Financier.

'Simon L. Brooks is the man you ought to see. He's behind God knows how many companies. But, mark you, my friend, he's no philanthropist. If, as you say, there's stuff in this Scottish genius, he'll probably buy him out of your crazy company, which will then be able to die peacefully, which would be, I imagine, its happiest end. If not –' D'Aynecourt shrugged his shoulders.

It appeared that the great man was in England at the moment. It appeared that D'Aynecourt was to meet him.

'I'll see what I can do. Well, well. How are you, when you're not attempting to reform the British Cinema? You look slightly fatigued. Have you gone over to Rome yet? Or are you still satisfied with the guidance of Sir William Joynson-Hicks, Bart., Defender of the Faith?'

'God forbid,' said Roger.

But he went back to the clergy house elated and expectant. It would really be rather exhilarating if he – the comic curate, the not-quite-real-man, could produce the financial god from the machine and save the company. He wanted to show Eleanor that he was not wholly without influence.

But the days passed and he heard no more from D'Aynecourt. Then, suddenly, that casual young man rang up to say that he had seen Brooks, that Brooks was quite amused, and that if he had time he might ring up on Monday night and ask Mortimer to take him down to see Macafee and the film.

Roger had a Boy Scouts' class at half-past eight on Monday evening, but he rang up and found a deputy. He refused to sacrifice the entertainment of escorting Simon L. Brooks out to Macafee's laboratory. Johnson's casual remark, that Miss de la Roux spent most of her spare time down there now, lit in him a faint hope that he might see her also. He did not know if he wanted to see Eleanor, but an entirely human and rather disgraceful sentiment made him anxious that she should see him visiting the laboratory as the escort of Brooks and D'Aynecourt.

'I'll larn her. I'll larn her,' swore he to himself as he fumbled among black clerical coats on the peg in the bleak passage. The wind howled through the bare hall. It was a wild evening.

Roger went out on to the steps and waited for the car which was to convey them all out to Annerley. The wind had torn the clouds to ribbons and scattered the earlier rain. It caught Roger's coat and whipped his face as he stood bare-headed, waiting.

'The Lord answered Job out of the whirlwind,' thought Roger. 'Where wast thou when I laid the foundations of the earth? Declare, if thou hast understanding! Well, it's a good whirlwind. But will the Lord answer me?'

A great car droned and purred up to the door. Roger went down and saw D'Aynecourt sitting with a large, spectacled personage, so amazingly like Roger's imaginary conception of film magnates that it was all he could do to keep from laughing during D'Aynecourt's laconic introduction in the little lighted saloon of the Rolls Royce. Mr. Simon L. Brooks drove at night with his car lit and its blinds down so that he was enclosed in a small and secret conference chamber like a ship's cabin, spinning through the rapids of the London traffic. He had an appearance of owlish benevolence. The eyes behind his horn-rimmed spectacles were kind rather than keen, and instead of questioning Roger about the company he told ribald tales with inexhaustible fluency and enjoyment. Roger listened half-heartedly, disturbed by the thought of Macafee's perversity, which might easily lead him to choose this evening to keep away from the laboratory. To his immense relief his sight of the battered hoardings screening the Chemical Works from the road was followed by a shaft of light from the uncurtained windows of the laboratory itself.

'It looks as though he were here all right. You'll have to leave the car outside, I'm afraid.' He found himself looking for Eleanor's Clyno, but no other car was there. Simon Brooks's light-grey spats twinkled on the pavement. 'I'm afraid you'll find it muddy inside,' Roger warned him. 'There's a sort of field to cross.'

'Is there?' Simon Brooks looked meditatively through the

gap in the hoarding. 'I feel like a bootlegger. Huh? Better take these off, eh?' he asked, indicating his spats.

'If you don't want them ruined,' said Roger gravely, and was thankful that D'Aynecourt's face was in the shadow when the great man leaned against the door of the car and with splendid absence of embarrassment tore off first one spat and then the other, and tossed them on to the seat.

'That's better. Huh? Come along, then. You'd better lead the way, Mr. Mortimer. Expect us when you see us,' he told his chauffeur. 'But if we're not back in about two hours, come to look for my dead body – with a gun.'

The wind was wilder than ever. It rattled and creaked in the crazy hoardings. It buffeted Roger as he pushed his way across the uneven ground, stumbling over broken pottery, and squelching into puddles. The land round the factory reminded him of France in war time, and his old phobia of treading on a decomposing corpse returned to him. Simon L. Brooks swore jovially behind him, and Roger strained his ears through the wind to hear, for though debarred from overt profanity by his cloth, he prided himself that his temperance was not due to poverty of diction, and appreciated opportunities of enriching his potential vocabulary.

But what a wind! Shut up in the Rolls Royce, Roger had failed to appreciate its ferocity, Here it swooped down on him, snatched at his hat and made his scarf a whip for his face. The factory itself seemed in the last stage of dilapidation. The wonder was that those high unsupported walls stood the strain of such assault.

'I don't think I envy Macafee his home to-night,' thought Roger, and turned to encourage the profane but pleasant Mr. Brooks.

Locating Macafee's light from across the field was one matter; finding his door in the darkness was another. Roger groped his way over piles of fallen masonry, and bruised his knuckles against several yards of wall before at last he knocked on what seemed to be a door. At first there was no response, but a gleam of light reassured him. He knocked, and finally kicked to save his knuckles, summoning his gently blaspheming companions. But at last the door opened, and Macafee, more rumpled, dusty and shock-headed than ever, stood before them, blinking through tinted spectacles. Stammering a little, but very conciliatory and polite, Roger introduced Brooks and D'Aynecourt, and followed them into the laboratory. Then, down the long lighted room, he saw the smooth brown head of Eleanor de la Roux, bent over a gas-jet in which she held a bubbling tube.

A stormy gust of emotion shook Roger. Joy, tenderness, dismay and anger broke down his valiant defences of irony and amusement. His benevolent patronage of Macafee was swept away in a gust of jealousy. So this was how she spent her evenings. This was where she came every night after her work at the Business College. This was the new hobby which had supplanted her enthusiasm for the I.L.P. There she sat, serenely indifferent alike to his anguish and to the possibilities of Simon L. Brooks, watching a vivid blue liquid which bubbled in her tube and noting on a slip of paper its reactions.

How was it, thought Roger, that ability to laugh at oneself proved so poor an armour against pain? He could see perfectly well the comic element in his distress. He saw how neatly he had conspired with fate to serve his rival. He had taken all this trouble to impress Eleanor, and had only succeeded in helping the detestable Macafee. Yet his appreciation of the comedy could not ease the torment of his mind.

His experiment, however, was succeeding. Mr. Brooks was accustomed to touchy and difficult young inventors, and apart from his financial ability, he really understood the technical possibilities of the cinema. Macafee discovered at once his capacity, and respected it. It was a relief to him to talk to a man who spoke his own language. He unbent and grew almost eloquent and obliging, explaining diagrams and chemical formulæ. When Brooks suggested a brief demonstration, he lifted his voice and called to his temporary assistant.

'Eleanor. Hi, Eleanor!'

Roger started. So it had gone as far as this. He called her Eleanor as though she were his maid, his chattel, his mistress. 'Absurd, absurd,' he told his raging temper. 'They are working together. He is an uncouth mannerless creature. He calls her by the name that comes quickest and easiest to him.'

He watched her adjusting the lights and setting up the apparatus. She was nimble, intelligent and quiet, intent on her job.

'Thou shalt not covet thy neighbour's house, thou shalt not covet thy neighbour's wife, nor his manservant, nor his maidservant, nor his ox, nor his ass,' thought Roger. But the commandment does not forbid one to covet that which is not yet one's neighbour's. It leaves the way open for free competition.

Eleanor turned down the lights. Roger found himself standing beside D'Aynecourt and Brooks, facing a softly luminous screen, tinted with pale ochre. Macafee's voice spoke from the shadows. 'In order to make a test film I made use of the Western Syndicate's studios in Hertfordshire, and simply took on the Tona Perfecta one of the settings of a talkie, simultaneously with theirs. This is the ordinary Western Syndicate Film.'

Roger had never been to the talkies, and he was astounded by the volume of brazen noise which emerged from the loudspeaker below the quivering screen. He was amused to see that Macafee, with his concentration upon technical problems and his contempt for artistic values, had been lured by an impish providence to choose for his test film a comedy scene of triumphant vulgarity. For the blaring syncopation of the music was followed by a vision of Bathing Beauties, splashing through synthetic shallows towards a rocking, if deceptive, fisherman's cobble. Their squeals of ecstatic discomfort, as they dashed into the cold water, broke like the notes of a high-powered saxophone through the orchestral accompaniment; but the music slowly died away to allow the dialogue to sound above the soft whirring of the apparatus.

'You will notice that there is no sense of inevitability about the relationship between the sound and the picture,' said Macafee. 'The speech might perfectly well not be speech by the people you see on the screen.'

The Scotchman was quite sure of himself here, thought Roger, and not at all ridiculous. Supposing that he had really done a good piece of work, was not Eleanor justified in admiring him? Was she not right to place herself on the side of technical progress? Was it not just in this control by man over his material environment that the triumph of the twentieth century lay? And was she not a woman of her age?

'She wants to master one kind of technical achievement,' Roger told himself, 'and to force herself into the competitive business world. She believes in power, money and efficiency. She believes that women and Socialists both suffer from lack of these things. They enjoy being victims instead of masters, and she disapproves of the enjoyment.'

The film danced and cackled in front of him. Suddenly Macafee switched it off and turned on the lights.

'I'm going to put on the Tona Perfecta. I shall use the same sound producers. I want you to notice the difference in synchronization.'

'Quite,' said Mr. Brooks. 'I get you. May we smoke?'

Eleanor came quietly forward with a saucer for an ash-tray, returning immediately to her place beside the instrument. Mr. Brooks watched her quiet movements.

'That's a smart girl you've got.'

'She will be when I've done with her. I've only had her a month and that for half-time. She's all right.'

From Macafee that was glowing praise, but Roger loathed the possessive patronage of his voice.

The lights went down again, and Roger found himself watching the same girls splashing and screeching through the same water. But this time, it was true, there was a difference. The photography was clearer and softer. The sunlight on the water gave an astonishing impression of vivacity. The sounds came with perfect accuracy as part of the picture. It seemed as though the girls really uttered their futile words, and the water really splashed about their feet.

'This is good work,' he thought. 'The man's clever, damn him; the man's clever.' He contrasted Macafee's mastery of his technique with his own halting incompetence as a

156

preacher, and the sick weight of depression settled upon his body till it became an aching physical discomfort.

But the demonstration ended, the lights went up, and Macafee talked again to the great man, while D'Aynecourt, supercilious and amused, wandered about the laboratory. Roger found Eleanor at his side. Her smooth hair was a little rumpled, and a smudge of oil had found its way on to her hot cheek.

'What do you think? Do you think it's good? Do you think he'll do anything?'

'I don't know. I'm no expert in these things. I don't know how good the Western Syndicate Film is supposed to be. Macafee's is certainly better. Do you want Brooks to like it?'

'Frightfully,' said Eleanor. 'When I talked to you the other day, in that restaurant at Earl's Court, you remember, after we met here for the first time, I told you I didn't much care. But since I came to work here, I feel enormously interested in the whole business and the Tona Perfecta's nothing to the new colour film we're making.'

She was a new creature, Roger thought. The self-interested Macafee had given her something that he, Roger, for all his love and anguish and solicitude, could never give.

'I believe that this is the thing I've been wanting,' she continued. 'Of course, I want to go in on the business, not the technical side of the film industry, but I must know something about processes first. I've got schemes for whole-sale manufacture of our improvement of the Van Dorn Kelley Pryzma films at astonishingly low rates. I do wish I'd learned more about optics. Oh – look – there's Hugh got on to his colour work. I do believe, I do believe your Mr. Brooks is interested. You know, the colour film is going to be *the* thing. It is indeed. I wish it were ready to show. How long is Brooks staying in England?'

'For another ten days, I think.'

'Oh, he must. Wouldn't it be gorgeous, gorgeous, if he really took up Hugh and gave him a free hand, and I got in sideways somehow? Wouldn't it be great?'

Roger looked down at her flushed happy face. He could

157

not do less than wish that her own wishes might be fulfilled.

'Yes,' he said, trying to believe he meant it. 'It would be
great.'

§ 5

Eleanor was right. Brooks was far more impressed by the
possibilities of the colour film than by the Tona Perfecta,
and Roger gradually realized that the outcome of this visit
might be very different from his intention. Brooks might
refuse to take any interest in the Tona Perfecta, and the
Christian Cinema Company would still be left with that
doubtful and unrealizable asset; but he might very easily
make some sort of offer for the uncompleted colour film. He
might persuade Macafee to return to California with him,
and Eleanor, who was clearly doing her best to persuade the
great man to accept her as an indispensable part of Macafee's equipment, might be snatched away by Brooks to
another continent.

'The best thing that can happen, of course,' Roger told
himself. But his heart and his nerves refused to respond to
the dictation of his reason. He stood just outside the group,
feeling ridiculously alien and unwanted. Nobody seemed to
remember that it was due to his initiative that Brooks had
ever heard of Macafee.

But at last D'Aynecourt and Brooks began to move.

It was arranged that Macafee should give Brooks a chance
to see the colour film directly it was ready for demonstration.

'Can we give you a lift, Miss . . . er . . .?' murmured
D'Aynecourt dutifully. He really disliked young women of
Eleanor's type, who became so much interested in light-
refractions and complementary colour-values that they
forgot the obligation of their sex to charm. 'Chemistry is
an unwholesome pursuit for a woman,' he murmured to
Roger.

'I've got to stay and help clear up and do one or two odd
chores, thanks,' said Eleanor. 'I'm all right. I always get
myself home.'

'May we have the pleasure of your company again, sir?'
Brooks asked Roger.

'Thanks. I'm seeing Miss de la Roux home.' Yes, by God, Roger told himself. Nobody shall deprive me of that half-hour's sweet torment.

The storm seemed fiercer than ever when Brooks and D'Aynecourt left the laboratory. While Roger waited for Macafee and Eleanor to put away the apparatus, he heard the wind whistling round the room. Once or twice there was a splintering clatter as slates fell, or as the broken fragments of glass still left in the gaping windows of the main building rattled down. He felt angry and depressed, resenting their indifference to his presence.

But Eleanor was ready at last, buttoning herself into her tweed overcoat.

'You've got a smudge on your nose,' observed Macafee.

'Thanks. Where? Here?'

'No. Here.' He took her handkerchief from her and rubbed her face with the rough familiarity of a brother.

'Damn him. Damn him. Well, in any case, I've got her now. For half an hour,' reflected Roger.

'Are you ready, Miss de la Roux?' he said aloud.

It took all his strength to push the door open. The wind howling through the factory slammed it behind them, and they stood in the darkness of the ruin. Blinking until he grew accustomed to this plunge from vivid light, Roger saw the jagged angles of masonry reared against the sky. Tattered wisps of cloud-like shreds of smoke blew across the stars. The crazy flapping of an old poster, partly torn away from the brickwork, made the wind visible. The whole bare building groaned and whined in travail. Slates clattered down. Gusts shook the straining walls. Right over the laboratory behind them swung the black menace of the tallest wall. Five stories high, with the supporting floors removed, it overhung the squat solidity of the one habitable room.

Dragging Eleanor away from this wall Roger turned and faced it. Even now it seemed to totter in the wind that blew its towering mass towards the laboratory.

'That doesn't look very safe,' he shouted. 'I think if you'll go out to the road, I'll speak to Macafee.'

He started back towards the laboratory. The wind buffeted the high wall in front of him, each successive gust striking on it like waves over a ship. It seemed probable to Roger that at any moment the whole mass might go down, crashing through the laboratory roof, on top of Macafee and all his cameras, perforators, projectors and loud-speakers.

The door stuck. Roger tugged at it desperately, but when he opened it he saw the young Scotsman standing in front of a large chest, rolling up papers covered with coloured diagrams.

'Hullo. You back?' remarked Macafee quite genially. 'Come and look at these – you didn't see them, did you? These are my improvements on the Pryzma film. Now, you see, in Van Dorn Kelley's work the negative film consists of successive pairs of identical images. . . .'

'Look here, Macafee,' gasped Roger, 'I think you'll have to get out of here. That old wall seems a bit shaky.'

'Oh, that's been shaky for a long time. You see, what I've done is to replace the "flash" exposure of the positive film. . . .'

'Yes, but you'd better just come and have a look.' Roger was acutely conscious of their danger. The laboratory gaped in front of him like a huge white trap. He felt the egg-shell fragility of the roof and the merciless mass of brickwork overhanging it. 'The wind's terrific.'

Accumulating exasperation maddened him. He saw himself shut into that trap with Macafee. He saw the inevitable buckling in of the laths, the crumbling avalanche of plaster, the final overwhelming ruin. So vivid was his consciousness of their danger that he involuntarily ducked his head. Yet he knew that while Macafee stood there, he could not save himself.

'Damn you, man,' he cried suddenly. 'Don't be a blasted fool. Do you want to be killed?'

Macafee looked up at him with supercilious amusement.

'Tut-tut-tut and you a clergyman. You'd better run away if you're frightened.'

But at that moment the driving hurricane detached an already-loosened brick from the masonry above. It crashed through the laboratory roof, falling on to the sink where recently Eleanor had been working.

'You see –' cried Roger, so anxious to prove his point to Macafee that he would almost have welcomed a complete catastrophe, if only the inventor would acknowledge himself in the wrong.

'Eh, well,' said Macafee, and maddeningly cool strolled across the room. They could hardly push the door open between them, but once it was open, it stuck against some obstruction outside, and through the open doorway, Eleanor was blown into the room.

'Hullo,' she cried. 'Are you two coming out? I really don't think it's safe in here, Hugh.'

'Go away. Get out of here at once, please,' cried Roger, beside himself with anxiety for her and fear and anger.

But Hugh calmly pushed his way through the door, looked at the threatening wall, and returned shrugging his shoulders.

'I'm afraid it does look a bit groggy. I know what we shall have to do. We'd better take out that chest with the reels and diagrams. We three ought to be able to move it.'

'Oh, but you can't.' Roger was about to protest, but Eleanor was already tugging at the bulky wooden cupboard into which Macafee had been thrusting his papers and specimen reels.

It was monstrous. It was inhuman. It was a nightmare of wanton horror, that Macafee should let her run that risk, when at any minute the wall might fall in on her.

The sweat started on Roger's forehead; he hurled himself at the cupboard, meaning at first to seize Eleanor in his arms and carry her off out of danger; but he realized that this was impossible. She would struggle and fight, and in the end more time would be wasted. He could do nothing but snatch at one corner of the cupboard and take his share in pushing the heavy thing towards the door.

Every second seemed like an hour. The chest stuck against the corner of a sink. Macafee, smaller and less muscular than Roger, stumbled once, and once caught his leg between the cupboard and a fixed table. They knocked over a tripod, and the crash made Roger start so violently that he almost let go his hold. He was conscious of Eleanor beside him, pushing and tugging like a small pony, completely unafraid.

The more they pushed, the farther the door seemed to recede from them. Roger found himself starting to pray instinctively that they might reach the door – only the door – alive. But his disdain for instinctive prayers of panic checked him. He would not, even for Eleanor's sake, fall into that abasement of spirit. He bent down and caught the weight of the cupboard more securely in his straining arms and stepped forward. With almost the entire burden of it leaning against his chest, he lifted the thing across the threshold and they went through.

They had still to cross the dark uneven floor of the factory, to stumble over fallen masonry, old wheels and bricks, but once outside the laboratory itself, the nightmare ended. On the waste land beyond the factory walls, they set their burden down in the mud and stretched their aching arms.

'Now which next?' asked Eleanor. 'Hadn't we better get the cameras?'

'You're not going back,' Roger stated.

'Why not? Come on, while the lull lasts. We'll all go and grab something,' she answered, darting off towards the building.

'Stop! Eleanor! Eleanor! Stop,' cried Roger, stumbling after her through the darkness and calling frantically as he ran. There is in the act of calling a sort of desperate pathos, which in itself augments desire. In his childhood, lying alone at night, Roger had sometimes started, out of a cold-blooded devilry, to summon his nurse or mother up to the nursery. But as he called the sound of his own voice, impotent and wild in the darkness, filled him with panic, until he was driven to real hysteria by the fears he feigned. So now, calling for Eleanor through the black wind, he found himself stricken by agonized and childish terror. The broken walls crouched like monsters waiting to pounce upon her. The wind buffeted him; a pile of rubbish tripped him and drove him on to his knees, scraping his skin through his thin clerical trousers.

'Eleanor! Eleanor!'

This was the nightmare of his childhood. He wanted to wake up and find himself in the lighted streets, with Eleanor safe beside him.

'Eleanor! Eleanor!'

He was near the laboratory wall again, groping his way along the wall. He found her tugging impatiently at the door. But the displacement of the wall had already pinned it. It would not open, though she set her foot against a fallen brick and pulled valiantly.

'Eleanor. Come away. Come away, you little fool.'

He tried to wrench her hands from the knob, and she, furious at his interference, turned round on him.

'Let go. Damn you – let go.'

Then, when he seized her by the arms and with a quick schoolboy trick snatched her away, she shouted, 'Get away – even if you're afraid for yourself. Let Hugh and me get in.'

But at that moment there was a new sound above the creaking of the brickwork and howling of the wind. Like the crack of a whip, the dry mortar let go its hold, and for a moment it seemed as though all the darkness before them stirred and shifted. It was such an extraordinary sight that Eleanor stood gaping, watching the black night move in front of her eyes. Then with an unexpected blow, Roger sprang on her and pushed her roughly to the ground, himself spread-eagled on top of her, sheltering her struggling, kicking body below his own, as with a thunderous roar, the wall went down in front of them.

It had, of course, fallen away from them on top of the laboratory, but a few odd bricks dropped into the factory, one hitting Roger on the ankle. They lay quite still, their mouths full of dust. The roaring seemed to continue for about half an hour, though really it only lasted a few seconds. It was followed by a complete and terrifying silence.

Then, very cautiously, Roger began to move. Eleanor, surprised and indignant, still squirmed with reassuring vigour underneath him. The dust was settling, and the wind, as though thankful to rest for a minute after its unprecedented triumph, held its breath.

'Are you all right? Did I hurt you? I do apologize,' cried Roger, helping Eleanor to her feet.

'My mouth's full. I know now what it is to bite the dust,' coughed Eleanor. 'I suppose it was the only thing to do. Oh, poor Hugh! Do you think it's smashed everything?'

As the dust settled, another and much lower profile of wall was arranging itself against the clear star-spangled sky. Roger looked round, coughing and blinking.

'We must get out of here. Before anything else – ugh!' For he stepped on to the ankle that the brick had hit, and found it gave way beneath his weight. He would have fallen if Eleanor had not seized his arm.

'What's the matter?'

'I think something hit my foot. I'm quite all right. You go on. I'll follow.'

'Nonsense. We'll go together. Lean on me.' Anything seemed better than remaining in that place; he limped forward, leaning on her arm. They found Macafee staring ruefully at the ruin.

'I'm terribly sorry. The wall's gone,' said Eleanor. 'Oh, Hugh, you mustn't go back there. It's no use. You can't see anything in this darkness, and you can't save anything if you could. And it's not safe.'

It certainly was not safe, and though they all felt rather stupid standing there in the wind, there was clearly nothing else to do.

'Well, what do we do next?' asked Eleanor.

Roger pulled out his watch, but it was too dark to see and he had no matches.

'Well, we'd better get out of here, anyway. I suppose the next thing to do is to tell the police.'

'Police?'

'Well, isn't that what you do when a building falls in?'

He started hobbling towards the street. The pain in his foot had subsided, so that when he stepped on it he could feel nothing but a dull pain from the knee downwards. Macafee and Eleanor walked one on each side of him.

It was curious to come out into the placid normality of the lighted street. What with the noise of the wind, and the

164

isolation of the old chemical works, nobody in Annerley appeared to have noticed that the gale had blown down a whole huge factory wall. All that noisy tumult and drama had not disturbed a single citizen.

Under a street lamp, Eleanor, Hugh and Roger looked at each other. All three were covered with mud, and brown as gypsies with brick dust, from which their red-rimmed eyes blinked foolishly.

Roger found himself suddenly obliged to sit down on the pavement with his back against the lamp-post. His ankle had begun to hurt intolerably, yet he felt elated rather than distressed.

It was at this moment that two policemen, rolling along with the majestic dignity of their profession, came upon the trio.

'Hullo. Hullo! What's this? What's this?' they asked.

Roger, remembering the responsibility of his cloth, sat up and tried to brush some of the dust out of his eyes, but he was covered with mud, he had lost his hat, and his clerical collar, having come unfastened, stood upright behind one ear.

'Ah, a very opportune arrival, sergeant,' he began in his formal Oxfordish voice. 'We were about to seek your aid. There has been a slight accident.'

Then, suddenly, Eleanor saw the absurdity of his pompous manner, and began to laugh, and Roger, though he had not felt amused until that moment, burst out laughing too, and rocked helplessly against the lamp-post.

'Come, come,' said the policeman, turning to Macafee as the one apparently sober member of the trio. 'We can't have this here, sir. You'd better tell me what's happened.'

'He's not drunk,' the Scotsman declared gruffly, 'he's hurt his foot. There's been an accident. The wind's blown in my factory wall. We were coming to report it.'

Macafee's sobriety was more convincing than Roger's laughter, but the policemen were still a little incredulous until Eleanor and Macafee escorted the fatter one through the gap in the hoarding and showed him the ragged outline of the factory. After that final gust, the wind was quieter. In the street they hardly noticed it. Convinced at last, the

165

policemen became helpful and almost animated. They took down pages of particulars from Macafee, and offered to look at Roger's crushed foot. At first he was reluctant, feeling shy in front of Eleanor, but when she brushed aside his scruples as nonsense, and herself got down on her knees to remove his boot, he at once preferred the attentions of the police, and in order to get rid of Eleanor, suggested that she and Hugh should go in search of a taxi.

The policemen, glad of a little distraction from their dull night promenade, and anxious to display their skill in first aid, inspected Roger's foot, and pronounced it to be nastily bruised.

'In fact, I shouldn't wonder if there isn't a bit of something broken here,' said one of them, sending little jets of pain up Roger's leg.

'No, I shouldn't wonder, either,' agreed Roger amiably. 'Well, we'd all better go home.'

But by the time Eleanor returned with a taxi he had been able to picture the housekeeper's dismay at finding an invalid on her hands in the Clergy House, and consented readily enough to be taken to the local hospital. He wanted Eleanor to go back to her club, but she declared herself to be wide awake. So in the end it was agreed that Macafee with one policeman should go to report upon the damaged factory, while the other escorted Roger and Eleanor to the hospital.

'Of course, it's perfectly absurd, going to hospital for a bruised ankle,' argued Roger in the taxi, 'but if one's going to be a nuisance at all, I suppose one is better there. In any case, a hospital seems the proper and artistic conclusion to such an evening.'

'What an evening!' Eleanor said. Roger could imagine to himself in the darkness how her eyes shone, and how her cheeks were bright with excitement. 'Oh, what an evening! But poor Hugh! I can't bear to think of all his lovely cameras and projectors smashed.'

'Well, we did save the films,' Roger consoled her.

They drifted into silence, as the taxi bumped and rattled down the gusty streets. At the main entrance of the hospital the policeman left them to go in search of the night-porter.

Roger, a little beyond himself with pain and shock and excitement, turned to Eleanor. Suddenly it seemed to him as though all the evening's events fell into their proper place. He felt tremendously confident and happy.

'I want to apologize for the way I behaved in the factory. I was grossly rude. But I was frightened for you,' he began in a polite conversational voice.

'It was perfectly all right – rather funny really. I suppose you saved my life. I'm very grateful.'

'You needn't be. You know, of course, I love you.'

'You what?'

'I love you. I don't want to bother you about it, but it may explain a little why I was so savage when I was afraid you might be killed.'

'Oh,' said Eleanor very softly. 'Oh.'

'I had not really meant to tell you,' he continued with conversational equanimity. 'But it occurred to me that no other explanation of my conduct was rational, and really there is no reason why you should not know. I mean, you see, loving a person puts one under a definite obligation to them. I have got so much happiness from simply knowing that you are in the world, that I naturally should be glad to have any chance of repaying it. Of course, I realize that this can mean nothing to you,' he went on, arguing with a sort of fierce good humour. 'But sometimes it might be convenient to know that there is somebody in the world who would give all he possesses for the chance of serving you. I'm not suggesting that there *is* anything I can do. But just in case.'

'Oh – er – thank you,' she said flatly.

'It's very good of you to bother with me. Now I promise not to refer again to this unless you choose. And now ought you really to be waiting here? You must be frightfully tired?'

'Oh, I'm perfectly all right. I wouldn't have missed it all for anything – the wind, I mean. But I see our friend the policeman coming back with a whole retinue of stretcher-bearers and whatnots.'

'Good. Excellent. Oh, by the way, if you happen to be seeing Miss Denton-Smyth within a day or two, would you be so awfully good as to tell her why I can't go round to-morrow? I think she was expecting me.'

'But, of course, she'll have to hear about all this. She'll probably come rushing round to see whether you're still alive. She thinks the world of you, you know. Poor Caroline!'

Chapter 6 : *Clifton Roderick Johnson*

§ 1

EARLIER that same evening Clifton Roderick Johnson, proprietor, manager, secretary, tutor and director-of-studies to the Anglo-American School of Scenario Writing, led his four pupils to the window of his Essex Street Office and bade them contemplate the view to their left.

'There,' he boomed, thrusting his vast head and shoulders through the window and gesticulating towards Essex Stairs. 'There's a bit of old London. That's Romance. That's Beauty.' He withdrew his body and one by one the clerk from Islington, the maiden lady from a Bayswater boarding-house, the retired jeweller from Streatham and the young woman from Barnes, who wanted to be like Pola Negri, strained their necks to look upon Romance and Beauty, then followed him back to their table. This was the Tutorial Class in Scenario Suggestion, Course II, a class which Mr. Johnson gave his pupils to understand was the most subtly advanced and select of all his classes, a class at which He Himself presided, and to which only his most promising pupils were admitted. The Chosen Four, who sat gaping at the deal table covered with apple-green casement cloth and ink splashes, thought that they were the star students chosen from a clientele of some hundreds, who in a larger, ruder, less eclectic hall heard words of wisdom from Mr. Johnson's Staff. They did not know, and indeed it is only fair to add that at the moment Mr. Johnson hardly remembered, that they were the sole pupils whose fees of six guineas, cash in advance, had been paid into the school account. They did not know, and indeed Mr. Johnson hardly knew, that their lecturer who spoke so confidently of technique, cuts, drama and royalties had himself been

169

able to sell for performance only one scenario and a set of captions.

Johnson was certainly feeling good that evening. Ideas flooded his mind so fast that they almost choked him, and the four pupils had no sense that they were being defrauded of their money's worth.

'Write down in your note-books, and engrave upon your memories,' roared Johnson, 'that you should never waste a good view. Every view looks picturesque from some angle. The dullest life gives scope for spot-lights somewhere. Bearing that in mind, let's turn to the Home Exercise. Got that view of the Essex Stairs in your heads? Right. Fire away. Design five different scenes suitable for

    (*a*) Silent films

    (*b*) Talking films

    (*c*) Colour – talking films

against the background of the Essex Stairs – making use of

    (*a*) The movement up and down the stairs

    (*b*) The teashop door half-way up the stairs

    (*c*) The view of the Embankment from the stairs

    (*d*) The busy life of Essex Street at the top. Think of Essex Street – movement – traffic – City life – street musicians – proximity to Fleet Street – Press – Strand – Law Courts – Temple – Business Offices. Then think of the Embankment – River – Romance – Roaming – London the biggest Port in the World – Gateway to the unknown – New London – Old London. Now think of different moods for a scenario.

    (*a*) Comedy – light – spring – love – pathos – human – sentiment. An April shower – primroses or violets sold on the pavement – a girl runs to shelter under Essex arch. The young man shelters too.

    (*b*) Farce – a chase – fat Jew hawker – absconding up and down the steps – cars parked by embankment gardens – motor-cycle – try to ride cycle down the stairs – fat woman at bottom selling toy ducks.

    (*c*) Tragedy – hero leaving the Law Courts – disgraced alone – all lost – river suggests flight – suicide – peace – between the indifferent hustle of the Strand an' the eternal peace of the river –

That no lives live for peace
That dead men rise up never – er – er
That even the weariest river
    winds somewhere home – down? home to the sea.

Look it up. Look it up. Always verify your quotations –
Remember that a little verse goes a long way in sentimental
comedy, drama, or tragedy – Keep it outa crook stuff an'
farce.

(d) Historic – that's the fourth – look up history costume
stuff. What would happen on Essex Stairs? You gotta find
out how old the Stairs are – what happened there. An'
what could have happened there. Remember that film history deals with possibilities rather than facts. Local colour –
time colour. Keep it vivid. Pep it up with a bit o' farce.
Love story an' so on. Keep your love stories light, without
any *sex* in them. I'm gonna talk straight. You're not kids,
nor'm I. Man to man. The public wants good strong
human interest, but it doesn't need *Sex*. Give clean humour.
Don't mind riskin' a tear or two. What do we take the
Missus to the Movies for but to give her a good cry, eh? But
keep it *strong* an' keep it *simple*. Now send me in those
synopses before next Friday; write on one side of the paper
only an' don't forget a penny-halfpenny stamp. That's all.'
He dismissed the class with much hand-shaking and saluta-
tion. 'Well – good night – So-long – Cheerio. Good night,
Mr. Simpson. 'Night, Miss Brodie. 'Night, Miss Elloway.
'Night, Mr. Loram. *Good* night.'

The pupils snapped up their dispatch-cases. They fumbled for their umbrellas, and off they went, clattering down
the steep stone steps, chattering: 'Well, *wasn't* he good this
evening?' 'Mustn't it be *marvellous* to have all those ideas?'
Even Loram, the jeweller, with masculine restraint, con-
ceded, 'Brilliant fellow. Very. Expect we shall hear more
of him one day.' Whatever else Johnson might do for his
pupils, he certainly gave them a sense of vitality. His enormous physical gusto invigorated them. He made them feel
that life was full of exciting possibilities; he made them feel
that they were in close contact with a cultured mind.

In his search for culture and beauty, Johnson had ac-

171

quired almost every kind of outline and selection that modern publishers' advertisements could recommend. On his shelves were Outlines of History, Science, Philosophy and Religion; Literature was served up to him in the *Hundred Most Famous Stories of the World*, in the *Thirty-Seven Forms of the Plot*, and the *Dictionary of Literary Characters*. He knew the characteristics of Mr. Micawber and Paul Dombey without having read a word of Dickens. He could adorn his tales with classical allusions and paint his morals from great fiction of the Continent. All modern labour-saving devices for recognizing allusions to Cervantes, Bellerophon, Cicero and Ella Wheeler Wilcox lay at his elbow, and if in the course of his headlong gallops through history, science, literature and religion, he sometimes misplaced an island, or swept an artist or composer into the wrong century, who among his audience was to question him? And, if challenged, had he not his perfect justification?

'Dates?' said Johnson. 'What are dates? An arbitrary division of time invented for the convenience of unimaginative men. 'Smy belief that in the future you'll never stop to bother about the date of this A.D. or that B.C. If you want facts an' dates, hop along the Strand to Somerset House. You'll get 'em there. You'll get nothing else. Dead stuff, I say. Dead stuff. I give you living knowledge. I give you Beauty – The Eternal Quest. The Eternal Question. I give you the key to the Universe. Culture –'

His breast expanded to the thought of culture and his eyes glowed. He soared high on the wind of his own words. His borrowed Americanisms infected him with a Great Glad sense of Pep and Progress. He forgot the unfortunate slump in Bolivian Minerals, the return of his latest scenario from his agent, with a brief note to say that they had exhausted all possible markets, the gnawing worry of accumulating debts, and the thought that Mollie was going to have another child.

It was so like Mollie to hang always a little behind his evolution. When he met her he was floundering splendidly in the shallows of a Back to Nature Phase. He had been working on a pioneer film of the 'Covered Wagon' type, and saw himself as the strong, virile man in the sheepskin coat, accompanied by his broad-hipped, broad-bosomed woman, mother of many children. Mollie had indeed followed him with daring confidence to the experimental pioneer life in a two-roomed flatlet at Haverstock Hill and their first child arrived with flattering promptitude. Johnson invented quite fascinating theories about child psychology and infant education. But after cluttering the living room with coloured cubes and squares, intended to teach the small thing how to appreciate tone and form values, he retreated to the office in Essex Street, and finally rented the flat in Battersea. For the Haverstock Hill establishment cramped not only his educational system, which required a background of great open spaces, but also his style of thinking, since a creative artist cannot afford broken nights with a wailing child, and days wasted in nursery disorder.

It was just then that he met Delia and began to create for her a scenario of London and Paris night life, with a background of cocktail parties and orchids and fashion shows and the Croydon Aerodrome.

Delia complicated everything, for Mollie grew less and less like his ideal Soul Mate the more she fulfilled the rôle he had designed for her. Johnson began to realize the difference between the economic situation of the pioneer patriarch, enriched increasingly by each addition to his family, and the city father, whose more numerous offspring simply result in larger bills. Moreover, Delia was extravagant. The best alone was good enough for her. Johnson began to feel a little tired of her. His imagination was already turning towards a new enchantment and the thought of a long epic poem embodying the Dream Woman of the centuries.

For he had met another woman, the perfect fulfilment of all his ideals in one. Strong as a pioneer, sophisticated as a cocktail, majestic, confident, splendid and conquering, Gloria St. Denis.

Because he was feeling good after the lecture, warmed with the heady wine of his own eloquence, Johnson let his thoughts dwell upon her – her slow indifferent smile, the rich curving lines of her body, her fund of admirably chosen anecdotes. He was thinking of her when he heard a knock on the door.

173

He glanced up, suddenly a little pale, for behind his rapturous dreams lurked the smothered subconscious worry of his financial difficulties. There were so many visitors whom it might be inconvenient to receive.

He sat for a moment, wondering if the caller would go away if he kept quite still and pretended that he had left the office.

But the knock came again, and the voice of Mrs. Franley, the office cleaner, shouted: 'Mr. Johnson, Mr. Johnson!'

'Oh, come in, Mrs. Franley,' he cried, relieved. 'I've been taking a class and I'm a bit late.'

'There's a young lady to see you, Mr. Johnson. I told her it was past your hours, but she said she saw your light in the window and knew you was still here, and she won't go away.'

'The devil she won't!' thought Johnson. 'Who is it?' he asked. 'Anyone you know?'

'Not that I know of. Not one of your regulars.'

'Oh, all right, all right; if you're going down you might ask her to come up. It's probably someone come to join the school.'

But within himself he thought that it was more likely to be Delia. They had had a tiff two nights ago at Pinaldi's. He had ordered the three-shilling table d'hôte in an unwonted panic of economy, and she, with angry hauteur, had messed up the *hors d'œuvres* with her fork and declared she never saw such muck in her life. What did he take her for? A servant girl on her night out? What did he think she wanted to eat: Herring bones in oil and some vegetables saved from other people's plate-sweepings? And up she got, and into her fur coat she wriggled, and out of the building she flounced, the little devil! Johnson had been left to pay, without rancour, the bill for her uneaten dinner. It would be just like her, he thought, if she came again to-night, and nestled up to him and begged him to take her to that nice, nice restaurant where the *hors d'œuvres* were made of herring bones and all the waiters had flat feet. Well, well, he would take her if she asked him, for in a melting kittenish mood she was delicious.

But the girl who came nervously through the open door

174

was neither the petted Delia nor the splendid Gloria. She glanced with scared, red-rimmed eyes through her pince-nez, and clutched a shabby dispatch-case as though it contained the secret of the universe. She was like the thousands of girls whom Johnson saw swinging daily down to City offices on trams and buses, narrow-chested, drooping, creatures with mud-splashed stockings, unbecoming brown felt hats and deplorable coats trimmed with worn fur. She looked at Johnson as though she thought that he might swallow her.

'Mr. – Mr. Johnson?'

'At your service.' He bowed, with his theatrical exaggeration. 'And what is there that I can do for you?'

'You won't know my face,' she stammered. 'But you will know my name. It's Miss Weller. Doreen Weller.'

A faint recollection of some slight discomfort stirred at the back of his mind.

'I'm very pleased to meet you, Miss Weller. This isn't the time I generally see clients, you know, but I stayed a little late after a special tutorial class, and as you are here, you might as well tell me what I can do for you. Sit down, won't you?'

She sat, drooping and unattractive, while he tried to remember which of the stupid girls who wrote to the school from time to time she might be.

'Mr. Johnson,' she said at last, with a sort of desperate rush. 'Why don't you answer my letters?'

'Ah, letters! letters! There, my dear young lady, you unhappily hit upon one of my congenital failings. I can't answer letters. I mean to. I mean to. I compose in my head wonderful phrases to dictate to my secretary. And they just fade away. They fade away.'

'Yes, yes,' she interrupted. 'But what about my novel? What's happened to my novel?' And without warning Miss Weller dropped her face in her hands and began to cry.

He stared at her with increasing disgust, but his voice was bracing and avuncular.

'Now, now, you're tired, I expect. What's gone wrong, eh? Oh, you city girls! You city girls. It's a sin – forcing

175

the sweet flower of girlhood to fade in the dark offices. Distorting the natural function of womanhood. Now, try to pull yourself together and tell me what's the trouble.'

Who the devil was she? What the devil was she?

Miss Weller removed her pince-nez and dabbed her streaming eyes. Johnson rose from his chair by the desk and began to walk the room with a lecturer's strides, giving her time to recover her composure.

'We call it progress, ye gods: we call it progress. We force our women to do things they were never meant to do. We wrench 'em away from their sacred tasks. We waste their lives. We waste their lives. And we call it progress!'

'But, Mr. Johnson,' gulped the girl, past all concern for the welfare of her sex. 'I *must* know about my novel.'

'Well, now, Miss Weller, I confess I don't at the moment recall exactly what it is about this novel.'

He had to go carefully, for the girl might have a real grievance. She might even, disquieting thought, have a legal case.

It happened that Johnson was not only the director of the Anglo-American School of Scenario Writing. He was also proprietor of the Metropolitan and Professional Correspondence School of Journalism. This school had been for a time a lucrative little venture. Johnson ran it with the aid of a man called Osborne, a broken-down journalist, a clever man but irresponsible and an intermittent and furious drinker. The correspondence school conducted its beneficent operations along the simplest lines. Johnson inserted from time to time in various papers his characteristically ingenious advertisements. 'Every Man, Woman or Child can sell at least *One* Story, if they know how.' 'There would never have been a Mute Inglorious Milton if he had known the Metropolitan and Professional.' '*You* can make people laugh and cry and make them pay you for it.' 'Manuscripts read free.' And so on. In response to these advertisements from Bath and Huddersfield, Peebles and Penzance, came poems, short stories, essays, plays and scenarios. To each correspondent Johnson dispatched, after a suitable interval, his standardized reply. The work submitted, he declared, was hardly marketable, but it showed undoubted promise.

The one thing needed to enable the writer to produce sale-able stuff was an intensive study of his little volume, 'How to make threepence into three thousand pounds,' to be obtained from the school at the trifling price of six and six, post free. As a matter of fact, the school had been designed largely as a convenient way of turning to profit the 1,786 remainder copies of his book which Johnson had been forced under his contract with his publisher to purchase. All manuscripts sent to the school were passed on at the rate of 2s. 6d. a manuscript to Mr. Osborne who, in his capacity as Director of Studies, glanced through the MSS. and scribbled half-legible remarks along their margins. But Osborne went off one day, as he always went sooner or later, with the Lord alone knew how many MSS. in his trunk; since that time Johnson had been too much preoccupied with his urgent private affairs to do more than cash the cheques and send off the books, and toss the MSS. as they arrived into a big tin box at the Battersea flat, to be handled by Osborne's successor, whoever he might be.

Among these papers, or among the papers irretrievably lost when Osborne decamped, it appeared probable that Miss Doreen Weller's novel lay.

The situation was awkward, but not irremediable.

'You told me that if I sent you £25,' Miss Weller sobbed, 'you would make it fit for publication. That was seven months ago. I've written and written. Why don't you answer my letters? What's happened to my novel? Don't the publishers like it? Have you tried them all? Where have you sent it? Oh God!' She was working herself up to a fit of hysteria. 'It's awful,' she gulped. 'It's been awful waiting every day for the post. Listening for the flutter of letters into the box. And then never a line. Day after day. I've got to have my royalties. I've got to. Or you must give me my money back.'

'But, my dear child, you can't do things like that.'

'But you must, or I shall go to prison. I took that money. You don't understand. I took that money. It was the petty cash for the month. I thought you said . . .'

'Oh, now, now, now. You don't mean that. You don't mean that.' Good Lord! The little fool! If this were true, and hysterical girls of her type could do anything, then there would be a police-court case, with inquiries about the Metropolitan School, and his revision service, and his method of handling manuscripts. And that was not at all what he desired. His patronage turned to paternal asperity, until his questioning extracted sentence by sentence the girl's story. She was plain. She was lonely. She was misunderstood. Nobody loved her. Her sisters married right under her very nose. Her brothers laughed at her. And all the time, she knew that she was talented.

'I know here!' she cried, striking with an ink-stained hand the flat breast under her brown coat-frock. 'I know here! I wrote poetry. I wrote plays. But nobody would look at them. Then I saw your advertisement. You said, do you remember? "You can make the world laugh and cry. You can pluck a leaf from Balzac's laurels. You!" ' She did not know much about Balzac, but she starved for laurels. She saw herself rewarded, rich, acclaimed, talking eloquently at the PEN Club, dressed in night-blue velvet and pearls, a famous novelist. She saw: 'The Book of the Year – *Destinies*, by Doreen Weller.' And her picture in the paper, without her pince-nez, and her hair nicely waved.

But twenty-five pounds was enormous, grotesque, impossible. How could she get hold of twenty-five pounds? She had five pounds of her own in post-office savings certificates. She was earning 30s. a week and paying out of that 10s. towards the housekeeping expenses; 5s. went on fares, and another 5s. on lunch out and incidentals. How could she save £20, save or borrow or make it?

Then her employer sent her as usual to the bank to draw £50 for the month's petty cash. And as usual, he did not ask her how much already lay in the box. She knew. She knew that the previous month had been unusually slack, that postage and messengers and incidental expenses had fallen off, and that a cheque of £10, paid in for a special purpose, had not been used. Twenty-three pounds already lay in the cash-box. If she took out her twenty, nobody would notice until the books went to the auditors, and that was not for another seven months. And by that time she would be rich, she would be famous, she would have repaid the paltry

178

twenty pounds, ten times over if necessary, and would have left the office for ever.

It was providential; it was obvious; it was ordained of God. She sent Mr. Johnson the twenty-five pounds and sat down to await her triumph. But triumph had not come; her letters remained unanswered.

And now confronting Johnson himself, alternatively fierce and apologetic, shuddering with fear, misery and apprehension, she delivered her tremulous ultimatum.

'If you don't let me have the twenty pounds by quarter day, I shall go to the police,' she said. 'I shall give myself up. But I shall tell them about you too. I shall tell them to find out what happened to my manuscript. What if you've sold it and kept the royalties yourself?'

This fearful, yet somewhat consoling thought had only just occurred to her. She sat with wild staring eyes watching for its effect.

But Mr. Johnson only smiled at her and patted her on the shoulder. He knew now what line to take.

'You little fool. You poor little silly fool. So, driven like a trapped animal you turn and bite the hand of the only friend who can help you, eh? Now, look here, look here. If you think we've got anything to fear from the police, you just go an' tell 'em whatever you like. You just go an' confide in 'em an' tell 'em all about everything. And don't be surprised if it all works out different to what you expect. My dear girl. The Metropolitan and Professional *welcomes* auditors and police inspections. If any of our clients are dissatisfied, we *invite* them to investigate our books. 'Smy belief there's not an establishment in London or New York with a cleaner record. But never mind that. The question for the moment is you, not us. Of course, you know, my dear girl, you've done a very, very silly thing. I'm not sure if for your own sake I ought not to let justice take its own course. It would be a lesson to you – a harsh lesson, I know.

'But I'll look into the business and think about it. You'd better come and see me, now let me see – quarter day's the 25th. Come on the 23rd. 267 Battersea Park Crescent Mansions. Come about half-past eight, and I'll see what I can do. I can't bear to see a woman in the dock – butterfly on

the wheel. Woman, woman, *Femina varians*. Well, well. I'll
see what I can do.'

He dismissed her on a high note of masculine unction, and
watched her take her way down the steps, then returned to
the chair by his desk and swore. For he had not twenty
pounds in the world, and did not know at the moment
where to lay his hands on it. Yet he did not want Miss
Doreen Weller to go confessing her guilt hysterically all over
London.

<h2 style="text-align:center">§ 2</h2>

The rain poured down. After the storm of the two
previous nights, the broken clouds accumulated and spilled
themselves over London. A silvery curtain obliterated Battersea Park. Rain pricked the flat grey surface of the river.
Along the road umbrellas bobbed ridiculously.

It would rain. It would rain. Johnson thought of California on a spring morning. He thought of sunlit snow in
Canada. He thought of the glowing, stinging warmth of hot
sand on a beach washed by the Pacific. Here in London it
would rain. Hell!

He stood by his window, a dilapidated brown dressing-
gown folded round his rumpled pyjamas, stroking his
bristled chin for the sake of the odd prickling discomfort
which was more in keeping with his present mood than
smooth silkiness. His head ached. Last night he had tried
to drown his worries in cheap whisky; but like kittens they
had nine lives and would not drown.

The post had brought him nothing but further food for
melancholy. Bolivian Central Stock was down again. Rex
Buckler wrote to say that if his loan of £500 was not repaid
before the end of the month, he would take out a writ – a
nice action from a friend to a friend. And to crown everything, Mollie had written one of her querulous, long, I'm-
very-unhappy-but-I-mean-to-be-brave letters.

'Darling, I know of course you can't be expected to give
up your work just when the book is getting on so well. But
of course it is lonely here and I think little Knud misses you
too. He says "Dad, Dad!" ever so often. Darling, don't
think I'm complaining for I'm not, but it is lonely here in

the evenings and I do wonder if I'm going to feel sick right on up to the time with this one.'

Hell, what a day, what a life, what a world! And then Doreen Weller went and got herself into police-court trouble for twenty pounds, to line the pockets of that swine Osborne.

'If I ever catch that son of a . . .' Johnson exclaimed aloud, but the shrill insistence of the telephone cut short his threat. Hitching his dressing-gown round him, he went into the dark stuffy hall.

'Hullo. Hullo. Hullo, blast you. Hullo.'

'Hullo. Good morning. You do sound bright and merry,' cried a rich lazy voice.

'Gloria. My dear. An angel told you I was gonna pass right away unless something nice happened. You've rung up to tell me I can take you outa lunch.'

'Have I? I didn't know it. I really rang you up to ask you to help me.'

'Help you? Ask? Don't think of asking; just say – "Clifton Roderick Johnson, come right over here," an' I'm there.'

'Oh no, you're not. At least not at the moment. Now listen. You know Basil hasn't been a bit well lately. What? No he hasn't. And I think the only thing for him is a spell in the South of France. But he's all worried up about this Cinema Company, and Caroline's been bothering him a lot because it seems that the wind blew in that old factory roof right on top of Macafee's laboratory two nights ago, and just at this very moment a man you'll know – Brooks, his name is –'

'Brooks – not Simon L. Brooks?'

'That's the creature – well, apparently he'd just been down to the studio and taken a fancy to the Tona Perfecta or something. Anyway, life being what it is, everything seems to have happened at once, and what I wondered is whether you, being a dear, wouldn't just trot round and find what has happened and come up to-morrow night and tell us all about it, because I want Basil to keep quiet until he sails – yes – yes, he's going by boat. It's more restful. No, I'm not sure which day. I'm at Hanover Square where I work, so you can't come and see me. I'm supposed at this moment

181

to be receiving particulars of a very exclusive order from a duchess.'

'Am I a duchess?'

'You're a duchess, and you'll be a duke too if you'll hop along and see what's doing.'

She had gone. The telephone clicked and crackled, and the air was robbed of the richness of her voice. Delia? Pshaw! Mollie? Hell! There was only one woman in the world, and she could turn a wet London morning into a golden day. She was regal and human and splendid. She was colour and warmth and light. She was worth even the discomfort of turning out into that rain to discover what had happened to the Christian Cinema Company.

Johnson made no attempt to go to the School in Essex Street. Newspapers commonly demanded cash in advance for advertisements and recently he had been able to afford no insertions. Without advertisements, his clientele declined immediately. He was in debt for the rent. His letter-box would be full of bills. Life simply was not worth living if one went to an empty office to read bills on a wet March day.

Instead, he shaved and dressed and made himself a cup of coffee, and went round to the garage for his car. Half-way round he remembered, with a queer shock of relief, that the car was his no longer. There comes a time when even a long-suffering dealer takes action if his instalments are not paid.

'After all I was always scared of the darn thing,' philoso-phized Johnson, and caught a bus for Annerley. He was in a less desolate mood, because Gloria had rung him up, and because he was going to see her to-morrow night. In the bus he noticed a young girl with dark bright laughing eyes and a scarlet béret pulled down over her black curling hair, a young Jewess, ardently and charmingly alive. He contrived to share her seat, and the contact with her warm firm young body cheered him. After all, there were compensations in the world. Even the chill of the rain on his face was quite agreeable when at last he jumped down from his bus and strode along the pavement to the place where Macafee's hoarding sagged below the weight of its damp flapping posters. A policeman stood outside the hole where Macafee usually entered.

'Greetings, Pyramus,' roared Johnson. 'Where's Thisbe?'

The policeman eyed him with the tolerant impartiality of the law. So early in the morning to be merry, thought he, and an American too. What price prohibition now?

'Can't I go in?' asked Johnson. 'I want to see Mr. Macafee.'

'What paper do you represent?' asked the policeman.

'Paper? I'm a friend.'

'Ho – well – I don't know there's any harm in going *in*. But you mustn't go beyond the ropes. It's not safe. Might all come down any minute.'

'Righto. I know. Sign along the dotted line, eh? Pass, friend, all's well.' And Johnson squeezed his huge bulk through the hole in the hoarding.

He saw an odd sight. The factory itself looked merely more ruinous than ever, but round its debris a rope had been drawn, with large boards marked 'Danger' hung along it at intervals. Inside the rope were housebreakers, working cautiously at the task of removing Macafee's precious apparatus from under the fallen masonry. Beyond the rope small boys, with their strange gift of ubiquity, scuffled in the mud, watching a little knot of people grouped round one diminutive gesticulating figure.

It was Caroline, and she had at length achieved one of her life's ambitions; she had captured the ear of the London Press. When Johnson came up to her, he heard her hurrying excited voice.

'And so he worked just in the old laboratory. Yes, on the Tona Perfecta, which belongs to the Christian Cinema Company – Cinema with the *C* hard as in the Greek *K*. Yes – yes, that's *most* important – to reform the moral and æsthetic standard of the British cinema.'

The rain poured down upon her feathered hat. It dripped on to her nose, her draggled fur, the large embroidered bag in which she carried papers, keys, smelling salts, lozenges and writing-blocks. She did not notice the rain. She did not notice the mud into which her small, ill-shod feet sank slowly, until it began to trickle over the tops of her battered

183

shoes. She did not notice the covert smile of the reporters, who had rarely in all their experience come upon so odd a figure.

She was touching glory. She had told her tale to four different young men, and 'saw the fame of the Christian Cinema Company spreading from pole to pole. Glory burned in her eyes. Glory loosened her tongue. Glory lent lyrical rapture to her words.

'The Church? Yes, of course the Church is interested. Wouldn't you be interested if you saw a movement for reviving the Golden Age of Athens, the Diamond Age of the Renaissance, empurpled with the solemn pall of Christianity?'

The young men were growing bored. It was cold, and they had heard all this before. They were polite, but the old lady was obviously a little cracked and the person whom they really wanted to see was the inventor himself.

'Now this Mr. Macafee?' asked one.

The flood-gates of another stream were loosened.

'Oh, he's a *most* interesting young man with such a romantic career, a crofter's son from Scotland where I always think they have such wonderful educational opportunities.'

She was muddling it, of course. Johnson, who thought in headlines and spoke in captions, grieved over her amateurish workmanship. She had not recognized him. Her shortsighted eyes saw only one more figure augment the group before her. Johnson knew as well as she did that there are few more exhilarating experiences than that of opening one's heart to the Press. The secrecy of the Confessional contains no comfort like the publicity of the Sunday paper. Caroline was visualizing front page after front page, blazoned with the sensational story of the Christian Cinema Company. She saw herself photographed impressively against the ruins. She saw her beloved Father Mortimer hailed as the hero of an exciting rescue. She saw the faces of the Marshington Smiths, blanching with disappointment as they realized that their interest in the Company had come too late. By the time they wrote from Yorkshire asking for shares, the capital of three hundred thousand – Caroline's present estimate – would have been over-subscribed. The days of hunger and fatigue and disillusionment no longer mattered. Nothing

184

mattered except the opportunity to convert these young men and send them forth into the world as missionaries for the Christian Cinema Company.

She spoke of Father Mortimer and of how he had been injured trying to rescue Mr. Macafee's work. She spoke of Eleanor, and the part which she had played. In her excitement she flew from point to point of her story, growing less and less coherent, until the four young men began to close their note-books and shift their cameras, and hope for a moment favourable to polite departure.

Then Johnson could bear it no longer. He stepped forward into the circle and raised his broad-brimmed hat.

'Good morning, gentlemen. Good morning, Miss Denton-Smyth. My name's Johnson. Clifton Roderick Johnson – proprietor of the Anglo-American School of Scenario writing, and one of the directors of the Christian Cinema Company. Now if there are any other questions you would like to ask, without keeping this lady standing here in the rain much longer, I am at your service. I'm prepared to answer any question, any question at all, about the company, or ourselves, or the Tona Perfecta Film.'

'Well, thank you very much, sir. But I think really Miss Denton-Smyth has told us everything.' The young man from the Penge and Annerley *Observer* was due at a local wedding in twenty minutes and wanted to catch his bus. The others were glad enough to follow his example. Indignant, with the chagrin of an outraged craftsman, Johnson watched the Ear of the Press vanish from before him.

But Caroline was in no mood for sorrow. She turned to him with a radiant face.

'Oh, Mr. Johnson, wasn't it *too* wonderful? I always knew an opportunity would come. But to come just *now*, when we so much needed something to uplift us. I can't *tell* you what I felt like yesterday, when I heard that the factory had fallen in, and the laboratory was ruined and *not* insured, and poor Father Mortimer in hospital. It just seemed as though everything were at an end. And then this morning *suddenly* everything begins to move. Mr. Brooks has sent for Mr. Macafee. The Press wants the whole story. Brooks will finance us I know and the Press will give us all the advertise-

185

ment we could *possibly* want, and I am going back to the office now to get out some new circulars and deal with the correspondence.'

'Have you seen St. Denis?'

'No. Didn't you *know*? He's ill again, poor man, at least not so very seriously I hope, but he has to go abroad, that's why I'm so *very* glad you've come because what I feel is that we must all get to work, and then about the signing of the cheques, that's another thing I wanted to say. You know that Mr. St. Denis and I had to sign everything that we paid out, but may I ask if while he is away *you* would do it, because Mr. Guerdon is very good, but he does rather fuss, you know, I don't think he's really *accustomed* to business methods and doing things quickly on a big scale.'

Johnson's quick brain was investigating possibilities. The signing of cheques for other people's money always offers opportunities for private enterprise. Things, as Caroline said, were certainly moving. At any moment aid might come from some unexpected source.

'Now you just leave everything to me,' he said. 'I can handle Macafee. I'll deal with the Press. I'll just see to everything. You get right back home an' get your wet things off, for we can't let you catch cold just now.'

'Well, that is kind. I *knew* you'd help me. Really it is a comfort, because single handed the responsibility really is rather great, and I've been so worried about Father Mortimer – you know he might so easily have been *killed*, I lay awake all last night shuddering to think of those *dreadful* walls. I can't bear to look at them.'

They were walking towards the buses. The rain still danced vindictively upon the shining street and pavement, but Caroline did not care.

'How soon do you think the Press will get out our story? Will it be in the lunch-hour edition? I can hardly bear to wait to see what they say. Oh, it's *too* marvellous.'

'Well, that depends on what papers you saw. I was gonna ask. What did those young men represent?'

'Oh – how stupid of me. Of course, I ought to have asked. I took for granted. Dear me, that just shows one ought never to get excited – well, agencies I suppose. I

186

really don't know. I thought the Press – I mean, one *does* tell the others, don't they?'

'Well, I expect you'd like me just to see about that for you, wouldn't you? You leave it to me. I'll see what I can do. Can't expect the ladies to do *everything*, bear all our burdens, you know?'

He put her on to her bus, and waited until she pushed her way up to a front seat and waved at him through the window. The bus carried off her small, draggled, jubilant person, and Johnson pulled out his watch. It was twelve o'clock. He had half an hour to spare before meeting Macafee. He looked hopefully along the road for a hospitable pub, feeling that what he wanted was a drop of whisky to keep the rain out. Signing cheques. Miss Weller's twenty pounds. St. Denis going abroad. Seeing Gloria to-morrow night.

He felt that he had done a good morning's work.

§ 3

Johnson walked along Elgin Avenue in the clear March night. From Maida Vale tube station the road stretched in polished darkness between its budding plane trees. Though it was only half-past eight, the pavements were almost empty. The straight tapering road, in day-time so commonplace, was disciplined by night to cool austerity. 'Elgin Avenue,' thought Johnson, and the word Elgin brought to him the thought of the Elgin Marbles. 'Greece,' he thought, and saw himself in a cool moonlit gymnasium, watching the pallid greenish light of the moon on naked figures. The glory that was Greece. He straightened his broad back, correcting the stoop which insidiously curved his rounding shoulders. The perfect development of mind and body – freedom both physical and intellectual. He could feel the muscles in his own thighs and stomach responding involuntarily to the fine tension of his mind.

The thought of Greece brought him a strong excitement. His vision of the age of Pericles was oddly compounded from pictures by Alma Tadema, the drop-curtain at the Regina Music Hall, an illustrated edition of Kingsley's *Heroes*, Isadora Duncan's autobiography, a lantern lecture

187

on the Elgin Marbles, and the film version of *The Private Life of Helen of Troy*. But from these ingredients he had built up so vivid and detailed a dream country that he could smell the crisp thymy scent of herbs in the sunburned turf. He could feel its warm prickling surface against his body as he threw himself down after the hot sweaty bout of wrestling. In the cool pillared hall behind him, Gloria reclined beside a low semi-circular table, on which stood goblets of wine, and bowls of goats' milk, cheese, and honey, and fruit piled in ample dishes. Three Nubian slaves fanned Gloria. Johnson borrowed the slaves from the bath scene in 'Kismet,' but that did not matter. Gloria's tunic slipped from one soft milky shoulder as she held out her hand with a parsley wreath to crown him victor in the games. Oh Greece! That was the time when men could live like men, unafraid in mind or body.

The soft padding of feet behind him echoed into his dream. He turned and saw, moving in and out of the long line of plane trees, now in gold lamplight, now in faint blue moonlight, the figure of a runner. It was a figure sprung to life from the Elgin Marbles, a young man's figure, white and lithe, loping with long free strides between the plane trees. His head was up, his chest wide, his hands clenched, his lean long legs cut the darkness with a beautiful easy rhythm. He ran as a youth had run from Athens to Sparta (or was it Sparta to Athens?) bringing news of War. He ran as boys run round the wide gymnasium. He was a miracle, a sudden unforgettable beauty, an uncovenanted gift from the gods, the old Greek gods. He was a clerk from Paddington Athletic Association, hurrying home after a late training, in his running-kit.

Johnson forgot his growing paunch, his lumbering weight, his slack muscles and unhealthy skin. He forgot his muddled shiftless way of living, and his doubtful honesty. Tears stung his eyelids, as he stared along the empty road, from which the fleeting vision slowly faded.

By God, that was a sight to see. That was a man's life. That was what the body should be like. Strong, dignified, sane, alive. They knew how to live, those Greeks.

Gloria lived. By God, that was what she was like. She

188

was a Greek. Mollie was a savage, Delia a Cockney; but Gloria was a Greek. She was large and splendid and unafraid. And Basil St. Denis was leaving England.

Johnson felt extraordinarily happy and hopeful.

During the past twenty-four hours, ever since he had watched Caroline interview the reporters, he had sought the key to his new mood. And now Elgin Avenue had supplied it. His happiness lay in the Greek view of life. He must tell that to Gloria. He had so much to tell Gloria. They must go away together. They must go to Greece. Why had he never seen the Acropolis? Why had he never raced knee-deep in asphodel? Why had he never stood, like Isadora Duncan, at the door of the Panthenon? Or was it the Pantheon? – well, anyway, they must go to Greece.

He had small doubt of his success. What could a fine woman like Gloria see in a little affected rabbit like St. Denis, a weedy delicate nincompoop? Fine women needed fine men. Yes, and they got them too, by Gad.

In a high exalted humour he climbed the stairs up to the St. Denis's flat. The steps were dark, except where the worn brass edging made a faint bar of light across them. Unworthy stairs, thought Johnson. Smelling of tom-cats and perambulators. Why doesn't she live in a grander place? St. Denis is probably mean. And she earns the money too. Well, soon she could live in a worthier home. Johnson was in an opulent mood. Nothing would be too good for her if she could come to Greece.

He rang the bell. Gloria herself came to the door.

'Basil's in bed. I've given him about seventy aspirins and made him go to sleep. Come along in.'

He followed her into the warm cosy room and stood on the hearth-rug looking down at her with bright compelling eyes. She curled herself like a great lazy cat on the divan.

'Well, what's your news? Mix me a cocktail for the love of Mike, and tell me something cheerful. I feel as mouldy as a wet week-end, what with Basil ill an' London like it is, an' everything. Tell me I've come into a fortune. Tell me the Christian Cinema Company's either made or bust. I'm tired of it. I'm tired altogether.'

But she did not look tired. She looked golden and grand

and placid. Her long gown of orange velvet made a warm moving mirror for the firelight. She held out a large handsome hand for the cocktail and Johnson saw that her painted finger-nails were bright as cherries.

He was a man of action. He was a Greek.

He stood with one elbow on the mantelpiece looking down at her, telling his news in crisp staccato sentences. He never muddled his own reporting. He was the unequivocal hero of his news.

'I always told Macafee to study Hollywood. He's like all specialists. Keeps his nose in his own work. Won't look around. I don't pretend to be an engineering expert. Ideas are my job. But I knew this right enough. Of course Brooks spotted it at once. The Tona Perfecta's no more use to any company to-day than a sick headache.' Johnson had quite forgotten his own enthusiasm for the film, and Gloria had ceased to take any interest in it. 'And we've paid five hundred for it. Aren't men businesslike?' she sighed.

'Of course, that doesn't mean Macafee's no good. On the contrary I pointed out to Brooks this new colour stuff's first rate. He'll do big things, that young man – when he's learned his lesson.'

'But we've got no rights over the new stuff, have we?'

'We? Who's "we"? Now look here, Gloria, honestly. Who cares a hoot for the Christian Cinema Company? You don't. St. Denis doesn't. Isenbaum never comes near us now. All he wanted was to make himself pleasant to your husband, 'smy belief. Now, honest, wasn't it? I guess old Guerdon won't care. He's scared stiff of everything. Won't blow his own nose for fear of germs on his handkerchief. The only person who'd really give a dime for the whole damn concern is Caroline, an' she's crazy. Well, I mean, you can't keep a thing going to please Caroline, can you? An' she's got her curate.'

'Got what?'

'Oh, she's sweet on that young curate. What's his name? Mortimer. The one who got hurt in the crash. Poor old bird. One of those old-maid-sweet-on-the-parson complexes. That'll keep her happy for months. You know, we never ought to have thought we could run a business concern with her as secretary. She's about as much knowledge of business as a flea has of higher mathematics. Of course, we didn't want to be unkind, an' all that. I quite see. But it's gotta come to an end some day. An' we're only losin' money. I've been going into the books a bit. We've been payin' money to printers, lawyers, God knows what. Hadn't you better call a meetin'; pay our bills with what assets we've got, an' wind up the affair, an' start afresh?'

Even as he spoke he saw himself as the strong practical man, coming to the rescue of these stranded idealists. He lifted burdens of responsibility from Gloria. He put St. Denis to shame. His energy was like a rushing mighty wind. He swept poor Caroline out of her incongruous position in Victoria Street and set her down in a nice suitable alms-house in the country, somewhere among hollyhocks and cabbage-roses, with a thatched roof and a cat, and a kettle on the hob. He swept Gloria out of Maida Vale and set her down in Greece among wild thyme and asphodel.

Gloria acquiesced in his rhapsodies. She was not really thinking about Johnson. Her thoughts were with Basil, whom she had kept in London through a dark chill winter when he needed sun and warmth. It was her fault that he was ill again. Without the Christian Cinema Company, he would have left for Nice last October, and stayed there until the warm weather came. The whole affair had been a stupid mistake. She ought to have seen from the beginning that a company run by Caroline Denton-Smyth was inevitably absurd. She ought not to have let Basil's sense of humour run away with her sense of business values. She fell into a mood of unwonted self-dissatisfaction. Tired of London, and of the Maida Vale flat and Hanover Square, she began to wonder whether a hat-and-dress shop in the Boulevard des Moulins might not, after all, be a good investment, now that Monte Carlo was developing a summer as well as a winter season. She hardly noticed when Johnson took her hand, still talking; but when his flow of conversation stopped, as he bent to cover her fingers and wrist with kisses, she raised herself on one elbow and looked at him, amused interrogation in her eyes. He interrupted his kisses to shout at her with tumultuous exaltation.

191

'We'll go to Greece – Athens, the Parthenon.'

'Athens is an awful hole,' she said. 'All the hotels have bed-bugs and you can't get a decent cocktail.'

She was not really surprised that Johnson kissed her, for men were taken that way quite frequently, it seemed to her. Indeed, she had been kissed so often and in so many ways that his boisterous onslaught hardly interrupted her speculations about Monte Carlo, and the word Athens only fitted itself into her plans for Basil's health.

But she consented to dine with him after Basil's departure, because she would then be lonely and she felt in need of some diversion. Johnson amused her, as a bear or a sheep-dog or a bad film might amuse her. She did not even object to his clumsy and grotesque love-making. She knew how to take care of herself. She had never been fastidious, and she could amuse Basil by recounting the big man's absurdities. Her solicitous and constant affection for her husband was a sentiment untouched by any casual adventure. It was the normal attitude of her heart and mind, the pole to which the needle of her life's compass swung. Basil was her child, her lover, her husband and her friend; he was part of herself, and she was part of him. Johnson, posturing dramatically on the surface of her consciousness, simply did not touch her. It did not even occur to her that he was taking seriously the possibilities of her promise to dine at his flat. But later that night she recounted his absurdities to her husband.

'And how was our friend Johnson?' asked Basil.

'More he-mannish, dirty, and businesslike than ever. I wish he'd trim his finger-nails before he tries to make love.'

'Did he make love to you?'

'Of course he did. A little. He wants us to dissolve the C.C.C. What do you think?'

'I don't care a damn. It was a farce from the beginning. I can't think why I thought it would amuse me. I suppose that we can cut our losses and just let the thing die a natural death. If Johnson wants to take the trouble of doing it, let him.'

And that, so far as Basil St. Denis was concerned, was the end of the Christian Cinema Company.

§ 4

Supper was ready, and not supper only. Fate was ready. Life was ready. All time and circumstances stood waiting with Johnson in his sitting-room at the Battersea flat. The lobster lay pink and exquisite, swimming in a bath of white wine sauce, needing only five minutes over a gas-flame to bring it to perfection. The table was spread with olives and cold chicken and salad and trifle in glass goblets. The champagne reclined opulently in a bucket of ice. Red carnations cast their shadows like purple petals across the damask cloth. The fire leapt on ruddy wings. The cigarettes lay in their silver box. Johnson stood gazing down upon his handiwork, and with jubilant appreciation found it good.

This was the night, and at any moment Gloria might arrive. She was coming, his own, his sweet, with the majesty of a ship in full sail, with the gallant port of a queen. The Battersea flat had known former festivals, but nothing could be like this. And to-morrow, to-morrow they would cross to Paris together. All the plans were laid. Gloria should have the whole day in which to pack her boxes, to tell her firm in Hanover Square that her husband had been taken ill, then she could join Johnson at Victoria for the night boat-train. Oh, it was easy, when the practical brain was lifted on the winds of high imagination, to devise, to risk, to scheme, to conquer. It was sublime. What if he had, while helping Caroline to straighten the affairs of the Christian Cinema Company, contrived to divert to his own pockets £437 17s. 6d.? What if, in the eyes of the law, he was no longer merely an adventurer, but a felon too? His love was greater than the law, and to-morrow he would have escaped. He was going to take his Gloria to Greece.

For the hundredth time he crossed to the window, brushed back the curtains and looked out across the park. The pale grey evening lay in delicate silence. Before her coming spring had cast a faint enchantment upon the air, so that the trees in the park and the hidden line of the river seemed to be hushed and waiting. Johnson felt that he too was hushed and waiting. He felt as though the black buds on the trees must swell with his swelling heart, that the ground must tingle with apprehension, while the crocuses unfolded and the flowers – he was a trifle vague about which flowers – pierced the dark soil with their green spears. All the world sang one song. She is coming. She is coming. She is coming. Spring? Gloria? Who knew, who cared? For were they not all one? Oh, this was ecstasy. He could have wept with pity for the poor, dull, lifeless creatures who had never known this rapture of expectation.

Then, just when his imagination had leapt beyond it, so that for the moment he expected it no longer, he heard the door bell ring. He dropped the curtains and stood facing the little room. Everything in it was perfect to his eyes. If never again he was to taste perfection, he would have had this hour.

He went down the passage, flung the door open, and saw, not Gloria, but Miss Doreen Weller.

'Good evening,' said Miss Weller. Her voice was high and unnatural. 'You were expecting me, weren't you?' And before he had time to collect his scattered wits, she was in the flat. She was in the sitting-room. She had seen the supper-table.

Johnson was horrified. His sense of decency was outraged by the thought that this ugly, untidy, stupid, revolting creature should peer through her pince-nez on to the room prepared for Gloria. There she stood gaping down upon the table, the carnations and the champagne.

'Oh,' she said. 'Oh.' And then her face hardened and a gleam of vindictive cunning lit her eyes. 'Oh, but you can't get away with it like that, you know. I haven't come to be made a fool of. I've got a boy friend now, and he's waiting outside, and I've come for my twenty pounds, and if you don't let me have it within ten minutes, he's going for the police.'

Thank God she was in a hurry. Thank God she would go soon.

'Now, now, young lady,' he said, with a mild severity. 'Now just remember that you've got no right here, and that you are in a very awkward position. If I chose to give you up to the police as a common thief, I could. I have no legal responsibility whatsoever for you or your manuscript. 'Smatter of fact, I've made inquiries, and your stuff is still on its way round publishers. One day you may be getting a letter to say it's been taken, and you'll be sorry then that you let yourself jump to conclusions.'

Johnson was playing for time. The truth was that until the moment when she entered his flat he had completely forgotten Miss Weller and her twenty pounds. Her visit to him had taken its place among the many other perplexities which he would escape by his retreat from England. England was full of troubles. Its civilization had become too complex. A man never knew where he was in it. At any moment Miss Weller might appear demanding twenty pounds, creditors might issue writs, or women like Mollie might write distressing letters.

'Do you realize,' he repeated, 'that this is blackmail, and that the penalties for blackmail are even higher than the penalties for theft? You can't come here and demand twenty pounds like this. You paid that money to me under legal conditions which have been fulfilled. You remember that in my prospectus,' his resourceful brain was supplying him with new expedients as he talked, 'I definitely declared that I only accepted manuscripts at my clients' risk. I cannot possibly undertake that every novel submitted to me will be published.'

'But you said you'd help me.' Her defiance was melting before his stern solemnity.

'Yes and I wanna help you. I don't like to see a girl like you ruin all her chances in life for an act of folly. I've been thinking a great deal about you since you came to me, an' how I could help you best. But it seems to me that you gotta face the music. If I gave you the money now, I'd be an accessory after the act, an' I hold myself in *patria potestas* –' He meant *loco parentis*, but one Latin phrase was really as good as another. 'I've gotta think what's the best for you in the long run.' He was temporizing, for he had not yet made up his mind whether to give her the money and get rid of her before Gloria arrived, or to get rid of her without paying. He had bank-notes in the house, but giving her these would leave him short for his journey. Oh Hell, what a life!

Wasn't it just too bad that this wretched sordid accident should break in upon his mood of ecstasy?

'But you must help me. I tell you, I've got a friend. I know your correspondence college is rotten – I've been to other girls. What happened to Miss Holden's stories, and Mr. Peter's? Where's Mr. Osborne now? Tell me that!' She was growing hysterical again. Her voice rose to a scream. All her doubts of the integrity of the Correspondence School returned to her. 'Why do you run that correspondence school? Why aren't you writing books yourself? Isn't it true that only the men who can't publish their own stuff try to teach other people how to write? How many of your pupils have you got into real jobs? How much have you ever really *done* for any of us? You cheat, you swindle, you take our money under false pretences. To buy champagne.' Gasping with sobs she seized the gold-covered neck of a bottle. 'Champagne. Champagne! and I shall have to go to prison.' Suddenly losing all control of herself, she flung the bottle across the table. It caught the vase of carnations and went crashing to the floor. Violence led to violence. Miss Weller caught up the tablecloth, and Johnson's supper fell round him in chaos. He lumbered round the table and caught the girl's hands, wrestling against her hysterical violence, as she snatched at his collar and tried to scratch his face.

'I'll kill you, I'll kill you,' sobbed Miss Weller. 'Thief! Swindler! Beast! Beast! Beast!'

'Well, really,' said a cool deep voice from the doorway. 'This is a pretty spectacle. Is it a private fight, or can anyone join in?'

Johnson and Miss Weller sprang from their struggling embrace, and faced Gloria, who stood contemplating them with calm amusement.

'The door was open, and hearing somebody sound all hot an' bothered I walked in. Is this the party you promised me?'

Johnson caught at his disordered collar and stared, and stared. For the first time in his life, he could find no word to say.

Miss Weller, with a final scream, collapsed among the

broken glass and crockery, and crouched sobbing on the floor.

'Don't you think you'd better say something?' asked Gloria. 'Or would you rather I did not disturb your confidential interview? No thanks, I won't come in. It looks rather messy, and I've got a decent frock on.'

It was a lovely frock. Never had she looked more rich and splendid and desirable. She held her cloak of golden tissue and brown fur tightly about her with one jewelled, cherry-tipped hand. The light from the passage glittered on her swinging ear-rings. She raised her eyebrows and looked from Johnson to the girl.

He still stared at her, speechless and ridiculous, seeing her as a goddess remote from mortal imperfection, as a bright loveliness, as the beauty and crown of life.

She shrugged her shoulders.

'Well, I suppose I ought to inquire whether you're murdering or seducing this young woman or something. But I'm tired, and I want my dinner. And as you seem to be otherwise occupied, I think I'll say good night.'

She had gone. He heard the door of the flat slam behind her. Only then did he find his tongue.

'Gloria! Gloria! Mrs. St. Denis! Come back.' He pushed the table over in his blind rush for the door, completing the ruin of his own room. He hurled himself down the passage, and fumbled with the Yale lock. But the catch had slipped, and it had always been difficult to open. By the time he reached the street, she had climbed again into the taxi which had brought her and had vanished among the jostling traffic. He knew then that he had lost her beyond all hope of recovery. He stood bare-headed and wild-eyed, staring up the street, but he had no hope of her return, and none of her forgiveness.

He climbed slowly and heavily up the stairs. In his flat the wretched Doreen Weller still wept among the broken tumblers. All that he wanted now was to get rid of her. He went to the desk, unlocked it, and from a leather wallet took out four five-pound notes. He had intended them for Gloria's expenses on the way to Paris. He had intended them to pay for Pullman cars and flowers. He crushed the

notes into a ball, and thrust them into the girl's damp
fingers.

'Here's your damned money; you little fool,' he said.
'Now get to Hell outa here.'

Slowly she opened her hand and unfolded the notes upon
her knee. Slowly the realization that she was saved reached
her dazed and angry mind. Slowly she climbed to her knees
and to her feet, pushed the notes into the shabby leather
purse which she had dropped on to the chair, and, still
sobbing quietly, found her way out of the room. Without a
word, she went off down the passage, and Johnson heard her
snivelling until the door of the flat slammed for a second
time, and he was left alone.

He stooped to gather up the red carnations, now drenched
in champagne, trodden upon and broken, and as he fumbled clumsily among the scattered olives and glass and
flowers, the sense of his desolation swept down upon him.

The telephone broke shrilly upon his misery. At first he
let it ring; then the absurd hope that it might be Gloria,
which even as it rose to his mind, he rejected, sent him to
the instrument. He heard a familiar voice.

'Hallo. Hallo. Is that you, old dear? I say. You know
who this is? Yes, Delia! Look here. You do anything to-
morrow? 'Cause I'm bored. This damn job's come to an
end. I've got the chuck. Couldn't we go somewhere?'

'Couldn't we?' Johnson responded to the old appeal.
'Look here, lil' old thing. What about Paris?'

'What, Paris! You don't mean it! Oh, boy. This is so
sudden.'

'Yes I do. You gotta passport? Good. I'll get two tickets
for the boat-train at Victoria 8.20 to-morrow night. Let's do
a little trip together. Yes. Yes. I've got the cash all right.
Need a holiday.'

'But honest. Not joking?'

'Abso-ballyutly. I was thinking of going off f'ra day or
two in any case.'

'Well, I don't mind. But how will all your good works get
along without you? What'll you do about your Christian
Cinema Company and poor Caroline?'

Johnson laughed into the telephone. 'I'm fed up with the

198

lot of 'em. You're the only woman in the world I can bear
to look at at the moment. You won't let me down, darling,
will you? We'll have a lovely time together. A lovely time.
We might go to Egypt. Cairo, you know, an' Alexandria.
'Smy belief I've been in London too long. Say, baby, we'll
paint Europe red, an' to Hell,' he was about to add 'with
Gloria!' but checked himself in time with a laugh that was
half a sob, and called to her, 'to Hell with your Poor
Caroline!'

Chapter 7 : *Caroline Audrey Denton-Smyth*

On Thursday, April 4th, Caroline faced her depleted Board across her pile of papers. From the chair, Mr. Guerdon blinked and cleared his throat. Hugh Macafee sprawled reluctantly on her right.

She despised both of them. Mr. Guerdon was a conventional man. At last she saw beyond his apparent liberality and progressiveness to his temperamental and invariable timidity. He could do nothing unsafe, and nothing that his fathers had not done before him. She had been deceived at first because, his fathers having been Quakers, pacifists, humanitarians and radicals, he had pursued these interests from filial convention and lack of initiative, just as in other circumstances he would have pursued imperialism, tariff reform, evangelicalism and fox hunting. Well, she knew him now. He was of no more use to her.

Hugh Macafee was purely selfish. He had never cared for the high ideals of the company. All that he wanted was to find someone who would finance his inventions.

She could manage them. That morning she had taken an egg beaten up with the remainder of Father Mortimer's brandy for her breakfast. She felt that she could face tigers on an egg.

'I – er – I suppose that we are all here,' muttered Mr. Guerdon.

'I looked up the constitution of the company,' said Caroline briskly, 'and so far as I can see, nothing was laid *down* about a quorum. Of course I'm not saying it ought *not* to have been but there it is, and until we have co-opted other directors, I suppose we must act alone.'

'Well, I suppose so. Really, there is not much to do. Let me see. . . .'

If Caroline had not prompted him, Mr. Guerdon would have let the whole meeting go to pieces. He did not care. He wanted to escape to his comfortable little home up at Golder's Green. Caroline knew. A high note of moral indignation rang in her voice as she began to read.

'A meeting of the Board of the Christian Cinema Company Ltd. was held on March 11th at the offices in Victoria Street. Mr. St. Denis was in the chair. Present, Mr. Macafee, Mr. Guerdon, Mr. Johnson and Miss Denton-Smyth, Honorary Secretary. The minutes of the previous meeting were read and confirmed. Under Correspondence the Honorary Secretary read a letter from Mr. Joseph Isenbaum announcing his resignation from the Board. The Board accepted the resignation with regret and instructed the Secretary to write a letter to this effect to Mr. Isenbaum.'

The formal phraseology of the minutes soothed Caroline as the familiar words of the Church service soothed her. Here lay security in a world of fleeting values. Disciplined by the ritual of business convention, the defection of Isenbaum appeared less tragic. What had these calm sentences to do with sleepless nights and days of aching misery? As she read the flat record of her own defeat, she found herself able to regard with something like complacency this retreat of her directors.

The minutes came to an end.

'Let me see.' Mr. Guerdon blinked and licked his lips. 'Any business arising out of the minutes which is not on the agenda?'

Nobody spoke.

'Well, then, I think we pass on to correspondence.'

Caroline drew from her file a large sheet of mauve paper, scrawled across with writing in brilliant purple ink. She felt perfectly calm now, though she was very cold and her throat hurt her.

'I have here a letter which I received since the last Board meeting from Mrs. St. Denis, and though I think we all know about it, I believe I ought to read it.' Her voice was even steadier than usual as she read: –

DEAR MISS DENTON-SMYTH,

I am writing on behalf of my husband to say that he has been ordered by his doctors to leave England immediately on account of his health, and is leaving to-morrow for the South of France. It is probable that he will not be allowed to spend another winter in England. As you probably know, his lungs were affected by his War Service. In that case he has asked me on his behalf to tender with great regret his resignation from the chairmanship of the Christian Cinema Company. He thanks his colleagues for their loyal and helpful co-operation, and wishes me to say how much he regrets the necessity for this step.

Yours truly,
GLORIA ST. DENIS.'

'Well,' said Mr. Guerdon. 'I suppose we must accept that. It comes to the same thing in the end.'

This was the first shadow of challenge. Caroline braced herself for battle.

'Don't you think, Mr. Guerdon, it would be *better* if I wrote to Mr. St. Denis and expressed the regret of the Board for his ill-health, and said that we should be delighted to appoint a *Vice*-chairman to serve during his absence but that we *very* much hope that, as soon as he is better, he will be able to rejoin us? You see, he has been ill before and got better. I understand that the Mediterranean is *very* beneficial to the lungs.'

'Well, I don't really see the point of that under the circumstances. It seems to come to much the same thing in the end.'

'I don't agree with you, Mr. Guerdon. It doesn't come to the same thing really, because in one case Mr. St. Denis remains our chairman, and in the other he *doesn't*. Of course you might say that he won't consent to remain as it were a sleeping partner, but I think we ought to give him the benefit of the doubt.'

She would not let herself know what the two men wanted to say. They were rats fleeing from a sinking ship. Rats. Or mice, rather. The Quaker with his long soft twitching nose and weak eyes was rather like a large lugubrious mouse.

'Well, Miss Denton-Smyth, I really think – What do you say, Macafee?'

'It's all one to me.' Hugh Macafee had heard nothing. He cared nothing. He was thinking about the bichromated glue process used in half-tone reproduction.

'Thank you, Mr. Macafee,' said Caroline. 'Very well then, I'll write to Mr. St. Denis to that effect.' She did not say to which effect. She was trembling with the secret ardour of the conflict. She hurried on to her next point. 'And I have another letter of resignation from Mr. Johnson. He just says that business has taken him abroad indefinitely and that he is very sorry to have to resign. I must tell the Board what a loss that is. He was *most* kind last month in helping me go through the books. I've missed him very much. Yes, it was March 26th he wrote that letter. I believe he left that same evening. I don't know where he has gone. Probably back to California. I understand that the Anglo-American School of Scenario Writing is closed. I went round to Essex Street, but the caretaker told me it was all shut up and some new firm was in possession.'

The two directors made no comment. Mr. Guerdon had his own fears about Mr. Johnson. He did not wish to be involved in that gentleman's business transactions. The sooner he escaped completely from his disreputable connection, the better. Hugh Macafee was thinking that if Brooks would not give him a free hand, he could always find someone else in the States who would be interested in his colour process.

Caroline was aware of their discomfort. She had no mercy. She was no longer afraid. Facing the worst brought her a sense of exhilaration. She was stronger than both of these stupid men together.

She read other letters. They dealt with the small change of public business.

There was a request from the Bishop's Council of Public and Private Morality, asking the company to pass a resolution in favour of a Children's Censor. There was a request from the Sabbatarian League, asking the company to send two representatives to a protest meeting against the Sunday Cinema. There were several invitations to Trade Shows of special films. All these signs of activity were reassuring. They proved to Caroline that the company had taken its place in society, that it was needed, that it was co-operating with all those other pioneers who strove to leave the world a better place than they found it.

Mr. Guerdon listened with impatience.

'Is that all the correspondence?' asked Mr. Guerdon. 'Secretary's report, then, please.'

Caroline gave it. Her reports were always long, detailed and optimistic. She loved writing them, and was continually surprised by the amount of work that she managed to achieve between the Board meetings. She had spoken at six drawing-room meetings and three conferences. She had interviewed eight firms. She had received such and such letters and attended such and such functions. If no very concrete result had come from all this activity, at least it proved that useful propaganda was being done.

Her fellow directors failed to be impressed.

'Have you the balance sheet?' snapped Mr. Guerdon.

'Well, I haven't exactly been able to prepare a full balance sheet,' smiled Caroline. She was not so happy about this item on the agenda, because she felt that she had fallen short of her standard of efficiency and helpfulness. But really one could not attend to everything at once. 'I have been very busy, as you know, and then Mr. Johnson was in the middle of helping me to put the books straight, which was very kind of him, when he went abroad, because as you know that is the part of the work that I have had *least* previous experience of, though willing to do my best until we could afford a permanent *trained* accountant. So of course he found that there were a good many accounts outstanding which he said must be paid off by quarter day. I expect he knew he might have to go abroad, and wanted to get everything straight for us, so he helped me to get the cheques made out, and so far as I *know*' – she brought up her lorgnettes and bent over the paper – 'our bank balance now stands at £35 4s. 7d., which is perhaps not very grand, but when you think what other similar societies have to do with, and then we have no salaries to pay out,' she added proudly.

Mr. Guerdon wanted to ask, 'Where is the £2,500 we had in January?' But his desire was for quiet and speedy escape. He suspected that Johnson might not be perfectly straight. He had never been sure of St. Denis. But Isenbaum had not cared what happened to his original investment and the de la Roux girl was Miss Denton-Smyth's cousin, and naturally she might be expected to look after her relative's own interest. The whole thing was a frost, and the sooner it was allowed to melt away the better.

'Well, we have to accept your statement, Miss Denton-Smyth,' he said. 'Now I come to the next item on the agenda, appointment of new directors, and as what I have to say seems to fit best in here, I have to offer the Board my resignation. I am very sorry, but these meetings have been a great tax upon my time, and I, personally, do not see that I can be of any further use to the company.'

Caroline looked up at him. She had suspected this. He thought that she would be frightened, did he? She smiled serenely, though her heart drummed a summons to battle.

'I am very sorry to hear you feel like that,' she said cheerfully. 'Well, Mr. Macafee, you and I seem to be the only directors left.'

'What's that? What's that?' asked Hugh, rousing himself. 'Oh, but I'm going to America, you know. I'm done with England, and I'm sure the Christian Cinema Company can do without me. You can make what use of the Tona Perfecta you like. It's a good film, whatever Brooks says. I'll have to see this new Hollywood one a good deal more before I'd believe it's better than mine.'

'You mean to resign too?' asked Caroline in a cold little voice.

'Well, you can take it as you like. I'm off. And I've wasted enough time here already. If that's all I'll be going.'

'So that seems to be the end of our business, I think, Miss Denton-Smyth,' said Mr. Guerdon. 'Well, it has been a very pleasant venture, and I am sure I have enjoyed it very

205

much.' One must get out of these things pleasantly, he was thinking. Caroline could see the thoughts scurrying about in his brain like mice, Mouse, mouse, mouse, she thought in scorn. 'I suppose it is really no use going through the other items in the agenda, because we may take it, I think, that the company must be voluntarily liquidated. We hope, I think, that our work together has done a little good by demonstrating to the public the need for a clean, decent cinema, and perhaps one day when things are more propitious and the state of trade justifies greater commercial enterprise, we may hope that something of the kind will be started again. I take it that the balance of – er – £35 odd will cover outstanding expenses. We shall have, as a matter of form, I take it, to call a shareholders' meeting. But as Mr. Isenbaum makes no objection to winding up the company, I suppose that Miss de la Roux will adopt the same attitude. There are no more shareholders of more than a pound or two, and I imagine that they will give us no trouble. A purely formal meeting, just to put everything in order. I suggest that we fix it for next week and then you can send out the notices, and if Miss de la Roux cares to attend, she can.'

'I see,' said Caroline. 'You mean that you both want to resign and then that we can wind up the company?'

'I think that it seems the only sensible thing to do. Of course –'

Mr. Guerdon hesitated, not because he had any qualifying suggestion to make, but because hesitation was part of his nature. Caroline took her opportunity.

'But just a minute, please, gentlemen. I want you to notice that I put down on the agenda that I had some proposals to make about the names of new directors I wanted to put forward for acceptance by the Board. I quite realize that we must replace Mr. Johnson and Mr. Isenbaum who have already resigned, and I was going to suggest the names of Father Roger Mortimer and Miss Eleanor de la Roux. They have both shown great interest in the company, and Father Roger Mortimer as a representative of the Church will be I am sure *most* helpful if we can persuade him to join us, and Miss de la Roux is as you know our chief shareholder and I always think that we ought to have the *younger* generation represented on a Board like this which is working for the *future*.'

She paused, because she could not for the moment continue. She was perfectly calm. Her brain felt cool and orderly. Why then did her mouth feel so dry, and her heart race so violently? She was not afraid. The company would not disappear if she chose to continue it. The half-hearted might fail her, but she would work alone. She would have a new Board, a new spirit. She would start again with spiritual rather than material power. She had been wrong, perhaps, to look for help among financiers and engineers. The power of the spirit could overcome the power of this world. Though a thousand fell on her right hand, yet should destruction not come nigh her.

'Well, Miss Denton-Smyth, if you act, you must act alone. My resignation is before you. I really am afraid I can't consider going on. It's out of the question, if you come to think of it.'

Mr. Guerdon began to gather up his papers.

'Would you both mind sending in your resignations in writing?' asked Caroline. 'We have to do this in order. And perhaps while you are still directors you would give your sanction to the co-option of Miss de la Roux and Father Mortimer, and, naturally, we must have others. Perhaps Mrs. Dawson Woodley and Mr. Maccullam Scott.'

'But, Miss Denton-Smyth, I think I must suggest that really it is no use now, just at present, while trade is so bad, trying to go on.'

'I intend to go on, Mr. Guerdon.'

'But the vote of the Board has gone against you; Macafee and I both think it wiser to dissolve – write off our debts – and so on.'

'Well, of course, gentlemen. You can both resign. But I don't believe that you can prevent me from reconstituting the company. I shall have to take legal advice, because I am not quite sure of *exactly* what are the proper steps at this moment. But I can assure you of this, that whether we call it the Christian Cinema Company or something else, and whether you choose to go or to remain, the work goes on.

I'm not going to give up now. If you won't help me, I shall carry on alone. That is all I have to say.'

Unnerved by open defiance, Mr. Guerdon looked round the room. But Macafee was wriggling into his shabby coat and gave him no help. Mr. Guerdon clung to the formula with which his position had supplied him.

'There being no further business, the meeting is now adjourned,' he said.

§ 2

Caroline breathed hard as she climbed the stairs. They always seemed to grow steeper while she was at the office. She sat down for a minute on the bottom step of the third flight.

From the basement came the shrill tuneless voice of Mrs. Hales singing 'The Church's One Foundation.' Caroline shivered. She wondered why she had ever thought of Mrs. Hales as a nice woman. Why she had even left her something in her will! But then you could never really trust any one in that class. Not really. In the old days in Yorkshire, of course, it had been different. She remembered Martha Whiting, who had been with her mother's family for twenty-nine years, a really faithful soul. People used to have faithful souls. Nowadays they watched instead to see how they could take advantage of you.

Her old friends were dead. Whoever said that old age was a happy time? Death and sickness lay in wait, not for oneself, but for one's whole generation. The 'Deaths' column in *The Times* became like a casualty list. One never knew who would fall next in the long-drawn war with Time. The only security lay in young friends – like Father Mortimer.

The thought of Father Mortimer lent her strength, so that she climbed the last steps quite quickly and entered her room. Once inside she looked round suspiciously. She was sure that Mrs. Hales had been there, spying on her, reading her papers, and perhaps trying on the hats that the girls had sent her from Marshington. Breathing heavily, she crossed to her desk, and looked to see whether the paper-weight she had placed over her letters had been moved. When she left that morning, she had set it down with the words 'A Present

208

from Bridlington' towards the bed. Now they faced the fire-place. Mrs. Hales had been upstairs, then, spying and ferret-ing. 'She wants to know about my will, I expect,' Caroline muttered. The thought of her landlady's curiosity exasper-ated her.

She ought to look for other rooms.

'I mustn't allow this to get on my mind,' Caroline told herself. It was absurd to let one's landlady become a terror. 'Oh, Lord, make us all charitable to one another, and give me a sense of humour, even about Mrs. Hales,' she prayed. Still, that paper-weight had been a good idea. It was as well to know where you were.

The evenings were growing milder. It was really extrava-gant to light the fire. And now that she was not paying for service and had to tidy the grate for herself in the morning, that was a consideration. Besides, she loathed having to carry down the ashes through Mrs. Hales's kitchen. It was humiliating, after having been on such different terms as a lady lodger.

She slowly removed her heavy feathered hat, and fluffed out the curls along her forehead. There always seemed to be much to do when she came in at night. She took off her coat and stretched it carefully on a hanger behind the door.

She unfolded her scarf and replaced her shoes by bedroom slippers. She set the kettle to boil, and produced from the cupboard a loaf, a jagged lump of margarine in a smeared saucer, a small pot of pinkish chicken-and-ham paste, and a small slice of stale Madeira cake, saved from a sixpenny tea for which she had reluctantly paid at a recent meeting. It had seemed a pity to waste the cake. After a nice cup of tea, she would feel less tired.

All the time she made her preparations and spread her paste across the bread and margarine, she held back by a desperate effort of will-power the memory of the Board meeting. She would not think about the company. When she had eaten and rested she would turn to face her future. Just now, she must rest, she must be tranquil.

It was the time of day she usually liked best. After an hour's rest she would pull herself together and go to her desk and mark the names of possible shareholders in a report sent her by the Evangelical Reform Association. But now she could sit and dream. She could think about her Friend.

The knowledge of his existence provided her with a constant solace and occupation. Whenever she had nothing else to think about she could re-live the memory of their last meeting, embellishing it with small added joys invented by her fancy. That time she went to see him in hospital, for instance, and he had come swinging down the long ward on his crutches, he had looked so happy, so young, just like a boy with his rebellious hair and his flapping blue dressing-gown. She had brought him a twopenny bunch of violets, and he had seemed so delightfully pleased. He was a person easily pleased by little things. He told her that his foot was out of plaster of Paris and that he was to be allowed to walk with a stick next day, and on Easter Eve he could go back to the Clergy House to help Father Lasseter on Easter Day.

They were friends. She had said to him: 'I wish I could do something to help *you*, Father, as you've helped me,' and he had suddenly looked so strange, as though he were happy and excited and yet in some way sorrowful, and said, 'Why, you have helped me, Miss Denton-Smyth. You've given me a lovely thing.' So that was what he thought of her. She had given him a lovely thing. She was getting old, but her spirit was still young. Age, after all, affected matter, not spirit. In spirit they belonged to the same generation. He realized that. Did he ever dream of her as she dreamed of him? Abélard and Héloïse were lovers. They too were parted by fate's cruelty, yet from her nunnery Héloïse cried out to Abélard. She, Caroline, was trapped in the nunnery of old age, and he, like Abélard, was a priest bound by his duty; yet they could give each other lovely things.

She hurried over the thought that what he actually had given her was a little wad of four ten-shilling notes screwed together. She had not meant to ask for money, but somehow, finding herself confronted by his sympathy, she could not help telling him about Mrs. Hales, and the lack of imagination displayed by her Marshington relatives, and the increasing parsimony of Eleanor, who had even asked her why she did not draw a salary from the C.C.C., Eleanor was efficient, but rather hard. She believed in competence and order and asking for one's rights. It had been a comfort to tell Father Mortimer all about her. Even the most charitable Christians had to relieve their feelings sometimes.

Of course it did not matter accepting an occasional small loan from Father Mortimer, because one day she was going to make him rich. For each pound that he had lent her, she could repay him back a hundredfold. He would be a bishop, perhaps an archbishop, before she had finished with him. How wonderful he would look in lawn sleeves with a swinging gold cross and an episcopal ring.

But even before then, she would make him happy. He loved beautiful things. She took pride in her discernment of his tastes. No wonder he was attracted by Rome, she thought, when he found such pleasure in deep rich colours, and heavy fabrics, and stately rooms. She would take a house for him in Little College Street. She knew the house exactly, an old house with high, beautifully proportioned rooms and an uneven roof.

She had found a new occupation. On her wanderings through the City she house-hunted for her friend. She knew of a labour-saving flat at Kensington, looking across the open spaces of Holland Park. He should have a study there warmed by central heating, and a drawing-room where he could give her tea – China tea, in delicate Crown Derby cups, with bread and butter, thin as wafers.

He should have chambers in the Temple, up queer creaking wooden stairs, with a double door on which former tenants had carved their initials, and oak panelling round an oval sitting-room. There would be deep window-seats in his study, on which one could sit among piles of crimson cushions, looking out to Fountain Court, watching the sparrows scattering water from their wings, and spring coming up the green gardens behind.

Sometimes she chose for him a country cottage. An old number of *Country Life* had given her splendid pleasure. She found Tudor Cottages and Elizabethan Farm Houses, Old Timber, Walled Gardens, and excellent Trout Fishing. She was not certain if he liked trout fishing, but the sport was at least suitable for the dignity of a priest. She would have walled gardens where William pears could grow. Her father had said that to eat a William pear properly you ought to sit all night to catch it at the moment of its perfect flavour. She could go down to visit him there, and there would be bees blundering among the hollyhocks and clarkia and lupins, and a rock garden, frothing with white arabus. She rocked backwards and forwards in her creaking chair, picturing the garden of his country cottage.

She must have fallen asleep, because she heard as though from very far away the tap-tap-tapping that might have been a woodpecker in the plantation at the end of the garden, but which was really Eleanor at the door.

She woke up with a shock of dismay to find the girl standing looking down at her.

'Hullo, Cousin Caroline,' cried Eleanor. 'Can I come in?'

Eleanor seemed younger and prettier than Caroline had ever seen her look before. Into the lapel of her tweed coat were pinned three perfect, slender, tightly rolled pink rosebuds. Her cheeks were flushed to match her flowers, and her breath, coming a little fast after her run upstairs, increased her appearance of youth and eagerness.

Caroline did not want to see her. In a day or two, she felt, she would not mind answering questions; later she could endure the unflinching catechism of efficient youth. Just now, she could not bear it. She had not yet taught herself to face the situation. How could she bear its exposure to Eleanor's bright, candid gaze?

'How are you, dear? I haven't seen you for quite a long time, though I'm sure I expect you're very busy even now that you have finished with the college, haven't you?'

'Well, yes. That was partly what I wanted to see you about.'

'Oh, yes. Well, now, let me see, have you had tea?'

'No, not yet. Can you give me a cup? I brought a cake along. I generally descend upon you like a ravening wolf and eat you out of house and home. But to-day I did remember.'

She produced the cake from a box in her dispatch-case. It was a handsome object, spangled with currants. Caroline looked at it with wistful disapproval.

'Thank you, my dear. I've had tea myself, in fact I was just going to clear up and sit down to some work I brought back from the office.'

'When I interrupted you? What a shame.' But the girl's eyes were twinkling, because she had seen Caroline asleep. Caroline's discomfort grew to positive dislike. Eleanor was begging her to have another cup, moving deftly and neatly from the table to the cupboard, cutting the cake, finding a second cup and saucer. She could see the piles of unwashed crockery on the shelf. She could see the disorder of the room. Caroline hated untidiness as much as anyone. She did not like to leave her cups unwashed and crumbs on her cupboard shelf. But there were days when she felt too tired to do anything but eat her meal and lie down on her bed, mornings when 'doing the room' became an intolerable burden. A business director, with heavy public responsibilities, should not have to wash up her own dinner and clean her fireplace.

'I was sorry you couldn't come to that concert last week,' said Eleanor, pouring fresh water into the teapot.

'Well, dear, it was *Passion* week, you see, and though I'm not so strict as I should like to be, there are some things one *likes* to do, aren't there? And a *secular* concert in *Lent* isn't quite the thing, is it?'

'Oh, Lent,' repeated the girl carelessly. 'I'd forgotten.'

Caroline felt a sudden anger against such light indifference.

'I know, dear, that you don't *believe* in the Seasons of the Church, but to us who do, there is something very beautiful and strengthening in the ordered procession of the year. Life can be so very disordered and troublesome, but if we submit to the pattern and discipline that the Church has designed as an eternal order –' She was groping for words spoken in a sermon by Father Mortimer, and because she tried to quote her Friend's opinion, her colour rose and her pulses fluttered.

'Oh, yes, I know all that,' said the girl. 'But I don't like external order imposed on me arbitrarily from outside. I like to make my own order.'

'You're very young and undisciplined, my dear.'

213

'Perhaps I am.' Eleanor paused, busy with the teapot. 'You will have another cup now it is here, won't you? Then I'll wash up for both of us.'

'Oh, well, as it is there.' She did not want to give way to the girl, but the hot tea steamed enticingly from the pot and the cake allured her. 'Just *half* a cup, then – and ever such a small slice.'

'You know,' Eleanor apologized, 'I'm sorry I upset you about Lent. I didn't mean to sneer or anything. I think sneering's beastly. But I can't help finding all that sort of thing somehow unreal. The seasons of the churches and the consecration of Bishops, and all these quarrels between Evangelicals and Anglo-Catholics, seem somehow so irrelevant – artificially created difficulties. I *can* understand the worship of Absolute Perfection – if it exists – and the desire to make reality in the noblest and strongest and loveliest possible form. But I can't see what this has to do with transubstantiation and the creeds and – I can't even see that the belief in immortality matters very much. I used to think about that desperately. But somehow – just lately – I seem to have passed right through that desire and come out on the other side. I don't even *want* anyone to go on living after they are dead. I don't *want* any more than this life.'

'You don't want this, and you don't want that,' flared Caroline. 'And you expect to find the universe and all eternity and God Himself arranged just to suit what you *do* want. I lose patience with you, Eleanor, I do indeed, and you a B.Sc. or nearly, and a very clever young woman, no doubt.'

It was terrible to grow excited like this about nothing. She must be calm. She must be tolerant. Eleanor had always called herself an agnostic, poor Eleanor. One must be sorry for agnostics and for all these poor young puzzled boys and girls who did not realize what they were missing. Father Lasseter and Father Mortimer would be patient. She sighed and looked across the table at Eleanor, who was crumbling her cake on to her plate and eating nothing. The girl looked less happy now. The flush had faded from her cheeks, and Caroline noticed, as she had not noticed before, the shadows under her eyes.

214

Caroline made an effort, coughed, and broke abruptly into another subject.

'Well, and what are you doing now, dear?' she asked.

The girl looked up almost gratefully, as though aware that she had been let off lightly.

'Well, you know the course at the college came to an end at Easter? We did an exam and apparently I didn't do so badly. I should have been a fool if I did. It was easy stuff. And I got Hugh to write me a letter to say I could do the laboratory work quite decently, and what with one thing and another, they're probably going to give me a chance at Perrin's – you know, they're the big people who work over here connected with Brooks in the States – and there's a chance – there's even a chance – that I might go to America with Hugh. Hugh's trying to wangle it, and it would be the most marvellous experience. And I should see Jan, my brother. He's in Pennsylvania now – and I could study all the American cinema and talkie processes. It would be *perfect*. And then I could come back here and – Oh, Cousin Caroline, wouldn't it be fun – *fun*, if I could one day be a big Business Magnate, like Brooks? There aren't nearly enough women in big industrial positions. I *must* be rich by the time I'm fifty – and then I'd go in for politics and really get what I want – with money and power and authority behind me. I don't mind starting at the beginning, but I *must* be a company director some day.'

That brought Caroline to the point. She leant forward.

'My dear,' she said. 'You can be a company director without waiting all those years and going to America.'

Eleanor shook her head. 'I wish I could. I'm horribly impatient. But it can't as a rule be done. One must begin at the bottom.'

'That's all you know!' cried Caroline happily. She was triumphant again, feeling herself in her rightful place, a distributor of largesse, a benefactress to youth. 'But supposing I offered you now – now, when you are only an inexperienced girl straight from a business college, what if I offered you now a directorship in an *important* company – a cinema company?'

'Why,' laughed the girl. 'I'd snap it up. You bet.'

'Well, my dear, you once did me a good turn, I'll admit it. Your investment of three thousand pounds helped to extricate me from a *delicate* – I won't say an awkward – but a *delicate* position. And now I am fortunate in being able to recompense you by giving you your heart's desire.' Why was the girl's expression so remote and puzzled? Caroline smiled in the sure knowledge of her triumphant benefaction. 'I asked the Board of the Christian Cinema Company to-day – only to-day, mark you – if they would approve of the appointment of two new directors – Father Mortimer, my dear, and yourself.'

She sat back in her chair and awaited Eleanor's thanks. She watched for the girl's confused and inarticulate delight. But instead of crying out with gratitude, Eleanor stared at her with something like dismay.

'The Christian Cinema Company?' she repeated. 'Father Mortimer – and me?'

'Father Mortimer – and you. There now! Of course I know you're very young, Eleanor, and naturally they were a little surprised, because of course it is a great honour, but then I always say that the more you expect, the more you get out of people. You have shown in a very *practical* way your interest in the company. My fellow directors agree with me that at least your appointment will *hurt* no one. And it would be a wonderful experience for you.'

'Oh, thank you,' stammered Eleanor. 'Thank you very much. But you know – I – I'm afraid it wouldn't do – it wouldn't do at all.'

'Now, now. Don't be so modest.' It was tiresome of the girl to take it like this. Caroline was too tired to contend with doubts and difficulties. 'Don't put difficulties in the way, dear.'

'But I'm afraid, you know – it isn't possible. I – I'd much rather begin at the beginning in a firm like Perrin's – I'm only just starting to learn what the business involves. Besides . . .' As though seeking comfort in her perplexity, the girl lifted the lapel of her coat and pressed her face against the pink roses.

A sudden intuition illuminated Caroline's mind.

'Is it because of Father Mortimer?' she asked. Good

heavens! Why had she not thought of that before? The girl was probably in love with him. That would explain a dozen little things that had happened recently. It was quite natural. What girl could avoid falling in love with so brilliant and charming a young man? Poor Eleanor! That would account for her oddness lately.

'Whatever do you mean?' asked Eleanor, but the tell-tale flush leapt again to her cheeks.

'You perhaps feel some difficulty about going on the same Board as him? Of course – I quite understand, but I think –'

'He's told you then?' It was Eleanor's turn to look astonished.

'Well.' He had told Caroline nothing, but he was her Friend. There were no secrets between them. Whatever remained to be told was in effect told already. 'Well, dear, I didn't know if you'd like me to mention it. But as you have done, of course, you know, I think I can say that we are *great* friends – almost like mother and son, and yet he is my father in God.'

'Oh, he's told you. Well – I'm rather glad really. But you see, don't you, why I want to get away if possible? I think that perhaps it's better for us not to meet – for a little, anyway. He'll get over it. He'll forget.'

So the girl had declared her love. How like these modern young women. Eleanor, for all her outward shyness, had strange moods of self-assurance.

'Oh, yes,' said Caroline. 'He'll forget. I don't think you need be embarrassed.'

'I shouldn't mind if it were only that. You see – so far as I'm concerned, I'd like to go on seeing him. I'd be a liar if I pretended that I didn't like him to send me flowers and write to me and everything.'

'Did he send you those roses?' asked Caroline quietly. Roses like that cost over a shilling each just then. 'He only gave me tulips,' she remembered.

'Oh, yes. I know I ought to stop him. I will too. Only – it's so much more difficult than I thought. I can't bear to hurt him. If he were a different sort of person. You know I'd always thought that nothing was easier than to get rid of a man you didn't want. All you have to do is to say "No" and go away. But this – well, he's different, isn't he?'

What was she saying? 'A man you didn't want?' Was she trying to imply that he wanted her and that she would not have him? Was it that way round? Caroline began to tremble. 'Has he *asked* you to marry him?'

'No. That's just it. He keeps on saying he won't ask me, because it isn't fair. And, of course, it isn't possible. I couldn't marry a clergyman. But I never thought, I never dreamed, that I should *want* to. It's like a sort of nightmare. Of all people in the world to love – an Anglican curate – me. It's comic. It's grotesque. When I've always found clergymen a little ridiculous. When I'm an agnostic, and dislike the Church and think it does more harm than good. And then to find Roger.'

What did she mean? What did she mean? She was staring at the black, unlit coals in the grate, and talking jerkily and shyly, as though she were arguing against herself, as though it were Father Mortimer who had fallen in love with her, and she who had rejected him. And yet –

'Do you love him?' asked Caroline.

'Love? Yes. I suppose I do. Though I find it harder than some people seem to do, to say straight out like that, "I love him." But I do love him. He is nicer than I had ever thought any man in the world could be – even nicer than Father. There's a kind of irony and humour about him that saves him from priggishness. There's something – something keen and fine about him. I suppose – you can't *help* loving someone like that?'

'Then what's the difficulty? It seems to me that you're taking a good deal for granted if you suppose he loves you when he hasn't asked you to marry him.'

'Oh – but of course – if he's told you – you know all about it. You see – that night of the accident at Hugh's laboratory – he told me then for the first time. I was so astonished I hardly knew what to say. Then next day he managed somehow to order for me some amazing carnations – a great box of them – with an apology for having bothered me. And you know – when anyone does that as *beautifully* as that, you can't just be indifferent. I went to see him. I've been to see him almost every day in the hospital. And we've talked and talked. He's almost incredibly nice. But, of course, it's all impossible.'

'What do you mean? Why do you go on saying, "It's impossible"?'

'Well, of *course* it is. How can I marry him? I know he says he'd be willing for me to keep my own name and do my own work and just come and stay with him whenever it was possible, and that he believes in divorce and birth control in spite of the present teaching of the Church, because the Church shouldn't pretend to be inspired on matters of social convenience. But that wouldn't do us any good, you know. I haven't somehow allowed for marriage in my life. I've never wanted it at all until I met him. I want to do things – to make things. I want to organize people. I'd like to organize a business like Perrin's, manufacturing cinema apparatus – and then use that knowledge of business in politics. There's so much I want to do and that I feel I can do. I can't just go and marry a curate.'

'I see.' Caroline felt quite cold now and very calm. 'He declares his love for you and you say you love him, but you are willing to sacrifice him and your love for your own selfish career.'

'You can put it like that, I suppose. But that's not really quite true. I do love him. I want to be with him. I should love to help him and look after him and – and have children by him, too, I think. He's so straight and keen and muscular. He'd have *lovely* children.'

'Eleanor!'

'Well – he would. I'm sure. They'd be darlings. He'd make a darling husband. But that isn't everything. There are all the other things. How could I make a slum curate's wife when the Franciscan ideal isn't my ideal at all? I want to change slums and poverty and maternal mortality and all that as much as he does. But I want to do it through power and rationalization and political control. I can't pray – I don't believe in prayer. I don't want to run girls' clubs. I want to organize a constitutional and rationalized revolution. You *ought* to understand, Cousin Caroline. You've always been a reformer. You ought to know that there are passions as strong and more lasting than individual love. There are. At least – for my sort of woman there are.'

'I understand,' said Caroline trembling, 'that your sort of woman can be completely selfish. I've always been a pioneer and struggler. But if I could serve Father Mortimer in any way, I'd give up to-morrow any of my *own* schemes. I've always wanted to help and enrich the people I love, and so I believe would all *real* Christians. And I always understood that love had some sort of connection with self-sacrifice, but probably I'm wrong and you're right. Only I think I'm getting too old to take in all these new ideas. You must go your own way. I can't help you.'

Caroline spoke bitterly. Her heart was bitter. She was angry and sad and tired. She got up from her chair and began to pile up the tea-things.

'Oh, let me do that,' cried Eleanor.

Very well. Why shouldn't she? She was young and strong and selfish. Let her work. She has everything, thought Caroline. Youth and hope and ambition and love – and love. Father Mortimer's love. And she did not want that. It was only an interruption to her. Caroline had nothing but the privilege of old age, to sit back in her rocking chair and let Eleanor wash up.

So he's been in love with Eleanor from the beginning and he's never told me, she thought. That was the lovely thing she had given him. He probably thought her a terrible old bore. Their friendship was all one-sided. He was young. He turned to youth. Why should she toil and work for him? He did not want to be enriched by her. He wanted Eleanor. There was no room for her in his heart, there was only room for Eleanor. Caroline might build dream houses for him at Westminster or Holland Park. She might furnish cottages in Kent and halls in Essex. But he would never come. He did not want to come. He did not need her.

Now she must face reality. The Christian Cinema Company was breaking under her hands. Her directors, one by one, were leaving. Her work was gone.

Her dreams were going. Father Mortimer had no need of her. He only wanted Eleanor, who did not care.

Everything was slipping away from her, because she was growing old. Her time was passing.

'Those cups don't go in there,' she snapped. 'And you might put the cake *properly* in the tin.'

'Sorry, Cousin Caroline,' said Eleanor humbly.

§ 3

The April evening lay green and tender across North Kensington. The long rows of pillars below the porches hung like stalactites in a submarine cave, and the people moving along the empty Sunday street glided quietly as fishes under water. Caroline hurried anxiously along the glistening pavements. It had been raining, and the streets were wet, although the sky now opened bland and clear beyond the spire of St. Cecilia's Church.

If she hurried, she would be just in time. Of course, it had been silly to come by bus. Buses always took longer than she expected. If she had gone by underground to Notting Hill and then walked, she might have been quicker. But even then, she was not sure. She did not want to be late, because she disliked people who came in after the service had begun and then insisted on clattering all the way up the aisle. Yet, if she sat at the back of the church, she would not be able to see Father Mortimer.

She had rung him up and arranged to meet him after Sunday evensong at St. Cecilia's. He was to take the service for the rector there, and to preach the sermon on behalf of his boys' club.

'Come and have supper with me afterwards. Then we can talk,' he had suggested.

She had forgiven him for not telling her about Eleanor. After all, she had been very hasty in jumping to the conclusion that he had any intention of keeping things back from her. He might have thought that telling was unfair to Eleanor. The story did not cast a particularly attractive light on Eleanor. And, in any case, Caroline could not bear to remain angry with her friend. It was her love for him, not his for her, which glorified her life. No feeling of his towards her could hurt her like the cessation of her love for him. She must love him or die.

She felt a sense of quiet emptiness and desolation. She had plans, but no spirit yet to change them into action. The Christian Cinema Company was dead; but from the ashes of the commercial failure a phœnix of idealism should arise. Caroline was meeting Father Mortimer that evening to ask him to join her new Board of Idealists. She had done with the taint of profiteering. If the new company made their fortunes, well and good. It was time that fortune favoured them. But this time there should be no ambiguity about her object. The C.C.C. was to be at last a pioneer association of idealists. Their one reward should be the consciousness of doing good. They were to challenge the enthroned and evil power of the Commercial Cinema by organizing a huge national demand for clean and healthy entertainment. No more Isenbaums, out for social advancement. No more Johnsons, or St. Denises, or Macafees. She would ask Father Mortimer to lend his lofty spirit to her enterprise. She would run the straight race by God's good grace this time.

She found the way round to the vestry door after the service, and saw Father Mortimer, very tall and remote in his long black cassock, talking to the vicar. He started when the verger announced that a Miss Denton-Smyth was waiting for him, as though he had forgotten the appointment. Then his face relaxed into its rare and charming smile.

He introduced her to the vicar:

'Miss Denton-Smyth's a gallant crusader for a higher standard of cinema entertainments,' he explained. 'Nobody but a very brave woman I think would dare to challenge the vested interest of the film world.'

'Cinemas? Never go. Loathe the things,' said the vicar, and hurried off with abrupt farewells to his Sunday supper.

'Now you must come and have supper with me,' said Father Mortimer. 'I won't take you to the Clergy House because we shall be late and our housekeeper has a short way with late comers. I should hate to offer you nothing but one pickled onion.'

Caroline laughed. It was wonderful to be walking beside her friend in the mild spring evening.

'How's your foot?' she asked. 'You still limp a good deal.'

'Oh, it's doing famously. I'm going to start swimming again next week. I have three pupils going in for a school-boys' competition and I've neglected them horribly. Look. This is the place. One can get quite a respectable meal here.'

They entered a small restaurant of the '2s. 6d. Table d'hôte supper – open Sundays' type. The tables were covered with green and orange cloths. A couple of Indian students were eating cold fish mayonnaise in a corner, and a large cream-coloured cat occupied the third chair at the table to which Roger Mortimer conducted Caroline. He fondled the cat with expert attention, running the tips of two long fingers down her vertebræ from her forehead to her tail.

Caroline waited for the waitress to take her order. She noticed that Father Mortimer treated the girl with the same serious and attentive consideration that he offered the cat. When he had asked for soup and pressed beef and salad, Caroline said:

'That's a wonderful text you chose from Ezekiel.'

'Yes. But what a rotten sermon I preached on it.'

She smiled. 'I'm going to pay you the compliment of not pretending I think it's the best you can do, because I always say that there's no compliment like candour. You know, I don't know why you don't let yourself go a bit more. You could if you liked. After all, the things that trouble people most are quite *simple* things – sickness and death and not having enough money. And the beautiful things are quite simple too, like truth and courage and love.'

'Is love simple?'

'Why – yes.' Caroline opened her eyes very wide and looked at him. Her pity and tenderness and admiration overwhelmed her. She loved him so much then that she wanted to smooth with her fingers his quizzical mocking eyebrows, to stroke his dear cheeks, to take his head into her arms. 'Why, yes – isn't it? Isn't it the only really glorious thing?' she said.

'I can't say that I've found it particularly glorious,' said he. 'I know, of course, that it should be. It may be true that perfect love casteth out fear, but imperfect love can play the

223

very devil. How can I preach about what you call simple things when I don't see them simply?'

She did not quite know what to say. Her anger against Eleanor raged in her heart. He sat so quietly, speaking with mild conversational amiability about love, and she found herself thinking, 'Eleanor's broken his heart. The little beast. The little selfish careerist.'

'But you could preach so *beautifully*. You can be so helpful, so understanding.'

'Well, that's very nice of you. I wish I could think so. But in any case it doesn't much matter. I've just accepted a mission job in Bermondsey where I shall have very little preaching to do, thank goodness.'

Bermondsey? Fear chilled her. She thought wildly of the Christian Cinema Company and of all her hopes for his co-operation.

'I've got a curacy there. The sort of job I really like. Lots of parish work and visiting and boys' clubs and things. It will do me good. Shake me up a bit.'

'But that's right across the river!'

'That depends how you look at it. It's across the river from one point of view. But it's on its own side of the river. It thinks of us as in the benighted North across the river.'

'But you can't go. You see – you can't.' Bermondsey for all practical purposes was as far away as Yorkshire or Berlin or Labrador. He must not go. She began to tell him her plans for the Christian Cinema Company, how it was to be reorganized entirely on a basis of idealism, and how much she counted on his help.

He shook his head slowly.

'I'm awfully sorry. And it's nice of you to want me. But it's no good. That sort of thing isn't really my line at all. And I shan't be able to belong to committees and things much outside the parish. I shall have to stick to my job rather closely at first. I've still got a lot to learn.'

'Oh, but you can't bury yourself down there.'

'I shan't be buried.'

'I can't do without you.'

'Why of course you can. You'll do splendidly. Look how you did before you knew me.'

224

'It's Eleanor,' cried Caroline in the bitterness of her loss. 'She's driving you away.'

His smile froze.

'What do you mean, Miss Denton-Smyth?'

'Oh, don't pretend. Don't draw away like that, it isn't as if I didn't know. I'm your friend, my dear boy, you mustn't mind my calling you that, because I'm nearly old enough to be your mother, and in any case I'm her nearest living relative at least in London, and I think she's a blind and selfish little thing. She's not good enough for you. She's one of these hard selfish modern girls who only cares about her career.'

He was looking down at his plate, and the hand crumbling his bread roll was still. Then he looked up, suddenly, and he was smiling cheerfully again. 'Do you know, I think I'd rather not discuss it, even with you?' he said, quite easily and pleasantly, as though he were asking her to pass the butter. 'But, of course, it isn't anything to do with Miss de la Roux – at least' – his instinct for truth urged him to definition – 'at least, nothing she can help.'

But Caroline would not stop. 'Of course she *could* help it. My dear boy, of *course* she could. She told me so. She told me all about it.'

That had roused him. He stared at her with wide astonished eyes.

'She told me all those ideas about marriage you both have and not living together and all that. Of course she *says* she loves you, and she *says* she would hate to spoil your career. But I told her that she hasn't begun to understand the first *thing* about love, because if she had she'd know perfectly well that none of her own silly little ideas about business would matter at all.'

'Oh, but they do matter. I think they matter tremendously.'

It was Caroline's turn to stare.

'I couldn't endure a wife who was prepared to "give up all" for me,' said Father Mortimer with vigour. 'I can't imagine a more humiliating situation. Think of the strain it would impose upon the husband, having to live up to some sort of ideal of value which would compensate to his wife for everything that she had missed. Good heavens! Just think of it, Miss Denton-Smyth. One would never have a minute's peace in life again, nor an undivided mind. One would never be able to enjoy advancement or work or achievement or anything. Why, one would come to loathe the woman!'

'Roger!' She had never said it before. Hardly even in her thoughts had she dared to call him that; but the shock of this revelation of his feelings called it out of her. She was dazed, shocked and disquieted beyond expression.

He laughed. 'Why of course one would. The ideal thing, I suppose, would be some sort of arrangement whereby neither husband nor wife need sacrifice their own work. And I believe it could be done. But one has no business to turn a wife into a laboratory experiment – and – well, in any case – that phase is all over and done with. But there's something I wish you would do. I wish you would try to persuade her to accept that American offer if she gets it. It would be a great chance for her to get really into the business. I want her to do it. I want her to do something that no woman has done before, but – I don't particularly want to see her again just now.'

'I can't bear it,' cried Caroline suddenly. 'Everything's breaking up. Eleanor's going and you're going, and the company's almost gone. I can't face it all alone. I'm too old.'

'Oh, no, you're not. You've got real youth and spirit. You've got all the courage you always had. You'll make a fine thing out of life somehow, and I shall look to you to cheer me on when I'm losing a grip on things, and we'll meet once a year and toast Eleanor's success while she's making fortunes in America.'

'Oh, these young people,' thought Caroline, 'with their glib cry of "once a year." These thoughtless young, squandering their opportunities. How many years shall I have in which to meet him?'

But she had regained her spirit, and only said brightly, almost coquettishly: 'Oh, yes, we must. Still, she hasn't gone yet.'

'No, not yet. But we might as well begin now.'

He raised his glass.

Caroline faced him across the table. She did not know whether the strange feeling that seized upon her was pain or exaltation. She had lost everything. Father Mortimer, her dear dear Roger, was leaving her. Eleanor was leaving her. The Christian Cinema Company would be wound up. She was back where she had been a year ago. It was all to begin over again.

And yet it was not the same. She had touched glory. She had found a friend.

She raised her glass.

'To Eleanor's success,' she said.

He smiled and drank.

'And to your health,' he responded with a polite bow.

'Aren't you going to drink to my success as well?' she bridled. 'I'm not at the stage yet when it's only my health that matters.'

'Of course you're not. Success to you and all your new adventures.'

Their glasses clinked again above the orange jelly.

But health was a condition of success which Caroline perhaps had not adequately valued. For on her way home, crossing the Bayswater Road towards Notting Hill Gate Metropolitan Railway Station, she walked still in the ecstatic trance in which the company of her friend had wrapped her; and she failed to notice a motor-car swinging round the corner from Westbourne Grove. It caught and hurled her to the ground, though it did not run over her. No address was found upon her person; her clothes and the sum of three shillings and fourpence in her bag proclaimed her poverty; she was carried unconscious to the Bayswater Infirmary.

§ 4

The infirmary ward was long and high and light and bleakly, brilliantly public. Caroline felt that she had less privacy there than if she had been put on the pavement in Piccadilly. In and out, up and down, passed the nurses and wardmaids, wheeling hand-lorries, covered with glittering bottles, with mugs of tea, with enamel plates of watery milk pudding. Occasionally a screen was pulled round her bed and she enjoyed a minute's seclusion, though even then her feelings were outraged by the familiarity of the pert probationer, who handled her without reverence and called her 'ma.'

She could bear the pain. Her thigh was broken, and she lay with her leg slightly raised under an iron cage like a meat-cover. Her body seemed to ache from her shoulders to her heel; but she had known before what pain was like. What she felt she could not endure was the publicity. Ever since she roused herself into consciousness and realized her plight, she had suffered anguish from embarrassment and humiliation. That a director of the Christian Cinema Company, the author of *The Path of Valour*, the friend of Father Mortimer, should be in a public infirmary under the control of the Poor Law, between a charwoman with ruptured varicose veins and a factory girl with pernicious anæmia, was too much. She disliked the pink flannelette nightdress provided by the institution; she disliked the mugs in which her tepid tea was brought her; the bread and butter, which was cut too thick; the coarse institutional sheets, and most of all, the free-and-easy patronage of the young nurses and doctors.

'I've borne everything, everything. Poverty and discouragement and loneliness. But this is too much,' she told herself. The hot tears burned her eyes. 'I can't, I can't bear it.'

Two days after her accident, Eleanor arrived, neat, solicitous, efficient.

'You must get me out of this. You must get me out of this,' cried Caroline. 'They tell me I've broken a bone, and I may be on my back for *weeks*. What about the company? How can I see the influential business men I must see and have important interviews in a pauper's ward? And it's just terrible here. Terrible. The language, you'd never believe what it's like. That thing there,' – she jerked her head towards the factory girl's bed. 'Her language. And the jokes she makes with the nurses. Horrible. Wearing so-called pearls too – over a pauper's uniform, and plastering her face up with lipstick. Eleanor, you *must* get me away. Find me a nursing-home. Ask Father Mortimer to come and help me.'

But the girl only answered with cautious sympathy.

'I've spoken to the doctor and your ward sister. I really

228

do believe that it's better for you to stay here. The quieter you keep, the quicker your leg will heal.'

'Quiet? *Quiet?* What sort of quiet do you think I have here? Being wakened up at five o'clock in the morning to be washed, and then – you see – all day long this continual traffic. I might as well be lying in Selfridge's Bargain Basement during sale week.'

'I didn't quite mean that.'

Oh, why had she ever thought Eleanor intelligent? She could not see that this place was unendurable.

'It's no use trying to argue with you. I can see you don't want to do anything for me. You don't want to help me, though I should have thought that even for old times' sake you might have been a *little* charitable. But I might have known.'

She remembered now that there was some particular reason why she was angry with Eleanor. What was it? The girl was obstinate and hard and selfish, of course, but there was something else. Caroline's head ached. Her mind was confused. She could not concentrate.

'I want you – I want you – I want you to write to dear Enid at Marshington and tell her what has happened. She must send me some money immediately and I want some butter and fruit too. Invalids *ought* to have fruit and they have a lovely conservatory at Marshington and a vine with grapes on it. I remember the William pears we used to have at Denton, they were splendid, not like the fruit *nowadays*, all pulp and pip, and then write please to Father Mortimer and ask him to come here at *once*. And then I shall want you to go to Lucretia Road, and to get my papers from the office in Victoria Street. I *must* attend to the business. I can't let the company down. All my directors – all my schemes. I want you to come here *every day* and bring my letters. Now it's a good thing you can do shorthand and typewriting, because there will be a *great* deal to do.'

The girl was stupid. There she sat fiddling with her block and pencil, taking down a few notes and looking miserable, instead of being bright and helpful as she could be if she chose.

'Cousin Caroline –'

'Well? Well? Now don't interrupt me. I've got to think.

It's very important. There are those particulars to be sent to the people who inquired. I had eight inquiries yesterday – no – not yesterday, Friday, I mean. I'm all confused. And then will *you* see the Bishop of Kensington-Gore for me? Of course, I *ought* to go myself. I always say, when you want a thing done properly, do it yourself. But here I am, tied by the leg.'

Oh, it was terrible to be dependent upon this obstructive and obstinate girl. She was trying to say something now – something about America and a man called Brooks. There had been a man called Brooks – Brooks – something to do with Macafee.

'I ought to have had a child,' wailed Caroline. 'My own child would never have grudged a few hours to help me if I were struck down in the middle of my *most promising* work, and though I always say that these things are sent to try our faith, I do think there are some occasions when a little sympathy would help us to bear the test.'

It was no use. Appealing to Eleanor was like appealing to a stone. She just sat there, looking white and troubled but mulish, not at all warm and sympathizing as she should look. There was something wrong about the girl. She had no ordinary heart at all. And those absurd clothes she wore – that old tweed coat. Girls should be as fresh as flowers.

'I don't like your coat,' Caroline said aloud suddenly.

Eleanor's solemnity broke into a dimpling smile.

'I'm sorry.'

'Next time you come, you might bring me a bed-jacket.'

'Cousin Caroline, don't you remember what I told you, about going to America? It's all fixed up. I heard yesterday – Monday – I can go – I sail a week on Friday. It's simply marvellous.'

'You what?'

'I sail a week on Friday in the *Ruritania* with Hugh and old Brooks – for six months – as Hugh's assistant.'

'On Friday? You're going to America a week on Friday? You're leaving me *here*?'

'But how can I help it? I'll do all I can to get you fixed up before I go. Couldn't Betty or Dorothy Smith from Marshington run up to see you? You have other friends. I can't play fast and loose with Brooks. It's simply amazing that he should have let Hugh take me.'

'You're going to leave me *here*? Oh, you can't, Eleanor – you can't. Don't you see – I must have you. I *must*. There's no one else who can run the company while I'm in bed. There's no one else. I can't – I can't. Oh, you're really only at the beginning of your career. You've got time in front of you, all time. But I'm growing old. This chance has come at the end of my life. You can't leave me alone.'

'But don't you see –'

'Now, now, now.' The ward sister bustled up officiously. 'Now then, we mustn't get upset, must we?'

'Time to go now. And you can come again to-morrow as a special favour, though it's *not* visiting day,' she whispered to Eleanor.

Caroline lay speechless. Eleanor was deserting her. Everyone was deserting her. Nobody cared. Life was running away from her.

Ah, but she'd fight for her rights. She'd fight to succeed. No one could take her work away from her. No one could take away the company that she had built up – she – she – she alone. Neither principalities nor powers could rob her of her right to work. Eleanor must stay. Father Mortimer would make her stay. He was her friend. She loved him. Perfect love casteth out fear.

'Milk pudding for supper *again*?' cried Caroline. 'I shall have a letter to the papers written about it. What do we pay rates for?'

The routine of supper, washing, thermometers and bedmaking rolled round on its accustomed circle. The lights were lowered. The stir in the ward sank to a subdued rustling as the night probationer went about her work.

The ward was a deep tank filled with greenish water. Caroline lay drowning in it. She was drowning in fear and pain and loneliness. Nobody cared. Eleanor was leaving her. Father Mortimer was leaving her. The company – she had the company.

She dreamed that all her directors resigned one after the other, and woke up with a gasping start to remember that her dream was true.

231

She had to begin all over again – from a pauper's bed in an infirmary. She had undertaken the Lord's work, and the Lord was testing her. But how could she sing the Lord's song in a strange land?

Could she draw Leviathan with a hook, when she must send out quite six thousand circulars? And Mrs. Hales would spy upon her will, but death, where is thy victory? She would summon Johnson for embezzlement of funds, for shall not the judge of all the earth do right? 'Nurse, Nurse, can't I have a sleeping-draught?' she called. 'If I don't sleep I shall never get through all the important business that I *must* deal with to-morrow. For women of the lower classes, sleep does not matter so much, but I always say that Mr. Lloyd George would never have got through all his *important* work during the war, beating the Germans for us, if he had not *slept*.'

'Hush, hush now. You mustn't be a naughty old thing. Disturbing the ward,' the night probationer admonished her.

'Stow it, you old bitch. Can't you let a girl get her beauty sleep?' grunted the factory girl from the next bed.

Caroline wondered if by any chance she had been killed in her accident, and lay in Hell already.

But next morning, things were better. The sunlight fell on the glass jars of daffodils crowded together on the white enamelled table in the centre of the ward. It moved like clear water across the whitewashed ceiling and the green-painted walls. And after dinner, Eleanor came, still in her old tweed coat, but carrying a bunch of primroses and a basket of fruit.

'Did you see Mrs. Hales about my rooms? You know, I've been thinking things over and if I am really to stay ill for a *long* time, I think you'd better pack up my things and per-haps you could store them in *your* club. There's always plenty of room at those girls' clubs, and then Mrs. Hales would let the room. Did you bring my letters?'

'Yes. I've them all here, from Lucretia Road and the office too.'

'You look very pale, child. It's all these late nights, I expect.'

232

'I'm all right. Look here, Cousin Caroline. First of all I want to tell you that I went to see Brooks and Hugh last night and told them I couldn't sail with them. Of course they were rather annoyed, but I can still get that job at Perrin's next month, and perhaps go to the States later.'

'Well, I'm very glad you've decided to do the sensible thing, because of course it was the only possible thing to do. As it happens I *can't* do without you at the moment. I should like to, but I can't. Now about the letters.'

They went over the correspondence together. Two Nonconformist ministers and an elementary school teacher declared their interests in the company. A gentleman who signed himself Widdall Plumer wanted particulars of the Tona Perfecta Film. The Hoxted Branch of the Women's Co-operative Guild asked Miss Denton-Smyth to give one of their Thursday afternoon talks on 'Purer Cinemas.'

'You see,' cried Caroline. 'You see, what it is. It's just beginning to catch on. The leaven is just beginning to work, to leaven the whole lump. Oh, don't you see why you can't desert me now? These chances may never come again. Now, what other letters are there?'

'There's one here with the Marshington post-mark. Shall I read it?'

'Please, dear – only come closer. I don't want everyone to hear. You've no idea how she' – a nod to the right – 'and she' – a nod to the left – 'try to spy into my business.'

Eleanor pulled her chair closer and began to read:

MY DEAR CAROLINE [the letter ran],

Robert and I are of course very sorry indeed to hear of your accident, and hope that you are getting on nicely and that the pain is not too bad. We are very glad indeed to hear that you have been sensible enough to stay in the infirmary, where I believe the nursing is always good as well as costing so much less. Of course this will no doubt mean an end to all your outside activities, which I dare say you will realize now is all to the good. I hope now that you will be sensible and apply for an Old Age Pension, which I am sure you deserve. As Eleanor is in London and looking after you, I expect she will be able to inquire about the proper steps.

Neither Robert nor I can come up to Town at present, as Robert has had sciatica, and I am very busy with the spring cleaning.

Times have not been good with the business, and now that there is this General Election coming on and some say that the Socialists may get in, and I hardly know what will happen then. We cannot of course help you much, as the calls on our purse are so heavy just now, but Robert sends you two pounds, which I am having changed into postal orders, and perhaps when you are convalescent, you could come to stay for a week or two. The girls are both well. Our love to Eleanor and all good wishes for a prompt recovery,

Your affectionate cousin,

Enid Smith.

'Rather a swine, isn't she?' asked Eleanor. 'I'd rather like you to make a fortune just to spite her.'

'Eleanor! Really. You must not talk like this, and I'm sure she means to be kind really, though of course she does not understand my position at all. Did the two pounds arrive?'

'Yes. The postal orders are here. I'll change them for you.'

'You'd better write and thank her for them.' Eleanor began to scribble shorthand notes on her block. 'Tell her,' continued Caroline, beginning to enjoy herself. 'Tell her about Mr. Plumer, and the two clergymen, and the Bishop of Kensington-Gore. Tell her I hope to get compensation from the motor-car for my injuries. Tell her I am already advancing my plans for the Christian Cinema Company.

'You know, I sometimes think that what is wrong with Enid is that she is a little *jealous*. Of course, I know she's comfortably off and has a home and children and all that, but what I feel is, she's never really *seen* life. She's always kept to the dull *old* sort of things. When you come to think of it, Eleanor, I've had a very remarkable life, really wonderful. I've been a pioneer in so *many* different ways – I mean, long before you knew me, I'd been fighting for progress in education and religion and diet and the Press and now the

234

cinema, of course generally working in the *background*, but then I *liked* to be the power behind the throne, and then think of the interesting personalities I've met. I'm sure when I lie here hour after hour I sometimes go over my adventures, and you know if anyone ever wrote them down I'm sure half of them would not be believed, for truth is stranger than fiction, I always think. That's probably one of the things I shall do when I grow old – write my auto-biography. Just think what a lot I shall have to say, I mean, take only one adventure. Take the Christian Cinema Company and all the personalities interested in it – Mr. St. Denis with his aristocratic connections and his lovely wife. You don't meet a couple like them every day, do you? And then Mr. Macafee. Well, he may become one of the really greatest inventors of the day, mayn't he? And if you really look at it in that light, I did discover him and as you might say the Christian Cinema Company did give him his first *chance*, didn't it? And then Mr. Isenbaum, of course Jews *are* rather a race apart, and I know he was less interested than some of us in the company, and I still don't know really why he ever came in or why he went out again, but I always felt that if one could know *everything*, there was something rather romantic about that man, and I suppose I shall know some day when the secrets of all hearts are revealed. And then Mr. Guerdon, who was at *least* a Quaker, though rather weaker than usual, I sometimes felt, Quaker and soda, I believe Mr. Johnson used to call him. And of course though Mr. Johnson *may* have been a crook, but I always think you haven't really *lived* until you've been done by a few crooks, have you? I mean, I don't suppose poor Enid ever met a crook in her life, leading that dull sheltered existence in the provinces. Well, you just write to her and make her a bit more jealous, Eleanor. Tell her that the C.C.C. is going to *sweep England*. Tell her Yorkshire isn't done yet!'

§ 5

Caroline's outburst invigorated her. By reassuring Enid, she convinced herself. After all, she had had a remarkable career.

The days that followed gave her ample opportunity for

recollection. They passed in dream-like and not wholly unpleasant order. Eleanor came and went, bringing fruit and fresh butter and the caramels and Harrogate toffee that Caroline loved; she took down letters and reported progress, and acted as substitute for Caroline at three conferences and two deputations. She still looked tired and white, and became suddenly silent if America was mentioned, but she was a useful if ungracious visitor.

Day and night slid in and out of the ward as water fills and empties a deep garden tank. Caroline lay subdued and peaceful, taking pleasure in the sweets and oranges that Eleanor brought her, in her distribution of largesse to the other patients and in the small tributes of respect she gradually contrived to exact from the nurses. They called her 'Miss Denton-Smyth' now instead of 'Ma.' The almoner came to visit her, and appeared to be duly impressed by her declaration of profession as 'Journalist and secretary.'

She gave her age as fifty-eight; for supposing, she thought, Father Mortimer or any of the directors were to hear that she was over seventy. The knowledge that she was three months off her seventy-second birthday appeared far less real and true than her conviction that she was good for another ten years of work. Perhaps if they knew that she was over seventy they would want to superannuate her. After all, a woman was as old as she looked and felt. 'Except for the pain in my leg, I feel about forty-five,' thought Caroline. When Father Mortimer came to visit her, bringing her fruit and flowers, she felt not a day more than seventeen.

Meanwhile, she was content to lie and dream. The green distemper of the ward reminded her of the green hills of her old home near Leyburn, patterned by grey stone walls. The farm at Denton lay spread out along the side of a hill. Above it the black moorland climbed to the sunny sky, below it the rough road wound to the dale. Behind the house the cowshed and fold yard snuggled beneath a small plantation. Caroline had always wished that the farm buildings were not so near the house. She wished that there was a separate carriage drive to the front door. Visitors had to take their gigs and pony carts straight into the stable yard, which was also the farm yard, and walk through a narrow gate in the garden wall to the front door. No one could call a house with such an approach a Gentleman's Residence.

Long ago, when Caroline travelled with the Bassett-Grahams, she had called her father a gentleman farmer, and had tried to console herself by reflecting that, since he had bought the fields between the house and the moor, he was a landowner. But to-day she was content to think of him as a yeoman farmer, to remember how he had slapped his friends on the back in Middleham market, and told Yorkshire dialect stories in a loud, hearty voice. The humbler her origin, the more remarkable her achievement. What other farmers' daughters from the dales had done and seen all that she had done or seen?

It was strange, but that child's life at Denton now seemed more vivid to her than all her subsequent adventures. She remembered squeezing herself into the hay rack above the stalls in the cowshed, eating cubes of raw turnip and composing poetry.

> 'What is happiness made of?
>   What makes it sweet and dear?
> Is it the things we look at?
>   Is it the things we hear?'

That had been real poetry, with rhymes and rhythm and the full blissful ecstasy of composition.

'If I'd had more time, I could have been a poet,' reflected Caroline, 'only between the claims of art and service I *had* to choose service, being by nature a pioneer and fighter.'

Still, she had written some good poems in her day. There was that afternoon on the Malvern hills with Adelaide. Oh, Adelaide, Adelaide Thurlby. How lovely in those days she had been. So tall, so willowy, so distinguished, with her white swan's neck, curving above the embroidered collarless square of her Liberty gown. A lovely neck, Caroline then had thought. No wonder she had dared to expose it when everyone else confined theirs in net and whalebone. It was sad that later those swan-like curves had developed into a goitre.

But when they picnicked together on the hills above the school, and Adelaide read aloud *The Lotus Eaters*, while

Caroline, who had carried the baskets, made the tea, nothing was missing from Adelaide's beauty.

'I am glad, I am glad, that I have known what a really intimate friendship can be,' thought Caroline. 'I am glad that I have known her even if it meant deeper suffering.'

For the days of bliss and art and companionship had been followed by months of anxiety, when one epidemic after another laid waste the school, and someone suggested that the drains were not quite right, and dear Adelaide grew nervy. Only Caroline knew what she had suffered from Adelaide's nerves when the pupils grew fewer and fewer, until at last only six assembled round the long dining-room table, and three of those were on reduced terms because their parents were abroad. Of course Caroline had put her own money into the school, and dear Adelaide had not paid her salary for three terms.

When the crash came – no, no – that was a time that Caroline did not want to remember. She had taken Adelaide up to Darlington to nurse her through her inevitable breakdown. Adelaide had recovered. From the moment Dr. Waddington had entered her room, Adelaide's recovery began. Ah, Sydney! thought Caroline, remembering that snatched kiss in the passage, when she was carrying a tray up for her mother's tea. It was the only time a man had ever kissed her like that. She dreamed of it for days and nights. She waited for his coming hour after hour. The clot, clot, clot of his grey mare's hoofs on the high road still echoed in her head.

She was in charge of two invalids then, her mother in one room and Adelaide in another, and she had had little time for dalliance. Afterwards, after the desperate day when Adelaide and Sydney announced their engagement, she had wondered bitterly whether, if she had spent more time with Sydney and less in looking after Adelaide, she might not have won him for herself. She had never believed that such a kiss could mean just nothing.

Ah, but that had been bitter, bitter. Deep waters had gone over her soul. Her mother had died in debt, and she had lost her lover, her friend, her mother, her home and her profession in one brief season. It seemed now so long ago, that it might have been another person who had sat after the funeral in the desolate house crying and crying, because she was left alone to wash up the dishes after the funeral tea. Her sister Daisy had had to catch a train back to Newcastle because her baby had whooping cough.

But in the anguish of her estrangement, she had written what was undoubtedly her best poem. It had been printed in the *Northern Clarion – Epigram on the End of Love*. By Caroline Smith.

> 'You said that death was not the End; most true;
> Death was not stronger than my love for you.
> But since sweet love so lightly goes, my friend,
> We are not dead, and yet – this is the End.'

It was strange that she could remember her poems so clearly now. Their rhymes sang themselves over in her mind at night.

It was something to have been a poet. Not everyone had been kindled by the divine fire. 'One day,' thought Caroline, 'I will write a long poem. All about pioneers.'

'Does the road wind up hill all the way?'

That was Elizabeth Browning, wasn't it? Or Jean Ingelow. Never mind. Caroline knew the answer.

> 'Yes, all the way and all the way,
> Above Frienze all the way,
> We'll climb for ever and a day,
>   But reach the heights to-morrow.
> We'll climb the hot and dusty road
> The paths where other pilgrims strode,
> And cast aside our heavy load
>   Of loneliness and sorrow.'

She had composed that, hurrying up the hot, dusty hill towards Fiesole, behind poor Dodo Bassett-Graham. Dodo's tall, gaunt figure had raced up before her, Dodo's skirt trailing in the soft Italian dust. Caroline panting behind in her tight shoes, and knowing that she would have to brush Dodo's skirt when they returned to the villa, had almost failed for a time to appreciate the privilege of being actually

239

in Italy, travelling with titled people. Poor Dodo had not, of course, been quite right in her head. It was sad that not even membership of the aristocracy exempted men and women from these afflictions. Lady Bassett-Graham had been an exacting woman, troubled, naturally, about her eccentric daughter, whose vagaries grew more and more impossible, until half-way through the Italian trip they had decided to place her in a nursing home.

But Caroline had seen Italy. She had seen Milan and Genoa and Florence. She had climbed the stairs of Savonarola's tower, she had looked at pictures in the Uffizi. She had learned how to say 'Dov'e?' and 'Duomo' and 'Grazie.' She had been to Paris. She remembered now the excitement of finding her way through the unfamiliar lighted streets, back to her small hotel.

Caroline was sorry for the sheltered, wealthy women who had never experienced the chill rapture of travelling alone. She was sorry for the vulgar little factory girl dying in the next bed, because she had never seen Paris.

Poor girl; she was rather like that naughty Barbara who had given them so much trouble at St. Angela's Home of Charity for Fallen Girls. Caroline had been secretary there for a whole year. It was then that she became definitely and blissfully a Catholic – an Anglo-Catholic, of course. The little chapel soothed and delighted her; the altar candles, the incense, and the quiet devotional movements of the Sisters in their grave black gowns, had been very pleasant to her. Yet even there she had felt a little superior to the Sisters. For they had fled from the world while she was still in it. She knew so well the sweet danger that had assailed the fallen girls. She knew so well, as none of the Sisters, she felt, could know, the startled delight of surreptitious kisses. Had Sydney not kissed her in the dark passage? Oh, she had been a pioneer in her sympathy with these poor fallen girls, even if she eventually quarrelled with Mother Ursula about the smoked haddock.

She had been a pioneer in the city. How well she remembered lifting her blue serge skirt with the braid binding to board a horse omnibus in Ludgate Circus. For nine months she had worked in the office of an educational publisher, drafting cultured little notices about history readers and First French Courses. He had been a difficult man. Oh, very difficult. It had been hard to lose her office job, but even that tribulation had led her to new experience. She had even ventured out to the suburbs as a canvasser for orders.

Poor Daisy, living in Newcastle with Edward growing fatter and balder. Poor Enid, so safe and dull and circumscribed at Marshington. What could they know of real experience and triumph? Of poetry and pain and loss and work? When had they sat up all through the night, drafting minutes, preparing reports, making coffee to keep them awake so that they might work on, with pricking eyes and aching necks and shoulders? All pain and discomfort and loneliness and failure became worth while if one had only a Great Cause to serve.

> 'What is the Cause? Oh Lord, I do not ask.
>   'Tis Thou appointeth, only Thou that guides,
> I only pray for courage for my task,
>   And strength to shoulder it, whate'er betides.'

That had been one of her poems published in the Parish Magazine. It had been a great success.

> 'I do not crave that I should always see
>   The winding road before my straining eyes,
> But only that Thy hand should beckon me,
>   Beyond the waning margin of the skies.'

A poem was company. If you had written poems, you would never go in want of a familiar voice of comfort.

> 'I do not ask that I may win the crown,
>   Only that I may still the Right defend,
> I do not ask to lay my weapon down,
>   Only to Fight unconquered till the end.
>
> 'I am Thy soldier, arm me with Thy might!
>   I am Thy pioneer; show me the way!
> I do not ask to triumph, but to fight,
>   To travel upward till the perfect Day.'

This world's imperfect day was coming now. The dawn slid slowly past the narrow windows. The night staff was beginning to stir at the other end of the ward. In another minute or two, the pert probationer would hurry along wheeling a tray of mugs of morning tea. Surely there had been one other verse, the best of all? One that explained everything, that answered all her questions?

She must ask Eleanor to see about the office rent – and the printing of the new circulars. She did hope the girl would come early. There was so much to do. One must be faithful over little things before one could become a ruler over many things. One must never give way, never relax one's standards when pioneering. Faithful.

Ah, that was the verse! she remembered it now.

'So when at last I reach the golden wall,
    Footsore and weary, stained with grief and sin,
Thy voice shall bid my heavy burdens fall.
    Well done, thou good and faithful Friend! Pass In!'

Friend, Friend, that was what she had been. And she had found a friend. A faithful Friend. She must make another verse for him, to show that she did not come lonely to the Golden City. Another verse.

'No nurse – not yet – not yet – just a minute – Can't you see – I'm busy?'

Why did the girl look so stupidly at her? Why was that water pouring in, in, in to the tank? They were drowning together, all drowning; someone must open the window and let the water out or they would drown.

She dragged herself up on one arm.

'Open!' she cried. 'Open! The Golden – Golden –'

And the gates opened.

Final Chorus

THE REVEREND ERNEST SMITH shifted his lace-trimmed surplice awkwardly. If he had known what mummery and nonsense he was going to be inveigled into, he'd never have come near the place. Good heavens! Couldn't they even bury her decently? There he was bobbing about in a dark stuffy church that smelt intolerably of incense, and incense always made him a little sick, watching a tall affected young curate with an Oxford accent patting Caroline's large purple-covered coffin with a ladle, while a small snuffling boy jerked a jangling censer. Not even the words of the service were familiar. He couldn't find his way about at all; he felt like a fool, and loathed the whole performance. He was not even given the orthodox verses to read. He'd write to the bishop. He'd complain to Robert. He'd . . . Good heavens, no wonder the country could not stomach these Anglo-Catholics. He had not taken any very active part in the controversy until now. He was a man of peace who preferred to let well alone; but really after this, it was time to put his foot down.

Naturally he had wanted to take some part in his cousin's funeral service; but if he had known, if he had had the slightest idea, of the discomfort and embarrassment to which he would be subjected, he would not have come near the place. What would Lady Bowsill think of all this tomfoolery, she, admirable Evangelical patroness of Flynders, who objected even to candles on the altar, and thought that fasting communion savoured of popery? What would his sidesmen think? What did he think himself? And after his hideous cross-country journey, and that absurd misunderstanding about the time of the funeral, he really deserved a little consideration. How typical of Caroline to cause as much trouble as possible, by dying, of a clot of blood at the heart after a street accident, so that she occasioned a post-mortem,.

an inquest, and an Anglo-Catholic funeral service! Fortunately Eleanor had seen to most of the arrangements; but he had little use for that young woman, a hard, difficult unwomanly young person who had not even had the decency to wear mourning. And what it was all going to cost, Heaven alone knew. The only thing to be said for the whole business was that this was the last time on which Caroline could trouble them. After this, they need never think of her again.

★   ★   ★   ★

Betty and Dorothy Smith nudged each other. 'That's her precious Father Mortimer,' Betty whispered. 'I say, doesn't Ernest look a scream in his little lace jumper?'

'It's rather impressive – the purple pall, I mean. I wish we had incense at Marshington,' murmured Dorothy.

'He's really quite nice looking, but too thin. I wonder what he thought of her *really*.'

'Hush! I say, I *do* think Eleanor might have worn at least a black *coat*, don't you?'

'Shall we go to a revue or to *The Lady with a Lamp* to-night?'

'I must get my hair waved – and we'll go to Marshall and Snelgrove's to-morrow morning.'

'Oh well, she's done us one good turn. I *had* to buy a new coat, and I do loathe shopping in Kingsport.'

★   ★   ★   ★

Hugh Macafee clutched the bookshelf in front of him and climbed awkwardly to his feet. This service was all gibberish to him, and he would never have dreamed of coming if Eleanor had not insisted. He did not like these mixed funerals. It was more decent in Scotland where only the menfolk attended; but really, if we came to think about it, all funeral services were offensive to the scientific mind. All this barbaric pother about a perfectly natural process disgusted him.

Well, to-morrow he would get away from it all. He was sailing for the States. It was an opportunity, but of course, he was not going to stand any nonsense from Brooks. Brooks was a clever fellow, and if he had the sense to give his men a free hand, Hugh would not object to his terms. The important thing was to perfect his own colour process.

Eleanor had been a fool to throw away her chance of going. Women were like that though, always running off to look after sick relatives or something. Well, she might still do something. She had ability and Brooks had taken to her. Probably Perrin would give her a job.

He'd write another letter. Perrin respected his judgment. If he said that she had brains and grit, and a few ideas of her own, they might find a use for her. Once in a place, she knew how to make herself useful. She was the one person in England whom he would be sorry to leave.

But not too sorry. His thoughts drifted away from her to Caroline, lying under the elaborate purple pall in the raised coffin. What a queer old thing she had been, odder than anyone he had ever met. Did she really believe that she was going to run a great organization that could rival the Brooks Combines and National Products? Ah, well, imagination played queer tricks with some of us. Engineering was safer than psychology. One knew where one was with it. This was the end, praise be. He'd slip away now. He was not going right down to Fulham cemetery. He had a lot to do to-day, and it was wonderful with all his many important engagements, that he had found time at all to pay his last respects to poor old Caroline.

*   *   *   *

Mr. Charles Fry Fox Guerdon stared out of the window at the passing traffic. Miss de la Roux had engaged only one car to follow the hearse to the cemetery, but the Reverend Ernest Smith, gazing with dismay at its congested interior, had whistled up a taxi, commanded Father Mortimer to share it with him, and at the last moment whipped Miss de la Roux inside with him to make sure that they, as the people principally responsible for the final ceremony, at least all kept together. Mr. Guerdon was left with the two other mourners, his legs screwed under the back seat of the car, endeavouring to prevent his knees from knocking against the shapely, but indelicately exposed lower limbs of the two Misses Smith. They, as the representatives of their parents, were seeing the ceremony through to its conclusion, and he,

245

as the representative of the Christian Cinema Company, believed it right that he also should attend. But he disliked the whole business very much indeed. He wished that he was comfortably back at Golder's Green, and he shrank from the unabashed interrogation to which Miss Betty Smith subjected him.

'This Christian Cinema Company's all off now, isn't it?'

'Er – yes – er – I believe so. Most of the directors have resigned owing to various circumstances, and I believe that the company is – er – in the process of – er – being wound up.'

'Didn't someone go off with all the cash?'

'Well, er – I understand that the accountant has found some irregularity. But Miss de la Roux is the chief share-holder and she has decided not to prosecute. The money is probably already dissipated, and the person whom we suspect has gone abroad.'

'Well, I know Mummy'll want to know all about it. Was this Mr. St. Denis really a genuine person?'

'Oh yes. Quite genuine, I believe, though really rather a *dilettante*. Of course Miss Denton-Smyth's enthusiasm was wonderful.'

'A bit too wonderful I think you'd say if you'd been one of her relations. Mum and Dad were always having to come in and wipe up the mess after one of her wonderful schemes had gone phut. I say – where have the others got to? Do you think we shall ever catch up with Eleanor and Father Mortimer? Isn't it silly to call him "Father" when he's such a boy? He's only a curate, isn't he?'

'I believe so, though – er – as a member of the Society of Friends I have not a very clear idea of the Anglican distinctions.'

'Are you a Quaker? How thrilling. We have some neighbours who are Quakers and awfully nice really. The girls are quite sporting, and one of them plays tennis for our club's first six.'

'I am glad that the Society of Friends meets with your approval,' Mr. Guerdon observed dryly.

*　　*　　*　　*

A shower fell as the three vehicles wound their way among

the traffic into Richmond Road and through the gates of the cemetery, but suddenly the sky brightened as at the foot pace they crawled down the long drive between the graves. The slanting sun lit the daffodils like golden flames in the green grass, and sparkled on the wet grass bubbles covering white china doves and posies.

A shaft of light came through the window, illuminating Eleanor's face, as she sat, stiff and silent beside the sullen bulk of the Reverend Ernest Smith.

Both she and the clergyman were staring out of different windows into the cemetery. Roger Mortimer, who faced them from the smaller seat, could look as long as he liked at her face, learning by heart the clear delicate line of her chin, her level brows, and the severe curve of her young mouth. He had need to look long and steadfastly at her, for perhaps after to-day their ways might never meet again. She was right, of course. He could not ask her to share, or even to understand his self-imposed obligations. She could go her own way, and he prayed that she would win success. For if she desired wealth and power, her ambition was not ignoble. She believed that society needed rich and powerful women, who had worked their way from obscurity to eminence, and she believed quite impersonally and firmly in her own ability to accomplish such a destiny. At least she had the courage to attempt it. No obstacle of personal or domestic complication must hinder her advancement. Her socialism would temper her ambition and her sense of responsibility would balance her egotism. He could regard her now with impartial detachment, he could see that there was a generosity and nobility about her which experience would develop. It had been fine of her to throw away her chance of going to America in order to look after poor Miss Denton-Smyth and to disentangle the finances of the Christian Cinema Company. It had been fine, though foolish, to throw away her security with such apparent indifference, especially when she had so keen a sense of financial values. She believed in holding tightly on to power and money. She believed in the necessity for taking risks.

There was none like her, none. He could thank his God always on every remembrance of her. His work would be

247

more tolerable because of his knowledge that humanity could achieve such grave and honest generosity. He would dislike futility and confusion less because at least he had known one woman whose mind was cool and clear.

He could thank Caroline too. Had she not brought them together? She always said that she wanted to enrich him. She had enriched him. She had given him something that he valued more than any other earthly experience.

These last few days had been very sweet to him. Ever since Eleanor rang him up to tell him of Caroline's death, he had seen her continually. She had let him help her with the arrangements for the funeral. She had let him go with her when she identified the body and gave evidence at the inquest. They had lunched together after the inquest in a little restaurant in Church Street.

This funeral service was the ceremony of his farewell, not only to Caroline, but to Eleanor. He believed that she too had been glad to know him better. She was not wholly indifferent to him, but he could be glad now that she had not loved him. There must be no pain for her in this farewell.

Afterwards he knew that he would have bad times, wanting her. He knew that he might grow jealous of her work and her preoccupations, and complain against the fate that severed them. But now he felt only pride and thankfulness for love.

'But oh, my dear, my dear, my dear,' his heart cried, as the car at last drew up beside the raw gaping cavern of an open grave, 'how shall I live without you?'

He climbed out of the car, and held the door open for her. As she sprang down, a blackbird in the wet thorn bush beside her broke into jubilant song.

*　　*　　*　　*

Eleanor stood beside the grave staring down at the dark hole in the earth. So this was the end of Caroline. This, she believed, was the complete and final end of one small individual adventure. Caroline was dead, and all her dreams died with her. The school which she had tried to found had failed. Her poems and *Path of Valour* lay unread and unremembered. The Christian Cinema Company had apparently existed in order to provide Mr. Johnson with a means of escaping his debts. Her many other plans had progressed no further than their conception in her fertile brain. This vivid unreliable April sunlight was the final comment upon her precarious and perishing activity.

On the tarpaulin covering the cast-up loam from the grave, lay wreaths and crosses, the conventional white wreath from the Marshington Smiths, and Mr. Guerdon's chaplet, a handsome cross bore a card 'From the Christian Cinema Company with gratitude and remembrance.' There lay Roger's scarlet carnations with an inscription in Greek. She must tease him about that. It was so typical of him to spend his money on red carnations, and then to decorate them with an inscription that nobody could read. Or did he think that Caroline's immortal mind, inhabiting her celestial body, was enfranchised into the vast liberties of classical learning? Did he picture her ghost peering down through her lorgnettes and taking pleasure in this tribute to her culture? Eleanor's own daffodils looked naïve and countrified beside his rich, defiant garland. But then Roger loved hot-house flowers, and heavy draperies, and purple, and incense and processions. He was not, like Eleanor, a stranger to this English spring, enraptured by its chill, dewy freshness and the surprising candour and bravery of its flowers. In this, as in so many other things, he seemed to provide the complement to her tastes and nature. Oh, they were made for one another. What folly, what folly to let a catchword part them. It was not a question of a future company director and Socialist member of parliament marrying a curate. It was a question of Eleanor marrying Roger Mortimer, the one person whom, since her father died, she could ever love.

After all, if one intended to conduct social experiments, was it not safer to share them with the most honourable and unselfish person whom one knew? Roger had that queer indefinable quality of goodness. She trusted him. Why, after all, should she remain celibate just because she intended to have a public career? She would not become an unpaid curate-housekeeper in Bermondsey. She would marry him and go off, just as she had intended, to Perrin's works in Manchester. She would go to America as soon as

249

she persuaded Brooks to take her. Roger would understand. He was the one person in the world who ever would understand, the one man she had ever met who wanted his marriage to be an adventure not a refuge. Why should she be so squeamish about his future when she knew perfectly well his odd ambition to remain a poor and overworked parish priest? Why should she be so timid about her own capacity? Surely strength to shoulder burdens developed with their weight?

'The present generation of feminists must marry,' thought Eleanor, listening to Roger's voice reading the funeral service. 'And if we fail, we can always separate. There's nothing final in this world but death. And after death . . .'

She looked down into the black cavern of the grave. Supposing it were Roger who lay there in the bright coffin? And supposing, from cowardice, she had kept away from him?

After all, marriage was not the only cause of failure. She thought of Caroline, and of her great desires. She thought of the tragic comedy of her will, remembering her wish to become a general benefactor.

And yet, was not Caroline's wish fulfilled? She had wanted to leave legacies to her relatives at Marshington, and here were Betty and Dorothy, very pleased with themselves, enjoying a shopping and theatre holiday in London. She had wanted the Christian Cinema Company to benefit mankind, and had it not done so? Mr. St. Denis had had his diversion from it, Hugh his advertisement, Johnson his romance, Guerdon the gratification of his conscience, and Isenbaum – well, Isenbaum was rather a mystery, but Mr. St. Denis had once said something about getting his son to Eton. It seemed probable, considering everything else, that he had done so. Caroline had wanted to leave a legacy to Mrs. Hales, and though she had quarrelled later with the landlady, Eleanor was sure that her sense of Christian forgiveness would have been gratified by the thought that the arrears of her rent had been paid at last, and that Mrs. Hales was browsing happily among the brilliant fragments of her wardrobe. She had wished for Roger his heart's desire. She had wanted so eagerly to enrich him, to make him happy. Why not? Why not?

Eleanor knew then that she could not let him go off alone to Bermondsey without knowing that she loved him. Life was so short, and justice so uncertain. Must one not take risks, living under the shadow of annihilation?

She looked up at Roger as though she had never really seen him before, and knew what she would do.

The ceremony was over. She followed Betty and Dorothy past the grave, throwing into it a bunch of primroses. As though she heard it now, she remembered Caroline's quick excited voice from the infirmary bed, crying, 'When you come to think of it, Eleanor, I've had a very remarkable life.' That was it. That was the way to live, acknowledging no limitations, afraid of nothing.

She returned to the car with the two girls and Mr. Guerdon. She remembered that Roger had to go straight from the cemetery back to St. Augustine's for a wedding. At the car-step, she asked Mr. Guerdon, 'Have you a pencil on you?'

He had. He produced one awkwardly. She found in her bag her little diary and tore a leaf from the end of it and wrote, supporting it on her knee, her foot on the step of the car.

'Please wait just a minute,' she said, and ran back to the undertaker's young man who still stood by the grave.

'I want you to give this to Father Mortimer *without fail*,' she said, folding her note very small and neatly.

'Very good, miss.'

She rejoined her cousins in the car, laughing softly to herself.

On the note she had written:

'You might at least pay me the compliment of asking me to marry you. I do love you, you know. ELEANOR.'

★   ★   ★   ★

Just as Eleanor handed her note to the undertaker's young man, Basil St. Denis sat on a terrace below the Casino at Monte Carlo smoking cigarettes, and watching the speed-boats scribble white curving lines across the deep blue bay. The sun poured down upon him like a benediction. He knew now that he had not been warm for months.

That was all that was wrong with him. He had been too cold. London in winter was intolerable. It had been stupid of him ever to think he could endure it. What one needed was sunlight. Well, thank Heaven the London adventure was over. Only that morning Gloria had written to him full plans for her hat-and-gown shop in the Boulevard des Moulins. Gloria, marvellous woman, would make it pay. The sooner she came, the better, for he missed her. He needed her rich and tranquil personality to invigorate him.

He drew from his breast pocket the deep violet envelope almost covered by her large sprawling writing. On scented paper, with bright purple ink, she wrote news of the state of her finances, her resignation from the Hanover Square house, the death of Caroline Denton-Smyth and the voluntary winding up of the Christian Cinema Company.

'Apparently, my dear, it was all in an awful legal mess, but the de la Roux girl is on to it like a ferret – all efficiency and company law and what-not. I hope it'll keep fine for her. It had really gone quite bust before Caroline's accident. Oh, well it was quite fun while it lasted, and nobody seems to be much the worse for it, and at any rate we have learned one thing from it all, that England in spite of Home and Beauty is no place for us.'

He put down the letter to light a cigarette, remembering as he did so poor Caroline's puzzled face bending over a tattered copy of the Companies Consolidation Act of 1908. He remembered her large innocent brown eyes full of wonder as she looked up to ask 'if we are an association to promote art, religion, charity and other useful purposes and *yet* we are for gain, if possible, which section of the act ought we to come under?'

Of course the whole thing had been a farce from the beginning. Caroline was a farce. All life was a farce. But Gloria would be coming out in another six weeks, and Gloria, even though she too was undoubtedly a figure in a farce, was a marvellous woman, and one of the few serene and unchanging certainties in a restless and unstable world.

★   ★   ★   ★

Not very far along the coast, passengers were scrambling

252

laboriously up the gangway from the Marseilles dock on to a ship bound for the East. Among them rolled Clifton Roderick Johnson, shouldering his way through American tourists, Dutch commercial travellers and French merchants. Behind him panted Delia, bumping a circular scarlet hat-box against the rail.

'You might stop. You might help a girl,' she scolded. 'Leaving me to carry everything. Call yourself a gentleman!' Johnson was already carrying two suit-cases and he did not call himself a gentleman. That boast at least had never been his. He called himself an artist, a pioneer, a teacher, an enemy of society, a benefactor of the Arts, an adventurer, a citizen of the British Empire, and a great lover. But he did not call himself a gentleman.

Three days ago, he might have explained this to Delia, but he was learning the futility of explanation.

'Second class? On a dingy little cockle shell like this? And you posing as a millionaire and going to take me a tour de-luxe round the Mediterranean? I've a jolly good mind to get you run in for White Slave Traffic. *I am* under age, you know.'

'Be quiet. Be quiet. Do you wanna get all the nosy-parkers on board on to us?'

But appeal was useless. Delia was tired already of adventure. She was cramped and dirty from her long journey through France sitting up all night in a second-class carriage. She was angry and bored and resentful, and she meant to let him know it. But she had to go with him to Alexandria, for he refused to give her money to return, fearing lest she should betray him, uncertain about the extradition laws, uncertain of the extent of his offences or the chaos he had left behind. He stood on deck looking at the gangway, and listening and half expecting to see an English policeman climb after him to arrest and take him back to England. But the girl at his side was merciless. The scolding voice went on and on, lacerating his nerves, tormenting him. But he would not leave her behind. He could not desert her in Paris, or Marseilles or even in Alexandria. She would make too much noise and he could not afford to face her vindictiveness while he was still uncertain whether he was a criminal flying from justice or a business man on holiday.

Fool, fool that he had been even to have attempted that mad journey. Fool, fool, to ask Delia to join him. For with her his money would last only half as long, and he was tired of her already. Her shrill petulance maddened him. And he could not shake her off.

He stood on the dingy deck looking back at Marseilles, wretched and fearful, a victim of his own temperament, of his upbringing, his tastes, and of the Christian Cinema Company.

★   ★   ★   ★

Joseph Isenbaum came late that morning to the office. He had been compelled to call upon an American client at Brown's Hotel, and arrived just in time to glance through his letters before he went off to lunch at Simpson's.

He was in admirable humour. Everything had gone very well with him. He was likely to make a profit of £18,500 17s. 6d. from his transaction with the American. The picture he had bought last week proved to be a genuine Sebastino Corea, a painter whose work, if now a trifle *démodé*, was at least worth acquiring. He would bid for those two Ming vases on sale to-morrow at Christie's if the dealers didn't run up the price too ridiculously.

He turned over his letters with satisfaction, jerking out to his secretary short notes for his replies. Then he came to one from an unfamiliar firm of solicitors, which for a few moments made him pause.

It stated that Messrs. Perkin & Warbeck were acting on behalf of Miss Eleanor de la Roux, a shareholder in the Christian Cinema Company, Ltd., and executor of the late Miss Caroline Denton-Smyth, also a shareholder in that company. Miss de la Roux had instructed them to approach him with a view to winding up the company, voluntarily if possible. Owing to Miss de la Roux's decision not to bring any action, it seemed unlikely that any litigation would ensue from the transaction; but in order to facilitate their action, the representative of Messrs. Perkin & Warbeck requested the pleasure of an interview with Mr. Isenbaum.

He put down the letter and chuckled softly. So this was

254

the end of the Christian Cinema Company Ltd. Ah well, ah well, and Caroline Denton-Smyth was dead. Poor Caroline. She had been so much alive, she had enjoyed with such pathetic absurdity her position as a business woman. She was such a queer old bird.

And she was dead. Well, he had reason to be grateful to her. Through her he had met Basil St. Denis and through St. Denis young Benjamin had been entered for Eton. What was there left now for the Christian Cinema Company to do? Had it not better, after that supreme achievement, fade out of existence with its founder? It had smoothed the path of life for Benjamin Isenbaum, a Jew. Was not that a Christian act? What better justification could any company require? 'Bless you, Caroline,' thought Joseph Isenbaum.

'Tell Perkin & Warbeck I can see their representative at 11.30 a.m. next Wednesday,' he told his secretary. 'Now, what about that order from Rumania?'

VIRAGO MODERN CLASSICS

The first Virago Modern Classic, *Frost in May* by Antonia White, was published in 1978. It launched a list dedicated to the celebration of women writers and to the rediscovery and reprinting of their works. Its aim was, and is, to demonstrate the existence of a female tradition in fiction which is both enriching and enjoyable. The Leavisite notion of the 'Great Tradition', and the narrow, academic definition of a 'classic', has meant the neglect of a large number of interesting secondary works of fiction. In calling the series 'Modern Classics' we do not necessarily mean 'great' — although this is often the case. Published with new critical and biographical introductions, books are chosen for many reasons: sometimes for their importance in literary history; sometimes because they illuminate particular aspects of womens' lives, both personal and public. They may be classics of comedy or storytelling; their interest can be historical, feminist, political or literary.

Initially the Virago Modern Classics concentrated on English novels and short stories published in the early decades of this century. As the series has grown it has broadened to include works of fiction from different centuries, different countries, cultures and literary traditions. In 1984 the Victorian Classics were launched; there are separate lists of Irish, Scottish, European, American, Australian and other English speaking countries; there are books written by Black women, by Catholic and Jewish women, and a few relevant novels by men. There is, too, a companion series of Non-Fiction Classics constituting biography, autobiography, travel, journalism, essays, poetry, letters and diaries.

By the end of 1986 over 250 titles will have been published in these two series, many of which have been suggested by our readers.

Also published by Virago

WINIFRED HOLTBY

Anderby Wold
The Crowded Street
The Land of Green Ginger
Mandoa, Mandoa!

VERA BRITTAIN

Testament of Experience
Testament of Friendship
Testament of Youth

TESTAMENT OF A GENERATION
The Journalism of Vera Brittain and Winifred Holtby
Edited and Introduced by Paul Berry and Alan Bishop

Other Virago Modern Classics

RUTH ADAM

I'm Not Complaining

PHYLLIS SHAND ALLFREY

The Orchid House

ELIZABETH VON ARNIM

Elizabeth and Her German Garden
Fraulein Schmidt and Mr Anstruther
Vera

STORM JAMESON

Company Parade
Love in Winter
None Turn Back
Women Against Men

ELIZABETH JENKINS

The Tortoise and the Hare

F. TENNYSON JESSE

The Lacquer Lady
Moonraker
A Pin to See the Peepshow

SHEILA KAYE-SMITH

Joanna Godden
Susan Spray

MARGARET KENNEDY

The Constant Nymph
The Ladies of Lyndon
Together and Apart
Troy Chimneys

ROSAMOND LEHMANN

The Ballad and the Source
The Gipsy's Baby
Invitation to the Waltz
A Note in Music
A Sea-Grape Tree
The Weather in the Streets

ADA LEVERSON

The Little Ottleys

ROSE MACAULAY

Told by an Idiot
The World My Wilderness

OLIVIA MANNING

The Doves of Venus
The Play Room

F.M. MAYOR

The Third Miss Symons

NAOMI MITCHISON

The Corn King and the Spring Queen
Travel Light

EDITH OLIVIER

The Love Child

KATE O'BRIEN

Mary Lavelle
That Lady

MARY RENAULT

The Friendly Young Ladies